J.T. Bock's

DAMA X

An UltraSecurity Novel

PepperLip Press

www.jtbock.com

Manufactured in the United States of America

Cover Design by Mike Parkinson © 2016
Interior Design by Mike Parkinson
Cover and Title page image from iStock photo.

Edited by Romance Refined and The Editing Hall

Published by:

PepperLip Press
Virginia

ISBN: 978-0-9888362-3-5

Acknowledgements

Thank you to my critique partners, Karen and Jessica, for plying me with wine and encouragement as we worked out the plot.

Thank you to Mike, Avi, Chris, and Beth for being my beta readers and giving me honest feedback.

Thank you to Rachel Daven Skinner and Chris Hall for your superhuman editing skills.

Thank you to Juan and Beth for reviewing the Spanish phrases for my Mexican characters.

Thank you to Rob for the paramedic and Hazmat information and providing the hilarious "crotch luggage" phrase.

Thank you to Stacia and Nick for your encouragement and your awesome writing parties.

Thank you to my family and friends for asking about my story and giving me the confidence to finish it.

Thank you to my readers, who enjoyed *A Surefire Way*, and gave me the boost to finish *Dama X*.

Thank you to my dog Woody for being a good listener.

Thank you to Mike for always being there whether I need a hug, a glass of wine, or a kick in the butt to get finished.

Dedication

This book is dedicated to the women in my life who are stronger than they realize. My three moms and my closest friends.

And you do it without superpowers.

Praise for A Surefire Way— UltraSecurity Book 1

"This was a fantastic take on the whole 'mutant' human storyline. I love the twist that the Aztec mythology added to everything. With a newsurprise around every chapter - the book remained interesting up untilthe very end."
--Jasmyn, reviewer, Bitten by Paranormal Romance

"I was quickly drawn into the story easily slipping into thepictures in my mind. The writing sparked a fabulous tableau of imagesthat easily flowed from the author's descriptive words through my mind's eye."
--Mindy, reviewer, Books, Books, and More Books

"With A Surefire Way, Bock provides an epic adventure jam-packedwith everything that makes reading a pure pleasure--a strong heroine, acocky hero, super powers, danger, skullduggery and laugh-out-loud humor."
--Kathy Altman, author of *The Other Soldier* and *Staying at Joe's*

"J.T. Bock has a wickedly funny and charming sense of adventure."
--Carlene Love Flores, author of *Sidewalk Flower*

"Colorful as a comic book, Bock mixes action and romance with Aztec mythology in this roller coaster ride of a story."
--Willa Blair, author of *Highland Healer*

Prologue
Lost My Charm

———————————

Not everyone responds to gene therapy the same way. Those born without the ability to walk, for example, may benefit more from an exoskeleton to aid their mobility than treatments that focus on the genetic level. Manipulating genes doesn't always work as planned. It's not the magic bullet for health and youth that some transhumanists tout. More research is needed, which is why our treatment isn't universally available.

—Dr. Victor Vivas, co-founder of TransGen, excerpt from an interview with *The Baltimore Sun,* 7 years ago

———————————

Perched on the edge of the sofa, Camille Jones slipped her hand into the pocket of her bulky sweater and fingered the cold cylinder inside. Her revenge. Her ticket to getting her life back. To making Jimmy Donovan, her soon-to-be-once-and-for-all-ex-boyfriend, see things her way. Feel her desperation during all those wasted years with him.

Across from her, Jimmy sat cross-legged on the floor of her apartment. Camille watched his face pinch and then relax as he stuck a needle into his arm.

"Damn, that's intense." Jimmy dropped the empty syringe onto the glass coffee table in front of Camille. He undid the shoestring tourniquet above his elbow.

Camille took a long drag from her cigarette. Her hands shook despite the two Xanax she'd popped earlier.

"You done good, Cams." Jimmy fell back onto the carpet. His arms bent like broken wings on a fallen angel. His face lit up with a drug-induced afterglow.

"It's all for you, hon." Camille flicked ash next to a joint and matchbox set on the table. "To say I'm sorry."

Sorry for leaving Jimmy and making him angry. Sorry for making him hit her and for making him stalk her during the last two months for her own protection.

So much to be sorry for, ever since she'd met him.

"All's forgiven." Jimmy gazed up at her with his large baby blues lined by dark, thick lashes.

Eyes she bet the snake used on Eve to make her take that first bite.

Camille turned her head and shut her lids tight. She wouldn't get sucked in again. Believing this gorgeous man could love her and that her love alone could change him. Such a load of crap. There was only one way to change a man like Jimmy.

"Where's your queer queen of a cousin? Finally got tired of him looking prettier than you?"

"He's doing a show tonight." Camille left unsaid how her cousin had moved out when he heard Jimmy was back in her life.

She snubbed out her smoke on the table. "I have a surprise for you."

"You know I hate surprises." Jimmy stretched his arms above his head. His gray T-shirt lifted to reveal a smooth stomach with a patch of dark hair trailing under faded jeans.

Camille jerked her gaze away from the jeans drooping low on his waist. She fisted her hands to stop from trembling. She hated herself for being weak and hated him for making her feel weak.

With her last ounce of nerve, Camille slid the vial from her pocket and placed it on the table.

"What's this?" He eased up and eyed the greenish-blue liquid, which twinkled in the light.

"A gift from Naomi for us getting back together."

"No, but what is it?" Jimmy leaned on the smudged glass table to peer closer. "I've never seen shit like that sparkle before."

"Naomi says it's new and hasn't hit the streets yet. It's from Mexico or somewhere . . . I don't know. Supposed to feel better than meth. Doesn't wreck your body."

Jimmy continued to stare at it. She couldn't tell if he was transfixed by the way it glittered or freaked out by it.

"Figured I'd give it a try." Camille reached for it. Jimmy slapped her hand away.

"You think you can handle this? Last time, you vomited a hundred dollars worth of pills all over my car's backseat. You ain't gonna waste this. Hell no, this must be primo brew by the looks of it."

"Fine. Go for it." Camille slouched onto the couch.

Resting his chin on the table, Jimmy eyed the vial more closely.

Try it. She willed him to pick up the needle.

His arm slithered out over the table. His fingers caressed the syringe then yanked back. "It's cold."

On the verge of losing her nerve, Camille blurted out, "Needs to be or it won't be as potent. But if you're too much of a puss to try it—"

His hand flew up. Fingers clamped around her wrist as she reached for the syringe.

"What did you call me?"

"Nothing." His fingers dug in tighter. Her wrist throbbed in protest. "I was saying that I need to put it in the fridge, if you want to wait."

"I'll do it now." He let go of her and snatched up the needle. "The other stuff's wearing off already. Just wanted to check it out first, that's all."

"Have fun." Camille shook the blood back into her hand. With her other, she grabbed the joint and matchbox with a blue jay cartoon from the table and stood. Walking toward the hallway next to the small kitchen, she turned her back on Jimmy to hide her hands, which shook so much she couldn't light the match.

Camille glanced over her shoulder in time to see Jimmy stick the needle into the same vein he had used minutes before.

A low moan escaped his lips, as his head dropped back. "Aw, man, this is the bomb. Here, you gotta try this." Jimmy held out the nearly empty syringe to her.

Pocketing the unlit joint and matches, Camille walked over and took the syringe from him. Several glimmering drops fell off the sharp needle and onto the carpet.

"It's like a million tiny fingers are massaging my body. All over." He laid back and jutted his hips in the air to accentuate the point.

Camille turned her hand over and stared at the vial.

Blood pounded in her ears. Naomi said it would take to the count of—

Jimmy screamed.

Camille dropped the needle.

"Jesu—" His body convulsed. "What . . . the . . . "

He curled into a ball. The skin on his arms and neck bubbled as if he were boiling from the inside out. From under his shirt, his chest enlarged with two balloon-shaped objects and then deflated.

Camille inched away.

"Help me!" Jimmy reached out to her. A gooey film covered his arms, matting down the black hairs.

She took a large step back.

"Oh, no, oh, no." He leaned on the coffee table to hoist himself to his knees.

He looked down at his crotch where a deep, red stain began to spread between his legs.

Jimmy struggled to his feet and pushed past Camille, stumbling down the hall and into the bathroom.

A deep, throaty wail echoed from the narrow corridor. Using the wall for balance, Camille took one, then two, then three steps toward the open door of the bathroom.

The wall under her palm vibrated with several loud thumps followed by the sound of boots kicking the wooden bathroom cabinet. Camille leaned into the doorway.

Then she heard a woman scream.

Chapter 1
Touch of a Good Woman

The case involving Surefire and Raven is still under investigation, so I can't comment on the specifics. I can say they both received pardons for whatever laws they may have broken in the course of saving our nation from a power-crazed criminal, proving once again that transhumans are working for the greater good.

—Sean Vivas, co-owner of U-Sec, at a June press conference

Cassandra trailed her tongue down the center of his chest and breathed in his scent—a combination of salt and sweat and a savory spice that always set her heart racing.

When her tongue reached the tight muscles of his stomach, his arms jerked and rattled the handcuffs around his wrists.

"Ticklish?"

"Maybe," he replied.

She lifted her upper body while she straddled his naked hips. Her fingers danced over his wide chest, then smoothed over his muscular shoulders.

Her eyes flicked to the cuffs holding his hands to her headboard. He could break them. Easily. He could even break her solid antique headboard without trying. But he didn't. He submitted to her. Wanted to submit. So much power under her control. Her pulse quickened.

"Uncomfortable?"

"Not now." He raised his head to kiss her.

She pulled back. "Not until I say so."

Cassandra's fingers combed through his thick blond hair that he'd grown out at her request. Her other hand cupped his cheek, rough with a few days of stubble. Then she let her thumb pass over his bottom lip. His tongue darted out and licked the tip.

She wanted to take him in. Take a mental picture of his gorgeous body. Because in real life, she didn't have him anymore. In real life, she could never see him like this.

In real life, she couldn't see him at all unless it was through another's eyes.

Cassandra placed her hands on either side of his face and leaned down, unable to resist kissing him, being nearer to him.

"Pax, I still . . ."

Her words faded into the lyrics of Madonna's "Like a Virgin." The song filled the room as if the pop icon was belting it out next to the bed.

"Matthews," she blurted out loud. The dream faded into reality. Her eyelids opened to the darkness.

The song continued to play, accentuated by a buzzing from the nightstand next to her bed.

Cassandra, UltraAgent Oracle as she was known at U-Sec, rolled over onto her stomach and scooted across the cool cotton sheets until her left knee rested over the edge of the mattress. She stretched her arm and felt for the hard edge of the nightstand. Her fingertips trailed along the lightly vibrating surface before knocking into the rubber case of her cell phone.

"What?" she grumbled into the speaker.

"Now you hurt my feelings. Thought you'd be happy to hear my voice," Detective Guy Matthews of Baltimore's Criminal Investigation Division, Transhuman Unit, teased her.

"What time is it, Matthews?" She stretched her legs out and her feet bumped a large, warm lump at the bottom of the bed. Her black lab, Nyxe, didn't stir from the light kick but kept on snoring.

"One o'clock."

"It better not be a.m."

"Would you believe me if I said it wasn't?"

She rolled onto her back and onto her soft, inviting feather pillow. "Are you okay?"

"So far, I'm good. But I need your help. I have a case—"

"No, no, no." Her voice rose as the grogginess lifted. "I'm off, Matthews. On disability, sabbatical, or whatever you call it when you get your butt handed to you by an ancient god."

"You're not going to let an Aztec a-hole keep you down, are you? That's not the Cassandra, I mean, UltraAgent Oracle I know."

What if this is the new me? Full of anxiety. Uncertainty. Fear. Someone who gets a pounding in the back of her head and bile rising in her throat because a colleague mentions work.

Work that required she open up her mind and let whatever evil was outside in the world inside her again.

She wanted to go back to sleep. And that thought sent a hot flush across her skin, when she recalled her dream starring a different man in an intimate position she hadn't considered doing with her current boyfriend, Matthews.

"Why did you wake me up about this case?" She yawned to accentuate the point that she'd been sound asleep.

"I have a possible transhuman suspect who has . . . well . . . let me put it this way, she puts Lorena Bobbitt to shame."

"She cut off her husband's penis?"

"More complicated than that. I'll brief you when I get there in thirty minutes."

"Matthews, I can't."

"I'm not accepting no for an answer."

"Bite me, then."

"Not that either, unless you're talking about what you'll do to me this weekend."

Oracle groaned and wished she had the sense to stop dating men she worked with. Tough, when she hardly had time to socialize with her friends and family let alone meet a man outside of work.

"You've been telling me for the last two weeks that you're starting to feel better. That you wanted back in the game. Well, here's your chance."

"I didn't mean now." Later. Much, much later.

"If anything happens, I'll be there. I wouldn't ask you if lives weren't at stake."

"You had to play the guilt card, didn't you?" Oracle sighed.

"What about the geek card: help us, UltraAgent Oracle, you're our only hope?" Matthews did his best Princess Leia impression.

Oracle groaned once more, louder to make sure he heard. Matthews wasn't going to let up, and she wasn't going to get back to that very blissful dream.

He was right. She could try. The old Oracle would try. Matthews wasn't one to exaggerate. She couldn't deal with a death on her conscience as well.

"Fine. I'll meet you outside my building in thirty."

"Less than twenty now. I forgot that there's no traffic in Baltimore this late at night."

Which meant she had time for either a shower or coffee. Considering the dream she just had, a shower it was.

Eighteen minutes later, Oracle deposited her rump in the front seat of Mathews's sedan and slammed the car door shut.

"This better be worth it." With a snap, she collapsed the telescoping cane she used to make her way to the curb.

"And *hello* to you too." Matthews welcomed her with way too much cheer for the early hour.

"I'm not a morning person."

"That, I know."

Oracle's face heated at his chiding tone. Thank the lord for her blindness, or else she'd have to face the suggestive expression that went with his suggestive tone.

"With less than four hours of sleep, barely time for a shower, and no time for coffee, your flirtatiousness is not helping my mood."

"Here. An apology for the abrupt wake-up call." A cup grazed the side of her hand. "Soy mocha latte. No whip. Double shot of espresso."

She wrapped her fingers around the warm cardboard-sleeved cup and took a sip. Burning hot. Just how she liked it.

"Better?" he ventured. The car jerked into gear then revved away from the front of her condo complex.

"A little," she replied, impressed that Matthews brought her coffee and even more impressed that he remembered the kind she liked. He was a good guy. A genuinely good guy, which made it even more difficult to find a reason not to fall for him.

"You're a hard one to please."

"Don't I know it." She took another drink then licked her lips. "Tell me about this transhuman suspect."

"*Possible* transhuman suspect. You were a bit groggy when I mentioned that part."

"Oh, no, you didn't." Matthews's good guy stock dropped several points. "Do not tell me that you dragged me out of bed for a *possible* transhuman case. You call me in when you have definitive proof."

Oracle took another sip of coffee, but it wasn't enough to wash away the now sour taste on her tongue. Laws were in place so people with extraordinary abilities like her didn't take advantage, hurt, or even kill N-Ts, non-transhumans, when they used their powers. The police needed a special order from a judge to bring a transhuman onto an N-T case.

"Just because we've dated, doesn't mean you can bring me in on a whim," she argued.

"You're using the past tense in case you didn't notice," he said, seemingly nonplussed by her biting tone. "We have plans for this weekend, remember? The cabin at Deep Creek Lake?"

"You'll be swimming in deep shit lake if you don't get me home." Oracle set her jaw though inwardly chastised herself for taking her frustration out on Matthews.

He blew out a breath and didn't argue the point anymore. Perhaps he would take her home after all.

The car slowed as they turned down what she assumed was a side street from the major road they'd been traveling. If she wanted to learn where they were heading, she could touch Matthews's skin and see through his eyes. But then she might hear his thoughts, and she didn't care to do that just yet.

Matthews stopped the car and turned off the engine. Oracle set her jaw tighter. He had no plans to return to her home.

"No man will go near the suspect or the victim," Matthews said, followed by the click of his seatbelt being released. "A female paramedic is on the scene, but even if they tested for transhumanism, it would take too long for the results. The paramedics called in a hazmat team. However, neither the vic nor the suspect should remain in the apartment much longer. The victim needs more help than what the paramedics and hazmat team can offer, but they need information on what caused his condition to know how to treat him, which the suspect is too far gone to give. After she called 9-1-1, she must've taken a narcotic that has rendered her incoherent. My team doesn't want to bring the suspect in until we know for certain she's a transhuman at worst. After what went down with Surefire and Raven, we're not taking chances that she isn't otherworldly."

Oracle's throat tightened when Matthews mentioned Surefire, a young UltraAgent whom Oracle had been mentoring. An agent who pursued a transhuman thief into a Baltimore warehouse and ended up battling an ancient god—something that shouldn't exist, something they still struggled to understand. Now one of those gods was using Surefire as a conduit, and it was Oracle's fault for not being strong enough to help her.

"What aren't you telling me?" Oracle demanded, because his voice held an uncertainty that created a slight stutter, a sign she recognized as Matthews carefully choosing his words.

She heard Matthews's slacks shift along the leather driver's seat until she sensed him facing her. Smelled his coffee-laced breath as it drifted across her face. The weight of his arm rested on the back of her seat. Its warmth lingered on her shoulder.

"Her boyfriend's penis wasn't severed. It . . . uh . . . ."

Oracle took a deep, relaxing breath, centering herself, trying to calm her prickly nerves as she had learned in yoga, as she had lectured her hot-headed boss Pax to do many, many times. Matthews was safe. She'd seen through his eyes and read his mind in recent weeks as she little by little began flexing her transhuman muscles again. Besides, how could Matthews believe in her while she continued to doubt herself?

"Here." She slid off one of the leather driving gloves she'd started wearing every time she left her apartment.

Pressure rose at the base of her skull. Her heart thudded so loudly she was certain Matthews could hear it. Over the past month, her anxiety had grown like an unchecked infection spreading to every nerve. Her psychiatrist claimed the psychic attack from an *unknown* force—the Aztec god, which authorities officially refused to acknowledge existed—had caused it, even if the effects hadn't manifested until weeks later. The anxiety pills he prescribed took the edge off, but ultimately she was responsible for finding ways to overcome it. Given her line of work—and talent—she needed to find a way soon or risk letting down those victims who needed her most.

Oracle took another deep breath and offered her hand to Matthews. His toasty fingers curled around hers.

"Close your eyes and picture what you saw," Oracle said.

A warm current vibrated against her bones, buzzed up her arm, across her right shoulder, and then along the base of her neck. When it reached her head, the current exploded into tiny pinpricks of energy that crawled inside her skull, until her mind rebuilt the scene as Matthews had seen it, one layer at a time.

Off-white walls, beige carpeting. A flat-screen television set on a low oak cabinet. Glass coffee table scattered with a bag of weed, wrappers, and a pill bottle. On a green couch sat a woman in a bulky sweater. She leaned over and screamed then sobbed. Her hands were cuffed behind her. Shoulder-length platinum hair veiled her face. Two officers pushed Matthews aside and ran past him toward the front door. Retching sounds erupted behind him as the men vomited outside the apartment. More screams echoed farther inside the home. Low male and then higher-pitched female cries erupted from the narrow hallway as Matthews walked past a galley kitchen. A tall, lanky male paramedic knocked into Matthews. From under the mask covering his mouth and nose, he grumbled about getting his turnout gear and breathing apparatus and calling in hazmat.

Matthews put his hand on a door jam and peered into a small bathroom. With a breathing apparatus over her face, a female paramedic in yellow bulky pants and jacket leaned over the victim's naked body sprawled across the floor with feet sticking out into the hallway. Crumpled jeans bunched at the victim's ankles. An IV line trailed from the person's arm. ECG leads kept slipping off the victim's soft, gooey skin while a heart monitor beeped on top of the closed toilet lid then fell silent. The paramedic jabbed a needle into an arm, reaching down between flailing legs. The victim's jerky movements stilled. As she let out a relieved breath from under her breathing mask, the paramedic flicked creamy goo off her gloved hand and onto the floor covered with more of the viscous solution.

Then Matthews got a clear look at the person finally at rest in the slimy substance. Face was male. Short, spiky brown hair. Cropped beard soaked with more goo. But his body was smooth under the sticky, slick mess covering him. Skin like a newborn's. Hairless, pale, translucent in places where veins and some kind of bladder pulsated underneath in his chest. Where his penis should've been was smooth, save for an indentation between his legs almost as if . . .

Oracle let go and pushed back in her seat. Her head banged into the glass window. "Was he—?"

"Turning into a woman?" Matthews offered. "That's what it looked like to me."

"What did the suspect say?"

"She's hysterical and barely has the vocabulary of a three-year-old. As I mentioned, we think part of her incoherence could be from drugs. We found a variety of narcotics in the apartment. Who knows what and how much she took."

"She showing any signs of infection or whatever has happened to the man in the bathroom?"

"Nothing so far. Neighbors were told to stay inside. Paramedics quarantined the area after calling the hazmat coordinator. Technically, I shouldn't have left the scene, should be quarantined myself."

"And not stop for coffee," Oracle added.

"Did the drive-thru. Small price for civilians to pay for me to get on your good side."

"Nice of you to sacrifice others for my happiness."

"My instincts told me that it's not contagious." Matthews opened the driver's door then said to Oracle before he climbed out, "But don't thank me too much—my instincts are right about ninety-nine percent of the time, so you might be infected now."

Oracle's gut clenched. When Matthews opened her passenger door, she opened her mouth to ream him out but he deflected her.

"You're scared, I know," he said.

Crossing her arms, she faced forward, not turning in his direction.

"This is your first time out in the field in months," he continued. "And I wanted you to hear a familiar voice and see inside a familiar mind. I wouldn't have called you in if we didn't need answers now to save the people inside that apartment. It would take too long to get another telepath here. You're our best bet for finding the right treatment in time."

Their best bet. Oracle's stomach clenched again. She swallowed down the acidic coffee inching back up her throat. She needed to get over her anxiety one way or another. And jumping into the deep end with drowning swimmers was one way to do it—or not.

She uncrossed her arms and put out her still-ungloved hand for Matthews to grab. Through his eyes, she received several image flashes of the area where they walked. They were in the parking lot of a three-story apartment complex near the suburbs but inside the city limits. Various police officers, a few FBI agents she recognized, and paramedics milled about on the lawn and pathway leading to the steps to the second floor, with police tape cordoning off an open apartment door covered by plastic. Tenants, some in boxer shorts and tank tops, and others in terry cloth robes and curlers, sat on their balconies or leaned over the metal rails to watch the activity on the lawn. Along the grassy area on either side of the pavement leading to the building, a hazmat crew was setting up a second shower and two women were taping up the edges of their white hazmat suits and then pulling masks over their faces.

"I told a teensy fib." Matthews bumped against her arm as they walked.

"Just one?" Oracle countered.

"I did get decontaminated before I left. Thought you might feel more special if I said that I ran straight to you first."

"A bit of advice on working with and dating me." She stopped abruptly and pulled Matthews to a halt. "Never put other people in danger for me. That's not love, that's stupidity."

"Duly noted," he said in a cheery voice, as if that's what he expected her to say.

She shook her head. Matthews led her forward.

"We'll have to get you a protective suit," he said.

One of the women in the hazmat suits paused while putting on her mask when she noticed them.

"Matthews," she shouted.

"Oh, boy," he muttered.

The woman stalked closer to them. Her puffy garment crinkled with every long stride. Her dark brows lowered over equally dark eyes. "Weren't you in the apartment earlier? You should've been quarantined and not left the scene. If this turns out to be—"

"Hey, Dr. JoJo, good to see you too," Matthews interrupted the doctor's verbal berating, and Oracle got a memory flash of a party and Matthews holding this woman's hand. But her hair was blood red and short in Matthews's memory, not long and black as she wore it now. "Have you met UltraAgent Oracle? She's here to help."

Before Matthews dropped Oracle's hand, she watched JoJo give her a once over. The doctor regarded Oracle with such intensity that she wouldn't have needed to see the woman's appraising stare to know it was there, especially when Dr. JoJo noticed her eyes. Oracle's skin tingled from the weight of her gaze. She had forgotten to wear her sunglasses and her grayish white eyes against her dark skin could shock those who had never met her.

But based on Matthews's memory, this was more than the good doctor being leery of a transhuman.

"Nice to meet you, Dr. JoJo." Oracle held out her gloved hand to the woman, who took it with a hardy shake.

"You're a transhuman?" JoJo said in lieu of a greeting.

"Yes." Oracle held her breath, steeling herself for a possible battle with someone prejudiced against transhumans.

"The one who can read minds?" she prodded in her direct, abrupt manner.

"When I touch them," Oracle clarified, not wanting to explain that she could hear everyone's thoughts in the vicinity if she fully opened her mind.

Which she wasn't about to do. Possibly ever again.

"Let's get you suited up." JoJo's tone perked up and Oracle relaxed. "I'll help you dress if you don't mind."

"Not at all."

JoJo grabbed Oracle's gloved hand and lifted it until her fingers pushed past billowy fabric and pressed into pliant flesh, what she believed to be JoJo's upper left arm near her elbow. With the uneven grassy area and the crowded crime scene, Oracle wrapped her fingers around JoJo's arm, accepting the doctor's gesture to guide her through the scene.

"My name is Dr. Johanna Johnson. But everyone calls me JoJo." She started to lead her away from Matthews and then paused and barked out, "Riley, get Matthews deconned now."

"I'm good," Matthew protested. "I was going to suit up and join you. Give Oracle some backup."

"No, you're not," she continued. "Into the showers with you—clothes and all."

"But I already—"

"That's an order. Go through once more to be safe," JoJo cut him off. "Don't want you to lose your crotch luggage too."

Oracle choked back a laugh.

"Oracle?" Matthews called after them, and she had to give him credit for not asking if she was comfortable going to the scene without him. She didn't want anyone else to know she wasn't functioning at one hundred percent.

"She's fine, Matthews," JoJo spoke for her. "I'm going with her. She's not a fragile China doll for Pete's sake. Let the woman do her thing."

She gave JoJo what she hoped was an affirmative smile, because inside, she was certain to break at any moment.

In record time, JoJo got Oracle into the protective suit and mask and led her up the stairs.

Before they entered the apartment, Oracle said, "I need to make contact with the suspect's skin to know what we're dealing with."

There was a long pause and then JoJo replied, "That's risky."

"It's the only way."

"You'll need to go through decontamination and be kept for observation until we determine it's not infectious."

"I understand."

"James Donovan, the victim, has been sedated with Haldol, so we can transport him as soon as you determine the cause. But I don't recommend getting your bare skin anywhere near him." She led Oracle into the room. The soft carpet gave way with each step. The hazmat suit sifted and crinkled, filling her ears with noise so she had to strain to hear JoJo talk though her mask. "I'm leading you to Camille Jones. She's on the couch, still dazed but not hysterical anymore. Should make your job easier."

"Let's hope." Oracle's shin hit into the pillowy edge of the overstuffed sofa she had seen in Matthews's mind. She sat on the cushion, through which she could feel the vibrations of Camille's rocking movement. She removed a hazmat glove.

"Miss Jones." JoJo leaned over and rested a hand on Oracle's arm. "Miss Camille Jones, I'm Dr. Johanna Johnson and this is UltraAgent Oracle. We need to make sure you're okay, and then we can get help for Mr. Donovan. You're going to feel her hand on yours."

A low babble was the only response to JoJo's statements.

An uneasiness settled in Oracle's stomach. She took in a deep breath and smelled Patchouli oil laced over a coppery scent, she assumed was blood. This wasn't the work of an ancient spirit. The air wasn't thick with a prickling energy like when the Aztec god had attacked her.

She rubbed her hands together. She wouldn't lose her nerve in front of JoJo. Wouldn't let her peers down again. She could do this. They were counting on her.

Oracle asked, "Can I touch her?"

She held up her ungloved hand in a signal for JoJo to guide her. She remembered from Matthews's thoughts that Camille wore an oversized sweater, but she wasn't sure if her arm was exposed now. JoJo's fingers encircled Oracle's wrist, right at the fabric, and moved her to touch Camille's hand still cuffed behind her back.

Oracle clasped Camille's fingers and a harsh current burned up her skin, pinning her back against the cushion with the shock of it. The hot energy passed over her shoulder and cruised up her spine to the base of her skull. Oracle braced herself for the images to come. But there was only darkness. Camille had blacked out the event.

"Tell me about Mr. James Donovan," Oracle said.

Camille let out a soulful wail and the darkness lifted.

James's face appeared, contorted with anger. His fingers dug into Oracle's biceps. Actually, Camille's biceps, but the memory was vivid. More vivid than she had experienced when reading a suspect in the past. The scene replayed in Camille's mind, bubbling up with emotions so raw Oracle choked back a sob.

Camille hated James . . . or Jimmy, as she called him. She wanted him to pay for what he'd done to her. In Camille's memory, Jimmy struck her. Oracle's own head whipped to the side.

"Oracle!" JoJo grabbed her shoulder.

"I'm fine." She shrugged off the doctor. But Oracle wasn't sure how convincing she sounded, because her left cheek tingled with the memory of the hit, and her arms throbbed where Jimmy had grabbed Camille. A bitter taste coated her tongue as if she'd just vomited. Oracle was getting the full 4-D memory experience with Camille. Maybe this woman was a transhuman, or maybe the drugs were causing the memories to be more intense than she'd experienced when reading others.

However, the memory wasn't from this evening, and they weren't in the apartment. It was a different time. Camille and Jimmy were standing on the pavement next to a shiny black Mustang.

"Focus on tonight," Oracle whispered. "How did this happen to Jimmy?"

The memory faded to a needle lying next to Camille's bare feet on the apartment floor. Jimmy's screams for help filled the room.

"On the living room floor there should be a syringe," Oracle told JoJo. "That's what Donovan used."

"I don't see anything," JoJo replied followed by the sounds of furniture being lifted and then slid across the carpet. "Wait. Here it is. Someone kicked it under the couch." She called to her team outside to get it to the lab.

"Who gave him the drug?" Oracle asked.

Camille's mind shut down. The memory faded once more to black. She stopped rocking, although the fingers Oracle clutched still trembled.

"We need to know so we can help you both."

Camille's body shook. She began to sob with a high-pitched cry that made Oracle's ears ring.

"We need to move them. Donovan's vitals are slipping. If you can't get more information, then you need to let go," JoJo said.

Oracle wasn't letting go until she finished the job. For the first time in months, she was beginning to feel in control. Her anxiety relegated to a corner the further she dug into Camille's mind. Matthews was right. She could do this. She needed to do this—and she wouldn't let them down. Not like when she lost Surefire and collapsed into a fainting mess at the warehouse. Or when she fell apart in the parking lot before Surefire and Raven had disappeared. Over this last month, after opting for desk duty in lieu of the field, she had heard the rumors. The whispers of others saying her ability had finally messed with her brain and that she couldn't control it anymore.

And she almost believed them.

"I got this." Oracle straightened her back and squeezed Camille's fingers.

She pushed her energy into the blackness of the young woman's mind like slipping a foot into a snug ballet shoe. Camille's body went rigid as Oracle's power spread through her torso and into her limbs. Through Camille's eyes, Oracle saw JoJo standing next to the sofa. Saw the table and the discarded drug paraphernalia. The swirling numbness of the suspect's narcotic-laced brain made Oracle dizzy. Her arms were sore. Cuffs cut into her raw wrists. Eyes burned with tears.

Then Oracle tilted her head, and Camille tilted her head.

JoJo gasped.

Oracle turned to face JoJo. Camille turned to face JoJo, who stumbled away from the couch, dark eyes wide under the hazmat mask.

What have I done? How am I doing this?

It was wrong. Deep down Oracle knew it was wrong to feel this much of Camille. She'd read another's thoughts. Saw through their eyes. But she'd never had control over someone else's body. Maybe it was the drugs that muddied Camille's mind and allowed Oracle to go deeper than ever before.

But her gut said otherwise.

Both Oracle's and Camille's hearts beat with the same frantic rhythm. Breath coming out in measured gasps.

Uneasy, she started to withdraw from Camille then stopped. JoJo needed answers and Jimmy needed treatment or he'd die.

Focus on Camille.

Later, she'd figure out why this was happening. Now, it worked to her advantage.

Where did Jimmy get this drug? She forced the question into Camille's consciousness.

A memory flashed in her mind. Camille waiting outside Columbia Mall, near the movie theater, in the suburbs west of the city. A beat-up Honda pulled up to the curb. Camille didn't look at the driver as she got in. Then the vision jumped ahead. The scent of cookies, chocolate cake, and a host of sweet, delectable desserts made Oracle's mouth water with longing. Camille sat in a sunny, cheerful kitchen at a polished wooden table. Her arm reached for a plate of cookies. A patchwork of purple bruises encircled her pale forearm.

A light touch lingered on her shoulder from a presence standing behind her.

"Naomi told me you could help," Camille said with a mouthful of warm cookie.

Turn around. Oracle tried to force her to look at the person behind her. But Camille didn't budge, just continued chewing the gooey treat.

"I certainly can," a female voice responded with a slight accent. Spanish, maybe?

Turn around.

"How?" Camille asked.

A wooden box carved with a circle—half sun, half moon—appeared on the table next to her hands. From over Camille's right shoulder, an arm reached in front of her and a manicured feminine hand lifted the lid revealing several vials filled with a blue-green, sparkling liquid.

Turn around.

"Diosa de la Venganza. It can make him see things your way. Understand what it's like to be you," the woman whispered in Camille's ear, making her scalp tingle.

"How much is it?"

"Compliments of the Sisterhood of Diana."

"Who?"

Camille spun around in the wooden kitchen chair. No one was there. After pocketing one vial, she ran out of the home.

Oracle withdrew her energy from Camille like sucking water up a straw. Warmth spread back into her limbs, which were surprisingly ice cold. She let go of Camille's fingers and sensed her body tilting away and then flopping onto the couch.

"Holy mother of all," JoJo exclaimed.

"Is Camille okay?" Oracle rasped, her mouth dry as sandpaper.

"She's unconscious." JoJo's voice came from the right, near Camille. "Vitals appear fine. We're going to take her to the hospital."

Oracle cleared her throat. She needed water. She'd never been so thirsty.

"I don't think Donovan's contagious. Whatever was in that needle caused his condition, and I didn't find evidence of it being preternatural. I saw several more vials of the drug used on him in Camille's memory. But I don't know who gave it to her."

"What you just did—" JoJo's words faltered. "I've never seen anything like that."

"That makes two of us." Oracle's head was as light as a balloon. The room began spinning and pitching around her like a fast-moving carnival ride.

"You need to lie down."

She sensed JoJo lunging forward to catch her. But it was too late. Oracle tumbled onto the floor and into a welcoming silence.

Chapter 2
A Complicated Woman

If I don't comment, you can't twist my words.

—Pax, co-founder of UltraSecurity, at a press meeting about Operation Bird Catcher (the Raven case assigned to UltraAgent Surefire)

Files handed off to his assistant Helena. Computer bag on his shoulder. Keys and wallet in his pocket. And his cell phone off.

Levi Paxton, Pax to everyone but his mother, took a mental inventory of what he needed so he wouldn't have to see his office again until Tuesday.

He rounded a corner. The door to U-Sec's garage came into view. Just a few yards away. He checked his watch. Twelve noon on the dot. Gorgeous late September weather awaited him outside that door. In four hours, he'd be sitting on the dock of his bay house with a beer in one hand and fishing rod in another.

"Pax!" The indignant, prep school voice of his business partner, Sean Vivas, echoed from the hall behind him.

He kept walking.

"Pax!"

Was it wrong to ignore Sean? It could be an emergency. It had better be an emergency. Pax had been working seventy hours a week for several months. He needed this break.

"Pax!"

He stopped with his hand on the gray bar of the metal door.

Hard-soled shoes skidded to a stop on the thin carpet behind him. "Are you deaf? I yelled your name twenty times."

"Three times." Pax turned and gave Sean the most heated glare he could muster.

Sean's smoothly shaved face didn't flinch. Pax must be losing his touch.

"You could've acknowledged me," Sean retorted.

"I just did."

"I tried calling your cell phone."

"It's off."

Sean crossed his arms over his gray suit jacket and a multi-colored, pop art tie that Pax wouldn't be caught dead in.

"I'm on vacation as of two minutes ago. As we discussed, I'm off noon Thursday through the end of Monday. Not on call. Not available at all." Pax pivoted back to the door and pushed it open when Sean spoke again.

"Felix Reyes from Mexico just called."

"Are you sure it was Reyes?" Pax released the door and let it slam shut.

"Unless you offered U-Sec's services for *free* to another Felix Reyes from the Mexican government . . ."

Screw me. He spun around and came eye to eye with Sean, who was an inch or so shy of Pax's six-foot-four height. He also had Sean by at least forty pounds of muscle, as he enjoyed reminding his business partner, who had a swimmer's lean build. No match for a linebacker like Pax.

"What did he want?" Pax couldn't process that Reyes had called. The Mexican general was ringing death's doorbell the last time he had seen him.

"He wouldn't talk to me. I told him I'd call him back as soon as I found you. He said it was urgent." Sean stepped back but his eyes bored into Pax's. "You'd just left so Helena transferred him to me."

Talk about timing. Some days, he couldn't win.

"We'll call from my office," Sean said.

"Makes sense to have a secure line."

"Why? Do we need one?"

Pax shrugged. He had no idea what Reyes wanted, but it better be important enough to warrant extra security if Pax was delaying his mini-break.

"I'm suggesting my office because we'll need to have a private discussion after this call." Sean squared his shoulders and ground out his point. "Without distractions."

As if this upcoming conversation with Reyes wasn't enough to smother his good vacation vibes, having a private talk with Sean was sure to extinguish them. With a frustrated grunt, Pax pushed past his partner and headed to the elevators.

"Is Reyes telling the truth? You promised to do a job for free?" Sean demanded.

"Yes." Pax punched a code in the keypad next to the elevator door and pressed his thumb against the fingerprint scanner.

The doors opened and Sean followed him onto the elevator.

"And you didn't think to tell Gloria and me about this?"

"Thought we were having this discussion after the phone call."

"We have a minimum to take in every month to keep U-Sec running." Sean wouldn't—or in his case—couldn't let it go.

They exited on the top floor, Sean close on his heels like a six-foot yappy dog.

"You're one of our top billable agents," he ranted at Pax's back. "Now you're going to work for free? For a government we don't have a standing contract with?"

"Lives are worth more than money. I made the choice to save Surefire and the others."

"I knew it." Sean clapped his hands together. "I knew you left something out of that report from Operation Bird Catcher."

"I made a deal with Reyes to save our agents and the hostages." Pax let out a relieved breath, glad Sean's assistant was at lunch. Never good for employees to see the owners arguing—even if it was standard operating procedure whenever they interacted.

"And you didn't think to mention this?" Sean paused at his office door to place his hand over the biometric reader.

"I planned to tell you after Raven and Surefire received their pardons and things settled down." Pax walked into Sean's office first. "Besides, I didn't think Reyes would pull through."

"Well, I hate to state the obvious—"

"Yet you will anyway." Pax deposited his laptop bag onto a leather swivel chair before plopping down into another.

"Agents Oracle and Surefire are down for the count because of supposed Aztec gods. Months later, I'm still getting emails and calls from the FBI, reporters, conspiracy theorists, and now a government security agency—one I've never heard of—wanting to investigate us. Things aren't going to settle down anytime soon." Sean sat at the head of the oblong, glass table.

"Our agents and hostages were underneath the ground, in a temple, along with our transhuman suspects and an unknown supernatural force." Pax locked eyes with Sean to convey the gravity of his words.

"I got that from the report," he bit out.

"Yeah, I could tell when you said 'supposed' ancient god that you completely got it." Pax rested his hands on the table and laced his fingers together so tightly, the strain began to numb them. But it kept him from hitting the table and accidentally breaking it in half as he had once before. An incident Sean never let him forget.

"This force took down Oracle and eventually knocked her out of commission. Another force would go on to possess Surefire. I didn't know what it would do to our other agents or hostages. We needed to act fast, and because it was an historical site, protected by the Mexican government, we couldn't storm in without permission. And Reyes, his army, and President Diaz weren't willing to give permission until I agreed to these terms."

Pax swiped his hand over the tabletop and a large keypad appeared in the retina display. His index finger poised over the buttons. "What is Reyes's number?"

"Ohhh . . . umm . . . excuse me," a feminine voice chimed.

Pax swung his head away from Sean to find his agent Kali, codename TimeTrap, standing in front of the shaded windows.

She edged closer with her long fingers splayed out in apology. "I thought it was safe to pop in."

"This is my office." Sean rapped his finger on the desk.

"Obviously, with fifty shades of blech. You really need to add some color to the space. A touch of red or—"

"Don't do it again. Use the front door like everyone else."

"Boring," she exhaled and sauntered toward the conference table. Her short sixties style dress hiked up her lean thighs as she sat on the table. She enjoyed spending her off days partying in the sixties. Not the best use of her ability, but who was Pax to judge?

"It's much more fun to make an entrance, and good practice too," she said. "If I don't use my ability, I may lose focus. Besides, you've been out of town on these secret missions with Gloria. It's been safer to arrive via QT in here so I don't displace anything or anyone."

"QT?" Sean inquired drolly.

"Oh, you know. Quantum-transference. I started calling it QT for short. Makes it easier to say and for others to get." She gave Sean's shoulder a condescending pat.

"Are you scheduled for work today?" Pax asked in a tone that implied, *Why are you here?*

"I need to talk with you personally . . . about some, uh, personal stuff," TimeTrap replied.

"I'm off this afternoon." He glanced at the clock, a quarter past noon now. "Was off, I mean."

TimeTrap's large brown eyes, accented with dark blue shadow, widened as Pax assumed she got the hint. "Right, well, that sucks. I'll just be . . ." her tall body slid behind Sean's chair and the wall, ". . . getting out of your way."

Sean huffed as his chair jerked forward when her boot kicked it.

"Sorry about that," she said in a not-so-sorry tone before she left the room.

When the door clicked shut behind TimeTrap, Sean said, "What was that about?"

"How should I know? I haven't heard from her in over a week. So, where were we?" Pax again swiped his hand across the glass table to make the keypad reappear.

"Here. I'll do it. You look frustrated, and I don't want you breaking the screen by pushing too hard again. This conference table was expensive," Sean said.

"That was once. Three years ago."

Sean waved Pax's hand away and rested his fingers over the tabletop tablet screen.

"Why did you call this meeting, Sean?" Gloria breezed into the room. "I've got a low-level security breach at TransGen to meet about. A new client proposal to send out and . . . what's Sean doing?" She pulled out a chair next to Pax.

"He's calling Reyes."

"Why doesn't he—?"

"Shh!" A soft blue light flickered across Sean's eyes and grew to a vibrant electric blue that obscured his dark brown irises.

"Did you shush me? Because I will personally shove that Warhol-wannabe tie down your throat, little bro."

"How did you get in?" Pax motioned to the locked door.

"I had them recalculate the scanner to read my print too. Sean's not keeping secrets from me."

Currents pulsated and lit up a maze of lines on Sean's hands. Electronic circuits followed nerves under his light brown skin and ended at his fingertips. The tabletop vibrated under Pax's palms as Sean connected with the circuits.

"Didn't expect you here." Pax swiveled his chair to face his other business partner.

"Sean texted that you were meeting in his office," she replied then asked, "Aren't you supposed to be at your bay house?"

"Supposed to be."

A black silhouette of a man appeared on the screen-top desk along with voice modulator lines. Reyes must've disallowed video conferencing on his end.

Sean spoke first. "Reyes, I found Pax, and our business partner, Gloria, is here as well."

Gloria mouthed "who?" to Pax, but he put up a finger for her to wait.

"Pax, my friend, good to finally talk to you." Reyes's cultured voice filled the room. "I heard mention of a vacaciones."

"Yeah, I heard mention of that too." He glared at Sean who shrugged it off. "How are you, General Reyes?"

"Ah, not General anymore. Retired. Forced into an early retirement."

"I'm sorry."

"It is what it is," Reyes replied. "President Diaz has reassigned me, moved me onto bigger things."

"How is it possible that you're even alive, let alone moving on to bigger things?" Pax blurted out. Reyes's strong, clear voice was at odds with the image etched in Pax's mind of a vibrant soldier in his early forties shriveled down to a thin, arthritic man.

Reyes laughed it off. "I didn't say I was recovered. But I'm reviewing opportunities as I continue to heal."

Pax never considered Reyes would call in the favor so soon. Over four months ago, Reyes was put into an induced coma after being aged thirty years in thirty seconds by an ancient Aztec god, which still sounded insane even though Pax had witnessed it. He'd heard rumors that Reyes had begun healing within a week of the incident as the spell had worn off. That notion seemed ridiculous, illogical, but given what Pax had witnessed—believable.

Gloria's high-heeled shoe ground into Pax's sneaker under the table. Her straight brown hair fell against his shoulder as she leaned over and whispered in his ear, "Is this the general from your report?"

Pax nodded.

"What the what?" she murmured.

Pax knew Reyes was a transhuman. Although he never admitted it, his actions spoke volumes. A small, graceful man, Reyes made Pax wince when he shook his hand for the first time. From what he could tell, Reyes's strength might match his own, which was ten times that of the strongest weightlifter. But could Reyes also heal? Regenerate his body and fight aging? Those were transhuman abilities that had eluded top scientists at TransGen—a transgenetic research facility owned by Sean and Gloria's father.

"Reyes, this is Dr. Gloria Vivas, Pax's other business partner," she spoke up when Pax paused to consider how to respond to him. "Are you a transhuman?"

Pax knocked his tennis shoe against her foot. Leave it to Gloria to sucker punch the elephant in the room.

"I read the report," she continued, ignoring Pax. "And there is no way for you to recover, especially in this short time, without genetic modification. What facility treated you? I'm aware of only one transhuman operation in Mexico."

Unless it wasn't science, Pax considered. Unless it was preternatural. During Operation Bird Catcher, UltraAgent Surefire had traveled to an underground temple in Mexico and partnered with her original target, Raven, to stop a god-like spirit from entering the world via a dimensional portal fueled by magical crystal skulls. Mexico and the United States had split the group of skulls used to call forth the Aztec god and placed them in secure locations to study their powers so no one could open the portal again. Could Reyes have accessed and harnessed power from one of those skulls to heal himself?

"With respect, Dr. Vivas, that has no relevance here. I would like to get to the point of my call," Reyes responded.

Taken aback, Gloria arched a brow at Pax.

He shook his head. Being a transhuman wasn't a crime, so why Reyes wasn't willing to admit it to other transhumans confused Pax as much as it did Gloria. Unless the facility that treated him was underground or a classified operation.

"I want to procure Pax's services for a personal assignment that is also of importance to my government," Reyes said. "Pax, you will follow through on our deal, I hope. President Diaz is counting on your help."

"My word is my bond. I told you and your president that I would be available when you needed me, and I meant it," he said.

Next to his ear, Gloria spoke in a quiet, harsh voice, "Find out how he did it. I'll make inquiries as well."

Pax nodded to shut her up. Reyes wasn't going to talk now. But he would question Reyes later if he wanted his help.

"Reyes," Sean cut in. "We need to draw up a contract and have it signed and sent back before Pax can do anything."

"It's acceptable for him to speak with me about the assignment, is it not? Considering you're not billing me for his time."

"True." Sean wagged his head in agitation. "But we'll have to bill for travel, other direct costs, and any additional resources that are required above Pax's time and expertise."

"Of course," Reyes replied.

Gloria rolled her chair around the table to Sean. In a voice low enough for Reyes not to hear, she began giving Sean the third degree about calling her into this meeting at the last minute.

"Tell me what you need." Pax grabbed a pen and pad of paper from his bag, preferring those to his SmartPad.

"Do you know of Dama X?" Reyes asked.

Pax glanced at Sean for confirmation that he knew the name, but he was too busy fending off Gloria's verbal barrage that had intensified from third to fifth degree.

"No," Pax said.

"She was married to Estabon Cortez, kingpin of the Mictlantecuhtli cartel, killed five years ago. Some speculated Dama X orchestrated his death, but there is no concrete proof. A few years later, she started her own cartel, La Hermandad de Diana, which gained a stronghold in Guerrero and Oaxaca on the Pacific coast and has threatened the drug lords in the surrounding areas."

Pax jotted down this information with notes to have his assistant, Helena, research the main players and confirm Reyes's statements. So far, he didn't know why Reyes would call him in on this case. Cartel leaders were killed all the time. By someone close to them like their wives, maybe more often than not.

Since Pax's time in the military, this cartel was considered a terrorist organization. Five years before Pax started U-Sec, his team from the Army's Enhanced Soldier Program (ESP)—co-developed by TransGen—had taken down a division of Estabon's crew that was smuggling terrorists into the United States.

"I remember the Mictlantecuhtli cartel. Estabon was a monster." Rape, murder, and even stories of cannibalism followed this group. Estabon's men destroyed any village resisting the cartel's advances to use their resources to set up shop. Pax's ESP team only put a dent in that crime organization.

"He was the devil incarnate. I experienced it firsthand twenty years ago when his *Cholos* decimated my hometown," Reyes said.

"I can't imagine what that was like for you and your family." Life in parts of Baltimore could be ugly. Nothing compared to the evil many cartels doled out on a daily basis. "But we're not in the business to protect criminals from other criminals. I doubt there was any love loss in your country with his death, unless his wife is worse than he was."

"She is a transhuman."

Sean and Gloria stopped their conversation and stared at the voice modulator on the screen. Pax shared a look with Gloria, whose face reflected the concern growing in his gut. Although there had been a handful of international transhuman crimes, usually the criminals were working alone, not heading an organized crime group.

"How do you know she's a transhuman?" Gloria demanded.

"We have witnesses to her abilities," Reyes replied.

Sean said, "If we're talking about an incident involving a transhuman cartel leader, you'll need more than Pax. We'll also need to contact at a minimum the FBI and DEA and coordinate with the Mexican military. This is not a one man—nor one agency—job."

"Our military is on standby, but I don't want those other groups involved," Reyes said with finality.

"That's not possible," Sean said.

"Reyes, we need more information. We can't send Pax alone— transhuman case or not." Gloria tapped a silver-tipped fingernail on the table. "We're bound by our contracts with these agencies to notify them of cases involving cartels."

"I fear she has spies in those agencies that could compromise this mission," Reyes said.

"We'll need proof other than your fears," Gloria countered.

"What has Dama X done?" Pax asked.

"La Hermandad de Diana is distributing a new drug in their region to be used on their enemies. Rumor has it that Dama X tested the drug on the remaining members of the Mictlantecuhtli cartel. These men disappeared soon after Estabon's death and are believed to be dead. In the regions that her cartel controls, several deaths and deformities have been associated with this drug. It was first known as La Santa Muerte by the cartels. But La Hermandad de Diana members referred to it as Diosa de la Venganza."

"Is that the Vengeful Goddess or Goddess of Revenge or . . . ?" Pax asked, trying to remember his high school Spanish class from twenty-odd years ago.

"What do you mean by deformities?" Gloria leaned on the table.

There was a pause over the phone and then Reyes said, "It's difficult to explain."

"Actually, it's pretty straightforward," a raspy voice spoke from Pax's left.

He turned to find UltraAgent Oracle propped against the closed door with TimeTrap next to her.

"The drug turns men into women," she finished.

"And on that freaky note, I'm out of here." TimeTrap disappeared.

♥ ☠ ♥ ☠ ♥ ☠

Gloria took her elbow and forced her to sit down, stating Oracle looked like "something my cat hacked up this morning."

No one could ever call Gloria subtle.

A whirlwind of questions followed. As Oracle folded down her cane and set her purse on the table, Sean, Pax, and Gloria spoke at once. Oracle could barely discern the questions, let alone who said what. If Reyes added anything, she couldn't hear over the cacophony.

"How do you know about this drug? Where were—"

"Who called you in? You should be home resting. I swear if Matthews—"

"You smell like a hospital. Have you been to the hospital? What's going—"

"Did you let HR know you're working again? What job is this—"

"Enough!" Oracle exclaimed louder than she expected, considering how tired she'd become. Adrenaline from the morning rush had receded, leaving bone-aching exhaustion in its wake.

"Give me a moment to collect my thoughts, and I'll tell you what happened." Oracle leaned back in the conference chair with a tight grip on the leather armrests. "And no questions until I'm finished."

Gloria fussed about the stipulation but offered no more protest as Oracle related the events of the early morning hours—omitting how she had passed out after controlling the suspect—before being quarantined at the hospital and then arriving at U-Sec to talk with Pax. When she walked into the building, she heard Gloria complaining to someone before the elevator doors closed that she'd have to deal with a possible TransGen security breach later, because Sean had called a meeting with Pax and a man named Reyes from Mexico. Fortunately, Oracle had bumped into TimeTrap, who knew where the meeting was taking place.

She recognized the name Reyes from Surefire's case. Nearly two months had passed since they'd heard from Surefire and Raven, who'd gone underground so the agent could gain control over her new goddess-fueled powers. She had wondered if Reyes had information about them, which is why she crashed their meeting.

"The mystery woman told Camille the drug was 'compliments of the Sisters of Diana,'" Oracle finished.

"Then it's spreading outside our country," Reyes's voice cracked over the speaker.

"Any reports from other U.S. cities or countries?" Sean interjected.

"None that the Centers for Disease Control knows of," Oracle said.

"Then why is this drug showing up in Baltimore?" Sean asked.

She shook her head. "I have no clue. Matthews is searching for Camille's dealer to find out who gave her this drug."

"Why were you there?" Pax's presence loomed at her right side. Even without seeing him, she knew he had drawn himself up to his full height, with arms crossed, jaw set, and a twitch starting at the edge of his mouth. "Didn't Matthews know you were on desk duty? I swear, I'll—"

"Before you go into Pax-smash-everything-in-sight mode . . ." Gloria butted in.

"What?" Pax exclaimed.

"The corner of your mouth is twitching, which indicates you're upset and are about to let us know it." Gloria's heavy steps stomped between Oracle and Pax. "So, before that happens, I need to know—" she tapped Oracle's shoulder— "where's the victim now?"

"At Johns Hopkins. Doctors from the CDC have him quarantined and stabilized." With great effort, Oracle stopped herself from giving Gloria a verbal beat-down for dismissing Pax, who showed more control over his super strength than Gloria or Sean ever gave him credit for.

"And the drug?" Gloria asked.

"Dr. Johanna Johnson of the CDC sent it to her lab."

"Why wasn't I notified?" Gloria demanded.

"I don't know." Oracle lifted her hands. "Matthews's department was officially assigned the case this morning. At first, they weren't sure it fell under our jurisdiction."

"They're going to ruin everything," Gloria uttered. "This is out of their league. I need to examine Donovan and move him to TransGen's facility before they screw it up."

Gloria marched away. A sweet perfumed breeze trailed in her wake, at odds with her agitated steps.

"We'll take the case, Reyes," Sean announced.

"We need more details," Pax stated.

Oracle let out a breath she'd been holding. What she'd overheard of this case after TimeTrap popped her into the office didn't feel right. More to the point, she didn't like Pax going it alone against an unknown transhuman—and a cartel leader at that, which tipped the meter into the danger zone.

"I will brief you fully once you are here. I need your consultation . . . your ESP military expertise . . . to handle this matter. That is all," Reyes said. "Let us work together to keep her—this drug—contained before it spreads further than your city and ours."

Oracle's ears zeroed in on the way Reyes paused as if he was choosing his words, deciding what to say and what to hold back, as Matthews had done earlier with her at the crime scene.

"What can Dama X do?" Oracle asked, trying to delve further. "I overheard you say she was a transhuman. What's her ability?"

Reyes paused long enough that Oracle assumed he wasn't going to reply.

"Reyes," she prompted.

A long breath filled the speakers before he replied, "We believe she can bend a person's will to her own. Witnesses saw Dama X whisper to three men who had been accosting and groping women at a discotheque she owns, where her late husband used to conduct business. Immediately, the men marched out of the bar as though in a trance. Hours later, police found them naked in the town square, wearing pig masks, and holding signs calling them out as chauvinists. The men had no idea how they got there or what happened to their clothes."

"Bet they didn't bother those women again." Gloria chuckled.

Oracle pressed back in her seat. This was more dangerous than she'd assumed. Could Dama X control a person's body as Oracle had done with Camille? If these witnesses told the truth, this transhuman had far more practice than Oracle did at being a puppeteer. In fact, Oracle wasn't certain she could do it again nor was she certain that she wanted to.

"How did Dama X get this ability?" Oracle asked.

"It's possible she always had this gift, but now it's enhanced," Reyes said.

A palm pressed over Oracle's gloved fingers. Even though she couldn't see who was touching her, she knew it was Pax, recognized his large, warm hand. She tilted her face up toward him where he stood at her side. He must've read the worry on her face. Noticed the tremble in her voice.

"Reyes, this is out of my expertise. I'll need help and more information before we meet." Pax's comforting hand left Oracle's.

"Rumor has it, her power doesn't affect transhumans," Reyes said.

"Rumor?" Oracle scoffed. "We need more assurance than that."

"You mentioned that her ability had been enhanced. Do we know when or how?" Gloria asked.

"No," Reyes said. "She toured Asia, Africa, the Middle East, and several European countries before Cortez died. We now believe this wasn't a vacation, but she was gathering women—many who are trained soldiers—from those countries to join her organization. Most likely, it was a facility outside Mexico that treated her."

Oracle's ears perked up. Reyes's words wavered when he said "outside Mexico." Like he added this as a side note, one he didn't believe.

Several registered transgenetic labs resided in the U.S. besides TransGen. Probably many more unregistered, underground facilities that didn't want to abide by government regulations. Some countries had loose or no regulations and didn't share their ethics-pushing findings through research papers in scientific journals.

Oracle would know. In college, her parents took her to one of those outside facilities, and TransGen had to fix her.

"Pax, you need to find out what you can," Gloria said. "If this is true, TransGen has never encountered or heard of the ability that Dama X has. Not to mention the damage this drug, Diosa de la Venganza, could do."

"If we can capture Dama X and get her to our labs, we could strip the gene that caused the mutation," Sean offered.

Oracle bristled. If her ability had expanded and she didn't cooperate with them, would TransGen try to strip it from her?

"TransGen has only stripped the transmutation gene a handful of times. There's no guarantee it would work," Gloria said. "Could others in her cartel be transhuman?"

"It's possible her inner circle is. Our police have seen several of her sisters, as she calls them, easily lift and carry objects an average woman, or even a man, would struggle with," Reyes replied.

Oracle's mind raced with scenarios as she half-listened to the conversation. Did anyone else besides Matthews and JoJo know what Oracle had done this morning? Did Camille know or had she been too far gone to realize? Had they told anyone else?

"How long have you known about Dama X and this drug?" Pax asked.

"Diosa de la Venganza came to our attention in the past year—at first as a rumor then via direct confirmation when we encountered its victims. She used it to harm and kill other cartel members and to threaten police and politicians she couldn't control."

"Considering what it does, no doubt the threat worked," Sean said.

"The drug's effects have worsened. At first, it caused impotence when administered to her rivals then came stories of penises shriveling up. A few weeks ago, we encountered a full-body transition where the man died."

"Now it's in our city. Why?" Pax drummed his fingers on the desk. Sean cleared his throat. Pax drummed harder.

"I don't know."

Pax stopped drumming and rested his hand on the back of Oracle's chair. "Then what do you know about this woman?"

Reyes paused for a few seconds before stating, "She's my sister, Xalvadora."

Oracle figured she'd misheard until Pax choked out, "Your sister?"

"We've been estranged for over a decade. I last saw her two years ago at our uncle's funeral. He cared for us when our mother died and left Xalvadora an island where she has recently moved her operation. There are plans in place to attack her compound, once it's located. An outside agency is funding this mission and working closely with the Mexican military. Our president and other leaders are backing this partnership and strategy. Partly because they fear Dama X, and partly because this agency is paying a handsome sum for access to her island.

However, I made a deal with them to reach Xalvadora first and get her to abandon the island before they attack. They'll kill my sister and all who are with her if we can't get them to leave. Families are living on this island. Women she's taken in who had nowhere else to turn."

"What are those families doing with a cartel leader?" Pax asked.

"Before she married Estabon, she ran a women's shelter."

"Why would someone like her marry a man like him?" Oracle frowned, trying and failing to fully grasp what Reyes was saying.

"I don't know," Reyes said. "We stopped speaking well before her wedding. I assumed she sought him out for protection. She was nearly killed by an offshoot of the Mictlantecuhtli cartel, but Pax and his ESP team saved her."

"I did what?" Pax interjected.

"A competing cartel took over a small town just over the Arizona border in Mexico. At the time, Xalvadora worked with an international aid organization, running the northern Mexican branch of this safe house for women and children. However, their property had been built over a system of caves, which ran under the U.S. Border, and the cartel planned to use these caves to transport members of a terrorist network."

"Those caves helped us track the town where that terrorist group had originated," Pax said.

"Xalvadora led the women in a battle with the cartel, who weren't expecting a peaceful organization to have firearms."

"I'm assuming she had help," Pax said.

"Perhaps," Reyes replied. "I pulled a few strings when I heard rumors of this cartel expanding their reach. For killing ten of his men, Juan Largo, Estabon's top general, planned to execute ten of Xalvadora's women, including her."

"I remember Largo lining the women up in the park at the center of town. If we had gotten there any later . . ." Pax let his words trail off.

He rarely spoke about his ESP experiences to Oracle. Mostly because there weren't many happy endings. If she had the power to erase those memories from his mind, she would've long ago. At times, she consoled herself that those memories were what had kept them apart. He'd failed so many; he didn't want to fail someone he loved.

Utter garbage, but it made the breakup hurt less if she believed this.

"Pax, remember when we first met, I mentioned how I heard about you? It was through Xalvadora. She once told me she owed her life to you. She carries this with her as our mother carried a medal of Santa Maria. She would listen to you and stop her madness, if we could find a way to get you in touch with her," Reyes said.

"We also need to understand what she's capable of. I'd rather not find out in a post-mortem," Gloria said.

Without reading her mind, Oracle understood what Gloria left unspoken. She needed to know how Dama X got her power, and if they could replicate it. Although a partner in U-Sec, Gloria's primary job was working with her father at TransGen, researching genetics to cure diseases as well as enhance the human condition. A portion of TransGen's funding came from the Department of Defense, the DoD. The military applications of Dama X's ability could win wars, or it could be a security threat to the United States if it fell into enemy hands.

TransGen failed to understand why Oracle had developed her ability from the procedure to restore her vision. No other patients had the same result. Biannually, they'd examine Oracle and run tests to understand the mutation. On occasion, the military called her in to assist with an interrogation. They'd claim the prisoner was a transhuman, but on several cases, Oracle had her doubts. However, her contract with U-Sec stipulated the DoD could call her in as needed on assignments they deemed a national security risk, and she didn't want to put soldiers—and civilians—in danger if her ability could keep them safe.

"I'll do it, Reyes," Pax said. "I'll meet with you in person, assess the situation, and see how we can help."

"I knew when we first met that you were a good man," Reyes said.

"Wouldn't go that far," Pax responded under his breath.

"I'll send you a contract this evening and book Pax on the next flight out," Sean said.

"Very good, and keep me posted on developments con Diosa de la Venganza in your city. My assistant will forward travel details. Vaya con Dios, Pax. Hasta luego." Reyes's line clicked off.

"I'm going to need backup," Pax said.

"I'll put that in the contract," Sean replied.

"And we need to inform Matthews and brief the DEA."

"I'll leave that out of the contact," Sean returned.

"After I arrive in Mexico, I'll assess the situation with Reyes and determine the type of backup needed."

"I'll accompany Pax," Oracle stated.

"No!" the three partners said in unison.

Oracle scowled in reply. If she was developing a similar ability to Dama X, then it made sense that she assist Pax. Of course, they didn't know about her possible secondary mutation and given their discussion about stripping Dama X's power, she didn't want to tell them.

"You look horrible," Gloria said.

"I appreciate your concern," Oracle replied.

"You're welcome."

Oracle rolled her eyes. She needed to up the sarcasm level when dealing with Gloria.

"You need to rest. Matthews shouldn't have called you in. You weren't ready for the field, and you certainly aren't ready to face what could happen in Mexico," Pax said.

Oracle straightened in her seat and lifted her chin. Sure, she barely slept last night and her power surge with Camille had drained her, but how bad did she look for them to treat her as if she should be kept in a bubble?

"I'm glad Matthews gave me that push. I needed it. It felt great to be back in the field and finally help again," Oracle argued. Maybe it was best that she didn't have a chance to tell Pax about what had happened with Camille. He'd probably side with Gloria and lock her up for her own protection.

Another reason their relationship didn't work.

"You don't believe I can handle it?" Oracle directed the question to Pax.

"That's not what I meant," he shot back.

Before she could respond, Sean said, "Let me get Reyes's contract written and a job number for Matthews. The three of you can work this out."

His chair rolled back from the table. "In other words, when I'm back from the bathroom, everyone needs to be out of here so I can get to work."

The door opened then shut as Oracle's phone rang out, "Like a Virgin."

"Did you . . . ?" Pax paused mid-question as if collecting his thoughts. "Did you add a new ringtone?"

Oracle pulled the cell phone from her purse and turned from Pax's voice. "Hello, Matthews."

"Weird freakin' day," Pax muttered.

Oracle didn't get a chance to ask what he meant, because Matthews went off about Oracle still being at the office when she should be at home resting—theme of the afternoon—and how he couldn't reach Pax or anyone, and how they had a lead from a matchbox found on Camille's person. Then Matthews put Oracle on hold as he took another call.

"Matthews, listen to me." Gloria raised her voice next to the phone resting against Oracle's cheek. "Don't do any—"

"He's not there." Oracle pulled the phone from her ear and hoped her face transmitted her annoyance loud and clear if her words didn't. "I'm on hold. If you don't mind giving me space."

Gloria's shoes shuffled against the carpet away from Oracle. "Tell him I'm coming to the hospital."

"Matthews, yes, I'm here," Oracle spoke into the receiver when he was back on the line. Matthews gave an update on the investigation before sharing news about the victim that drained the blood from her face.

"What's wrong?" Pax shifted close as Oracle hung up.

She moved her pinky and touched his hand resting next to hers on the table.

"It's Donovan. He's fading. They're not sure he's going to make it," Oracle said.

"I knew this would happen. I'm going over Matthews's head and calling Dr. Knowe at Hopkins to move Donovan to our facility. He just made Chief of Staff, and he wouldn't want a death like this on his new watch." Gloria's heavy steps paced to Oracle's left. "Oh, and I think my dad's playing golf with him today. Bonus! He'll agree to anything to get off the phone and back to his game."

"Whoa!" Oracle lifted her hands for balance as her chair suddenly rolled back from the table.

"And you're going to the hospital with me," Gloria said.

"No!" Oracle and Pax answered.

Oracle glared in his direction. In his defense, he didn't say anymore.

"Gloria, I'm exhausted," she said. "I need a shower and—"

"Coffee. And you smell fine, somewhat stale and there are some odd stains on your shirt, but otherwise fine." Gloria wrapped her surprisingly strong fingers around Oracle's upper arm. "I have cologne in my purse, and you can borrow my U-Sec blazer."

She fisted her hand. Gloria could be pushy but grabbing at her arm and trying to force her up was not acceptable. She tried to figure out the best way to tell Gloria to back the hell off when she felt Pax's jeans brush against her arm as he leaned across her. Gloria's hand dropped from her bicep.

"She's obviously worn . . . " Pax began to say then corrected himself, ". . . worked hard this morning helping Matthews get a lead on this case. Why do you need her?"

"Oracle was in Camille's head and saw what happened. From what little she learned from Camille's drug-hazy memories, Donovan was an abusive ass, but Camille didn't want to kill him. She didn't know what that drug would do to him. Probably thought it would make him somehow see her perspective on things. Like experiencing how a woman feels would change a man like him." Gloria's hard truth soured Oracle's already unsteady stomach.

"I want Oracle as backup for me, in case things go wrong more so than they have already. Now that Camille's detoxed, maybe she can get a clear memory from her that can help Donovan. Or maybe she could pull insight from Donovan to save him."

Oracle focused on controlling her breathing. Her hands clenched, nails digging into her palms at the idea of diving back into Camille's—or worse—into Donovan's memories.

"The longer we debate, the less time we have to stop this," Gloria continued.

Gloria needed her. Camille needed her. Donovan, no matter how much Oracle despised him from what she experienced through Camille, needed her. This would allow her to test her ability even if it broke her. She couldn't say she didn't try, and she'd know for sure.

"I'll do it," Oracle said. "But Matthews just gave me a request for Pax."

"You have two minutes while I call Knowe." The door closed behind Gloria and her flowery lilac scent followed her out.

"What does Matthews want from me?" Pax asked.

"They found a matchbook in Camille's sweater pocket from Flock of Blue Jays." She'd been to the club a few times with Pax when they were dating. Pax's friend and former ESP soldier, Jay Jones, owned it.

"Matthews thinks Jay's involved?"

"He's not sure, but he wants you to visit Jay tonight. Matthews received a tip-off about Camille's supplier, but she's disappeared, and now they're out of leads. Camille is still sleeping off the drugs, so they haven't interrogated her. Her mom isn't talking to the cops."

"I'll leave now and catch Jay before they open," he said.

Oracle slung her purse over her shoulder. As she unfolded her cane, she decided to ask what had been needling her. "Why don't you really want me to go to Mexico with you?"

"Why are you still using that cane?" he countered.

"I'm blind."

"You didn't need it a few months ago."

"I chose not to use it. There's a difference." She stood up. In her flats, she was only three inches shorter than Pax. He used to hate when she wore heels.

"And the leather driving gloves? It's eighty degrees outside, and you don't drive a British motor car."

He had her there. She hadn't worn gloves since Pax had helped her control her ability.

"It's a new trend," she quipped, and he snorted.

"If that were so, then Gloria would own a pair in every color." He stepped closer.

The heat from his body caressed her upper arm and shoulder. She smelled the citrus spice of his cologne. The one she had bought for him when they were first dating. In spite of her exhaustion and stress, she recalled her dream and his taste and his body underneath her. She bowed her head and hoped he didn't notice her discomfort. How she could feel giddy in the midst of everything that had happened was ridiculous and annoying.

"Two weeks ago, you took time off. You haven't returned my calls, and now you show up looking more tired than I've ever seen you. Did you come to the office to talk with me?"

"It's nothing. Merely wanted to show you that I was back on the job."

"Bullshit. Something happened this morning that you couldn't tell me over the phone."

If she told him now, he might put her on permanent leave. As an owner of the company, he had that power. Then she couldn't go with Gloria, couldn't help Camille or Donovan if they needed her. Whatever happened to them or anyone else affected by this drug would be on her. Whatever was happening with her power was secondary to doing her job. Pax's protectiveness grated on her when they were dating. But they weren't dating anymore. He'd broken up with her long ago.

"I needed to get something from my office and see HR about being taken off desk duty and working in the field. I hadn't been to the office this week, so I wanted to say hello. Nothing more."

The door slammed open, making Oracle jump. Gloria yelled, "Donovan's vitals are slipping. We need to leave now."

Oracle turned from Pax. The bottom of her cane rolled along the floor on an electronic ball sensor that sent different pulse types when it closed in on an obstacle or encountered an opening. Within a few paces, the cane sent a vibration up to her hand, indicating an open doorway. She walked through, and Gloria's perfume filled her nostrils. She heard the woman's agitated breath as she impatiently held the door.

Without turning, Oracle stopped and said to Pax, "Matthews trusted me. He believed in me. Why can't you?"

Gloria grabbed her hand, forcing Oracle to take her arm. The door shut behind her, muting Pax's reply.

Chapter 3
All-Time High

I am a model for how transgenetics can save a life. Without these modifications, I would've been dead by ten. I owe my life to TransGen—and the owner, my father, Dr. Victor Vivas.

—Sean Vivas, co-founder of UltraSecurity

"You look down and out, my man. Let me get you a beer on me." Jay "Jaybird" Jenkins waved over a Katy Perry lookalike wearing a white tank dress adorned with lines of large multi-colored dots. Pax's Army buddy had been a participant in the same Enhanced Soldier Program that gave Pax his transhuman super strength. After Jaybird retired from the program, he opened this club, happy to leave his fighting days behind him.

"You called for a teenage dream." Katy sauntered over and rubbed a large hand over Jay's shoulder. Her wide shoulders bulged out of the sleeveless outfit, showing off muscles that were anything but feminine.

"Two Natty Bohs for old time's sake. Unless you want something stronger?" Jay lifted a sculpted brow at Pax.

Katy tilted her pink-wigged head while her eyes sized Pax up. If he ignored the Adam's apple and masculine physique, she could be a dead ringer for the pop starlet.

"I might be leaving for Mexico tomorrow morning, so one beer is good," he replied.

Katy winked a heavily lashed eye at him before drifting over to the bar.

"I think she likes you." Jay smiled with a twinkle in his own made-up eyes. Dark hair caressed his rosy cheeks, ending in a smooth bob just before his bulky shoulders sprouted out of a black corset-like top with thick sheer straps. An umbrella hung from the back of his chair for a dress rehearsal, which Pax had interrupted.

"Who, Katy Perry? I'm leaning more toward Winehouse myself," Pax joked and nodded to an Amy Winehouse performer, looking like a Baltimore Hon in a brown beehive wig.

"Oh, you don't fool me. You were scoping out Beyoncé next to her. You love the brown sugar lovelies like me." He winked.

Laughing, Pax shook his head. "You know I don't have a type. I like who I like."

Pax tried hard not to think about Cassandra. She'd come to the office to confide in him, despite what she'd said. Something had gone down that morning with Matthews. His gut was never wrong, especially when it involved her. And then he'd hurt her when he refused her offer to go to Mexico with him.

Matthews trusted me . . . Why can't you?

It had nothing to do with trust and she knew it. Maybe he could use something stronger than a beer.

While singing the lyrics to "Hot 'N Cold," faux Katy brought over two beers and set them down.

After the waitress managed to skip away in platform heels, Jay turned serious. Although, it was tough to focus on a serious conversation with a very bass voice coming from a well-made-up Rihanna impersonator.

"You're still hung up on that Cassandra woman, aren't you?" Jay cut to the chase.

Pax took a long swig of beer to buy time. Jay could always read him like a SAT image.

"That's not why I'm here," Pax replied.

"It may not be why you dropped by, but it's why you look mopey."

"I don't look mopey."

Jay shrugged. The gold glitter on his brown skin sparkled in the light. "Whatever, man. I thought that woman was trouble. She worked for you and that's one strike. Then she's from an ambassador's family. All strutting around here like she was Nefertiti whenever you came for a show."

Pax took another drink to keep himself from defending Oracle and being derailed even more for the reason behind this visit. Although Jay was partly right. Oracle did carry herself with an air of confidence that many mistook for arrogance. But Pax knew her demeanor came from growing up in and navigating the Hill's political community. Her dance background gave her a graceful and confident stride. Her aloofness was a mask to shield herself from the fear her transhuman ability instilled in N-Ts, non-transhumans.

"Then there's Jolene," Jay said.

"What does your sister have to do with this?"

"Just saying is all. You have a way with the ladies. You rub some kind of scent on them, and they can't get you out of their system. But I know there's the right one out there for you, if you take a break from work for once."

Yeah, the right one works for me, and I'm definitely not in her system anymore.

Jay pursed his red-painted lips. "Jolene still asks about you. Even with that ex-baller husband, two J.Crew-looking kids and a medical practice, she hasn't forgotten you. I think she sees you as the one that got away."

"Jolene broke up with me."

"Exactly. Just like that other one, Gloria."

Jay had to go there.

"That's in the past. She's my business partner now," Pax clarified.

"When Gloria was just an intern working on us at the TransGen lab, I thought something was off with her." Jaybird twirled a finger next to his temple.

"That was over fifteen years ago."

"She change at all?"

He considered Jay's question then shrugged. "Gloria's a 2.0 upgraded version."

"Told you that chick was crazy. Not sure what you saw in her. Then you had me double date with her friend Lucy. Loony Lucy, if I recall. And you still owe me for that one."

Great, now he got Jay started. Pax took a few more swigs of his beer. He'd forgotten about Lucy and for good reason.

"She looked like one of those gals from that singer's video back in the eighties. Hair slicked back, dead-eyed stare. I captured terrorists more pleasant than her."

"She wasn't that bad," Pax said before adding with a wink, "She baked a mean fudge brownie and chocolate cookies."

Jay grunted. "Yeah, I'll give you that one. But, man, you didn't have to talk to her. She kept staring at me, eyeballing me, not like she wanted to do me, but like she wanted to open me up, take me apart, see how I tick. Then she kept saying that we all have parts to play in this stage called life or some bullshit like that. Not sure what she meant and didn't care. I was lucky to get away from her without any bits missing. That was the one and only time I went on a double date with you. I started to worry that you set me up because I'd really pissed you off. Thought I saw her the other day at the mall. I ducked behind these grandmoms to avoid her."

Pax laughed at the image of his badass platoon partner, a running back to Pax's linebacker build, diving behind a group of elderly ladies to avoid someone.

"Lucy's long gone. Left the country years ago with no plans to come back. You don't have to worry about her."

"Good to know." Jay tipped his bottle at Pax. "Let's get back to why Cassandra is making you mope around here like Taylor Swift missing her red lipstick."

"Can we focus on why I came here and not discuss my love life—or lack of? I'll need a few more of these"—Pax held up his empty bottle—"to do that and I'd like to get home and packed before midnight."

"Okay, okay. I have to get back to practicing for tonight's show anyway." Jay took a drink. "Fire away."

"Cassandra encountered a male victim last night missing . . . well, in the words of one official . . . he was missing his crotch luggage."

Jay exploded in an uproarious laugh that turned several of the faux starlets' heads from their conversations. "Someone Lorena Bobbitt his junk? Don't know if any man deserves that."

"Appears he was abusing his girlfriend."

He lifted a shoulder then downed the rest of his beer. "May not blame her for that one. What does this have to do with me? I'm not in the business of cutting off men's privates."

"It wasn't just that. His penis . . . well, it . . . melted off."

Jay's mouth dropped open. "That's some sick shit."

"Gloria's at the hospital to get the victim moved to TransGen's care. Oracle read the suspect's mind, the vic's girlfriend, and found she gave a syringe filled with a narcotic to her boyfriend. We believe this drug attacked and altered his DNA, changing him from male to female."

"And you think I may know about this drug because I own this place and like to dress up as a woman?" Jay lifted his hand, waving it around the room. "Most men working for me aren't looking to lose their essential parts."

"Whoa, Jay." Pax held out his palms in defense. "I didn't mean it that way."

Pax was the only one from ESP whom Jaybird had shared his secret with. Pax had encouraged him to open this club and follow his dream. One of Pax's new rules in life after his military service was to keep an open mind. He'd seen friends deal with enough prejudices, and he dealt with them as a transhuman. Most of his associates outside of U-Sec had no idea what he was capable of.

"I know, man." Jaybird shook his head. "I get tired of explaining myself. Why it makes me happy doing this. Hell, I'm lucky I found a lady who accepts me for who I am."

"I only came to you because the suspect, Camille Jones, had a book of matches from Flock of Blue Jays on her person when she was taken into custody."

"Camille Jones," Jaybird muttered then shook his head. "Doesn't ring a bell. Could've been here for a show one night. I'll check through our reservations. If not, I'll ask around to see if someone knew her or heard of this drug. I know of a few people who are transgendered and not a transvestite—there is a difference." He looked hard at Pax to make his point.

"I got it." He pushed his empty bottle away.

"One is close to the end of her hormone treatments. However, she got laid off a month ago from the day job and might be desperate to pay for the operations. Wouldn't be surprised if she looks into this as a shortcut."

"Thanks." Pax stood to leave, eager and apprehensive to make one last stop before he went home. "I appreciate whatever you can find."

"I'll walk you out." Jay pushed in his chair and grabbed the long black umbrella.

They threaded their way past the stage, jutting out in the middle of about thirty cocktail tables. Jay didn't speak as they walked to the exit, and Pax assumed his friend was processing what he'd revealed.

When they reached the door, he shook Jay's hand.

"There's one more thing I want to mention," Jay said as he let go. "I wasn't going to say anything, but Jolene is insistent I get tested, and that's one of the reasons why your name came up with her the other day."

"Okay," Pax replied tentatively, not liking what the word "tested" could mean.

"Several in our ESP troop have developed cancer. Tumors in their brains and thyroids. Jolene heard that Ben Tucker, one of the first guinea pigs from ESP, is dead."

"Cancer as well?"

"Appears so." Jay glanced behind him in an obvious gesture to make sure no employees were close enough to hear. "I'm not getting the injections anymore. I left that shit behind when my early retirement came up. So far, the only side effects have been a decrease in strength back to pre-injection levels and a few minor blood clots that were absorbed back into my system."

"Gloria's been monitoring me," Pax said. "I get a booster once a year now, not monthly like we used to."

"You always took to it better than most. I hated being on that stuff. I remember having migraines at first, followed by stomach cramps. Then random muscle aches and weird twitches for days after."

"I don't know why it never happened to me."

"Be glad. Maybe you won't be affected. But I think you should talk with Gloria about getting a body scan. It's pricey but Jolene could hook you up if Gloria can't."

"I'll think about it when I have time."

"Yeah, right," Jay chided as Pax stepped out of the theater and into the late day sun. "You better make time, or I'm sicking Jolene on you."

Pax cringed and raised his hands in defense, feigning terror over Jay's sister coming after him. They shared a laugh then Pax rounded the corner, and the smile dropped from his face.

He glanced at this watch. Oracle should be home by now. If she wasn't, he was driving her back from the hospital whether Gloria was finished with her or not. Oracle and he needed to talk—and not just about this job.

♥ ☠ ♥ ☠ ♥ ☠

Oracle rotated her shoulders and stretched in the straight-back, cushioned, waiting room chair that was becoming more uncomfortable as the minutes ticked by. It didn't help that the sleeves of Gloria's ill-fitting U-Sec blazer constantly rode up her arms, and the midsection lifted around her waist, forcing Oracle to tug it down every so often to no avail. Gloria was shorter than Oracle, although her attitude could fill a dinosaur's skin.

Where is Gloria?

She listened for her boss's heavy gait. How long did it take to bully hospital staff and law officers to move the victim to TransGen headquarters and their private medical facility?

Her chest tightened. Her pulse rate elevated the longer she remained powerless in the chair. She took a deep breath and slowly released it.

Her anxiety was rooted in a lack of control, her therapist had told her. She couldn't save her agent Surefire. She couldn't combat the psychic attack by the supernatural force. The effects from it lingered within her mind months later.

Then there was her blindness. That had been out of her control when it first manifested in college, and no amount of her parents' influence and money could've changed it.

Her fingers dug into the vinyl armrest. She screwed her eyes closed behind her sunglasses and tried to relax, but her mind kept playing the *"If"* game. *If* glaucoma hadn't taken her sight at twenty-one, and *if* her body hadn't rejected corneal implants, her life would be different.

She'd be a ballet dancer or teacher, and she'd probably never have met Pax.

Oracle leaned forward and rubbed the back of her neck. A throbbing pain at the base of her skull clawed its way forward, drudging up memories of the transgenetic facility in Vietnam, her mother's birthplace. Her frustrated parents had dragged Oracle there hoping the experimental gene therapy would regenerate her eyes. Instead, it put her into a coma. Oracle's father implored his friend, Victor Vivas, to save his daughter and allow her into TransGen's test group for a new genetic procedure that Vivas promised would restore her vision.

If she had known the type of vision she'd get with TransGen's procedure, would she have agreed to it?

An invisible hand squeezed at her lungs. She struggled to breathe. The room teetered.

Damn it, she was not having a panic attack. Now. In the middle of a hospital. With Gloria nearby.

She rested her head in between her knees and raised her arms.

Breathe. In and out. You are in control.

When had she last taken her anti-anxiety medicine? This morning? No, she was at the hospital with Matthews and had left the bottle at home.

Push away the triggers. Focus on the positive.

Oracle heard the unmistakable click-clack of Gloria's heels against the floor.

So much for positive thoughts.

"He's dead." Gloria sat down with a thud in the chair next to Oracle.

She winced at a sharp pain slicing through her brain. "What happened?"

"What are you doing?" Gloria asked.

"Yoga. Chair pose," Oracle lied and stretched her arms out, fingertips reaching out in front of her while her head rested between her knees. "My back was killing me in this seat. I needed to stretch."

"Okay," Gloria replied with hesitation. "Are you sure you're not sick? Looks like you're trying not to vomit."

"I'm fine." Oracle eased into a seated position, careful not to rise too quickly. The mounting pressure in her head subsided to a dull throbbing at the base of her skull. Crisis averted for the moment.

"What happened?" Oracle asked once more.

"What do you think? His body rejected the change. It was too much, too quickly. He had a heart attack, of course."

Oracle concentrated on keeping the pain at bay, while Gloria kept chattering.

"I told them it would happen. They needed to induce a coma as soon as he arrived. Then cryogenically freeze his body to stop any further change. Unfortunately, this hospital is too conservative—and cheap—to have cryo technology on hand."

Oracle bit her tongue. She didn't need to get into an argument with Gloria about the ethical questions surrounding cryogenics and why the mainstream had yet to fully embrace it.

"At least they're letting us examine the body and run tests since no family has come forward to claim it. I'm still trying to get the syringe in question for analysis. I'll be ticked if those CDC lab rats contaminate it."

The pounding subsided. Her throat no longer constricted, Oracle couldn't stay silent anymore.

"A man is dead, and his girlfriend will be charged with murder. Two lives are over, and all you keep talking about is how your precious specimen might be ruined. They're human beings in case you've forgotten."

"No need to snipe at me."

This woman hasn't heard me snipe yet.

"But you're right." Gloria grabbed her elbow with fingers mere inches above Oracle's exposed lower arm. "I'd forgotten about Camille. She's still here. I want you to talk,"—Gloria emphasized "talk" and Oracle got the impression she used partial air quotes when saying it—"to Camille while things are fresh in her mind. I doubt her lawyer's been by yet."

"That's not a good idea." She stood then yanked her arm from Gloria's grip.

"You said you would help."

The tightness renewed in her chest. "I changed my mind."

"You're not ready to go back to fieldwork, are you? Pax was right, Matthews shouldn't have called you in."

"It's not that." Oracle composed her face, hoping the rising anxiety and headache didn't show.

"You're not all right. I told you to let me examine you. What if that supposed god—or whatever—screwed with your ability and it changed just like Surefire's did?"

"Nothing's changed. I'm fine." Massaging her neck, Oracle tried to pry loose the vise-like grip stress had on her head.

"Then I thought you wanted to help Camille. Didn't you just say she's a human being? One whose life is on the line?"

She rubbed harder and shook her head as Gloria used her own words against her.

"But if you can't do your job, I'll take you—"

"I'll go to Camille."

Oracle's mouth went dry. It wasn't the idea of invading Camille's mind that made her anxious. It was facing Camille after what she had done to her. What if Camille recalled how she had possessed her body? What would Gloria do if she found out?

The room teetered again. Oracle widened her stance for balance.

Breathe.

The only way to overcome this fear was to gain control over this situation and stop playing the *If* game. She should talk with Camille. Better to control what happened now than have Gloria and others hear it from someone else.

The tension in her neck slowly receded, although a tingling lingered at her shoulders, letting her know she wasn't in the clear yet.

She rested her hand in the crook of Gloria's arm covered by a silky material. She gave thanks for her gloves and the blouse, extra protection against touching Gloria's skin because heaven help her if she saw into that woman's mind at this moment.

Gloria led her down what she assumed was a hallway and then onto an elevator after twenty-five steps. It took to the count of ten for the elevator doors to swish open. They took twenty steps past a group laughing before they drifted ten paces past a woman crying. They rounded three corners and stopped. Gloria barked orders at someone—a nurse, Oracle guessed—who sighed loud enough for the patients on the floor above to hear her agitation before saying the suspect was in Room 411.

After twenty more steps, they paused again. Gloria's arm pulled out of Oracle's hand. Then she heard a zipper being undone—from a purse, perhaps. She assumed Gloria was retrieving her U-Sec ID to show an officer stationed at the patient's door. Oracle followed suit and held out her ID.

"Oracle, hey," the officer's tone turned from business to casual after giving Gloria the okay to proceed. "Matthews told me you had gone home. I can't believe you're still here."

"I'm supposed to be home." Oracle relaxed upon hearing a familiar voice. Officer Max Shane was one of Matthews's closest friends, and someone who never treated her like a freak as many on the force did. "But someone wanted backup."

"Let's go. We're not here to interview him," Gloria said.

Oracle heard the room's door open and then click close after Gloria marched inside. Officer Shane chuckled.

"Now, I understand," he said. "I heard rumors about that woman. Guess some of them are true."

"Want to place bets the rest are as well?" Oracle smiled. Max's friendly voice was a balm to her frayed nerves. "So, what am I walking into? Is the suspect conscious?"

"She's awake and responsive. Her mother is in there and not too"—through the door came a muffled yell of *get the fuck out of here*—"fond of anyone interrogating her daughter."

Oracle closed her eyes and took a fortifying breath. She wouldn't gain anything, least of all control of this situation if she ran away.

"I better go in before Gloria causes another tragedy."

And before I lose my nerve.

"My chips are on the mom. Hell, I'm scared to go in there. Based on her build, I think she might've wrestled Hulk Hogan back in the day."

Running her hand along the door, Oracle found the handle, wrapped her fingers around the cool metal, and forced herself to open the door. Then she carefully counted her steps into the room.

"Who the fuck are you?" Came the loud-mouthed, thickly accented Baltimore greeting. "Cammy's told youz already. She don't know anything."

"Christ, Mom, shut up. These women aren't cops. I know the black one. She was at my apartment. She's cool."

Oracle relaxed, relieved that Camille didn't scream when she entered the room or her mother didn't body slam her to protect her daughter. Was it possible she didn't remember or know what Oracle had done to her?

"Don't you tell me to shut up. I'm doing this for your own good. If you'd just listened to me once, you wouldn't be in here." Labored breathing came from the far corner of the room.

Oracle sensed her boss's body heat and smelled the alcohol in her hairspray as Gloria sidled up next to her. It wasn't a good sign if Gloria backed away.

"And why she got sunglasses on in here? Think she's special or something? Too hoity to look me in the eye?" Camille's mother continued to rant.

"She's blind, Mom."

"Oh." Her reply dropped into welcomed silence.

"Can you get me a Coke?" Camille cleared her throat.

"I ain't leaving—"

"Mom, please. I know what they want, and it's not what you think."

Metal springs creaked, followed by a chair's feet scraping against the floor. "I'll get your Coke, but you promise to say nothing that'll dig a deeper hole for yourself. That goddamn lawyer gonna cost enough without having to deal with any shit you let slip."

"Move." The mother's breath reeked of beer, and based on its proximity to her face, Oracle could tell they were close in height. Oracle sidestepped, and she heard Gloria do the same. The mom's heavy steps stomped by and out the door, which slammed behind her.

"How are you feeling?" Oracle edged closer to the bed and put out her hands to feel for any obstacles.

"Better than when you last saw me. Thought I was going to die," she said then added in a quiet voice, "Almost wish I had."

Oracle nodded. "I'm sorry for what you've been through."

"What did you give him?" Gloria's heels clacked across the floor as she moved behind Oracle.

"Your agent's been in my head. She saw the vial. It was turquoise and sparkled," Camille replied.

"You remember me reading your mind?" Oracle swallowed down the rising panic.

"Not that part. But I saw you walk into my place with that CDC chick. She came by this afternoon after I woke up and told me what you had done."

"She did?" Oracle squeezed her hands together until the fingers numbed.

"Don't worry. I signed the waiver, so I won't sue you for reading my mind. It was to help me and Jimmy, I know."

Oracle relaxed.

"She told me I passed out after you read me. Probably was too much for me to handle with the drugs I'd taken."

JoJo, I owe you one.

"She needs to go in again," Gloria stated. "Now that you're clear of the drugs."

"No way. Freaked me out enough someone was inside my head. I can't let you do it again, especially sober."

"If you can't tell me what was in the vial, then she's going in," Gloria countered.

"I don't know, and that's the God's honest truth. Some woman gave it to me when I dropped by Naomi's. Said it was on the house."

"Can you describe her? Any name?" Gloria asked.

"She was Mexican," Camille stated. "I already told Matthews this. Thought you were here for something else."

"What is that?" Oracle asked.

"To tell me how Jimmy really died."

"It was a heart attack," Gloria replied.

"No, not that. You saw him. I know you did. That was something more than a heart attack. I've seen people die of that. But this . . . this time there was goo and his junk just melted off and he started screaming . . . oh, God, I'd never heard a man scream like that, and then . . ." Camille's voice cracked. The bed shook as she started to sob.

"It's okay. You don't have to say anymore," Oracle said.

"He didn't just OD," Camille asserted between her sobs.

"Did Naomi's friend say anything about this drug?" Gloria asked as Camille sniffled.

Oracle took a tissue out of her purse and held it out to Camille.

"She said it would make him understand what it was like to be me." She took the tissue and blew her nose. "She said he'd know what it felt like to be a woman, and he'd never hurt me again. I just thought it would give him a crazy trip. Freak him out so he'd leave me alone, and I'd stop having to look over my shoulder all the time. I should've listened to my mom when she said he was no good. God, I am stupid." Something hit the mattress that rattled the metal rails. Her fist, maybe? "He was sweet at first, you know. Bought me tons of stuff. Took me places. I'd never had a guy that hot even look at me before. But he never loved me. He never gave a shit about me." Her words shook along with the bed again. "He was just using me."

Gloria brushed by Oracle to stand closer. "Did he do this to you?"

"Yes," Camille choked back a sob.

Oracle fought the urge to take off her gloves and touch Gloria's hand to see what made her breath hitch after examining Camille.

"I'm so sorry," Oracle offered again.

"Where did you meet him?" Gloria asked.

"I was waitressing at Drew's, that steakhouse downtown. He was a regular with a shit ton of money. Thought he'd be different than the losers I'd dated from Essex."

Gloria cursed under her breath then mumbled something Oracle couldn't make out.

"I didn't mean for him to die." She wailed.

Oracle wanted to touch Camille, comfort her, but she was afraid even with the gloves on, she'd somehow get inside of her again. She didn't want to relive the terror of not only the past night but also Camille's past relationship.

Then she heard the unthinkable. Gloria shushed Camille as a mother would comfort a child. She heard the bed creak, and then Camille's cry softened. Was Gloria actually hugging this women?

"I didn't mean for it to happen," Camille whispered.

After a minute, but what seemed like ages, Gloria's heels clicked against the floor as she slid off the bed.

"I didn't mean it," Camille repeated.

"Trust me, he got what he deserved." Gloria pushed past Oracle and left the room.

Chapter 4
Balls for the Job

Some UltraAgents use aliases and wear masks to protect their identity and their families from the prejudices perpetrated by media fearmongers, who only want to sell more ads and get more airtime. Many of us were born with disabilities and disorders that science has helped us overcome. In a few cases, certain side effects occurred that enhanced senses or expanded our abilities. But we just want to live an ordinary life. We don't want world domination. We want to live in peace. Spend time with our families. Have barbecues with our neighbors. Grab a beer with friends. Go to our kids' plays. Mundane stuff like that.

—Sean Vivas, co-founder of UltraSecurity, at a Congressional hearing on transhumans

---

"How's my girl, Nyxe?"

Oracle stepped into the foyer of her condo then closed the door behind her. Nyxe's nails tapped against the hardwood floor as she pranced around Oracle's legs in a greeting that warmed her heart.

"You know how to make a woman feel special." She squatted and ran her fingers through the fur around the nape of her gentle black Labrador retriever.

Nyxe responded by licking her cheek, and Oracle smelled a familiar cologne. She nuzzled Nyxe's head and inhaled. Citrus with an earthy spice—

The toilet off the hall flushed.

Oracle bolted to her feet. Her hand burrowed into her purse feeling past lipstick, her U-Sec badge, and then a wallet before reaching her Mace. Nyxe trotted away from her toward the sound of water running in the sink. The door opened from the half-bath.

"Pax?" Oracle ventured with a finger poised above the trigger of the aerosol can.

"Hey, you're home," came the familiar male voice, commanding like a stage actor, although he hated public speaking.

"Seriously, Pax." Oracle slumped against the wall. She lowered her weapon and clutched her chest. "How did you get in?"

"The front door still reads my biometrics."

"That is for an emergency. Otherwise, you have no right to be here without my permission." He'd relinquished that right two years ago. Two years ago *today,* if she wanted to be precise.

Dropping the Mace back into her purse, she shoved off the wall and pressed past Pax, heading down the hall to the kitchen. She prayed she hadn't left her anti-anxiety pills on the counter.

"I didn't mean to upset you." Pax followed her into the kitchen. "When I knocked, I heard Nyxe doing that high-pitched whine she does when she can't hold it anymore. Figured you didn't need to deal with a mess on top of everything else. So I took her for a walk and fed her. That counts as an emergency, doesn't it?"

"I guess so," Oracle conceded, having a hard time staying angry when he meant to be helpful.

She threw her purse onto a kitchen stool. A cheesy aroma drifted past her nose. "Is that pizza?"

"Yep." The refrigerator door opened and the delectable scent intensified. Oracle's stomach growled. "I guessed right. You haven't eaten. I picked it up from your favorite place during Nyxe's walk. I can warm it up, if you want."

"I'll eat it cold." Oracle felt along the counter near the stools where she usually kept her prescription. It wasn't there. Did she leave it on the nightstand?

"Here. Sit down." His large palm rested in the middle of her upper back, creating a warm ripple along her spine that she tried and couldn't ignore. He nudged her forward. She put out her hand and grabbed the wooden spindle of the dining room chair.

"What do you want to drink?"

"Water's fine." She sat down and found he had set out utensils, a plate, and a napkin.

His thoughtfulness sent another pleasant ripple through her body, and she felt herself relax, truly relax for the first time since Matthews had woken her that morning—from a very vivid dream about the man now sitting in the chair across from her. Oracle felt along the place setting for her napkin and hoped Pax didn't notice her fidgeting.

Collecting her thoughts, Oracle savored the veggie slice Pax had placed on her plate. With Matthews's long, odd hours, he was rarely at her house for dinner. In fact, they only saw each other twice a week. She missed having someone waiting for her when she returned from a rough day. Someone who took care of the house and dinner, and even her dog, so all she had to do was unwind. Only problem was that it felt too good, too normal, and brought back too many painful memories of why she missed Pax. He hadn't come here to take care of her and ease away a stressful day, with a foot massage and then cuddling on the couch while they watched a movie.

No, that wouldn't happen again. He had an ulterior motive.

"I appreciate you doing this. But why are you here?" She set down her crust.

"I wanted to help."

"Then it's not because you didn't believe what I told you at the office?"

"About what?"

He was so bad at playing dumb. "About me feeling fine and just stopping by to check in with HR."

"I heard what happened to Donovan. Gloria called me from the hospital."

Oracle arched a brow at Pax's abrupt change of the subject. "The whole situation tears me apart inside. Although Gloria had other thoughts. She told Camille that Donovan deserved it."

"Why would she say that?"

"Donovan physically hurt Camille. Gloria saw the bruises. They were probably worse than what I'd glimpsed in her memories."

"Hmph," Pax responded between the sound of chewing.

Oracle frowned. Was there more to Gloria's story to make her say that to Camille? Of course, it wasn't any of her business. But still, it left her curious.

"As much as I enjoy your company, this is awkward," she said. "We're not dating anymore. In fact, I'm dating someone else now."

She heard rattling followed by a small, hollow object being set on the table.

"If you're fine, then why do you have these?" Pax inquired gently.

Oracle slid her hand across the table until her fingertips touched the pill bottle. Her suspicions confirmed.

"How dare you go through my things?"

"It was on the counter," Pax said, but his defense was weak, and she was sure he knew it as well.

"Because I didn't expect my snooping boss slash ex-boyfriend to be here." Nyxe rubbed against Oracle's leg as her voice rose.

"I didn't mean to pry."

"Yet you did. These pills are none of your business." She snatched up the bottle.

"I'm worried about you."

Something in Pax's tone made Oracle pause, made her heart skip a beat.

"I'm sorry. You're right. I shouldn't have looked," he said.

She pictured his shoulders slumping forward with a shameful look that softened his features whenever he realized he'd been wrong.

Oracle bowed her head. Pax sounded sorry, truly sounded as if he didn't know that bringing up this subject would upset her, so she said, "Sometimes a person needs a little help, especially when an ancient god scrambles their brain. It doesn't mean I'm unfit for duty."

For several seconds they sat in welcomed silence. Pax's water bottle crackled as he took a long drink. Oracle scratched Nyxe's head, assuring the nervous dog that she was okay.

"I have something else to talk to you about. It's the main reason I came here besides wanting to check on you," Pax said.

"Just tell me." *Can't be any worse than what we already discussed.*

"Matthews told me what happened with Camille at her apartment. How you scared the hell out of that CDC doctor."

Yes, it could be worse. Oracle bit the inside of her mouth to keep from spouting a slew of curses. Matthews had no right to speak for her.

"He said Dr. Johnson is keeping quiet. She was the only one who saw what you did and doesn't want to cause departmental panic over it."

Oracle tasted blood as she bit harder on her inner cheek.

"She said you told her it was the first time you'd ever done that to someone. Is that true?"

Oracle nodded.

"Dr. Johnson is planning to issue a cease and desist request with U-Sec so that you don't use your power anymore until we understand and catalog what you are capable of."

"What?" Oracle started to shake. "She can't do that."

"She's scared of what she saw."

"She's scared of me."

Pax let out a long breath.

"Admit it. She's scared of me." Oracle threw her napkin down. Nyxe again rubbed against her shins then lay across her feet in an effort to calm her.

"What happened?" Pax asked.

"Matthews told you, so why would you need my side?"

"You're not on trial here."

"Certainly feels like it, and judgment has already been passed."

"It hasn't. I need to know how you did it."

"I don't know how I did it." She kept her tone calm and even. A true feat considering the outrage boiling inside her. "I don't even know if I could do it again. It could be a side effect of my anti-anxiety meds. Or the drug cocktail Camille had taken that weakened her will and made her susceptible. Or maybe coming in contact with that damn god Tez-whatever-the-hell-his-name-was changed the way my synapses fire. This was the first time my power has controlled another human being. As far as I know, it will be the last."

"Before we send you back in the field, TransGen needs to examine you."

"No."

"It's part of your contract. A physical once a year. An assessment of your ability and you're due for yours."

"Get out."

"Oracle, listen. I'm worried—"

"Out. Now." She stood abruptly, knocking down her chair. She jabbed her finger toward the door.

A sudden image flash of the room disoriented her. She saw herself through Pax's eyes. Wisps of hair floating out from her loose bun. Skin ashen and eyes sunken. She felt his guilt, his pain at seeing her lips trembling, her arms shaking. She grabbed the table for balance. Her drink tipped over. Cold water spilled across her hand.

"What was that?" She heard the scrape of chair legs being pushed away from the table. "Were you just inside me?"

Oracle shook her head, her power retreating inside her body. "For a second, I was."

Nyxe whimpered and scratched a paw down her leg.

Oracle hadn't felt her power rise. She hadn't focused it on Pax, as she normally needed to do, to see through his eyes when she wasn't touching him.

Pax's solid presence loomed next to her.

"Don't touch anything. I'll clean it up," she said, grateful her voice didn't crack.

Pax stood not a foot away. If she lifted her hand, she'd touch his waist. She sensed his hesitation as if he were debating whether to hug her, comfort her.

She set her jaw and pointed to the door again.

"I didn't mean to upset you," he said. "I wanted to tell you in person so you didn't hear about it from someone else."

Oracle swallowed down the lump inching up her throat. She prayed the tears building behind her eyes wouldn't fall before Pax left.

"Well, you did. Now go." How dare he act as if he wanted to take care of her and help her this evening? He only cared about U-Sec and protecting it. He never once asked how she felt or if she was scared and how he could help.

She trailed him to the foyer.

"Oracle, I'm sorry. I—"

She slammed the door, cutting him off.

She slid to the floor as tears slid from her eyes. She opened the pill bottle then screwed it closed. Until she knew this power surge wasn't a side effect, she wasn't taking any more medication. Oracle pitched the bottle down the hallway then groaned at her stupidity. She needed to find that bottle before she slipped on it and twisted her ankle.

But not now, because now she wanted to sit on the floor and stew. Let her anger simmer and frustration percolate, so she didn't focus on the loneliness left in Pax's wake.

Her condo seemed emptier with Pax gone, and she felt more alone than she had in years. Pax didn't love her anymore, so why wouldn't her feelings for him go away? Then it wouldn't hurt as bad when he treated her like any other employee.

Nyxe trotted over and licked Oracle's face, already wet with tears.

Then there was Matthews, who hinted that he loved her, even if Oracle couldn't return the sentiment no matter how hard she tried. Considering how Matthews had ratted her out to Pax, maybe she should give up on men altogether.

Nyxe snuggled against Oracle's side before plopping down next to her. She ran her fingers through the soft fur along Nyxe's back.

"What would I do without my sweet Nyxe?" Oracle scratched under the dog's jaw. "You'd never hurt me or leave me or tattle on me."

Nyxe placed her head on Oracle's lap. "You're not scared of me, are you?"

She'd been inside Nyxe's head. At times, Oracle used her dog to get image flashes of her condo when she spilled or broke something. Nyxe provided vision when Oracle wanted to check her hair or see how a dress looked. A companion through it all. Never abandoning Oracle when she needed support the most.

Seized by an idea, she withdrew her hand from Nyxe and took off her glove.

"I need your help, Nyxe. Are you up for it?"

Thump, thump, thump. The dog's wagging tail hit the floor.

Flexing her fingers above Nyxe, she wiggled them through the fur until she came in contact with warm flesh. Then she dove in.

♥ ☠ ♥ ☠ ♥ ☠

Pax was an idiot. With a broom and dustpan in hand, he looked down at his punching bag. Not so much a punching bag but a mound of sand and fake leather pummeled to a sad, sagging pulp.

Which is how he felt after Oracle kicked him out of her home last night.

Now his morning consisted of cleaning up sand and getting ready for his trip to Mexico the next day. The first flight out was at six on Saturday morning. Nothing available on Friday, giving Pax a day to prepare—and sulk.

He should've done yoga when he got home last night. Instead, he decided to expel his frustration with a cardio workout, and he forgot to pull back his punches, because Oracle wasn't pulling back hers. She was doing the one thing she knew irritated him the most whenever they argued.

Ignore him.

Oracle wasn't answering his calls. She was home. He knew it. There were only so many times he could apologize to her voicemail. He'd only wanted to help. Try and understand her side. Protect her from what he feared could be a backlash. Instead, Pax made things worse by hurting the person he cared about most. He found her anti-anxiety medicine and didn't understand why she hadn't told him. Even though yesterday had been two years since Pax had called it off, they'd always been honest with each other. At least, Pax assumed so until Matthews called about the incident with Camille.

He bent down and swept sand into the dustpan.

Was that why she'd come to the office? Did she want to talk to him about it? If so, then why did she lie to him, hurting him even more? Had their relationship devolved so much that she thought she couldn't trust him?

Pax poured sand into a trash bag as his smartphone rang. He dropped the dustpan and fumbled to remove the phone from his back pocket.

"Hello."

"There's another victim," Gloria said.

Pax sat on the floor. "Where?"

"Found him in Columbia. A John . . . err . . . maybe Jane Doe at this point? He's alive but unconscious. Just moved him to TransGen. My staff is prepping the cryochamber now."

"Do you need me?"

"Aren't you going to Mexico?"

"Tomorrow morning."

"I'll call if I do. I want to get him settled first."

"Anything else?" Pax prompted when the line went silent save for a car horn in the background and what sounded like a radio announcer.

"Sorry, I'm driving to Oracle's. I took a wrong turn."

"You've spoken with her?" Pax tried not to sound surprised.

"She's not answering her phone. Matthews said he couldn't reach her either."

Pax's phone buzzed with another call. He glanced at the screen. Jaybird. He hit IGNORE.

"What do you need with Oracle?" he asked. His phone dinged indicating Jay left a voicemail.

"I want her to read our Doe."

"That's not going to happen."

Gloria let loose a loud, judgment-heavy sigh. "What did you do?"

"Why do you assume I did something?" Pax stood, wiping the sand from his jeans.

"Because Matthews said you went to her place last night, and he hasn't heard from either of you since, save for a text from Oracle canceling their plans for this weekend."

Pax rubbed the back of his neck and wondered if Matthews had submitted Dr. Johnson's request to Gloria or told her about the Camille incident. Considering Gloria was planning to ask Oracle for help, he assumed Matthews hadn't spoken to her.

He'd avoided Matthews's phone call this morning. He figured the detective was calling to ask what Pax had done to upset his girlfriend. Replaying his conversation with Oracle over and over again, Pax tossed and turned in his bed last night until he came to a conclusion that his thick head didn't understand at first: Oracle needed a friend last night, and Pax had acted like her boss.

"We had a disagreement," he finally said.

"A disagreement, huh? Tell that to Matthews. He's swearing you two ran off together." From Gloria's end, Pax heard a car door shut and keys jingling.

"Are you serious?" Pax stopped midway up the stairs to his bedroom.

Gloria thanked someone for holding open a door then said to Pax, "You're lucky he got called into work. He'd probably be breaking down your door if this new victim wasn't keeping him busy."

As if Pax was afraid of Matthews. "He doesn't have anything to worry about. Oracle isn't interested in me."

"Are you sure about that?" Gloria asked, a teasing lilt to her voice.

"Positive." *Especially after last night.*

"Guess I'm losing the office pool, then. There goes fifty dollars. Knew I should've saved that money for the Nordstrom sale."

"What?" He kicked off his tennis shoes.

"Got to go." An elevator dinged. "I'm entering a dead zone."

The line clicked off, leaving Pax to stare at the phone. Did he misunderstand Gloria? Employees and his business partner placing bets on his love life? They must not have enough work to keep them busy. He could certainly fix that.

People sticking their noses in his personal business was the last thing he needed today. Although, it hammered home one of the reasons why Oracle's and his relationship couldn't work out. Granted, it was the bottom reason on the list. He didn't give a crap about what others thought of their dating. But he knew it hurt Oracle's relationship with employees, who assumed she received favors by dating the boss. They didn't care that Pax and Oracle had started dating before he became her boss.

But that was irrelevant. Breaking up had been the best way to protect her in the long run, whether she'd understood or forgiven him for it. The decision had been necessary. End of story. Their story anyway, even it if did continue on in other less intimate ways.

At least Pax could still spend time with her. Talk to her. Joke with her. Watch her million-watt smile light up a room.

Pax pulled off his T-shirt then pushed off his jeans. He reached for his button-up shirt, black cargo pants, and U-Sec blazer that had been draped over his open suitcase.

Even if Pax couldn't touch her or hold her or make love to her, he could be with her in his dreams. When he was at Oracle's house, he'd peaked into her bedroom. Feather comforter. Soft, deep-red duvet cover. Carved antique headboard just as he remembered, with slats perfect for handcuffing him to. Just like the dream Pax had the other night before Madonna's song interrupted them. The same pop tune playing on Oracle's phone at U-Sec yesterday.

An old-fashioned ring tone sounded from his jeans, crumpled on the floor. Retrieving the phone, Pax glanced at the screen and immediately became concerned.

Jaybird's name popped up in bold letters.

"What's up?" Pax grabbed keys from his nightstand.

"I have a situation. Can you come by or are you flying out today? It may be nothing but—"

"On my way."

"Appreciate it, man." Jaybird hung up.

He planned to check out the Doe at TransGen, despite Gloria saying she didn't need him. He wasn't missing a potential opportunity to apologize to Oracle in person before he left. But Jaybird never asked for help. Calling twice in less than fifteen minutes meant something was wrong. Pax hoped he could still track down Oracle after he'd helped Jay out.

He stepped outside his townhome, and his foot kicked a small wooden box lying in the middle of his welcome mat. It skidded off his front stoop and landed in the azalea bush to his left.

"What the . . . ?"

Pax squatted down and reached under the leafy branches. He found a box about the size of a small jewelry case. Carved in the center was a half-sun, half-moon circular design.

He bolted up and faced the street. His eyes scanned the sidewalk and the rows of tri-level townhomes. No unfamiliar people or cars. Nothing out the ordinary. Most of his neighbors were at work. Odds were that no one had seen the person who delivered the box.

His thumb pressed against a metal latch. The lid popped open. It was empty. On the inside of the lid, Pax noticed words carved into the wood, "To creating a new world. Love, Xalvadora."

He went back inside for a Ziploc bag and his gun.

Chapter 5
Thrust of It

You want the truth? Talk to Sean. He's good with telling you the truth you want to hear.

—Pax to a reporter ambushing him outside U-Sec about Surefire and Raven

---

Oracle wiped the sweat from her brow as the notes of Act IV, no. 28 Scène of *Swan Lake* segued into the final part. She swung her right leg onto the ballet bar. Leaning over, she reached forward and grabbed her foot in a much-needed stretch. Several years ago—at Pax's urging—she'd turned her third bedroom into a mini-dance and yoga studio. Practicing ballet after breakfast was a positive way to expel her negative energy. Her mind and body dipped into a lethargic ease. A good tired, as Oracle's ballet instructor used to say, and she no longer had the energy to throttle two of the men in her life.

Oracle hadn't seen Nyxe since this morning when she took her for a walk, and she was afraid she'd pushed her loyal friend too far. It took much coaxing with several types of treats until Nyxe agreed to Oracle slipping on her harness and leash. After their walk, Nyxe balled up on her bed in the corner of the living room. Usually, she followed Oracle everywhere. Now the sweet dog kept her distance, which broke Oracle's heart and made her feel worse, so she had sought out Tchaikovsky, dancing until her legs wobbled, and she was too tired to feel scared about what she'd done last night.

She had controlled Nyxe. Power had surged through her fingertips, burning like an electric shock into the dog. She saw through Nyxe's eyes as she normally did. Saw the hallway in grayscale. The track lights illuminated the kitchen. The pizza box lay open on the counter.

But she didn't stop with a mere image flash. She pushed further into the dog's mind until it seemed her spirit left her body and filled out Nyxe's torso down to her legs and paws. When Oracle dropped to all fours and wiggled her butt, Nyxe's tail wagged. She made the dog's legs stretch. Her paws twitch.

Her head moved back and forth with as much thought as Oracle applied when using her own appendages. The animal's body stood. Wobbly at first. Testing out the feel of the wood floor underneath the pad of her paws and then walking a few steps before Oracle was pushed out. A metaphysical shove against her power, causing it to snap against her hand before it coiled back inside her.

Nyxe stumbled and fell. The room pitched and Oracle slapped both palms on the floor for balance. This time, she didn't pass out. Nyxe snorted then sneezed. Metal dog tags rattled when Nyxe shook her body. Then her nails had scraped rapidly against floor, seeking leverage as she darted from her master.

Oracle finished her stretches. She left her stereo on to play the last set. The soothing, classical notes offered more comfort than silence.

On her way to the shower, she grabbed her phone charging on the kitchen counter. A female voice sounded from it. Robotic and indifferent.

Ten missed calls, five separate voicemails, and a slew of texts. The majority from Matthews and Pax. She skipped over those. She wasn't ready to give up this calm sensation to let loose a storm of emotions again. Another call was from her mother. She'd forgotten her parents were back in town. Ever since Oracle's father retired from the Department of State, they'd been traveling for the non-profit her mother ran. She couldn't keep track of where they were: Russia, Japan, Vietnam, India, Mexico, and many other countries.

When Oracle was a child, she covered one wall in her bedroom with a world map. Whenever either of her parents went away, she'd mark the spot on the map to keep track until countries became a sea of blue and red dots. Now they were back in town to support her brother's campaign for Congress. No doubt they wanted Oracle to attend one of the fundraisers they'd set up for him.

She skipped over their message to the last one.

Gloria.

Knock. Knock. Knock.

She froze.

Pushing past Oracle, Nyxe ran down the hall and let loose with her big, bad dog voice. Her nails clicked a nervous beat against the floor.

The knock came again. Harder, more insistent.

Nyxe barked louder. Tchaikovsky's no. 29 Scène Finale came to a crescendo behind her. Louder than she'd remembered setting the volume.

"Oracle, I know you're in there," Gloria yelled through the door. "Tchaikovsky gave you away. Open up."

Oracle hung her head and pinched the spot between her eyes where an ache formed at the sound of Gloria's voice. So much for keeping the storm at bay.

"I'm coming." Nyxe kept insisting on being first at the door, so Oracle had to nudge her aside.

"To what do I owe this pleasure?" Oracle held onto Nyxe's collar as she opened the door.

Floral cologne assaulted her nose. She pulled back after her boss stepped inside.

"Is that thing friendly?" Gloria asked.

Ninety pounds of dog jerked forward with a nose going a million sniffs a minute. Oracle used both hands to restrain her.

"As long as you're friendly," Oracle responded.

"I'm not a dog person."

"Explains a lot."

"Honestly, is she going to bite me?"

"Not unless you bite her first." Oracle couldn't help herself and smiled for the first time that day.

"Ha, ha. I see you're feeling better." Gloria's shoes made a shuffling noise against the hard wood. She sensed Gloria had pushed herself against the foyer's wall to ease past them.

Now she felt bad for teasing Gloria, whose actions screamed she was truly leery of dogs. Nyxe continued to pull forward, giving Oracle's arms a workout. "I got Nyxe. Go by us and sit down in the living room. She only wants to smell you and make sure you're okay."

Gloria's heels smacked along the wooden floor. The sound grew muffled when she rounded the kitchen corner into the living room.

"I'm sitting. Let loose the hellhound. But if she bites me, I can't be held accountable for whatever I do."

Oracle rolled her eyes and let Nyxe go. Paws scrambled against the floor past the kitchen and into the living room.

Hearing an *"umph"* come from Gloria, Oracle jogged into the living room.

"Nyxe, go lie down. Now," Oracle raised her voice, assuming the worst. Nyxe trotted past her. Her nails dug at her dog bed before she flopped down with a grunt.

"Did she jump on you?" Oracle asked. "Usually she's good about staying down."

"No, but she did violate me. Stuck her snout right between my legs. Good thing I'm wearing pants or else this would've been very awkward. Please let her know that I'm not into women, not that there's anything wrong with that."

Oracle chuckled, surprising herself. "You're a strange bird, Gloria."

"Think about it. How would you like it if a person greeted you like that?"

A quick flash of Pax giving her that greeting made her giggle at the absurdity. Then it made her body flush, her mind wandering to places she'd rather not go.

She stopped laughing. "That's how dogs socialize and get to know you. Besides, men aren't animals."

"I beg to differ."

"Can I get you anything? Water? Tea?" Oracle asked to direct the subject away from the other sex.

"Thanks, but not necessary. I'm here because I've been trying to reach you since this morning."

"I'm sorry. I was—"

"Reliving *Flashdance.* Yeah, I can tell from your outfit and the sweat stains on your leotard."

And just when she thought they were getting along. "I was working out. Practicing ballet. I was about to shower when you started knocking."

"There's been another victim."

"What? Who?" Oracle dropped into an armchair across from where Gloria sat on the couch.

"We don't know who he is. The man was found on the street in partial transition. Matthews's team and the CDC were able to move him to TransGen before he went into cardiac arrest. We're prepping him for the cryochamber."

"Then why do you need me?"

"He has no identification. We showed Camille his photo, but she didn't recognize him. Could be because his face was bloated when they found him. We checked missing persons reports. None have been filed in the past few days that fit his description. We need you to go inside his mind and find out who he is."

"I can't. Didn't you hear? There's been a cease and desist placed on my ability. Dr. Johnson from the CDC had Matthews submit the request to U-Sec. I'm sure one of them has spoken with you about it." Oracle dug her fingers into the chair's cushioned arms, preparing for an argument with Gloria over the physical exam that Pax insisted she do.

Instead, Gloria replied, "I never received her order."

"But Pax told me last night that I couldn't—"

"As I said," Gloria reiterated. "I . . . never . . . received . . . it."

Oracle got the hint. Gloria was pleading ignorance.

"You aren't scared about what I did?" Oracle asked.

"Are you a good person?"

"I believe I am."

"I believe you are too. In the years I've known you, you've never done anything to deliberately hurt another human being. You've never used your power to manipulate or take advantage of someone. I trust you. In fact, I trust you so implicitly, I will offer myself up to test your new ability if it would make you feel more comfortable."

Shocked, Oracle exclaimed, "You're not freaked out?"

"Should I be?"

"No." She scrubbed her palms up and down the soft armrests. "I don't think so."

"Telepathic transhumans are more common than other types but far less dangerous than those with other abilities I've encountered and even violent N-Ts. Despite the public backlash several years ago, I'm not afraid of you or any other telepathic transhumans."

Oracle nodded, recalling that stressful time when Sean and Pax testified to a Senate subcommittee regarding laws determining how and when they could use their abilities. Stories of transhumans with mind powers, encroaching on the rights of N-Ts—namely the right to privacy—became a hot topic. The media reported on every incident, making it appear as if thousands of telepaths existed when less than a hundred resided in the world. Thankfully, her parents' influence and her U-Sec alias kept Oracle out of that spotlight.

"I'm personally not aware of anyone else like you who can see through another's mind by touching them, or reach out to search for their consciousness, or control another person's body as you've done," Gloria continued. "Transhumans with lesser telepathic abilities than yours couldn't handle the power. Some of them were institutionalized. Considering how advanced your power is and you haven't yet gone bat-shit crazy, I believe you can handle this power evolution."

Gloria giving her support and not Pax. She'd never believe it if she hadn't just heard it from her boss's mouth. "Can you tell Pax? He isn't convinced. He ordered me off the case until I had a physical."

Ordered was a strong word. Possibly stronger than how Pax actually relayed Dr. Johnson's request to her. But the implication was there. She didn't have a choice.

"A case of FIMS," Gloria said offhandedly.

"What is that?"

"Foot in Mouth Syndrome. Pax is known for it particularly when he's upset."

"He's upset?"

"Just forgive him and move on."

Oracle sucked in a breath and considered relating to Gloria her conversation with Pax. But thinking about last night was upsetting enough, Oracle didn't need to relive it verbally.

"He can't help himself. *Male-itis.* Another disease afflicting him. Men tend to think they know best even when they don't. It's a dominance reaction to protect those they care about."

"I'll take your word that Pax cares about me." If he did, then why was Gloria the one who trusted and believed in her?

Several dings interrupted their conversation. "My father just texted," Gloria said. "The victim is under cryo at TransGen. I need to go."

"I'm coming. Give me ten minutes to get ready."

Forty minutes later, Gloria led Oracle through TransGen's maze of corridors. From inside her purse, Oracle's phone rang out with "Climb Every Mountain" from her mother's favorite musical.

"Do you need to get that?" Gloria asked.

"It's my mother. I'll call her after we're finished. I'm sure it's not important." Weeks could pass before she spoke with either parent. Not because they weren't close. It was fundraising season for her mother's non-profit, along with her brother's Congressional bid, which meant long hours and a frantic social schedule. Oracle couldn't remember if she'd told them about the Surefire incident. Besides, there was nothing they could do for her that she couldn't do for herself. She didn't want to worry them unnecessarily.

Gloria halted. "We're keeping the victim in here."

Oracle let go of her elbow. She heard the slip of a card being swiped, along with five high-pitched beeps from the biometric reader analyzing her handprint.

The door opened with a puff. Ice-cold air hit Oracle in the face like the arctic blast from a freezer. Goosebumps broke out along her arms. Gloria positioned Oracle's gloved hand on her elbow and walked her into the room.

Oracle shivered under her U-Sec blazer.

"I should've told you to bring a sweater."

"I lived in Canada for a few years when my dad worked for the Department of State. I can handle the cold." Oracle rubbed her arms. Of course, it had been thirty years ago.

"I want you to take a look at him. Know what to expect when you see into his mind. Can you handle using me to get an image flash?" Gloria asked.

"Yes," Oracle replied when she wanted to say no. Last time she'd seen inside Gloria's mind, she'd gotten a memory flash instead of an image flash of their surroundings. The memory wasn't one she'd cared to see. Gloria and Pax kissing. Granted, it had been eighteen years prior. They'd dated when Pax was first recruited to ESP. But still, knowing that her boyfriend at the time had dated his business partner was hard enough to swallow. Seeing it replayed in vivid HD was another matter.

Oracle often wondered if Gloria had forced the memory on purpose.

"I don't know if I can control it yet, so I suggest we sit down in case I go too deep."

"And end up using me as a meat puppet?" Gloria added.

Oracle's lips pinched in disgust. "That is not a descriptor I would use. It's a bit grotesque."

"Don't like that? What about telepathic marionettist?"

Oracle cracked a smile. "You're wasting too much brainpower on this."

"Not wasting brainpower, only thinking like Sean. How to market your ability." A chair rolled across the hard floor followed by another one.

"Gloria, this isn't a power I want the public to know about."

"Not the public, just U-Sec's clients."

"It could be dangerous," Oracle asserted. "There might be health implications for the person I'm tele-marionetting—or however you label it. Using this ability may even affect *my* mental well-being. I would appreciate it if you kept this development between the partners until I understand it and can control it."

"I can respect that. After this case is over, I'll call a meeting with the four of us to discuss how you want to proceed."

"Thank you," Oracle replied, grateful for Gloria saying that she'd include her in the meeting.

A chair's cushioned edge tapped Oracle in the back of her calves. She sat down and removed the glove on her right hand.

"How do you want to do this?" Gloria asked.

"Give me your hand and relax." Oracle saw the irony in ordering Gloria to relax when pins and needles pricked nervously at her own skin. A month ago, she'd only needed to touch a person's hand to get an image flash of her surroundings. She didn't need to think about her ability. It became automatic like breathing or moving a toe. Her fingers had only needed to skim an N-T's flesh, jolting them with a mild static shock, and momentarily, the darkness she lived in would brighten with an image of a hallway or a park or wherever it was the person was looking at. She likened it to a camera flash going off in a dark room.

But now she didn't know her ability anymore. She didn't trust herself no matter how much she pretended otherwise. She still reeled from the raw hurt of Nyxe forcing her out. She'd never experienced that rejection before from her faithful companion.

I can do this. Focus. She dragged in a breath and blew it out with smooth control.

"Should I be breathing like that as well? Is this a type of Lamaze technique?" Gloria fidgeted making her chair roll back and forth.

"No, just shush, okay."

"Yeesh. Didn't meant to—"

"*Shhh.* Keep your mouth closed and your eyes open."

By the grace of a higher power, Gloria did what she was told.

After three more controlled breaths, Oracle's heart rate lowered and her nerves fizzled to a gut-tickling twinge.

In the beginning, this was how she'd practice using her ability. Slow and easy. Baby steps on a metaphysical plane with Pax as her willing test subject.

My, how times have changed.

Warm energy eased from Oracle's core. She let a trickle of the vibrating power drop into Gloria's hand to test the receptacle. Gloria jerked back. She tightened her grip around thin, cold fingers to hold her boss in place. Gloria again shifted in her seat. The muscles in her hand tensed before Oracle opened the floodgates, pouring the energy into the other woman.

Gloria's mind remained blank, giving Oracle the lightheaded sensation of entering a vacuum. The feeling of weightlessness she'd experienced on twisting roller coasters.

Emerging from a dark tunnel, she looked out of Gloria's eyes onto herself or what appeared to be a replica of herself, a realistic looking mannequin akin to a wax figure at Madame Tussauds. Sunglasses obscured her eyes. Back ramrod straight under the U-Sec blazer over a red blouse and pressed black pants. Left hand covered in a black leather glove with the other outstretched, resting on Gloria's lap. Dark fingers wrapped around Gloria's pale ones.

Although she was inside Gloria's mind, she continued to feel the cushion of the swivel desk chair under her and the soft support at her back. Unlike when Oracle went deep with Camille and Nyxe, she remained fully connected to her own body, projecting her subconscious but not going far enough to control Gloria. This was her version of an out of body experience, with an invisible energy-fueled lifeline tethered from Oracle's spirit in the center of her chest—her solar plexus chakra, as her mother referred to it.

Move your head toward the victim, Oracle requested, but her lips didn't move. Her words formed as a thought in Gloria's mind.

"This is weird," Gloria spoke out loud.

Her head swiveled to the left. A cylinder came into view. The bottom half constructed of shiny metal with curved glass on top. A display case for the specimen inside. Gray steel walls encased the room. Vents on the ceiling kept the space a brisk thirty-two degrees, according to the digital display next to the entrance opposite them. A glass window appeared in the center of the door.

"We keep this room cold to give us time if the cryochamber fails. Inside the chamber, the body is kept at negative ten degrees," Gloria explained.

A glass monitor blinked and beeped behind Gloria. Next to the coffin-like cylinder, a tray with medical instruments had been placed.

"Did you get the lay of the room?" Gloria asked.

Yes, Oracle replied, again from inside the conduit's mind.

Gloria's attention turned back to the cryochamber. Her cool, scientific eye assessed its controls. For the first time, she heard Gloria's internal dialogue, pleased that the victim's vitals were at the right levels and the cryo temperature remained stable.

Gloria let her eyes trail over the naked man. Pale skin with a bluish tint. Black, shaggy hair. Veins running like circuits under his thin skin. Patches of hair lined his arms and his chest, which protruded as if he'd had breast implants. She wondered if they had pulsated as she'd seen on Donovan through Camille's and Matthews's memories. Oracle noticed his genitals were missing with a vaginal opening beginning to form in its place like Donovan. Both his knees were purple with bruising.

Gloria's eyes wandered back to his face. Soft, petite, very feminine. No trace of stubble. Smooth, porcelain skin. He reminded Oracle of someone. The image wavered on the edge of her brain, but she couldn't get a clear picture.

"Seen enough?" Gloria asked.

She pulled her power out of Gloria's mind and dropped her hand.

"How did that feel?" The chair's squeaky wheels rolled along the floor when Gloria stood.

Oracle rose and took stock. No dizziness. No anxiety gnawing at her gut like a gremlin.

"I'm fine." The trick seemed to be baby steps. First connecting with someone she trusted in a safe environment, as she had with Matthews in the car when they'd arrived at the crime scene. She'd taken her time tapping her telepathic line into Gloria's mind. She didn't lose control or go too deep.

"Then you're ready for our Doe?"

"Bring it," Oracle said with confidence that wasn't a front.

Hard heels echoed off the metal floor and walls as Gloria walked away. Oracle rubbed her palms over her arms. The blazer and silk blouse were not enough to protect against the cold. Inside her ballerina-style flats, she wiggled her toes, trying to stop the icy discomfort from creeping into them and making her bones ache. She couldn't wait to get back outside to Baltimore's warm fall weather. Definitely a first for her.

"I lowered the temp in the room so I can open the cryochamber." Gloria stood at her side. "The opening will be large enough for you to make contact. It'll get a lot colder in here soon, so brace yourself."

Oracle flexed her fingers then blew hot breath on them to stave away the aching effects of the cold. The idea of it getting even colder caused a preemptive, full-body shudder before she heard the hiss of the cryochamber's lid being released.

"There is a six-inch gap by his head." Gloria explained. "Are you ready?"

Oracle nodded. She lifted her hand. Gloria's fingers wrapped around her forearm. She guided Oracle's arm forward. Frosty air bit into her skin.

"You only have two minutes before I need to shut it."

Oracle nodded again. Her teeth chattered. The side of her hand scraped past the glass case, which was thicker than she'd realized. She reached inside the cylinder, much like sticking her hand into a bucket of ice. The cold bit into her flesh. Joint pain followed before numbness set in. Surprised at how quickly her hand turned numb, she forced herself not to pull away. She could barely perceive his smooth forehead under her fingertips. His skin was frosty and harder than she expected. His flesh jerked when the psychic link flowed from her hand into him.

It was hit or miss when she touched an unconscious person. Although their guard was down, their thoughts were jumbled, much like Camille in her drugged state. Oracle would see their dreams, but it was hard to discern true memories and experiences from REM-produced fantasies. When she touched a conscious person, she viewed what they saw and could read their thoughts, if they didn't block them, and any memories they replayed while she was inside. Trying to read thoughts of someone unconscious was like sitting down at a computer and wanting to view the most recent file the previous user had accessed. If they hadn't left the file open, then it would take time to hunt through hundreds of folders to find what was needed.

And the brain didn't come with a search feature.

Once Oracle connected with the victim, the darkness parted to reveal a side street near Columbia Mall where the police had found him. His mind was stuck in replay mode. A perpetual nightmare of his last waking moments. Soaring pain cut between his legs. The man staggered. Flesh expanded across his chest to the point of tearing away. He screamed and fell. Knees cracked against the pavement. The scene faded and then restarted again.

If Oracle wanted to find his identity, she needed to go deeper than she had with Gloria. Taking a breath, she dove in, concentrating on swimming into his subconscious. Just like with Camille and Nyxe, her spirit filled this Doe's vessel. She sensed his numb, frozen body, right down to his toes, lying prone on the hard, uncomfortable table.

"Your legs are wobbling," Gloria said, her voice far away.

Oracle tried to respond but couldn't. Her mouth was frozen shut.

No . . . not her mouth, the victim's mouth. It was his voice she'd tried to use.

How was she doing this?

"Get out of there," Gloria ordered, although she heard it only as a whisper. She had the vague sensation that Gloria's arms hugged her waist.

But Oracle couldn't pull out. Not until she did her job and learned who he was.

Blanking out her boss, she focused solely on the Doe's mind. Images flashed quickly as if she were holding down the channel button on a remote control and watching television shows blur by. She caught snippets of voices and pictures but not enough to understand the context. What Oracle couldn't see, she could feel. As the memory flashes flew by, emotions crashed like roaring waves against her telepathic line, bringing with it a deep depression that made her want to cry.

Oracle shoved past these emotions. She needed to be specific if she wanted answers, and she couldn't drown in this emotional tide.

Where did you get the drug? She forced the query into his thoughts.

The blob of images slowed down like a reel of a slot machine. It stopped on the jackpot: a familiar feminine hand holding a vial containing a sparkly liquid. Flexing her mental muscles, Oracle tried to force the Doe's memory self to look at the woman.

He didn't budge, so she asked, *Who are you?*

Music played in the background, growing louder as the room took shape around them. Pop music. Brittany Spears, maybe? Another song started to play. Pop as well. Possibly one she'd heard Pax play in his office when he thought no one was listening.

Dark walls came into focus with a high ceiling and track lighting. Cocktail tables surrounding a stage. It was a bar. No. A nightclub.

And the room looked familiar.

What is your name? She forced the thought.

Women chatted and laughed around the Doe. No, not women. Men. Wearing women's clothes. Stage makeup exaggerated to create the image of pop and Hollywood starlets.

The victim walked to the bar past Pax, who was sitting at a table.

Pax? Oracle jerked her hand back along with her power, which snapped back inside with the force of a giant rubber band.

She had the sensation of falling into a black hole devoid of sound and feeling, filled with nothingness.

A hissing noise, followed by a click brought her back to reality. Was that the sound of Gloria sealing the cryochamber?

Slowly awareness crept into her limbs. Hard floor beneath her back. A painful knot at the back of her skull. Legs and arms bent.

Oracle rubbed her head.

"I tried to catch you, but you're heavier than you look." Warmth emanated from Gloria's body when she crouched next to her.

Oracle moaned. Why did Gloria insist on insulting her when she wasn't able to shoot back? She pushed up her glasses and pinched the bridge of her nose.

"Can you stand?" Gloria asked.

"Give me a second."

"I could try to help you up or call an orderly."

"Because I'm heavier than I look?" Oracle offered.

"You fell like a huge sack of potatoes."

"And the compliments keep coming."

"A bag of sweet potatoes then? Is that simile better?"

"Stop talking and help me sit up." She put out her arms. Fortunately, Gloria's floral perfume had faded during the day, so it didn't make Oracle's headache worse when she leaned in close, wrapping her arms around Oracle's upper back and helping her to a sitting position.

"Do you think you have a concussion?" Gloria pushed Oracle's glasses on top of her head. Her warm breath cut through the cold air and along Oracle's cheek while Gloria's frosty fingers held open her eyes.

"I don't think so." She held her power inside when Gloria touched her.

Gloria gently touched the growing knot below Oracle's bun. "Doesn't seem bad. But I want you to stay at our facility under observation for a few hours."

She couldn't argue with that.

"You went too deep, didn't you?" A chair rolled toward her, and she heard it creak as Gloria sat down.

"I had to so I could sift through his memories. I couldn't do that unless I went deeper."

"You need to be careful. Take small steps until you understand what you can handle."

Oracle shrugged off her comment. They could discuss that later. "I saw Pax."

"Pax? Why was he inside this guy's memories?"

"He must've seen Pax at a club somewhere. It looked vaguely familiar. You may want to call him and see if he can ID him since the Doe didn't provide any images that revealed his identity."

"I'll need to call him from the lobby. There's no signal in here. Are you well enough to stand?"

Nodding, Oracle placed her palms on the floor and lifted herself up while Gloria put her hands under her armpits to steady her.

"Can I lie down somewhere while you call Pax?" The same exhaustion she felt yesterday after reading Camille made an encore appearance. So bone-aching tired that she'd sleep on a metal floor if she had to, as long as it was in a warmer room. Plus, she preferred to be tucked away in another area before Pax arrived.

"There's a room down the hall." Gloria's arm snaked around her waist.

The door swooshed open.

"Hey, Gloria," a man exclaimed. "I didn't realize you were here today."

She cocked her head, honing in on his voice as Gloria allowed Oracle to lean against her for support.

"I brought Oracle in to help ID the victim," Gloria replied. Oracle sensed a nervousness to her words that she'd never heard in Gloria's voice before.

There was a pause, and then Gloria touched her shoulder. "Oh, you've never met, have you? This is Oracle. She's an UltraAgent at U-Sec. Oracle, this is Dr. Ronald Smith, one of our best cryo doctors."

"You flatter me, Dr. Vivas," he said. Even without seeing him, Oracle could tell he beamed at Gloria's compliment.

"Trust me, I'm not one to give out false praise. Ask Oracle."

"No," she said flatly. "No, she isn't."

Oracle extended her hand and immediately realized her mistake as Dr. Smith accepted it. She'd forgotten to slip her glove back on. An image flash of her and Gloria standing in front of him cut through the darkness. As he shook her hand, his eyes strayed from her face to Gloria in her pristine lab coat over a green pantsuit. Heels that would torture Oracle's feet added at least four inches to Gloria's height and brought her head on a level with Oracle's chin. She pulled away but not before a thought grazed his mind about how attractive Gloria looked, followed by a few more love-struck thoughts Oracle wished she could bleach from her memory.

"Did you know the victim? Is that why Gloria brought you in?" Dr. Smith asked.

"No, I can read minds."

"Oh." His voice dropped before he responded with a worried, "Oh, huh. That must be . . . uhh . . . interesting."

"You have no idea," she replied. Oracle knew he was probably turning a shade of red. Did Gloria know this man had a huge crush on her?

He coughed.

"Are you well?" Gloria asked. "You look somewhat flushed, which is fairly impossible in this cold."

Nope. Gloria had no idea.

Oracle's lips twitched into a smile. She looked down so she wouldn't embarrass him more by showing her amusement. Of course, legally she wasn't supposed to read minds without consent. However, at times it couldn't be helped when the person wasn't actively blocking their thoughts or was distracted.

Or when she was dealing with a power evolution.

"It's okay. I didn't see anything. I'm too exhausted," Oracle lied.

"Ah, good. I mean that's fine. Doesn't matter if you did," he said quickly and coughed again.

"You got some secrets you're keeping from me, Ron-Ron?" Gloria asked.

"No, I'm a book. Wide open," he said.

"Exactly what I prefer," Gloria responded playfully.

Oracle cinched her lips to suppress a laugh.

"What did you find out about 'Teenage Dream' over there?" Ron asked.

"What do you mean?" Gloria sounded perplexed.

"You know the song, 'Teenage Dream' by Katy Perry," he replied. "That guy could easily pass for Perry's brother. He's a male version of her for sure."

Chapter 6
My Second Life

Crystal skulls? TransGen would never waste resources researching those things. We aren't in the business of proving fairy tales exist.

—Victor Vivas in a *CNN* interview

Shaking his head in disbelief, Pax stared at the nude male lying inside the cryochamber, which reminded him of a prop from a sci-fi movie. Pax had last seen the victim, Andrew Cook, dressed in drag as Katy Perry only yesterday. Now his skin was whiter, preserved in the freezing cold of the chamber. Lips tinted blue and not because of lipstick.

Matthews stood next to Pax, scribbling on his electronic notepad. In the fifteen minutes since they'd entered the room, Matthews had taken several photographs of the body for his records, along with one he'd emailed to Camille. Now that the swelling on the victim's face had diminished and they knew his name, Matthews hoped Camille could recognize him, and they could learn of any connection between the two.

"Does Jaybird have an idea who gave Cook the substance?" Matthews asked.

"No, but Jay's asking his employees if anyone saw a Hispanic woman with our victim last night," Pax replied.

Pax was at Jay's home, helping him file a missing person report for his employee, when Gloria called to tell him the victim had a memory of Pax. He headed straight for TransGen and was shocked when he recognized the man right away—he was the same man Jay was searching for.

When Pax broke the news to Jay, he blamed himself. He swore that if Katy Perry's drag double hadn't overheard them talking, this wouldn't have happened. Pax tried to calm him down, arguing that Oracle had seen inside

Andrew's mind and believed the same person who'd given the drugs to Camille had given them to Andrew.

"You said Cook was diagnosed with gender dysphoria?" Matthews asked.

"Yeah." Pax studied the sleeping man's face, which appeared more feminine than it did when in full makeup. He wondered if it was the relaxed nature of his face in the cryo state or if the drug had softened his masculine features that quickly. "Jay spoke with his parents and learned Andrew had been diagnosed when he was a teenager. A friend of his worked at the club and introduced Jay to Andrew, who started hormone treatments for his transition last month."

"She," Matthews corrected him.

"What?"

"If Cook was making the transition into a woman, for all intents and purposes, she was a woman. Knew without a doubt that he should've been born a she. Part of the transition is having others refer to them with the feminine pronoun. I'll check with Jay when I interview him. Out of respect, that's how I'll assume Cook would like to be referred to."

"How do you know this?" Pax asked.

"My younger brother is now my younger sister. Went through the transition last year. Never seen her happier."

Pax stared at Matthews as if it was the first time he'd met him. "I never knew this."

Matthews lifted a shoulder. "You never asked."

Pax didn't know how to respond because it was true. He'd never asked about Matthews's personal life because he'd never given him a second thought outside of work—until Matthews started dating Oracle. Then he tried not to give Matthews's personal life any thought at all.

"I'll talk to Cook's friend at Jay's club." Matthews snapped the case closed on his SmartPad.

Pax started for the door, relieved to leave the room. Not because of the cold, that never bothered him. It was seeing someone with whom, less than twenty-four hours ago, Pax had interacted, a person who vibrated with life, now reduced to a frozen mannequin on the verge death. During his time in the Army and ESP, he'd buried enough of his friends and members of his squadron. Seeing Andrew in that state brought back memories he didn't have the bandwidth to deal with.

"Have you spoken with Oracle today?" Matthews asked.

"She didn't run away with me, if you were wondering," Pax tossed over his shoulder.

"No. What? I'd never think that. I was only asking because she's been in hiding since I arrived here. Gloria mentioned she was resting and resetting her power."

"She's been avoiding me too." Pax pressed a button and the door hissed open.

"Hey, Pax." Matthews touched his arm.

"Yeah?" Pax half turned as he walked into the hall.

Matthews plowed his hand through his unruly red hair.

Man, he needs to get that cut. Since he stopped dating Cassandra, Pax kept his short, less mess, less fuss.

"A question for you about Cassandra," he said.

Matthews using her real name got Pax's attention, doubly so with the way he lowered his voice while his glance shot behind Pax as if he were making sure they were alone. Pax stopped in his tracks and faced him.

He was taller than Matthews, though not by much, but the man was lean like a basketball player. Gangly. His white button-up shirt bagged out on him and caused a poof around the top of his dark gray slacks.

"What about her?" Pax's chest puffed up and his back straightened automatically. His body tensed, readying for a fight, although he didn't know why.

Matthews took a step back, although his bright green eyes held Pax's. "You know Cassandra and I have been seeing each other."

"Yeah." Pax's arms folded across his chest.

"Her birthday is coming up, and I want to do something special for her."

Shit. This summer had blown by. September was almost over. November fourteenth would be here soon enough. Not that he planned to do anything, but he could at least acknowledge it. Maybe send her flowers. Or a card. Or her favorite bottle of wine. Was it appropriate to give a gift to an ex for their birthday? Yes, he decided. They were still friends. Colleagues. He done it in the past. Why stop now when she was dating someone?

Pax nodded, giving Matthews the okay to proceed.

"I know you two used to . . ." Matthews hesitated then said, ". . . be close, so I hope you don't find it inappropriate, but I was wondering if you had any suggestions."

Pax wanted to say that they were still close. Then he realized it wasn't true. Especially after last night, when he learned she'd been keeping secrets from him.

"I don't know, Matthews." Irritation caused Pax's words to come out fast and clipped. "Tastes change. I don't remember what she likes."

Medium-rare filet with Béarnaise on the side. Salmon with a drizzling of lemon. The Outer Banks in the fall. White roses because the scent doesn't overwhelm and the petals are soft against her skin.

"Worth a shot." Matthews's shoulders slumped. "With all she's been through, I wanted to make this birthday special."

A flicker from behind Matthews's back diverted Pax's attention. The lights from the connecting hallway momentarily blinked on and off. At the crossroads of the corridor stood a security guard looking up at the ceiling as if he'd noticed it too. Behind the guard was a metal door. A red light above it. Authorized personnel written in bold block letters.

When had TransGen added that secure room?

Matthews started walking away.

"Wait." He grabbed Matthews's arm. "I remember this necklace she mentioned a few years ago. Not sure if they still have it, but my mom might have the catalog it was in. Tiffany's sold it. Something Cassandra wouldn't buy for herself, and something totally impractical because we know how practical she is."

Matthews's ruddy face broke out into a wide grin. "Thanks, dude."

"I'll email it to you if I find it," Pax offered.

"Much appreciated." Matthews matched Pax's pace down the corridor. They walked by the guard, who nodded at them.

"Do you know why Oracle is avoiding us?" Matthews asked.

"Could be that I told her about Dr. Johnson's cease and desist request," he said.

"Are you kidding me?" Matthews halted. "Why would you do that? I was planning to tell her."

"I'm her boss," and friend, he added silently. "I thought it was best coming from me."

"Was it?"

"What do you think?" Pax countered, annoyed at his mistake.

"We need to do major damage control. You know that, right?"

"We?"

Matthews hurried toward Gloria, standing at a doctors' station, reading text scrolling over a glass screen held in her hands.

"Gloria," Matthews called out. "Where's Oracle?"

"Resting, why?" She kept reading.

"I need to talk to her."

"Good luck with that one." She shot an unkind look at Pax. "Especially with this FIMS sufferer hanging around."

"FIMS?" Matthews furrowed his brow and looked at Pax, who shook his head at Gloria's dig.

"Why did you ask Oracle to read Cook? We could've called in Mary Night from the DC office." Pax leaned down to Gloria's level.

"Pshtt." She waved him away from her. "Mary couldn't read a person if their life story was etched on their forehead. Oracle is our strongest telepath, and we need the best if we're going to find the person behind this drug. Besides, it would take Mary too long to get here. DC traffic sucks."

"But Dr. Johnson issued a—"

Gloria slapped Pax's chest with the glass SmartPad as several staff members walked by. "I don't know what you're talking about."

Gloria pointed a finger at the open door of her office further down the hall. Fanning the electronic device over her head, she beckoned Matthews and Pax to follow her.

"Matthews hasn't *officially* submitted the request, so we *technically* haven't received it, and I *technically* don't know what you're referring to," Gloria stated once inside her office with the door firmly closed. "There is no official reason to not engage Oracle's services."

Pax's ears burned and most likely turned red, his anger having reached the boiling point.

"Matthews," he somehow managed to say calmly. "You told me Dr. Johnson submitted the report."

"To me personally. No one else in my department knows about it yet. I've only told you and Gloria at U-Sec." Matthews had sense enough to step back from him.

A stream of curses coursed through Pax's thoughts but couldn't escape from his mouth, which was clenched shut.

"I didn't ask you to tell Oracle. I was planning to speak with her at the cabin this weekend. I sure as hell wasn't going to pull her from the case," the detective argued.

"Matthews, why don't you check in on Oracle? She's in the Banerji wing, Room 700." Gloria wedged herself between Matthews and Pax, and he could feel the corner of his mouth beginning to twitch.

Matthews caught Pax's glare above Gloria's hair and bobbed his head in agreement. Pax gave him props for meeting his gaze, especially when this petite woman was the only thing holding him back right now. How could Matthews let him take the fall like that? The man did it on purpose. He was sure of it. If Matthews wanted to place a bigger wedge between Oracle and Pax, he succeeded.

After directing Matthews to Oracle's room, Gloria closed the door and turned to Pax. "You didn't have to tell her."

He rested his hand on the edge of a hard-backed chair in front of Gloria's expansive glass and metal desk. At least, he thought he was resting it. The wooden corner broke off, splintering in his palm.

"And there goes my new chair." Gloria threw her hands up. "Of course, you did me a favor. You wouldn't believe how many people make themselves at home in it to chitchat while I'm trying to work. I ordered the most uncomfortable chair possible to dissuade people from hanging out in here. But, whatever."

She sat down behind the desk, swiveled toward her laptop, and began typing. Two flat monitors on the wall behind her chair flashed on to reveal 3-D wire skeletons with arms outstretched. Underneath the images appeared the names Donovan and Cook. A stream of text flowed down the sides of both screens.

Pax crossed his arms and waited for Gloria to acknowledge him again.

"What do you want, Pax?" She stood up and put her back to him as she studied the screens. "I need to review the imaging and toxicology reports."

"Am I the only one worried about Oracle?"

"There's a difference between worrying about someone and making decisions for them." She touched both monitors and the text stopped scrolling.

"I wasn't making decisions for her. I was following protocol."

Gloria drew three fingers over the screen, and Donovan's 3-D body image filled a monitor. "Did you ask her what she wanted? Did you even ask her about what happened with Camille Jones?"

"Matthews told me what happened. Oracle didn't say anything to me, even when I pressed her at the office when I could tell she wasn't well. She lied."

"Then that explains everything." Gloria spun around and pointed at him. "You're pissed because she lied to you."

"I'm upset, so what?"

"I'm going to make an assumption here and my assumptions rarely make an ass out of me, although I'm certain it will make one out of you, so here goes: Your feelings for Oracle are clouding your judgment. If this was any other employee, you wouldn't be so quick to tell them what to do. Men love to think they know what's best for the women they care about."

"Don't play the gender card with me."

She went back to reading the screen. "Basic behavioral psychology. It's an alpha control thing. You can't help it."

"You're not a psychologist, you're a geneticist."

"More specifically a transgeneticist and one who is about to lose her mind if she can't find out how this transformation occurred. Delivery was viral, targeting the Y chromosome, reconfiguring its proteins, I'm assuming in the SRY gene. Won't know until I can compare DNA sequences before and after transition, which will take a while since we're in the real world and I'm not playing a forensic pathologist on *CSI: Baltimore.*" Tapping the screen, the image shrunk down and the text enlarged, revealing numbers and symbols Pax recognized, but he couldn't tell one chromosome from the next.

"In a short time, the body was inundated with estrogen and proteins like in a cell forming a female fetus. But in this case, the fetus was a grown male with already formed male organs that—" Gloria sighed and hung her head. "You're still standing there. Sulking."

"I'm not sulking."

"If I had a penis, you wouldn't be standing there."

"I have no idea what you're talking about."

"I recently read a research paper that stated women are interrupted far more than men, as if what they have to say or do isn't as important. The study stuck in my craw."

Pax decided it was best not to comment.

"Get over it." Gloria motioned to the screen. "I have work to do. Just admit that you're wrong about Oracle."

"I'm not."

She twisted around and scowled at him. "You worked overtime to ensure Surefire got her pardon. She asked that TransGen leave her alone as she worked out her new abilities, and you gave that time to her—with pay. Now you're asking, no demanding, Oracle gets examined by TransGen before she goes back on assignment based on an overblown cease and desist."

"Stephen St. John wanted to use Surefire as a weapon."

"The DoD is our largest client. The income from St. John's DoD special interest committee is what keeps U-Sec afloat. Grants from this same group fund research at TransGen. There's nothing in Surefire's contract that states she can't be hired out on military operations." Gloria planted her hands on the desk and leaned toward him.

"Surefire's his daughter."

"And that's for them to work out as a family. This is his committee. St. John helps pay your salary and funds U-Sec. Something you negotiated to give us oversight of transhumans and shut down the off-the-books transhuman research that our government previously had done. It was in our best interest—and Surefire's too—for us to monitor and understand her transformation."

"And you're doing what in Oracle's best interest by keeping her on this case? How far are you going to push her?"

Pausing a beat, Gloria replied in a calm voice, "That's up to Oracle."

And Oracle would continue pushing herself, so she didn't let anyone down and no one could see her as weak. He'd seen it before when she first started with U-Sec. He'd worked with her to control her ability. He'd work with her again if it meant keeping her safe.

"She needs to be examined and monitored to make sure she isn't pushed over the breaking point. That she doesn't end up in the psych ward or dead." Pax jabbed a finger in the middle of her desk then checked to make sure he hadn't cracked the glass.

"And I will. I am. I completed an exam before you arrived. My assistant performed an MRI. Vitals are normal. No irregular brain patterns to indicate an impending stroke or hemorrhage as has happened to other telepaths."

"I heard she blacked out after reading Andrew."

"For a few seconds, nothing too abnormal."

"Too abnormal? She's passed out twice after two different readings in two days." Gloria raised her brows at Pax's condescending tone. He lowered his voice. "Something isn't right. How do you explain her sudden power evolution?"

"I don't know. She allowed me to take blood samples today. Plus, I hooked her up to an EEG. I have more tests scheduled for next week, and we're not ruling out the medication the psychiatrist prescribed."

Oracle submitted to an examination for Gloria but not when he made the request? That fact hurt Pax more than he cared to admit.

"She agreed to the tests, because I left the decision up to her, which is the secret in dealing with women," Gloria answered as if she'd read his thoughts.

Pax needed to work on his poker face. Granted, he did handle the situation with Oracle poorly. But Gloria was reading his reaction the wrong way.

"We need Oracle, and I want her to believe that we have her best interests in mind. That we're working with her as a team, not as someone who owns her," Gloria said.

He flattened his palms on Gloria's desk and leaned down to meet her at eye level. "Just what are you insinuating?"

"Nothing." Her lips twitched into a smirk, contradicting her response.

"If seeing an employee as a person and not how I can make money off of them is wrong, then I will freely admit my error."

Gloria shrugged.

"I see . . . I'm the one who's acting like he owns her? Are you fucking kidding me? You and Sean are always on about the money and the company's income. Do not pull this shit on me now. I'm the one who cares about Oracle."

"So . . . you do still love her, then. Glad we cleared that up."

Pax pushed up from the desk. There was no getting Gloria to see his side once she had an idea permanently carved into that hard head of hers. Until she realized that his feelings for Oracle didn't impact his actions, there was no discussion to be had with her.

Lights flickered in the office. Gloria's computer rebooted with a ding.

"What was that?" Pax glanced around the room.

"Fudge it!" Gloria exclaimed. "I forgot to save." She hit a few keys before explaining, "Construction. Down the street. They keep banging into power lines. Been like this all week. Keeps causing blips in our firewalls and security panels but nothing major. Fortunately, we have backup generators for the cryo rooms."

"I need to talk with Oracle," he said.

Gloria blinked. Three times. Pax's teeth ground together.

"Haven't you said enough?"

From the interior pocket of his blazer, Pax pulled out the wooden box sealed in a plastic baggie and tossed it onto Gloria's desk.

"What's this?" She scooted away from the object as if it might nip at her.

"Found it on my front stoop when I left this morning. I think it's the box Oracle saw in Camille's mind. The one containing the three syringes."

"And what was inside?" Gloria lifted her eyes from the box.

"Nothing."

"Double fudge." She beat a path to the door.

"Exactly what I thought." He grabbed the box and followed her into the hall. For a short woman, she walked fast. Pax hurried his steps to keep pace with her.

"Why did they bother leaving it with you?"

"To intimidate us. Get our attention. Just wanting to be dicks." Pax shrugged. "I didn't tell Matthews yet. I wanted to be sure it was the box Oracle saw."

Gloria stopped outside a closed door, muffled male and female voices coming from inside.

"If Oracle saw three syringes and two have been used already, then we're waiting for the third case to drop. Triple fudge balls," Gloria said again and opened the door without knocking first.

Pax relaxed his fingers before he crushed the box in his hand. Matthews was sitting next to Oracle on the bed with his arm around her shoulders and his free hand holding her gloved one.

"No pantyhose on the door, so we thought it was safe to enter," Gloria said.

"Excuse us." Matthews jumped off the bed.

He could feel himself glaring at Matthews. No matter how hard he tried, he couldn't maintain a neutral I'm-okay-with-this expression. Besides, Oracle—like Pax—was never one for public displays of affection. Unless she'd changed her stance with Matthews.

"I was helping Oracle. She got a pain in her head when the lights flashed. Then that machine spiked."

"Indeed, it did." Gloria checked the flat-screen next to the bed. A multi-colored web of wires spread out from the back of the monitor and onto a swimmer-type cap fitted to Oracle's head.

Oracle's hands fidgeted on her lap. "Is Pax with you?"

"As a matter of fact, he is," Gloria replied as she removed the cap.

"Oh." She laced her fingers, cracking her knuckles.

"What do you want?" Matthews shoved his hands into his pockets.

Pax wished to speak to Oracle. Alone. To properly apologize face to face. But how to make that request without looking like a schmuck to her boyfriend was beyond him. "I found this in front of my townhouse. I wanted Oracle to feel it or get an image flash to see if it looks familiar."

Pax set the box on Oracle's lap.

She unclasped her hands and ran her gloved fingers over top of the plastic bag, along the sides of the box and the metal latch. She took off a glove and pressed her thumb over the engraving on top.

"I don't have to see it to know it's the box containing the vials," Oracle stated. "Is it empty?" She balanced the box in her hand as if assessing the weight.

"Yes," Pax and Gloria said in unison.

"Inside the box lid is an inscription with Xalvadora's name."

"She knows where you live," Oracle stated in alarm.

"Why would she leave that box on your step and incriminate herself?" Gloria asked.

"To send a threat, maybe?" Pax shook his head.

"Well, it worked," Oracle said.

Matthews's phone beeped. He excused himself and walked to the far corner while he took the call. Gloria fiddled with the machine next to Oracle's bed. Pax stared at Oracle as she closed her eyes.

"That was Camille." Matthews stood at the end of the bed. Oracle's eyes popped open—an old habit. "She recognized Cook from the photos I just sent. He's her cousin and used to be her roommate until he moved out because of Donovan. He'd been helping her get clean for the past year. She stopped at Jaybirds a week ago to see Cook perform and get away from Donovan after they had a fight. That's where she ran into Naomi again."

"There's the connection," Pax said.

The lights went out followed by the slow hum of the building A/C quitting.

"Son of a bastard!" Gloria yelled. "The emergency lights should come on in . . ."

They waited several seconds. When the darkness remained, Gloria continued, ". . . or not."

Footsteps and shouts echoed outside the door. Pax reached inside his jacket for his cell phone.

"My phone's dead," Matthews said.

"Mine too." The short hairs raised up on the back of his neck.

"Pax," Oracle ventured. "Do you feel it?"

"Yes."

Oracle didn't have to explain what *it* was. Months had passed since he last experienced this uncanny, unsettling feeling tripping over his skin. "Is it affecting you?"

"So far it doesn't seem as strong as outside the warehouse with Surefire," she replied.

"What's going on?" Gloria bumped into him.

He rested a hand on her upper arm to steady her. "The air's changed in here. Charged like during a lightning storm. It's what the environment felt like before the Aztec god broke up the ground beneath our feet."

"That wasn't a god," Gloria said.

"Then what was it?" Pax asked.

"The supernatural, including gods, is the unexplained that hasn't been explained by science yet," Gloria said with authority.

"Then explain it to us," he replied.

"I said *yet to be explained*. We're almost there," she said with less authority.

"It's gotten quiet in the hall. I don't hear any movement," Matthews said.

From the crack underneath, a deep red light shown through, allowing Pax's eyes to adjust to the dark and see Matthews' outline near the door.

"That should be the emergency lights. Finally." Gloria felt past Pax to where Matthews stood at the door.

Pax laid his hand on his sidearm in the holster underneath his jacket.

"Pax and I should go first," Matthews said.

"Okay, but I doubt it's necessary. Probably a downed wire outside." Gloria stepped away.

Back to back, Matthews and Pax sidestepped into the hall. Pax had his gun out and pointed down at his side, safety still on. Matthews had his in hand and positioned similarly, although Pax couldn't tell if his safety was off. Dull red emergency lights cut a line along the ceiling in the direction Pax faced.

"No one down this way," he said.

At the far end of the corridor, a green light illuminated the letters spelling out EXIT that hung over a door leading to the emergency stairwell. Pax blinked and the light faded, then brightened. He craned his neck to peer in Matthews's direction and noticed the emergency lights had faded and some were completely blacked out.

"What happened out here?" Matthews whispered.

A cold gust blew past Pax's face. He eyed the ceiling, wondering if the A/C had kicked back on.

"Someone's coming," Matthews said.

Pax flattened himself against the door to Oracle's room. Matthews pressed against the opposite wall.

"I don't see—" Pax began to say before he noticed several people huddled together on the floor lit up by a green-blue ethereal light glowing from the hall, perpendicular to the one where they stood.

Then shots rang out and a man screamed. Pax unlocked the safety from his gun and ran down the hall. Matthews trailed behind him. Before they rounded the corner, the guard he'd seen earlier walked out in front of them. He shot round after round at the ceiling. Glass shattered and rained down on him. A doctor exiting a room dropped to her knees and covered her head.

An arctic gust slammed past them again, pushing Matthews's hair back from his forehead.

"Stop. Put down your weapon," Pax ordered. Arms extended. Gun aimed. Finger resting at the side of the barrel.

The guard dropped his arm to his side but didn't drop his weapon.

Pax watched the doctor scoot back into her room and shut the door. His finger lowered onto the trigger. Was this guard from one of the extremist groups that had targeted TransGen before? Those groups that believed science shouldn't alter DNA and transhumans were aberrations of the natural order? They'd protested outside TransGen last fall. Up to now, they'd been peaceful and orderly. Threats relegated to online forums.

"Stop," a woman yelled.

The guard's gun dropped from his hands. The green-blue color grew, painting the walls with the serene hue. Pax noticed a tennis shoe first. Then a woman's jean-clad leg came out from around the corner.

The woman's chest was the source of the overwhelming light that obscured her face and torso so it appeared as if a ghostly figure stood facing them—a glowing orb standing on human legs with curly hair creating a black halo. The bright light hurt his eyes. Pax squinted and looked down. The odd turquoise shade stretched across the floor to his feet.

He hazarded a glance at the woman and saw that her body wasn't glowing. Instead, she held an object in her hands at chest level.

No, it couldn't be.

He lowered his gun.

Was that a crystal skull? One of the skulls used to summon the Aztec god and turn Surefire into something more than human?

"Stay where you are," Matthews told the woman. Pax glanced at him and noticed he'd put on sunglasses to block the glare. Smart.

"Matthews, get back from her."

"Lower your hands," the detective said.

The woman stopped a foot from them. Pax continued to stare at the linoleum floor darkened from its normal cream to an eerie teal.

"No," she replied.

Pax detected an accent but couldn't be certain.

"Put the glowing skull down," Matthews ordered.

"No," she repeated. Pax strained to hear what she spoke next. A phrase in Spanish directed to Matthews.

"Lo siento, Pax," she uttered and truly sounded sorry.

"Who are—"

Matthews's fist connected with Pax's jaw and cut off his question.

Chapter 7
Properly Introduced

There was nothing otherworldly or supernatural in the case involving Raven and Surefire that can't be explained by science—eventually.

—Sean Vivas in a *Washington Post* interview

"What the hell, Matthews?" Pax shouted.

Matthews tore a fire extinguisher off the wall and whirled around to slam the edge into Pax's solar plexus.

"Oof!" Air coursed out from Pax's lungs. A dull ache radiated from the impact. He staggered back into the wall. If Pax wasn't an exceptionally strong transhuman, that hit would've buckled him to the ground. He clicked on his gun's safety and holstered it as a determined Matthews came at him once more.

With a roar, he blocked Matthews from slamming the metal cylinder into his face. Pax's other arm swooped up and he tagged Matthews's bicep with his knuckles. Matthews's arm fell limp at his side. He dropped the extinguisher. Pax shoved him back until he tripped over his own feet and landed on his butt.

Pax tore down the corridor toward the mystery woman, who continued her steady pace to the exit.

She glanced at him over her shoulder and gave a half-smile that was a carbon copy of someone else's smile he knew.

"Espero verlo pronto," she said.

"Stop!" He reached out. The skull's energy leapt from her and burned along his hand. His fingertips brushed the cotton hood of her black jacket.

From behind him, someone slammed a shoulder into Pax's hip as the woman sprinted forward. Off-balance, he teetered to the side and banged into a closed door but remained on his feet. Looking down, he found the guard, who had been shooting at the ceiling, holding onto his torso. Beefy arms tightened around his waist. Pax strode down the hall and dragged the man with him. His attention not wavering from the target.

Pax lurched forward as an awkward weight landed on his upper back. A knee hit his spine. Fingers dug into his shoulders. Hot breath hit his cheek. He smelled Matthews's spicy deodorant. Arms covered by a white dress shirt wrapped around his neck.

Pax barreled on with his mission. Eyes on the prize, now breaking into a jog. He worked his fingers under Matthews's wrists and loosened their grip from his neck. But with Matthews's viselike grasp, if he broke the choke hold, he risked breaking bones.

The guard at his waist struggled to stand. His shoulder pressed into Pax's lower back. Pax stumbled.

Enough.

He paused and landed a back kick into the guard's stomach. Or maybe it wasn't his stomach but a bit lower, because the man let out a high-pitched cry and let go.

One down.

Matthews's arms tightened over his neck, and Pax's breathing became shorter, shallower. Reluctantly, he tore his gaze from the woman. He slammed against the wall to dislodge the human backpack.

Something snapped and Pax prayed it was only a rib. Matthews's grip relaxed. Hands unlocked from around his neck. The detective slid down Pax's back onto his feet.

Pax started once again toward the woman, who'd reached the end of the hallway. She opened the door leading to the emergency stairwell and disappeared inside.

Behind him, he heard shoes scraping then slapping against the floor. He looked back to find the guard plowing forward. Head down. Arms pumping at his side, creating a human ram. At the same time, Matthews pushed away from the wall where Pax had left him and bolted forward. His pleasant, friendly face devoid of emotion. No anger or pain. Just a blank, pale slate. Pupils so large his eyes appeared black.

"Sorry, Matthews," he muttered as the detective lunged. Pax put out his hand and planted it onto his chest, holding him at bay. Matthews's mouth snapped at Pax's forearm.

Bite me? Really?

Using Matthews's forward force, Pax pivoted and pushed him into the wall. He grabbed the back of Matthews's shirt and pants and flung him around at the guard, knocking both to the ground to reveal Gloria standing stunned in the middle of the corridor.

"What are you doing?" she yelled.

Ignoring her, Pax ran in the opposite direction. The power churned back to life. Lights turned on and he blinked to adjust his eyes to the sudden brightness.

He rammed into the door to the stairwell. It tore off the hinges falling with a bang to his side. Behind him, he heard people screaming and Gloria calling out to him. He paused, wondering whether to go up or down. No unearthly glow pierced the dimly lit stairwell. No other footsteps echoed against the concrete steps and walls.

Slam. A door shut below him.

He took several stairs at once, then finally leapt down to the bottom to find one door. Hitting the metal handle, he spilled out into a service alley. To the right, it ended at overflowing dumpsters and a brick wall, so he took off for the street at his left.

A warm fall day, no one wore a black hoodie. In fact, he didn't see one woman. Only men on the street.

Sirens sounded in the distance, getting closer the longer Pax ran up and down the street in the hope that a clue would stand out to indicate where the woman had gone.

Police cars, a fire engine, and two ambulances pulled up to the building.

Defeated, he walked back up the exit stairs and picked his way over the crumpled door at the second floor.

Employees milled about in the hall and appeared dazed as they rubbed their eyes or leaned against walls or tentatively cracked open doors to peer out. Others stooped down to help their colleagues caught unawares when the guard started shooting. At first glance, it appeared those huddled on the floor were shaken, not wounded.

Gloria knelt next to Matthews. He winced when her fingers probed his chest. Near her a man in a lab coat, whom he recognized as Dr. Smith, attended the security guard. Oracle stood over them with her arms crossed. She turned in Pax's direction when he approached, probably recognizing his footsteps.

"What did you do?" she asked, and he cringed at her accusing tone.

"They started it," Pax said then cringed again. His explanation sounded like a kid justifying a fight.

Oracle shook her head as if disgusted with his response.

He shrugged. It was the truth.

"Are you okay?" Gloria looked up at him.

"Fine." He brushed her off.

"You have blood spattered on your face and hair. Are you sure you're not injured? Or did you smash someone on your way out the door?"

He rubbed a hand over his face and looked at the red smears. "I don't know where this came from. Is Matthews all right?"

"He has broken ribs and nose. Sprained wrists and fingers. No concussion. Vertebrae seem fine, but I need X-rays to be certain and make sure there's no internal bleeding," Gloria said.

"This sucks," Matthews said. Voice hoarse. "What happened?"

"You punched me in the face then continued to attack me after that woman whispered something to you," Pax replied.

"What woman?" Oracle asked.

"Really? Then that explains it." Matthews shook out both swollen hands and grimaced. "Last I remember is the woman walking toward us holding this Halloween skull prop and then I wake up next to this dude feeling like a train hit me." He jerked his head toward the guard behind him.

"What woman?" Oracle asked again.

"Did you say skull?" Gloria croaked out.

"Yeah, he did," Pax replied, as the gurney arrived. Two paramedics gingerly lifted Matthews onto it and immobilized his neck and back.

"You need to tell me everything," Gloria said.

"I was about to say the same to you," Pax replied.

Oracle grabbed his and Gloria's arms. "Am I not speaking English or are you just ignoring me? What woman are you talking about?"

Green eyes and dark, curly hair. Delicate face with high cheekbones. Narrow nose. Willowy frame. The puzzle pieces clicked together, and he knew why she looked familiar.

"Reyes's sister," Pax said. "Dama X."

♥ ☠ ♥ ☠ ♥ ☠

"I saw nothing in Matthews's mind. He retained no memory of the event. Recorded no images of what transpired during his attack on Pax. It's as if he'd blacked out." Oracle addressed Gloria, Sean, and their father, Dr. Victor Vivas, owner and CEO of TransGen, in a conference room attached to his executive office on the top floor of the TransGen building.

Oracle had skimmed through Matthews's thoughts with precision and control without going too deep or passing out. In fact, she felt rejuvenated—at odds with the experience of reading Cook. Perhaps the difference had to do with how much self-awareness the person retained when she connected with them. Perhaps it was the adrenaline kick-starting her system when she heard her ex-boyfriend had beat up her current one. So badly that Matthews and the guard had multiple broken bones and contusions. Whereas Pax sustained a red mark on his jaw, scratches on his collarbone and neck, and a light purple bruise the size of a fist below his chest.

Oracle teetered between being upset over Matthews's injuries and impressed at how well Pax maintained control of his strength. It could've been a lot worse—for Matthews and the guard.

"Although spotty, the security footage corroborates Pax's account. The cameras were on a backup grid along with the emergency lights," Sean said. "I believe the skull emitted energy bursts that interfered with our electronics. Whenever the woman neared the cameras while holding the skull, the image wavered then faded to black."

"Or the skull was tapping into the building's grid to power itself," Oracle added. "It happened when we were on the case with Surefire. Although the suspect Ari didn't possess the skull at the time, he used the preternatural force connected with a crystal skull to cause an earthquake. Moments before the quake, our cell phones died. The lights went out around the warehouse. Batteries in several cars were drained dry. Pax also experienced this force in Mexico when he located our agents and the hostages along with the missing crystal skulls."

"Our skull never emitted light or interfered with electronics. Our staff measured its thermal infrared energy. Although higher than expected for the elements comprising it, there was nothing to indicate a power source," Gloria said.

"Maybe you needed to expose the skull to its conduit," Oracle replied.

"I don't follow."

"Surefire gained power when she was exposed to the circle of skulls in Mexico. She became a conduit for its energy, which we are still trying to understand. When Surefire touches the skull associated with her new abilities, it not only glows but enhances her power and her contact with this otherworldly being—the Aztec goddess Xochiquetzal."

Gloria snorted in response. Oracle shook her head at her boss. She could refuse to believe these beings existed but denial didn't change the facts.

"And this woman who stole our skull and who we believe is Xalvadora Reyes, Dama X, is tapping into a similar energy?" Dr. Vivas inquired.

"It's a theory based on my experience. Maybe she's possessed by the spirit associated with the skull as Ari had been? When the lights went out in this building, the environment became charged like during a lightning storm. Energy pricked against my skin. I experienced that same jolt when Xochiquetzal's skull appeared in Baltimore," Oracle said.

"Then why didn't you feel it when you entered this floor, or the building for that matter?" Gloria asked, a challenge not a question.

"After what happened with that god Tez, I've kept my ability blocked for the most part, which might explain why I didn't sense the skull. It could also be that the holding room was enough to mask the skull's energy from me."

"Obviously, that room wasn't enough to keep Dama X from knowing about the skull or from taking it. Gloria, why wasn't this object more secure?" Dr. Vivas inquired in a calm, measured manner.

"It was secure. The contractor we hired is the highest rated SCIF builder in the country—that is Sensitive Compartmented Information Facility, for those not in the know. For several weeks, they dedicated their entire team to constructing the SCIF with the equipment we needed to study the skull and the access controls and alarm system per federal code for highly sensitive facilities like this one. When we encountered reoccurring power outages, I stationed a guard—"

"How did she get past security?" Dr. Vivas interrupted.

"I don't know," Gloria replied. "She must have someone working inside TransGen because two biometric scans are required to access the room. The cameras showed her entering the building via the front door. Then the cameras appeared to malfunction, going in and out, losing her image. She doesn't show up again until she exits the SCIF. Tech was called in to fix what they thought was a wiring problem—"

"Dr. Smith, among others, contacted you with their concerns about a security breech. They were ignored," Dr. Vivas said.

Oracle shifted in her seat. She wished Vivas's words would offer a hint of what he felt. His neutral tone left her uneasy.

"I didn't ignore them. They called one meeting after the first victim was found, and I've been working thirteen-hour days—"

"If it's too much for you to handle, then get help," Dr. Vivas cut her off yet again.

Oracle was getting agitated listening to this exchange and longed to find a way to cut Vivas short. Sean had spoken for at least fifteen minutes about Felix Reyes and his ties to Dama X and this drug. Vivas never once interrupted him.

"I assure you, it's not." Gloria's measured tone cracked, showing her agitation.

"I've tried contacting Surefire. Since her new power is connected to the skulls, I'd hoped she could help," Oracle said in an effort to distract Dr. Vivas from further berating his daughter. "But she hasn't returned my calls. Has anyone else heard from her?"

"She asked for time off. She wanted to do a sabbatical or hide out from her dad or something like that. Gloria had finished with her physical so she didn't think it would be a problem," Sean replied.

"You let a girl who possessed that kind of power just go on *vacation?*" Vivas spat the word "vacation" as if spitting out sour wine. The first time his tone lost its neutrality and displayed displeasure.

"It's not like we have the facilities to keep her even if we wanted to," Gloria said. "She can teleport like TimeTrap but by using physics in a way my colleagues—and even she—can't comprehend. Synthia and Raven allowed me to run physicals and draw blood, which I sent to an outside lab for a secondary analysis to supplement our findings."

"Which were?" Vivas prodded.

"Inconclusive. They're transhuman . . . but not. I'm supposed to meet with the other lab but they keep postponing—"

"I don't need a detailed report about Surefire or more excuses now. If she can help in this case, then we need her here. Someone find her. We can't let loose a person of her ability. What were you thinking?"

So much for deflecting Victor from Gloria.

Oracle grimaced. She should offer to help Gloria by opening up and reaching out her power to find Surefire. She could possibly sense the UltraAgent if she were in the vicinity. But she wasn't comfortable doing that just yet.

The best she could do was say, "Surefire went back to Mexico to research the Aztec and skull legends. She also mentioned traveling to the Garden, some kind of alternate universe or dimension, which I don't fully understand, to learn about her power. If she went there, no one can reach her."

"Then get UltraAgent TimeTrap on this. Do I have to think of everything?"

Under the table, Oracle clenched her hands, holding back the power that suddenly surged up and wanted to slap this man square in his spiteful mouth.

Dr. Vivas fortunately turned his attention away from Oracle who resorted to calming breaths to hold her power at bay. "Sean, reporters are setting up outside our building. Probably heard about this incident on the scanners. They want a statement, and I want you to give it to them."

"I plan to. I've been pushing them back since yesterday after an anonymous caller reported seeing Oracle at Camille Jones's apartment with the police and CDC. Appears another person called in a tip about what occurred at the hospital, and they have questions about James Donovan's death," Sean said.

This reminded Oracle of several missed calls she'd received this afternoon from phone numbers she didn't recognize. No messages had been left. Her mom had also called, but Oracle hadn't had the energy to listen to that voicemail yet.

"Do the reporters know of his condition? How he died?" Vivas asked.

"Just that the official cause of death was a heart attack. They asked about reports of body modification and even Donovan losing his penis. I offered no comment."

"Good. Although we won't keep those wolves from our doors much longer with this travesty today. Do they know about Andrew Cook?"

"Not that we're aware of. I don't think any of our employees would be willing to risk a lawsuit for breaking their non-disclosure agreement and losing their Top Secret security clearance."

"Everyone has a price, son. Who could've leaked information about the skull or given her access to the SCIF?" Without seeing his face, Oracle knew Vivas directed this question to Gloria.

Oracle sensed a subtle shift in tone from one sibling to the next. Vivas's way of speaking wasn't entirely neutral as she first suspected. Her ears picked up a hardness to his consonants. A sarcastic lilt at the end of his question directed at Gloria.

"There's only a few of us who knew about the crystal skull, which arrived two weeks ago from Mexico," Gloria responded with an uncertainty Oracle rarely heard from her. "We're launching an investigation with Dr. Smith's team leading it."

"Glad to hear Ronald is heading this. I know it will get done," Vivas said.

Oracle inwardly squirmed. Did he realize how condescending his statement was? Most likely, he did.

"Reyes told us Dama X has the ability to bend a person's will," Oracle spoke. "That theory has been proven by what just happened in your building. If she can make two men attack another, and suppress their memories of it, then she could force someone on your staff to let her into the SCIF—and they wouldn't remember it."

"Then she could be privy to other TransGen projects. Who knows what she's learned about us?" Sean cursed under his breath.

"What is so important about this skull?" Vivas asked.

"Our lab reviewed samples scraped from it," Gloria replied. "I sent you the reports this morning. Silicon and quartz as we suspected. Trace amounts of calcium phosphates, which could indicate biological remains from a mammal. We found evidence of primary proteins and one percent of an unknown substance. Dr. Smith sent samples to the lab that was helping us analyze Surefire's and Raven's blood. They cross-referenced our results and found nothing more than we did."

"How does this relate to Diosa de la Venganza?"

"I haven't received a sample of the drug to test for any relationship," Gloria explained to her father. "The syringe from Donovan's crime scene was lost in CDC's bureaucracy, and there was no syringe found on Cook's person, in his vicinity, or at his apartment. I was comparing the results of Donovan's and Cook's toxicology reports when Pax came—"

"Ah, here's Pax," Vivas announced. The glass door to the office opened with a swish. Pax's telltale stride sounded across the room, followed by the scent of his cologne, which he must've refreshed when he cleaned up after his ordeal.

Oracle took a deep breath.

"I spoke briefly to Reyes, and he knows nothing about his sister's whereabouts," Pax said. "Yesterday, one of his people thought they spotted Dama X outside her club in a town near his home. Matthews's team is checking flight manifests and airport surveillance to see if anyone fitting her description flew here within the last twenty-four hours." A chair rolled out next to Oracle and then creaked under Pax's weight when he sat down.

"You're still traveling to Mexico tomorrow to meet with Reyes?" Vivas inquired.

"That's the plan," Pax said.

Oracle offered up a silent prayer. After witnessing this woman's power, she'd hoped Pax would change his mind about meeting with Reyes alone.

"Are you going with backup?" Vivas asked.

"I'm happy to go," Oracle found herself suggesting once more, surprising herself and most likely everyone in the room.

Pax's warm palm rubbed across the top of her gloved hand sending a shiver up her arm, although it felt like the heat had kicked on in the room. His fingers grazed her exposed wrist, giving her an image flash of the room. Everyone was clustered around one end of the oblong glass-top meeting table, nearly the length of the large rectangular room. Video images played along the glass surface. The surveillance footage, she guessed. Pax faced the floor-to-ceiling windows that looked out over a stone patio.

"Thanks, Oracle, for the offer to help," Sean responded. "But we have Pax covered."

Does this mean you forgive me? Pax forced the words into her mind like they used to when they were dating. Where normal couples communicated with a look across a room, they would do it with their thoughts.

Oracle slid her hand away. Let him stew for a bit more. Work for her forgiveness. Never mind that she forgave him after she finally listened to his first apology left on her voicemail.

"Let's get to it," Vivas said. "I leave tomorrow for a conference in Amsterdam. I want hourly updates on our progress with this case. I expect a full chemical workup of this drug within two days."

"But dad, we don't have—" Gloria began.

"Two days." His footsteps retreated from the room along with the oppressive vibe hanging over the group.

"And there goes my effort to drop less f-bombs in the office," Gloria uttered after spewing forth a series of curses that would make a sailor's ears burn.

"Glor, it's not a big deal. Once you review and compare the toxicology reports from Donovan and Cook, I'm sure it will be apparent," Sean said.

"You don't know. You never studied human biology. It's not that simple. Try reviewing thousands of lines of code to find a computer virus and then remove it in . . . oh, I don't know . . . less than ten minutes. Then create a counter virus that fixes any software issues caused by this virus. That's what he's asking me to do. Without the drug, it will take months at least to narrow it down, and that's working 24/7," Gloria argued.

"I'll see what evidence Reyes has. They may have samples from their cases," Pax said.

"I tried that already. The evidence was destroyed or contaminated beyond salvation. Except for one, their victims didn't have the symptoms of Donovan and Cook. They experienced some body transmodifications but nothing to the extreme of ours. Appears our drug is the next evolution."

"There has to be something in this footage," Gloria said, followed by hard finger taps that led Oracle to believe they were reviewing the videos displayed on the tabletop again. Perhaps slowing down, and then zooming into the images.

"Yeah, this woman is not what I expected," Sean noted.

"What do you mean?" Pax asked.

"She's supposed to be this badass transhuman drug lord, and she's just . . . well . . . a woman," Sean said.

"Excuse me," Oracle and Gloria said in unison.

"I mean," Sean backtracked. "I expected her not to be wearing jeans, a hoodie, and red Asics, especially with a name like Dama X."

"Sean," Gloria began exasperated. "This isn't a comic book, it's the real world. Villains don't go waltzing around in leather bikini tops glued to their D-cups, which incidentally would not give them proper support in a fight or when stealing crystal skulls. Nor do they wear high-heeled boots when doing kung fu. They'd sprain an ankle when they kicked *your* butt. They want to be comfortable and *blend in.* Which is probably how Pax lost sight of her."

"Trust me, if she had a leather bikini top pasted onto D-cups, I wouldn't have lost her," Pax added in mock seriousness.

Oracle shook her head, trying in vain to suppress a smile.

"Whatever, Pax," Sean said followed by another tap. "If you look at these photos of her in Mexico, you'll see why her appearance today surprised me."

Oracle felt Pax leaning away from her, as if trying to get a closer look at what Sean was showing them on the table.

"Who's that?" Gloria asked.

"Dama X," Sean replied.

"Is she going to a Halloween party?" Pax said.

"Hmm . . . possibly a comic convention. I saw something like that in a Red Sonja comic once. Do they have cons in Mexico?" Gloria said.

"Is that a bra made from fingers?" Pax asked. "That's got to be fake."

"I agree. Although it might be comfortable. Well-proportioned hands on your breasts can feel nice but weird. But the idea of dead fingers on my boobs . . . yuck."

"This is killing me." Oracle removed a glove and reached out until she felt Pax's pinky finger. An image flashed in her mind of the glass table. Digital pictures—large, small, fuzzy, and clear—were displayed across the table's surface.

If Sean hadn't said the woman in the photos was Dama X, Oracle would've thought she was a performance artist or maybe a cos-player or even a knock-off Lady Gaga, depending on the costume. Some outfits were full of feathers and dark makeup, giving Dama X an owl-like appearance. In other images, her face and body were painted like a skeleton. Another photo showed her in bright colors and billowy skirts with bone patterns. Thick black circles painted over her eyes reached up to her hairline with dark curly hair teased out.

"She looks like a witch." Oracle let go of Pax and fell back into darkness.

"A bruja," Sean replied. "That's what they're calling her."

"They?" Gloria inquired.

"Media outlets. Locals. Internet trolls. There's even a website devoted to her supposed mystical powers and exploits," Sean said. "I think she has several social media fan pages. Not sure if she personally runs them, but some are buzzing about her island being a sanctuary for women."

"I've never heard of a cartel leader with fans," Pax commented.

"She's helped a lot of people. Well, mostly women in the villages where her cartel operates. They praise her for cleaning out their towns. She built schools. Gave money to local hospitals. According to the site, she made the cartel's men disappear."

"And replaced them with her own," Pax said.

"As much as they respect her, they fear her," Sean said.

"I don't blame them. These outfits are enough to freak anyone out." Pax's chair creaked.

"That's the point," Gloria said. "It's brilliant. She's a woman in a man's field. Like any female in a male-dominated world, she needs to work harder, not only to be respected, but in her case feared. She doesn't want them to see her as vulnerable or as a sex object. She made herself over to be a mythical creature. A supernatural one. A bruja. Someone more than human."

"If she's a transhuman, then she is," Oracle added.

"Today she proved what Reyes said about her. The power to persuade, bend people to her will," Sean said. "But I still can't figure out how she hid the crystal skull in the crowd. Even in the bright sunlight, I doubt a shirt or a bag could hide a sparkling turquoise skull. It would stand out."

"Did you say sparkling?" Oracle titled her head.

"Yeah, why?"

"The drug in the vial. What I saw in both Camille's and Andrew's memories. It sparkled and was a blue-green color."

"Then there could be a correlation between Dama X taking the skull and this Diosa de la Venganza," Gloria said.

"Why would Dama X want this skull otherwise?" Oracle leaned forward, excited as these puzzle pieces clicked together. "Why did these cases occur in Baltimore and not anywhere else in the United States? Why did our victims have serious damage to the point of a total change? Maybe she needed the magic—"

"Not magic," Gloria corrected. "Go on."

She shot Gloria a look then reiterated, "Maybe X needed the *element*—the uncategorized element—found in the skull sample to perfect this drug. If she got her hands on one of those samples, maybe she ground it into the serum."

"If she's planning to turn men into women without killing them, she isn't there . . . yet," Sean pointed out.

"It doesn't make sense," Gloria said. "Why waste the drug by testing it here?"

"Maybe her main distributor is in the city? Earlier Matthews told me Camille's dealer, Naomi Moore, left the country for Mexico. His unit is working with the local authorities to track her down," Pax said.

"Dama X could be sending a message," Oracle suggested.

"What message and to whom?" Gloria exclaimed.

"To us, perhaps?" Sean said. "I don't know. Camille didn't have anything to do with TransGen or U-Sec, but both victims knew her."

"And the victims were very different. Donovan, I can understand. He represented everything that X had fought against. Maybe she learned about Camille's situation from Naomi. As far as we know, Andrew was nothing like Donovan. He wanted the drug because he couldn't afford the sex change operation. Why sell it to him?"

"Could Andrew have been a test? The drug didn't work on Donovan so maybe they tried another route." Oracle felt they were on the path to the truth but the road was still foggy.

"Like someone who welcomed the change," Pax said.

Oracle nodded.

"That didn't work, either," Gloria declared. "And we suspect there's a third vial based on what Oracle gathered from Camille's memory and the empty box Pax found. Who knows when that's going to drop and if there are any more we don't know about."

A chair rolled back from the table across from Oracle.

"I need to talk to these reporters before they start spouting their own theories that then become fact," Sean said before a door swooshed open. "Keep me posted on what you learn and what I can tell the press. And, Pax, after you reach Mexico call me ASAP. I need to know what backup you want, so I can work out compensation with Reyes."

"I got it the first twenty times you told me."

"I'll call him if you prefer," Sean shot back.

"That's not what I,"—the door closed as Pax spoke—"meant."

"And I'm going to hook a vein to an IV full of caffeine and try to pull an answer out of a gene's ass, which would be a lot easier if they had asses." Gloria punctuated the sentiment with a yawn.

Oracle echoed her yawn.

"Pax, can you take Oracle home?" Gloria asked.

"I'm fine with a cab—"

Pax rested a hand on Oracle's shoulder. "I got you covered. Unless you're planning to see Matthews at the hospital."

"His parents and sister are with him. I'll just get in the way when he needs his rest."

What Oracle left out was a change in Matthews's attitude after she'd read him. He became distant, which she attributed to the sedatives. He even turned his head as Oracle kissed him goodbye. She got the impression he wanted his space. Probably embarrassed by the whole episode with Pax.

Oracle stood along with Pax, who guided her now gloved hand onto his arm.

"I should probably send Matthews a fruit basket or something," Pax muttered.

He guided her out of the room. Gloria's heels slapped the hard hallway floor in front of them.

"Of course, you should," Gloria joked. "Nothing says 'I'm sorry for breaking your bones' more than a fruit basket."

"Give it a rest," Oracle admonished. "You know Pax held back and did what he had to, considering two good-sized men were attacking him. A less controlled transhuman would've killed them. He's come a long way."

"True," Gloria said, followed by the ding of the elevator. "I'm sorry, Pax. It's been a long several days with no shiny light in sight."

"It's all good," Pax replied and patted Oracle's hand.

"Ron's a good transgeneticist, but I need someone who can think outside the norm to make significant movement on this case." Gloria stepped onto the elevator, and Pax and Oracle followed.

"Like Lucy?" Pax suggested.

Oracle's shoulders tightened as if someone had stomped over her grave in spiked heels. She hadn't heard that woman mentioned in years.

"I never thought I'd hear that name from you," Gloria said.

"Jaybird brought her up when I met with him. Thought he saw Lucy at the mall."

"Doubtful. Last time I spoke with Lucy, she'd bought out her father's shares in a pharmaceutical company they started in Costa Rica."

"Wasn't there a rumor that—"

"No, she didn't kill her father," she cut off Oracle.

The elevator settled to a stop and chimed as the doors slid open. Pax stood firm, letting Oracle know this wasn't their stop.

Gloria stepped out but kept talking, apparently holding the doors open. "Although, I wouldn't blame Lucy after her own father took credit for her research. I'm still angry with my dad for not sticking up for her. He knew the truth, but it was easier to get funding with a senior geneticist's name on the project."

"That wasn't the only reason she left," Oracle noted.

"Lucy was set to get her license revoked by the board from running unapproved trials. I assumed that's why she left the states pretty quickly." Pax shifted closer to Oracle.

"Ever since we were in high school, Lucy pushed the limits. She's ahead of her time. Politicians in the states aren't as open-minded as they are in other countries."

That was adding a cupful of sugar to it. From what Oracle recalled, Lucy had run tests on transhumans without their permission or knowledge. Two had to be institutionalized. Her father had left the country with her to avoid a lawsuit. Dr. Vivas and the government made the cases disappear to protect TransGen's reputation. Oracle assumed they paid off the victims' families as well.

The elevator buzzed, indicating the doors had been held open for too long.

"That's my cue. But I'm glad you mentioned Lucy. I should call her. She may have insight on this, given her recent business venture. But you didn't hear that from me." Gloria's voice echoed from the hallway, as the doors shut.

"Not even going to ask what she meant," he said.

"Good choice."

Pax didn't speak anymore as they rode the elevator down to the garage level. Oracle welcomed the comforting silence after the hours spent talking— both verbally and mentally.

The doors opened, and Pax broke the silence, chitchatting with her on the way to his truck. Generalities. Safe, innocuous subjects. The weather. His mother. Her parents. Sean's love of stupid ties. Gloria's lack of social skills. The normal topics they brought up when they were skirting larger issues.

As Oracle climbed into the seat of his SUV, her phone rang. Her mother again.

"I have to get this." She was glad for the distraction since they'd run out of safe conversational turns.

"I'm sorry I didn't get back to you," she said as she answered. Oracle's mom didn't let her say anymore. Without a pause, she accelerated from relief to concern to agitation then finally putting on the brakes when she got to Oracle's brother, Alex. At his campaign dinner, which Oracle had misremembered as taking place next weekend, a reporter inquired about his sister working at U-Sec on a case where a Senator's son had been killed. It appeared James Donovan's body was claimed by someone after all.

Oracle propped her elbow onto the armrest and leaned against the window while cradling the phone. In a hushed voice, Pax asked if she was all right. Oracle nodded when she really wanted to tell him to keep driving West to the Appalachians and beyond and leave this mounting craziness behind them. Muscles tensed in the back of her neck. A headache would follow right . . . about . . . now.

Her mom stopped for a breath, allowing Oracle to assure her that she'd call Alex when she got home.

After Oracle hung up, Pax said, "I'd forgotten how much your mom can talk."

"And how fast. She threw in a few Vietnamese phrases when the English ones took too long to describe the point."

"Is everything okay?"

Oracle sighed and shoved the phone back in her purse. "Alex is running for Congress."

"I saw his ad on TV. Meant to ask you about that."

"They held a fundraising banquet last night, which I'd forgotten about."

Oracle hoped Pax wouldn't say anything about last night and their fight. He didn't, so she continued, "Sean will have his hands full with those reporters outside TransGen. I didn't know Donovan was the son of a former Senator."

"That's news to me."

"Someone at the hospital must've tipped off the media, or maybe Camille's lawyer did, once they found out. Camille didn't know much about Donovan's background, just that he came from money and was estranged from his family."

She wrung her hands together, popping a few knuckles.

"I'd hoped that my being a transhuman wouldn't put Alex's political career at risk. It didn't come up when he was in the state legislature. Now a few of his large backers are concerned about our connection."

"You're working for U-Sec, so what?"

Oracle lifted her shoulder. "You know how it is. Ever since that one police chief used her transhuman telepathy to get confessions from suspects, politicians have been leery of us."

"Probably afraid of what transhuman telepaths would find out about them." Pax snickered.

"Sean's been making a play to help people understand what transhumans can do to help our country. He's been meeting with a PR agency, but the general public is frightened of us."

"The general public is filled with idiots."

"No, they're just ignorant."

"Same thing," Pax said as the truck slowed down.

"Now this ignorance could be hurting Alex's chance at a Congressional seat."

"What do you plan to do?"

The truck rolled to a stop. Based on the time they'd spent in the car, Oracle assumed they were in front of her condo building.

"I'll talk to Alex. See what he suggests. I'll need to fill him in on as much of Donovan's case as I can. I won't give him any names or compromising details, only enough to field any questions that may come up in the future if we have more victims."

Pax's phone rang with the *Jaws* theme music.

"Gloria?" Oracle asked with a half-smile.

"Yep." Pax didn't answer.

"I should go and call Alex." Oracle felt along the door for the handle.

"I appreciate what you said to Gloria about me."

"It was the truth." Her fingertips rested on the metal door release.

"Yeah, well, I feel bad about what happened."

"Don't. Matthews will be okay."

"I'm glad you're okay."

"Why wouldn't I be?"

"Because you're with him and we were . . . you know."

"You know, what?" she asked. Pax brought it up so he needed to say it.

"Together."

She wondered if his face flushed from saying that, because hers did, which only made her skin become even more heated with frustration.

She turned away from him. But he surprised her by grabbing her hand, which was naked since she'd removed the glove to call her mother.

With a start, Pax jerked away but not before she caught a memory flash.

Of them in bed together. Her on top of Pax, who was cuffed to her headboard. Same image as her dream last night, down to the black fuzzy handcuffs and the sheer red negligee she'd never had the opportunity to wear for him.

"What was that?" Oracle snatched her hand away.

"What was what?" Pax's words faltered, as if he hoped she'd answer first.

The big bad shark's theme music filled the car again.

"I better . . ."

"Yes, you better." Oracle fumbled to find the door handle again. "We'll talk about this later."

Her feet touched the curb. She slammed the door. The purr of the window rolling down made her pause.

"Hold on, Gloria," Pax said before he called out to her, "Seriously, what did you see?"

"You know what I saw. We'll talk when you return from Mexico. Privately." She made a circle with her finger to indicate Gloria was listening.

Turning on her heel, she squared her shoulders and snapped out her cane. The bottom rolled from side to side along the walkway to her door while her heavy steps carried her forward. The cane vibrated when she neared the entrance. She placed her hand on the door handle, and it read her handprint and unlocked for her. Pax's truck continued to idle next to the curb. She didn't give him the satisfaction of a friendly wave goodbye. She wasn't in a friendly mood.

Oracle threw open the door and marched into her condo complex. When she entered the empty, quiet elevator, she could no longer avoid the questions stalking her.

Where did that image come from? Had she pushed it inside Pax's mind when she read him, which could happen when her guard was down?

No. She shook her head and pressed the third button up from the bottom. She hadn't been thinking about her dream when she'd touched him.

Then maybe he'd dreamed the same dream too? She shook her head harder.

Impossible.

She slumped against the wall. The elevator rose.

Did this mean he still dreamed about her? Still thought about her, wanted her?

Maybe.

Chapter 8
Cleaning up the World

I deal in science, not miracles.

—Dr. Gloria Vivas, co-founder of UltraSecurity and lead transgeneticist at TransGen

Pax gripped the steering wheel as he stared at Oracle's retreating back, his heart dropping with every angry, stiff step she took away from his truck.

"Pax," Gloria's voice sounded from the truck's speakers.

He didn't reply, too busy debating whether he should walk Oracle up to her place or not. She wouldn't be happy for the escort, but she'd deal.

"Pax," Gloria implored once more.

The building was secure. Cameras positioned outside and in. The front door keyed to each tenants' handprint and up to three guests per unit. He was surprised that Oracle kept his on file.

"Pax!" Gloria screeched.

Through the glass wall, he watched Oracle get into the elevator from the lobby.

"Yeah," he finally responded.

Gloria's labored breathing filled the car, followed by people shouting in the background.

"What's going on?" His attention snapped to her.

"My father's been attacked."

He stepped on the gas, and the truck lurched from the curve. Pax turned it around in the middle of the street. Wheels squealed against the asphalt.

"Who did it?" He accelerated through a yellow light.

"We don't know. We found him by the south entrance five minutes ago. I'm rushing him to cryo."

"Cryo?" Pax took a turn too tight, causing the truck to dip to one side.

"We have the third vial, Pax, and it's empty."

"Shit."

"Ron, take the service elevator, not the lobby one. I'll take the stairs." Gloria's voice became faint as she issued this order. Pax heard the squeak of a gurney's wheels.

Over the line, a door creaked open then slammed shut.

"Ron's taking care of him with my oversight," Gloria said.

"What can I do?"

Pax listened to Gloria's heels echoing through the stairwell as she hit each step. He wasn't sure she heard his question until she responded, "Just be a friend."

"You got it."

He called Oracle. He didn't think she'd answer but she did. "Dr. Vivas was attacked."

"Oh, my God. Gloria and Sean . . . ?"

"Gloria is getting her dad prepped for cryo." Pax sped through another yellow light. "Stay inside, don't go out until we know this attack is isolated."

"I will. Call me when you know more."

"Will do."

He turned down the street in front of TransGen. Reporters and camera crews swarmed the building's entrance. Three security guards were positioned between the glass entranceway and Sean, who stood on the pavement in the spotlight with microphones bunched in front of him. The throng edged into the parking garage's entrance. Pax couldn't drive in without drawing attention and possibly allowing a few journalists standing on the fringes to sneak past the gate. He looped around and saw Dr. Vivas's town car parked by the south entrance without its driver. With Sean occupying the reporters up front, the side street was devoid of life. He pulled behind the shiny black sedan. His truck lights illuminated dark, wet blotches on the sidewalk.

Pax flashed his badge to the two guards stationed at the side entrance. Taking two steps at a time, he took a guess where he'd find Gloria. And he was right. She was working alone in the lab adjoining her office.

"How's your dad?"

"Frozen." Gloria didn't look up from the microscope.

Pax halted next to her and crossed his arms. "How far along was he?"

"He didn't lose his penis if that's what you're angling about." She entered digits into her computer tablet then adjusted the microscope.

"That's good news."

Gloria lifted her head from the eyepiece. Her eyes, puffy and bloodshot, rested wearily on his face. "Dillon, his driver, saw my father leave the building. In the second it took for him to get out of the driver seat, my father was on the ground with a woman in a hoodie standing over him."

"What did she look like?"

"She had the hood up. It obscured her face from his viewpoint. Dillon slid over the car to get to her. Must've surprised her because she dropped the needle and took off."

"Dama X?"

"Who else would it be?" Gloria shrugged. "But they'll check the vial for fingerprints as soon as I'm finished extracting what I can from it. They're reviewing the security footage now."

"Do you want me to see if they found anything?" Pax pivoted to leave when Gloria grabbed his arm.

"Stay. I want the company." She motioned for him to sit on the stool near her.

Pax scanned the three long metal tables filled with beakers, microscopes, test tube plates, and centrifuges. Spaced out above the tables, glass monitors hung suspended from the ceiling. He didn't recognize several machines, from the size of shoeboxes to taller than him, that aligned the tables and floor. In the corner of the room, one machine emitted a whirring sound.

"Where's everyone?"

"I kicked them out." She removed a glass slide from the microscope and slipped in another. After peering through the lens, she pulled back, frowned, and leaned back in to study it again.

Pax drummed his hands on the underside of the stool. He wanted to do something to help. In here, he was useless.

"Maybe I should—"

"I'm watching this virus attack my father's cells. But it's not having the same effect as it did on Donovan and Cook. His cells are fighting it and not changing. I don't understand unless this isn't the same serum." Gloria touched a button on the side of the microscope's base and a screen lit up above her head. To Pax, the image looked like a bunch of red bubbles churning in soda water.

"Want me to get someone?" he asked.

With a yawn, she stretched out her arm along the table and rested her head on it.

"I don't trust anyone else right now. That's why I called you. I need a friend to talk with me."

Talk. Gloria knew that wasn't his expertise. "What about your mother?"

"Sean politicked to keep her out of the loop until we know what's going on. Fortunately, she's in Amsterdam. She sits on the board for the bio-engineering conference my father was supposed to attend. They're six hours ahead of us."

Pax glanced at his watch reading nine thirty p.m.

"If we don't have an answer by the time she's awake, then we'll tell her." Gloria closed her eyes, and Pax thought she was going to nap until she said, "I have a confession."

"Okay."

"I knew James Donovan." Gloria rubbed her eyes.

"How?" Pax pulled back in surprise.

"High school. It's been twenty years since I last saw him. When Camille mentioned the steakhouse where she worked and meeting Donovan there, I put it together. His parents used to own the restaurant."

"Did you contact his family?"

"They told me to keep his body for as long as I needed then cremate the remains."

"That's harsh." Pax crossed his arms.

"They wanted his death kept under wraps, which is why I didn't mention this before. Unfortunately, Camille's lawyer learned that Donovan's mother is a retired Senator and told the press."

She stared at the blank wall across from them before saying, "He'd dated two of my friends. One broke her ankle when he shoved her down stairs outside the school. Another ended up dead after she left him."

"Why wasn't he arrested?"

"My friend was too embarrassed to press charges, afraid her mom and dad would blame her, see her as weak." Gloria grunted and combed her fingers through her hair. "Such bullshit that we believe when we're young, always trying to be strong and not realizing what real strength is."

Pax watched as she rubbed her eyes again. He wasn't sure what this had to do with the case but figured Gloria needed to talk, so he let her.

"She regretted not going to the police when our friend's car ran off the road," she continued. "They couldn't prove it was foul play, although we had our suspicions. Jimmy switched schools after the accident. Then I heard he got into drugs, and then there were run-ins with the law before his family disowned him. Paid him a large sum to disappear."

Gloria dragged herself up from the table.

"But enough about the past. Jimmy can give some contrition now by helping solve this case." She raised her arms above her head and stretched out her back. She caught herself on the stool as it teetered to the side.

"Glor, maybe let someone else take over for tonight. Get a few hours of rest to clear your head."

"Would my father leave before finding an answer?"

"He would ask for help and not do it on his own."

The whirring sound cut off, followed by three consecutive beeps.

"Who said I don't have help?" Gloria slid off her stool and walked over to a large glass monitor above a machine the size of a freezer.

Pax followed her across the room. Above their heads, rows of genetic code began to stream down the screen.

"Sean surprised me with this software to reverse engineer the drug and create an antidote. He developed it today."

"How long did it take him to create this?"

"Two hours." Gloria isolated a line of genetic code by tapping it with her fingers. The code enlarged, and she wiped her fingers across the screen to move it onto a secondary monitor. "He didn't want to give me the software until he had tested it, but with what happened to our father, he figured I could do the testing now. He's getting faster at programming for sure."

"I'd say he interfaces better with computers than with people, but he does a helluva job with those media vultures."

"Better him than you and me," Gloria said.

"Agreed."

Pax watched as Gloria tapped on a few other letters and swished them over to the other monitor.

"What are you doing?" he asked.

"I'm highlighting similar abnormalities. These are areas where genes are being switched on and others off to cause this transmodification . . . hold . . . on." Gloria flattened her hand on the screen. "My father and Cook have the same marker. It was missing in Donovan."

"Okay."

Gloria's tired face lit up; she grabbed his upper arms, dug her fingers into his biceps. She shook him.

Tried to.

"Don't you see?" She slapped her hand across Pax's chest to make her point.

"See what?"

"That's a key piece. But I still need to analyze the serum. Dammit, what's taking so long to do that?" She tapped the screen. Pax took another step back. Gloria tended to express her excitement and frustration with her hands.

"What's this key piece about?" Pax asked.

"It's something found in many transhumans, but we weren't sure what it meant. You have it. Oracle has it. Surefire does, too, along with most of U-Sec's agents. I was still testing my theory so I couldn't publish my paper yet. Still building up the evidence."

That got Pax's attention. "I have an abnormality."

"Of course, look at you." Gloria flapped her hands at him.

"Look at what?"

"Your skin's a bit tougher than normal and heals faster than a year ago. Your muscles are denser. You can take the blunt trauma of a rhino without being killed, besides being able to lift the thing. None of your ESP buddies responded as well to the enhancements. And your last physical showed another uptick in strength."

Over the last few months, Pax recognized changes in his body but had been too busy to bring it up to Gloria. He noticed that he was healing faster. Only a small bruise remained from the blow Matthews landed with the fire extinguisher.

"But let's get back to business here. This isn't about you. It's about these genes and saving my father. Although, if my theory's correct, it won't kill him like Donovan. Just turn him into a woman."

"That would kill him," Pax said.

"As much as I want to save him, there is a sense of poetic justice if I let that happen."

Vivas never hid his prejudice toward women in the sciences. How his wife, a respected entrepreneur and heiress, put up with his chauvinism was beyond Pax. Must be a generational thing.

Gloria's phone buzzed.

"Sean, you're on speaker. Pax is here."

"What's he doing there?" Sean's words came out weary, tired.

"Helping me. He's acting girlfriend for tonight. My sounding board."

Pax rolled his eyes. Maybe he should add that to his job description.

"Ron told me dad's stable. Appears we stopped it in time," Sean said.

"Now we need to reverse it, or else Mom will need to reevaluate her sexual preferences." Gloria furrowed her brow at the monitor.

"Really, Glor? You had to go there."

She waved her hand, dismissing Sean's comment.

"What did the reporters know?" Pax changed the awkward path this conversation was taking.

"Skewed facts. Sensational assertions mixed with a drop of truth. The usual," Sean replied.

This was one of the few times he would love to buy Sean a beer for dealing with this side of the job so Pax didn't have to. "Oracle's brother Alex Cross is running for Congress. Last night at a fundraising dinner, he was blindsided by reporters asking questions about Donovan."

"Got a few of those questions, too," Sean said. "I wish you would've told me he was *that* Donovan."

"I was sworn to secrecy by the family," Gloria replied.

"Like that ever stopped you."

"Whatever." Gloria held the phone for Pax to speak into as she zoned out of the conversation. Mumbling to herself, she swiped past the thousands of lines of genetic code.

"Any word on the woman who did this to your father?" Pax asked.

"Nothing. It's like she's a ghost," Sean said.

"Or a bruja," Pax tossed out. "But why target Dr. Vivas? And why risk coming back here when she already had the skull."

"Dad was in too much pain to provide a description to his driver. By the time Gloria and I arrived, he'd blacked out."

"Anything in the security video?"

"There's no picture. The security camera is dead. Not sure when it happened. I asked U-Sec's tech crew to investigate the camera."

"That is interesting," Gloria muttered with her nose to the screen.

"I'm going to check with our tech department, then see our father," Sean said.

"Go on, then." Gloria gestured with the phone in her right hand as she placed her other on her hip. She leaned closer to the monitor.

"This is it," Gloria whispered so low Pax had to strain to hear her. She hung up on Sean, who kept calling out, "hello" after Gloria dropped the phone on the table.

Pax squinted at the screen. There was a pattern in the codes Gloria had isolated on the smaller screen, but he would have more luck translating Egyptian hieroglyphics than understanding what this structure meant.

"It's the missing link." Gloria pocketed the phone in her lab coat. "Literally." She faced Pax, her brown hair falling haphazardly out of her ponytail.

If Gloria needed a sounding board, then he was more than happy to oblige. "Good job."

"*Pfft.*" Gloria blew the strands off her forehead. "Good job will be finding a way to keep these codes from rearranging the body's biology."

She touched a shiny black desk below the screens. It lit up with a keyboard touchpad. Gloria typed several commands, and the smaller screen projected a 3-D model of a DNA strand between them.

"I finally got the Donovan vial from the CDC. They weren't as incompetent as I thought," she said under her breath. "Although there is a slight difference between the samples gleaned from that vial and the one used on my father. I think the Donovan vial was contaminated. Ron's team is running a more thorough comparison."

"But what we do know is this." Gloria enlarged the image. "Both vials contained a protein that acts like a converter switch. It attaches to this part of the DNA code."

"The abnormal one that I have."

"You were paying attention."

"If it has to do with me, of course I was."

Gloria shook her head as if he were serious. Maybe he was a bit serious.

"Oracle said the vial in Camille's memory sparkled with the same coloring as the crystal skull. That's because the drug residue inside both vials comprises the same biological components as the skull, namely the primary proteins," she circled a string of letters with her fingertip.

"However, Donavon's vial contains a substance that the serum used on my father doesn't, along with a few other differences, which is why I need to rule out sample contamination. What's interesting is how this substance acts like a binding agent with the proteins and the abnormal port."

"So a skull, used in religious ceremonies hundreds of years ago, contains a protein that fits a gene port in my DNA?"

"Possibly, but with the aid of this unknown substance to bind it together."

"What about this *unknown* substance. Where did this come from?"

Gloria wagged her head. "I have no idea. That's why I need that skull back. It may also hold the key to how Surefire got her powers."

She whirled from the screen to face him. Mascara smudged around her eyes, making them appear even more sunken and tired as she gazed up at him with an intensity that cut him to the core.

"What I do know for sure is that skull holds the key to saving Cook and my father. We need to get it back."

Pax gazed down into her bloodshot eyes. He didn't recall ever seeing Gloria appear so vulnerable, so needing of his help. His chest tightened at her misery. His temper rose when he considered how Dama X's selfish, cruel act put his partner—his friend—in this situation.

"I'll bring you that skull and Dama X, with or without Reyes's help or permission."

♥ ☠ ♥ ☠ ♥ ☠

The car inched along the packed streets and past vendors selling brightly colored sombreros, scarves, and tchotchkes to tourists—some toting children, some toting several cervezas, if not tequila shots, based on how they staggered through the crowd. The weekend meant tour groups and twenty-somethings were making their way to the Pacific coast of Mexico to soak up the sun, food, and booze. Reyes's driver informed Pax it may take longer than usual to arrive at their destination with so many tourists clogging up the streets.

Pax popped open a can of soda from the small fridge in the back of the limo sent to pick him up from the airport. He bypassed the beer and top-shelf booze lining the small bar in favor of staying professional and alert. Three hours of sleep last night and none on the plane, crammed next to two dude-bros who tried to one up each other about how much they'd drunk and vomited last time they were in Mexico. Then they'd given a detailed list to make *Playboy* editors blush of what they'd like to do to a woman they had passed by in first class. Sleek and modern, she was well out of the frat guys' league and belonged in New York City, commanding a boardroom full of executives, and not in their beach bunny fantasies. She reminded Pax of Gloria's corporate style except for the wraparound shades and felt hat worn over her short hair. At one point she got up to stretch and looked their way—or somebody's way, it was hard to tell where she looked with those sunglasses—and the dude-bros snickered like teen boys ogling a hot teacher.

Pax was never that obnoxious in his twenties.

On a positive note, he was too distracted by their inane conversation to think about Dr. Vivas in cryo, his own genetic abnormalities, or Oracle. Or the fact that he had dreamed of Oracle once again during those few stolen hours of sleep. This time he'd followed her from the truck, stopping her before she disappeared into the building. Then he kissed her as he wanted to kiss her nearly every time he saw her. Told her how much he still cared when he shouldn't, before a Godzilla-sized Gloria appeared and screeched then stepped on them.

Pax shook his head. *Man, I need to lay off those sci-fi classics before bed.*

Of course, last night wouldn't have gone so poorly if Oracle hadn't touched him at the same time the dream had entered into his thoughts. Something she said made him think about that dream. What was it?

Pax scratched his jaw. More importantly, what were the odds of Oracle touching him at that precise moment when it popped into his memory?

Possibly the same odds as seeing UltraAgent TimeTrap hitchhiking on the side of the road in Mexico.

"You've got to be kidding me," he mumbled then looked down at the can in his hand to make sure it was indeed a Coke.

Clothed in a floral peasant-style top, TimeTrap held her arm out to the road. Thumb pointed up to the bright blue sky. Hip jutted to the side. Long legs covered in bellbottom jeans. A satchel slung over her shoulder. He couldn't see her eyes behind the large round sunglasses, which obscured most of her face, but he knew his agent. Her sixties style outfit and tall, lean frame stood out among the board shorts and beach style of the tourists streaming around her.

"Pull over, Bruno," Pax told the driver.

The car eased into an empty spot past the open-air market where TimeTrap stood. Pax opened the door as she ran up in her platform sandals.

"Hola, mi jefe!" She threw her canvas satchel along with herself into the seat across from Pax.

Once settled, she swiped away the sweat from her forehead with her cotton sleeve and exclaimed, "Hace mucho calor."

Pax agreed. It was indeed very hot outside. But it was getting a hell of a lot warmer in the limo even with the cold A/C blowing directly on him.

"Oh, me siento especial." TimeTrap took off her sunglasses and reached for a bottle of real Mexican tequila and a shot glass.

Pax closed the privacy divider on the driver. "What are you doing here?"

"Sean sent me to help you."

Pax grabbed the tequila bottle and glass from her hand and set it back on the bar. "No alcohol if you're on the clock."

Dejected, she slumped back in her seat. "What's the fun in helping you in Mexico if I can't imbibe the local beverages?"

Pax gave her his most stern boss stare. "How did you get here?"

"Sean was too cheap to pay for my airfare. Something about it being a waste on me with my QT ability and all. Apparently, he was ticked because he wanted me to pop you here last night, but he couldn't reach me because . . . well, you know . . . I was out of the universe and all that." TimeTrap reached across and procured a bottled tea from the small fridge. "Of course, traveling via quantum transference this far drains my mojo, so I won't be able to pop anywhere else until I eat some food and wait a few hours. And, later, if I have to transfer you as well, then . . ." She made a wide motion with her hands as if to indicate Pax's bulk.

"Hold on." Pax put up his hand for her to stop. "Let's start from the beginning."

TimeTrap made a rewinding noise like an old school tape machine. With jerky movements, she re-screwed the cap onto her bottle and placed it back in the refrigerator and slumped into the seat.

A real comedian this one. Too bad he was boiling over with frustration at Sean to find any of this amusing.

"Sean sent you," Pax stated.

"Yes."

"How did you find me?"

"Sean did his thing"—she wriggled her fingers in the air—"and hooked into the tiny GPS in your shirt button." She pointed to the third button down on his shirt. The top two were open. "We triangulated your route from the airport and figured where you'd eventually pass by, based on Reyes's directions. Otherwise, I would've called for you to pick me up. Fortunately, there was a clear space not far from that market where I could safely pop into."

"Sean never told me any of this."

"He caught up with me this morning after what happened to his old man. That's totally trippy. Although it would be nice for Dr. Vivas to experience how the fairer—yet stronger, I might add—sex lives."

"And why did he send you and not tell me?" Pax asked. TimeTrap tended to go off on tangents, losing her way in conversations. It's a wonder she was able to find her way home when she traveled through space and time.

"Who knows why Sean does and says half the stuff he does? Take those ugly ties he wears for instance—"

"Why did Sean send you?"

She reached for her iced tea once more and spied a gift basket of goodies on the bar. "Yum, bananas and Chiclets and mini-wafer candies and weird spicy mango pops. Oh, double yum, salted apricots."

She stuffed two bananas and a pack of Chiclets into her satchel, and then proceeded to dig into the bag of apricots.

"TimeTrap," Pax bit out, his patience as thin as the cotton top she wore over a tie-dyed tank.

"Oh, right. I'm here to help you get the skull back from Dama X," TimeTrap said between bites of the dried fruit.

Gloria's last words for Pax were to locate and acquire the skull and Dama X—both preferably intact. But there was one obstacle to this plan.

"We don't know where Dama X or the skull are. Reyes is meeting with me and—"

"Plans have changed a wee bit now that Reyes's spy has made it onto her island."

"Spy? He never mentioned this."

"Yeah, well, Sean gave him an earful about not telling us, but Reyes wanted to make sure it worked first—and it did, sort of. They got an approximate location of the island before the spy's tracker went dead. Satellite surveillance picked up a few large objects in the area where her signal last . . . ahhh . . . signaled." She rummaged through her bag and unfolded three printouts.

"These could be X's island or freight ships or massive sea monsters, which would be seriously cool." TimeTrap pointed to the grayish blips taken at sunrise this morning based on the timestamp in the corner. "An insider who defected from X's camp will meet us at Reyes's place to give us the lowdown."

Pointing at the second page, she said, "But it's kind of weird because several of the items appear in one sat photo and then disappear in the two others. Like they were spirits or aliens or something."

TimeTrap made a high-pitched wooing noise, which Pax assumed was supposed to mimic a moaning ghost. Sounded more like a sick goat to him.

"Sean said you prefer paper to electronics, so these are for you." TimeTrap handed Pax the photos.

It was true. Digital readers were easily destroyed in the field, and data could get lost from energy expelled when TimeTrap popped from one place to another.

Pax's cell phone buzzed from inside his duffle bag. He pulled it out and rolled his eyes when he saw Stephen St. John's name. He didn't want to answer it but knew St. John would keep calling until he did, as if Pax couldn't possibly be doing anything that was more important than speaking with him.

"Yeah," Pax answered, not hiding his agitation.

"Are you in fucking Mexico?" came an equally agitated reply.

"I never heard of a town in Mexico called fucking, sir. Is that near Baja?"

"I'm not joking here, smartass."

"Neither am I." Pax took a sip of his soda. In spite of the situation, he smiled. It always felt good to upset his old Army commander who deserved every bit of his smartassiness, considering what happened the last time they were in Mexico together.

"It's that Reyes guy, isn't it? He called in that favor." Like a dog with a juicy bone, St. John didn't want to let it go. "I've run background checks on him. They come up short. As if he were born at twenty-five. Can't find anything about his earlier life except how that tech tycoon Antonio Suarez had adopted him."

"This is my cell phone. Not a secure line, St. John."

TimeTrap's eyes widened into brown pinwheels. She fluttered her hands at Pax, who raised his eyebrows, not understanding her wild gestures.

"I'm not worried about this shit getting out," St. John went on. "But when you find a secure line, we need to talk more. I don't like you going there without alerting me first."

"Going where?" Just because St. John's special DoD committee was U-Sec's largest contract, didn't mean that he—and the government—was privy to all their cases.

St. John didn't reply so Pax took this opportunity to put his hand over the receiver and mouth to TimeTrap, "What are you doing?"

"He"—she jabbed a finger toward the phone—"is why I needed to talk to you the other day."

Pax nodded when he remembered how TimeTrap had disrupted his meeting with Sean and Gloria when Reyes had first called, saying she needed to talk with him. With all that had transpired since Reyes's initial phone call, her request had slipped his mind.

"He keeps bugging me to get a clearance," TimeTrap whispered.

"Pax, are you there?" St. John's voice bellowed over the speaker.

"Yeah." Pax moved the phone back to his ear.

"He's pushing me to use my power for things I'm not comfortable with. Stuff not in my contract," TimeTrap continued in a hushed tone.

Lack of sleep on top of current events meant Pax had no patience for this kind of overstep. "What did you say to TimeTrap to upset her?"

Her pale face lost even more color. She recoiled from Pax, as if afraid St. John could reach through the phone and grab her.

"What? That she's a pothead?"

Pax snorted. "I doubt she'd find that offensive. No, you asked for help outside her scope of work."

"She needs to clean up her act and do what she is paid to do. I don't know how you kept that woman a secret from my committee—let alone the government—all these years."

"TimeTrap wasn't ready for the field until this past year. She was working with TransGen to develop her ability before training with U-Sec to help us out as needed and when available."

"She can do more than help on occasion. I know of several military operations that could use her."

"As long as it's within her contract and you go through the proper channels at U-Sec. You may represent our largest client, but hiring one of our agents still requires approval from the partners even for government assignments."

"We'll see about that. She has a specialty that, so far, no one else has. It's her duty to use it for the public good."

Pax massaged his forehead, trying to soothe the tension over the "public good" argument that St. John trotted out whenever one of U-Sec's agents refused an assignment. Not all transhumans came into their powers with a career in law enforcement on their minds. Some were looking for solutions to ailments or handicaps. Others were caught up in an accident and were able to work out a deal with TransGen and U-Sec for a job, afraid the public sector wouldn't accept them.

"It's her duty to do what she believes is right. Just because someone has a power you want to put in use doesn't mean you can pull eminent domain and claim it. Being a transhuman doesn't mean that person gives up their freedom to choose the life they want to live."

"But what if that freedom is in jeopardy?" St. John countered.

Pax blew out an exasperated breath. When weren't the freedoms of American citizens in jeopardy? Seemed it was the age-old spin politicians and the military used to sway public support to whatever cause they were selling.

"You need to be more specific," Pax replied.

"You know I can't do that."

"I can't sanction you approaching TimeTrap about any assignments before going through me or Sean first. I'm asking you to respectfully back off."

"All I can say to you on this unsecured line is don't agree to anything with Reyes until you here from me. In fact, use TimeTrap and leave now. Return to Baltimore."

"No," Pax replied.

St. John hung up, not one for goodbyes or recognizing the word "no" being said to him.

Pax's fingers tightened around the phone. Fortunately, he stopped himself before he snapped it in two. Yoga had helped in anger management, but there were times when what he considered a squeeze was strong enough to shatter a phone. Which he learned twice this year, to Sean's annoyance, when the company had to buy him two new phones.

"Thanks." TimeTrap crossed her arms.

"He needs to learn that U-Sec is not his company. My employees are not his to bully." Every nerve buzzed in Pax's body, no longer sleepy but wide awake. Funny how a conversation with St. John could get his adrenaline going. More invigorating than the most potent energy drink.

Outside the window, Pax notice the road split and watched as another limo, identical to theirs, accelerated then peeled off to the right. Screeching tires kicked up a dust cloud as the vehicle veered from the road before it straightened out. He wondered if it was the same one he'd seen at the airport that the corporate woman from first class had gotten into.

"It's hard to believe he's Surefire's father. No wonder she never introduced us until the Mexico incident." TimeTrap sipped her iced tea.

"She still hasn't spoken with him?"

"Do you blame her after what he did last time we were here in *fucking* Mexico?" TimeTrap swept her hands in a circle, spilling drops of her iced tea.

"He loves her," Pax said then added, "in his own way."

"If you're talking about a narcissistic, what-can-you-do-for-me way, then you're right on." She saluted him with her drink.

The engine churned as they chugged up a steep incline. Bottles and the food basket slid along the bar.

Pax put his hands on either side to keep from tilting. TimeTrap pressed back into the seat.

"Are we getting ready for a launch?" she asked.

The car accelerated followed by a loud pop. It lurched to the side and spun around. Bottles flew from the bar and hit Pax in the chest and legs. His body plastered against the window behind him. With a squeal, TimeTrap slammed into his shoulder. His feet lifted off the floor. His upper back slid further up the window as the car rolled over and his body followed suit. He put out his hands to brace himself against the roof. Pax's palms slipped and the top of his head busted the plastic dome over a light. Stars exploded across his eyes before his body came to rest along with the car. He rubbed then blinked his eyes into focus.

"TimeTrap." He flipped over onto his stomach.

She didn't respond. Her straight brown bob hid her face turned the other way. Long limbs splayed at awkward angles.

"Kali," Pax said her given name. Over broken glass and the pungent smell of alcohol, he crawled to her.

He felt for her pulse. She was still alive. But he was afraid to move her. Her neck or back could be hurt or broken.

"Bruno!" Pax yelled to the driver. The privacy screen had cracked during impact. Pax slammed a hand into the thick plastic, breaking it apart. Through the opening, Pax spied Bruno suspended by his seatbelt. Blood dripped from his mouth to the ceiling. Breath came out in wheezes. He was alive but unconscious. Probably for the best.

Branches, thick with leaves, lay across the broken front window. Pax couldn't see the road or outside. Gas fumes hit his nose. He covered his mouth and pulled back through the divider into the passenger area. The vehicle teetered. Pax froze. They must be wedged against trees and other foliage that was keeping them from tumbling further down the steep incline.

With the engine cut off, the interior heated up like a sauna set to high. Humidity pressed its hot sticky fingers against his neck and back, soaking them with sweat. He patted his pockets for his phone. Gone. Jostled free during the topsy-turvy ride. A buzzing noise startled him. Outside, branches creaked and scraped against the roof. Pax remained still and evened out his breath, fearing a deep inhale would be enough to topple them further down the hill.

The buzzing sounded again. Past TimeTrap, broken bottles and glasses, and various sundries that had fallen from their bags onto the roof, Pax spied his phone near the back window. The screen lit up with a name he couldn't make out. He wiped his sleeve across his brow to stop more salty sweat from stinging his eyes.

"Down there!" a woman shouted.

Pax cocked his head. Branches snapped above their car. Someone must've seen them lose control and go over the edge.

He cupped his hands around his mouth. "Two seriously injured. Approach with caution. Vehicle is unstable."

The rustling moved closer. More voices spoke from front, back, and sides. All female.

"Quien habla?"

"El conductor?"

"No sé."

"Es voz de hombre."

"Un hombre? Nos equivocamos? Chocamos con otro coche?"

Every muscle tensed along his spine until Pax swore he'd break apart. Did he understand them correctly? No, his Spanish was shoddy. They couldn't have said they targeted the wrong vehicle.

More snapping and crunching sounded from outside the limo. It slipped an inch or so. Pax's hands shot out to either side of him.

"It's unstable!" Pax yelled. Dammit, what was the Spanish phrase for that?

He heard rustling underneath the roof. Was a person crawling underneath the limo?

Palms flattened against the padded roof, Pax felt vibrations from objects being wedged underneath.

"Estamos en el lugar. Es seguro."

Again, Pax racked his brain trying to find the right translation.

The vehicle jerked to the side when one of the rescuers tried to open the passenger door. Pax slid over to TimeTrap. He felt her pulse. Gingerly, he ran his fingers along her skull to feel for any knots and found one on the back of her head. Odds were good, she had a concussion. He looked for something to help stabilize her head.

Metal ground against metal. They were wedging a crowbar or another object into the door, which was jammed shut. The car swayed. Women shouted from . . .

Pax put his ear to the ceiling under him. Were there people—women—underneath the car, holding it up?

No, it couldn't be. They had to have wedged a large branch underneath.

The door gave way. Fresh air flowed over Pax followed by a sweet coconut scent.

A rifle barrel slid through the open space.

Pax crawled over TimeTrap and reached for his bag containing his gun. Because of Mexico's strict gun regulations, he hadn't planned to strap it on until he was at Reyes's home. At the airport, he was held up for a half hour while they cleared it with their government that Pax could bring a weapon onto Mexican soil.

He pulled out the Beretta M9 and magazine from his bag and loaded a round into the chamber. Taking a steadying breath, he pointed it at the open door.

Then they fired at him.

His shoulder whipped back and an object bounced off his shirt. A stinging sensation followed. He unloaded a round out the open space as a warning. The long barrel his only target.

Another shot fired at him, grazing his cheek. The next shot hit into a button on his shirt and cracked it. Not a bullet but a dart. He lunged forward. Another shot hit his chest where his shirt gaped open. He grabbed the end of the gun, shoved it toward the shooter, and accidentally twisted the barrel, bending it up. A female voice bellowed, cursing him in Spanish mixed with English. He tossed the weapon out before flattening himself against the interior next to the open door.

An argument started just outside the limo. Two, maybe three people yelling. All women.

He shook his head as his vision blurred. His fingers felt through the hole in his shirt and found an object protruding from his skin. Not metal like a bullet but a dart with an empty vial attached to it.

Pax would've panicked if not for the pleasant warming sensation wrapping around his body like a down comforter.

One voice rose above the others, reminding Pax of his Army drill sergeant, except higher pitched. He tried to make out what she was saying, but his hearing was fading along with his vision.

"Hello in there." The same voice called to him, this time in English. No longer gruff with giving orders but friendly, almost singsong. A mother coaxing a child from their hiding spot.

"We want to help you," she said.

"Could've fooled me." Screwing his eyes shut, he shook his head hard to clear it.

"There's been a mistake."

"I'd say." Pax pulled the dart from his chest. A drop of creamy liquid mixed with blood rolled down the side of the vial. It didn't sparkle and wasn't turquoise. One positive in this screwed up situation.

Pax's phone rang again. Through his wavy vision, a name flashed across the screen. *Felix Reyes.*

"I have two people injured in here. The driver and a passenger. Both probably concussed and with possible spinal injuries," he said.

"My people are assisting the driver. You'll need to let us in to help your friend, Pax."

Did she say his name? The world was tilting in and out. Her voice faint then becoming louder, like a radio being turned up and down and then up again. Whatever was in that vial was affecting him faster than three of Jaybird's Rum Grenades. He pulled the other vial from his shoulder.

"How do you know my name?" Pax grabbed TimeTrap's compact lying next to his thigh. Flipping it open, he slowly held it out until he could see through the partially open door.

A woman stood holding another rifle. Her dark hair yanked back from a face painted white with black designs creating a skeletal mask. It wasn't evil Halloween makeup but feminine, with swirling flowery designs. Two others with faces similarly painted appeared behind her. Rifles resting on their shoulders.

"Who are you?" Pax asked.

A shot came from the front of the limo. The dart traveled through the broken divider and into his neck.

Soft fingers gently stroked his cheek as his head dipped to the side and his body went numb.

"We're La Hermandad de Diana. But you can call us the Sisters."

Chapter 9
A Woman of Many Parts

The cases of Sergeant Richard Parker and Captain Elaine Evans are why we passed the law to limit transhumans from working with N-T suspects. Parker lost control of his power when pursuing a suspect, who died from an electric shock emitted by Parker. Evans entered the minds of suspects and illegally attained confessions. In both cases, rights were violated. We can't allow this to continue, and we need to protect our citizens from further violations.

—Former Senator Janet Donovan during a news panel with candidate Alex Cross

---

"Oracle, wait." Pax ran from the truck. He grabbed her arm, spun her around, and pulled her tight against his chest.

In her dreams, her ex-lover broke out the smooth moves.

Oracle lost herself in Pax's eyes. Diving deep into the cool blue depths reminding her of Turks and Caicos, where her family vacationed before everything went dark. At times, Oracle loved her dreams more than reality, because in her dreams she could see every last detail.

Pax tilted his head. His hand held her cheek, while his thumb caressed her jaw before his lips brushed against hers.

"I want you to stay," she whispered. "Don't go to Mexico."

"Then what do you want me to do?"

"Take me right here." Oracle shoved him against the wall, grinding against him. She dug her hands into the back of his neck to hold him in place, exactly where she wanted him, and kissed him. His mouth opened. His tongue tangled with hers. His hands pressed against her lower back, dropping to grip then massage her cheeks.

It started to rain. A hot, steamy mist that drenched his blond hair and made it stick to his face. She liked envisioning him with long hair the way it was when she used to call him Thor-Bear.

"Do it. Here. Against the wall. Show everyone how much you still want me."

In the back of her mind, a whisper of a name: *Matthews.* Wasn't she supposed to be dreaming about her current boyfriend, not her ex? The main man who was recovering at the hospital because of Pax?

No, it was only a dream. The second time today she'd had this one. Not like she could control it . . . that much, anyway.

Oracle ignored the guilty prick and concentrated on the man she ground against, whose body jumped and stiffened as her hand slid over his shirt and ripped it open. Buttons flew off. Her nails scrapped over his wide shoulders, cut chest, abs, and lower to the top of his jeans. She tugged down the zipper and—

A loud screech and giant footsteps pounded the ground.

Godzilla.

More specifically, Gloria-zilla. The same way this dream ended this morning. With a giant Gloria breathing fire and stomping the city.

She has the worst timing. Dream Oracle backed away and sighed as the glorious image of her half-naked hero faded, and she awoke in an awkward position on her couch. She'd been asleep on her arm, which she shook to regain feeling as she rolled toward the phone screeching with the ringtone Oracle had programmed for Gloria.

Godzilla's battle cry. Matthews's idea, not hers, to use this ringtone for her boss. It was funny after two glasses of wine. Now . . . not so much.

"Pax is missing," Gloria announced before Oracle could utter a greeting.

"Tell me what happened." She swung her legs over the edge of the couch and kicked a blanket onto the floor along with the remaining euphoria of the dream. Her pulse thudded in her ears. She strained to hear what Gloria said next.

"Pax's plane landed. He went through customs, got his bag. Reyes's driver picked him up. Then nothing."

"What about TimeTrap? Wasn't she supposed to be there?"

"Missing as well. Sean received a text from her that she'd spotted Pax's car and flagged him down. That was her last communication. Then there was St. John."

"What does St. John have to do with this?" Oracle put Gloria on speaker as she entered the bathroom. Cool tiles under her feet provided a contrast to the wood floor in the hall. She ran cold water over a washcloth.

"He spoke with Pax while on route to Reyes. Based on the timestamp of St. John's call, they were halfway between the airport and Reyes's house. We triangulated the cell signal before it went dark. Reyes's team is searching the area now."

"Was Pax wearing his U-Sec shirt with a tracking device?" Their tech genius Oliver had been working with nanotechnology to develop a GPS signal that fit inside a button.

"The signal's dead same as TimeTrap's locator."

Dead. Oracle shivered and it wasn't from the cold cloth pressed to the back of her neck.

"Are you okay?"

"I'm trying to get my bearings after waking up from a nap to this news."

"A nap? At 10 pm?"

No wonder she felt disoriented and her muscles stiff. "I fell asleep on the sofa when I got back from the office. Hadn't planned to sleep this long."

"Exhausted from reading my father?"

"Among other things." Gloria had brought Oracle into the office this morning, waking her up from Pax's embrace, for another gender-bender nightmare, this time involving Dr. Vivas. Oracle wasn't much help. Dr. Vivas didn't get a clear look at the assailant, mostly because white makeup with black markings covered the woman's face, reminding Oracle of her mom's Day of the Dead dolls she'd collected during frequent business trips to Mexico.

The phone connection cut out momentarily.

"Call you back." Gloria hung up.

Oracle dabbed the washcloth against her cheeks and forehead. She stretched out her legs, which ached from being curled too tightly on the couch. She scrubbed a towel across her face and let herself enjoy the comfort of the soft plush material drenched with cold water.

When did her life become like a bumper car ride? Hit and pushed from all sides.

Last night, talking to her brother had been the sour whip on top of her stress sundae. Alex wanted details he could feed to the press. Enough to show that he was ahead of the other candidate in the race on this topic. She gave him what she could. It wasn't enough. He went even further and insisted Oracle sit in an interview with him and reveal to the public once and for all what she could do and show they had nothing to fear from transhumans.

But transcriminals like Dama X were making this hard to prove. Fortunately, the media hadn't learned there was a transhuman suspect behind Donovan's condition. She didn't tell Alex either.

Oracle jumped at Godzilla's shrill cry and seriously reconsidered this ringtone. She felt along the smooth granite counter, knocking over her toothpaste in her haste to grab the phone.

"Reyes found their limo down the side of a cliff not far from his house," Gloria stated when Oracle answered.

"And?" She slid down the wall onto the bathroom floor, not trusting herself to stand.

"Pax, TimeTrap, and the driver are missing. The tires were blown. They found a spike strip thrown into the brush off the road."

"Someone did this on purpose?"

"La Hermandad de Diana. They found small vials inside the limo from a dart gun."

"What kind of vials?" Nyxe trotted into the room and nuzzled and licked Oracle's tear-streaked face.

"Reyes said he encountered this drug before. The Sisters used it to incapacitate officers during a police standoff."

"So, it's not . . . ?" Oracle couldn't say it. Pax would not make a good woman. He was a perfect man. In many ways.

"He'll have all his man parts. For now anyway."

Nyxe scampered from the bathroom and ran down the hall. Her big dog voice boomed from the corridor.

"Hold on. Nyxe is barking at something." Oracle pulled herself up and out of the bathroom. She put her back to the wall, sliding along it toward the door. Her thigh bumped into a small stand where she kept her purse, which held her Mace.

Oracle rummaged through the zippered compartment then tiptoed down the hall. Bottle of Mace clenched in her hand.

"Someone's at the door," she whispered into the receiver.

"That would be me."

"What?" Oracle swung open the door. Gloria's flowery cologne tickled her nose. As Oracle lowered the phone from her ear, Gloria shoved past her into the condo.

"Your dog's sniffing my crotch again."

Nyxe's tail whacked against Oracle's shin.

"Just push her away." Oracle bent down and felt through Nyxe's thick, soft fur for her collar. "Get back Nyxe, you don't know where that's been."

"I wish it's been somewhere. Trust me, it hasn't seen any action in a year."

"TMI." Oracle held onto Nyxe as the three of them trudged down the hall.

"You're grumpy when you wake up, aren't you?"

"When I wake up to news about friends being abducted by a transhuman cartel leader, I would use a stronger word than grumpy. Why are you here, Gloria?"

"We're going to Mexico. My mom procured a private jet from one of her friends. So pack up. We'll fly through the night and get there in the morning."

"I thought no one wanted me to go." She released Nyxe, who bounded away and, judging by Gloria not throwing a fuss, ignored her nether regions this time.

"Sean has no say in this. It's my show, and I want you with me."

"What do you need me to do?" Oracle gripped the edge of the kitchen counter.

"I don't trust anyone else besides Pax to find this skull and save my father—and Pax is missing so it's up to me. I'm going to make sure we get it, if I have to pry it from Dama X's hands myself. My mother's flying back from Amsterdam. Sean's meeting her at the airport and will thankfully deal with her. With my father and Cook on ice, there's nothing I can do until I get that skull." Oracle heard Gloria walking around her living room, not in her usual click-clack heels but shoes with thick rubber soles that let out random squeaks against the wood.

"But mostly, I don't trust Reyes or his associates. Which is *one* reason why you're going." Gloria's words grew closer. Oracle sensed she stood next to the kitchen island where Oracle had parked herself.

She also sensed a dip in Gloria's tone as she said "one reason." Gloria was holding back, choosing her words.

"I want you to read Reyes," Gloria continued. "And the others working with him."

"Others? What others?" She frowned.

"Just others . . . you'll see when we get there. The situation has changed a bit so I'll need you to get into their minds and find out what's really going on. For now, Reyes won't let us bring backup agents—save for you—and is refusing to call St. John's troops for an extraction once we find Pax. He wants to use his own team. After dealing with St. John on the Surefire case, Reyes doesn't trust or like him."

Oracle couldn't argue with Reyes on that point, but she could argue with Gloria on the points that she was glossing over. "What aren't you telling me? You mentioned getting into 'their' minds. Who are the others?"

"I'll explain later. But first I need to know I can count on you to help find Pax, TimeTrap, and the skull."

Oracle blew out a breath. It didn't matter who else was involved with Reyes and the secrets they were keeping: what mattered was saving Pax and their agent and Dama X's other victims.

"I'll go. Let me get my passport. Clothes. Toiletries." Oracle tossed the last word behind her as she headed for the bedroom.

"What's this?" A rattling sound followed Gloria's words.

Please tell me those are not my prescription pills. Oracle knelt next to her bed.

"You tell me. I can't see, remember?" Oracle stretched her arm under the bed and felt along the floor until her fingers hit the handle of her roller bag.

"They're your pills for anxiety. I nearly slipped on them in the hall."

With the stress of these last few days, she'd forgotten that she pitched her pill bottle down the hall the night Pax stopped by.

"You knew they were prescribed to me after the Surefire case." Oracle bristled. She was not going to have a conversation about her meds with Gloria.

"I knew you were given this drug, but what I didn't know was the name of the lab that distributed it."

Oracle grabbed several panties and put them into the bag. "I don't pay attention to those things."

"It's Lucy's company."

Oracle's spine tingled as if Gloria had dropped a tray of ice cubes down it.

"The pharmaceutical company she started with her father?"

Don't panic. Take a breath. The room isn't closing in on you. Oracle opened a drawer and focused on feeling for the right bra.

"An offshoot of that company, which she relocated to Mexico. She started her own TransGen-type business there."

Oracle swallowed once, then twice, but the bile continued to rise even as her throat started to constrict. She turned to her closet.

Find my U-Sec jackets. Matching pants.

"Lucy's company, Circe, cured Felix Reyes after he was injured during Operation Bird Catcher. She just told me when I called her about our current case."

Oracle rolled up her spare jacket and blouse and placed them in her bag along with her bra. She continued packing so Gloria would see that this news wasn't stopping her from fulfilling her duties. She wanted Gloria to think that nothing was wrong, and Oracle's head wasn't pounding and her stomach wasn't clenching and her chest wasn't tightening. She planted her hands along the edge of her suitcase and squeezed. The zipper dug into her palms. The discomfort offered a small distraction.

"What's in my pills?" Oracle squeezed harder trying to center herself as the room pitched.

"Thirty milligrams of Lexapro according to the drug info on the label. But knowing Lucy, she spiced up the mix if it was prescribed to a transhuman. This could explain your power boost." The bed bobbed and creaked as Gloria sat down on the opposite end from where Oracle was packing.

She wasn't sure how much more she could take. How many more fingers she'd need to use to plug up the cracks in her emotional dam.

"How do we find out?" Oracle walked into the adjoining bathroom. Well, walked was generous. She staggered as the room teetered and her shoulder hit into the door jam.

"I don't trust her to be upfront about her proprietary blend. I'll have Ron run diagnostics on them while we're away," Gloria elevated her voice to be heard from the bedroom.

She sighed with relief that Gloria didn't follow her into the bathroom.

Against the back of her neck, Oracle pressed the cold washcloth she'd earlier discarded in the sink. After a few deep breaths, the room straightened out. She made it back into her bedroom without running into the wall. She tossed her cosmetic bag along with toiletries into the suitcase.

If she just centered herself, focused, she could push through it. Concentrate on one thing at a time. Avoid one swinging sword above her and not think about the lot of them.

"Thanks for asking Ron to look into it." Oracle zipped up her suitcase then turned to her closet to change out of her tank top and shorts and into her work clothes.

"You need to tell me if there's anything else you're experiencing. Any other side effects."

Oracle thought about her dream and how Pax had the same image from this dream in his memory. But she had no desire to share this intimate fantasy with Gloria. Until she spoke with Pax and verified what she'd seen, she'd keep it to herself.

"Taking over someone's body is a major side effect. Don't you think?" She reached into her closet and knocked several shirts from their hangers, her hands trembling too much to hold onto them.

"Lucy believed we could push the limits further than what we'd been doing."

Oh, no, Gloria didn't just express admiration for Lucy. With her back to Gloria, she threw off her shorts and tank and shoved her arms into a blouse and legs into linen slacks.

When she felt calm enough to speak rationally, she said, "It would've been nice if Lucy had informed those whose limits she was pushing. I can't believe charges weren't leveled at her after two transhumans lost their minds and one lost control of their power during a routine bust. She was the main reason that politicians passed those laws."

"People forget that Lucy did save several transhumans when their powers nearly overwhelmed them."

"Based on my current issues, I wouldn't be surprised if Lucy had caused their power spike." She let her voice rise, let the anger clip her words. "Pushed the limits so far that their bodies couldn't take it. Transhumans may have special abilities, but our bodies are still human."

"For the most part."

"What does that mean?" Oracle whirled around then sat, actually plopped, onto the bed. The movement was too much. The anger too much. The news on top of everything else too much to take.

"Just that there is a unique code inside each transhuman that helps the special abilities manifest and grow, where others without this marker have adverse effects. Lucy's trials helped set the groundwork for this research. In fact, I'm still trying to understand this code more thoroughly."

"You act like you respect her for what she did." Oracle's power flared. A bright heated blip that was here and gone in the span of a second.

"I don't condone what she did. But she was my colleague and my friend at one time."

"I'm not having this conversation with you right now." Oracle rubbed her temples.

"Afraid you'll say something you'll regret?"

"Nothing that I'll regret, I promise you. But it might make our time on the plane very unpleasant." Again, a flare up of her power burned along her skin. She hadn't concentrated on bringing it forth. Was it feeding on her anger?

"When do you take these pills?"

"In the morning."

"When was the last time you took them?"

Oracle pressed her fingertips gently over her eyes. Cool palms cupping her cheeks gave some comfort against her heated skin. "I don't know. Since this case started, my sleep schedule has been severely off." She shook her head. "Maybe the day before Matthews's call. I don't remember."

"Then it's been a couple of days at the very least. You've missed two doses possibly more. No wonder you're on the verge of a panic attack."

"I'm not on the verge of anything."

"From across this king-sized bed, I can see your breathing has increased. Your hands are shaking."

"This situation doesn't make you upset? What we've experienced in these last few days, doesn't it make your blood pressure spike?"

"Of course it does, but I'm not letting it overtake me. I'm in control."

Oracle slammed her palms on the bed and yelled, "I'm in control."

Except she wasn't. Her power flared up, burning up her back and down her arms and arcing over the bed and into Gloria. She got an image flash of the room. Of herself sitting on the edge of the bed. Chest heaving. Nostrils flaring. Skin dulling with an ashy sheen. The window shade drawn behind her. Yellow light from the street lamps peaking around it.

"I thought you weren't opening up anymore?" Gloria's breath stilled. Her mind an empty picture box.

I don't know how I'm doing this, Oracle confessed, not out loud but in Gloria's mind.

She slid her power out of Gloria then slumped against the headboard.

"You're right. I'm not in control." She was too numb to care if her words made her sound weak or pathetic. It was the truth and Gloria, as a doctor, was one of the few who could help her.

"You need to continue to take the pills until we return."

"No." Oracle shook her head hard as she pulled her hair back into a loose bun. She sat up straight, testing her equilibrium.

"They're SSRIs. You shouldn't go cold turkey, especially under this kind of stress. I would give you a generic version. However, until we know what or if there is a power booster mixed into these pills, I'm afraid of what will happen if you simply stopped. You may need to be weaned off. If the only side effects are enhanced abilities, then it's my opinion you're safe to remain on them."

"No." Oracle shoved her feet into her flats. She'd plow through. That's what she did. That's how she survived. When she became blind, did she let it make her weak? No, she figured it out and restructured her life. When she gained this ability, she embraced it, learned to control it so she could help others. If her ability had changed because of the pills, she'd deal. She only needed to learn to read the signs, her triggers.

"What about Pax?" Gloria asked.

"What about him?" Why wouldn't Gloria just shut up so she could figure out what to do next?

Yoga pants to sleep in. Check. Passport. Check. Text dog sitter. Check.

"If you crash without your pills, mentally and physically, you'll be of no use to Pax or TimeTrap."

As much as she wanted to tell Gloria to stick her opinion where the sun didn't shine, Oracle knew she was right. She'd researched anti-anxiety medication and how stopping suddenly could cause adverse health risks, especially with the dosage she was given. That didn't take into account what else was in the pills.

Gloria was only giving her medical opinion. Although Oracle couldn't help but sense Gloria was observing her from a clinical trial standpoint. A bit excited at the possibility that Lucy could've added an element to this drug that enhanced Oracle's abilities and could enhance other transhumans as well.

The power rose again. This time Oracle was prepared and tamped it out before it caught fire. She was learning. So far, it appeared anger, extreme emotion, awoke this energy surge. A new wrinkle caused by the pills *or* by forgetting to take the pills? Would it get worse if she stopped altogether?

"Give me the pills." Oracle held out her hand

"Take one now."

A plastic bottle tapped against Oracle's palm. She wrapped her fingers around it and tried not to squeeze enough to crack it.

She didn't trust the pills. Not with Looney Lucy behind them. She'd survived the last few days without the medicine. She was strong enough to help Pax on her own. Oracle pretended to pop a pill into her mouth and made a show of swallowing it down. Then she tossed the bottle into her purse at the same time "Like a Virgin" started to play from her phone stashed in an interior pocket. She hesitated with her hand on it.

"Why do you use that song for Matthews? You know what it means, right?" Gloria asked.

Oracle turned her back to her.

"Matthews, is everything okay?" she answered, surprised he was calling so late.

"As well as it can be after being hit by a human Mack Truck."

Oracle would've smiled if she wasn't so stressed.

"I couldn't sleep, figured you were in the same boat. How's Dr. Vivas?"

"He's still in cryo. No change since this afternoon when I read him."

She slid her small suitcase onto the floor and extended the handle. "Listen, Matthews, Pax and TimeTrap are missing. Gloria and I are leaving for Mexico to find them."

"I'm sorry to hear that."

"So am I," Oracle replied.

Gloria's steps stomped a path from the bedroom. From the hallway, she bellowed, "Come on."

Oracle grabbed the handle of her suitcase and rolled it into the hall. "Can I call you from the plane?"

"If you're going after Pax, I'd rather say this now before I lose my nerve."

"Okay." Oracle knelt down next to Nyxe and scratched her chest. The dog's tail hit a low, sad beat against the wall.

"When you find him—and I know in my gut you will—promise that you will get back together with him."

"Excuse me?"

Something tapped impatiently against the wood floor. Gloria's foot?

"Your power went both ways when you read my mind at the hospital."

"How so?"

"I saw into your thoughts and your feelings. When you asked me to replay the fight with Pax, I felt what you felt for him. It was a blip, but I recognized what it was."

Oracle buried her head in Nyxe's fur, but she couldn't hide from the guilt.

"I didn't tell you this," Matthews went on, "but a week ago when we fell asleep on the couch together, you said Pax's name in your sleep and woke me from a dream which I thought was mine at first, but I think . . . I think it was yours."

She wanted to blame her power surge for hurting Matthews, but she couldn't. She loved Pax when she started her relationship with Matthews. She'd hoped a man as good as Matthews would help her move on.

"I'm sorry. I . . ." What could she say to make this better?

"Don't say you're sorry. I tried to make you happy. Remember what I said about being right ninety-nine percent of the time? Well, this is that one percent where my gut is wrong. I thought you were over Pax but you're not. I need time to heal, and the pain of knowing you still care for him isn't helping. If you need anything, I am here . . . but as a friend."

"I understand."

"Goodbye, Oracle. Good luck."

Pax noticed two things simultaneously: the hard floor and a pounding headache.

He'd woken up in this condition before but usually from a night out with Jaybird, and the last time was a decade ago. There was a reason why he stopped partying with him.

Pax tried to move his arms and found them secured behind his back with zip ties. His right cheek pressed against damp tiles. His shoulders were twisted and stiff from lying on the floor with his hands tied back. He rolled into a sitting position and kicked out his feet—tied together as well. Plastic ribbons cut into his ankles.

With rapid blinks, his eyes adjusted to the pitch black room. Or maybe the room became brighter. He shook his head. It was hard to tell.

He spied a slice of light, no wider than a pencil, shining between what appeared to be stones making up the wall. The rest of the room was bare from what he could tell. Four duplicate stone walls with no noticeable way in or out.

Pax stared into the black hole above his head, unable to see the ceiling and determine the height of the room.

With a wince, he stretched his arms up behind his back—and gave a silent thanks to his yoga class for making this possible. He pulled his arms outward while he slammed his wrists down against his lower back. The motion snapped the ties. A burst of pain followed, spreading up his spine. He'd have serious bruising—the least of his problems. Pax worked his fingers into the ties around his ankles and popped those off. Holding his breath, Pax listened for something, anything to clue him in on where he was and who or what could be outside this cell.

Through the wall with the small crack, did he hear a splash? Like waves crashing along a shore?

He hauled himself up onto his feet and paused, testing his equilibrium. The pounding in his head let up, but the room felt as if it were moving. Pax rubbed his palms into his eyes. Then he carefully walked over to the wall and ran his hands along it. Cold and damp just like the floor. He walked the length of it until he reached the corner. Again, he followed the next wall to the next corner all the way around. The other three walls were solid. No entrance or exit that he could see or feel. When he knocked, the sound was muffled. The room was insulated. Pax felt as if he were trapped in a dungeon from a Conan movie. He just hoped he wouldn't find a Snake god waiting for him on the other side.

Pax hated snakes.

But he hated being trapped even more. In the dark with no clue where he was or where TimeTrap was and if she were still alive, which he didn't want to consider. He forced his thoughts away from that dark route. First things first. Get out of this damn room. Despite the cool, damp stones forming the walls, beads of sweat pooled on Pax's forehead and on the back of his neck.

He undid the buttons of his shirt. Several broke off in his fingers.

Shit.

He dropped the button containing the crushed GPS chip. Oliver, U-Sec's master of tech, was working on a GPS nanochip as tiny as a cotton strand that could be woven into their uniforms and withstand impact. He wished he had that now.

He wondered if anyone knew he was missing yet, and if they had any lead on where to look for him. Most likely, Sean had told his assistant, Helena, also Pax's mother's best friend, which meant his mom was aware and at church praying for him. Judging by his situation, he'd need all the prayers he could get.

Briefly, Oracle crossed his mind. Did she know what happened to them?

Yes, she did. He knew with a certainty that should surprise him, but it didn't.

Pax wrapped the shirt around his fist, making sure to place the buttons to the back. He twisted the bottom button and the threads expanded, puffing out to cushion his hand. Besides the extra padding, the shirt was made from a special polymer, strong threads that could protect his hand and body by swallowing the impact of a punch. He pulled back and slammed his fist into the wall above the crack. Wind blew past his arms and into his chest. The shirt took the brunt of the blow and threw the energy out into the room instead of rattling his bones too much.

Pax looked over his shoulder. Did the walls blink on and off like a television screen? He screwed his eyes closed to clear his vision. Better get out of here now with his mind somewhat intact.

He opened his eyes and hit the wall again. Around the radius of the hit, the stones faded to black with cracks spreading out into a web.

Pax ran his fingertips along the cracks. Thick glass, not stone. But when he'd punched it, when his palms slid along the walls, it had been stone.

What kind of drug had they shot him with?

A large chunk fell out from the middle of the web-like crack. A yellow beam of light followed.

He pulled his arm back and threw his body into another punch. His fist went straight through glass. Broken shards sprinkled across the floor.

"What the—?" Pax leapt back and shook out his hand, the shirt falling to the floor. The polymer threads dissipated the harshest impact, but his knuckles still throbbed.

The scent of salty water flowed through the hole in the wall along with bright sunlight. Fresh air, warm and humid, blew across his face. He spun around and stared at the cell walls. No longer stones but a gray-black shiny glass. Each was a large plasma screen.

How it felt like stones under his hand freaked Pax out as much as it made him curious. It's one thing to fool the eyes but another to fool the sense of touch.

Oliver would love taking this room apart.

Pax returned his focus to the hole in the wall, several inches larger than his fist. He rewrapped the shirt around his hand and knocked out the loose glass shards making the hole big enough to poke his head through.

He peered out and was no longer surprised by the holographic room.

A hill thick with green grass and tropical fauna sloped down five or six stories before it ended abruptly at a metal edge that overlooked the blue water. Occasionally, waves slapped against an object below, sending foam over the metal border. It floated and bobbed over the water as if it were a ship covered with a jungle, which is exactly what Pax believed it was.

The hill stretched in either direction lined by more vegetation. Pax looked above to find the vegetation spreading upward, ending at a sharp ledge. Large rectangular windows broke through the lush greenery as if nature had grown over a building underneath. They formed a line below the lip. In between two of these windows, Pax spied a balcony laced with copper vines to mimic the surroundings.

The sun's angle told him it was morning. Possibly 8 a.m., maybe later, which meant he'd been out for more than twelve hours.

He swayed, grabbing a branch to hold steady. Grinding and grunting, the vessel or island or whatever it was ground to a stop. Steam hissed from somewhere below. Loud clicks followed. The island appeared to rise, water sloshing below. Then the entire structure vibrated before it settled into position.

He ducked back into the chamber and threw on his shirt, fastening the remaining buttons. The material had thinned from taking the brunt of the punches. Another hit and the shirt would fall apart, but it would protect him from the morning sun, growing harsher as the minutes ticked by. He stomped against the floor with his thick-soled combat boots. Short, sharp blades popped out from the front of both shoes. Using his hard heel, Pax kicked away at the crumbling bits until he could safely wiggle through the opening without being cut.

His fingers found where the soil met the metal pane holding the glass he'd broken. He crawled to the side of the room's glass wall, partially obscured by soil and plants. Reaching up, he grabbed a green stalk of a large fern, strong and thick enough to hoist his body. He shoved his toe blades into the moist soil covering this strange structure and began his ascent, picking his way around ferns and brush. The sun burned against his neck and shorn head. Perspiration streamed down his face and neck. Several times, he slowed to wipe away the sweat burning his eyes.

At last, Pax reached the side of the balcony. The hill seemed to have grown around it as if this terrace had been part of a hotel swallowed by nature, leaving this remnant as a reminder that humans had once lived there.

He grabbed the railing and hoisted himself over it. His feet hit the metal with a thud. Shoe blades retracted. Flattening himself against palm leaves and exotic flowers, he peeked into the opening. A short cylindrical corridor led from the balcony to a glass door, from which the corridor continued, but in metal, contrasting sharply to the green hill outside. At the end of this passage was a frosted glass door. He couldn't see beyond it.

Pax shaded his eyes and turned to look across the open water to the horizon. He thought he spied a tiny speck in the distance. A helicopter or plane, maybe? Or the heat had half-baked his brain so he was seeing a mirage.

Out of the corner of his eye, he spied a speed boat cruising away from under the grassy slope and into the open sea. Pax took it as a good sign that the mainland wasn't too far away. He hoped more boats were docked inside this structure to provide a getaway. That is, after he radioed for help; hopefully, he could reach Sean to request backup. Hell, he'd even grovel to St. John if it meant a safe extraction for him, TimeTrap, and the limo driver, Bruno.

Of course, that was *if* there was a boat docked somewhere. And if he could secure the crew. And if they didn't have guns. And if he weren't severely outnumbered.

He could play the *"If"* game forever, as Oracle used to say. He needed to see what he was up against and then plan his next move.

How he was going to get down to the water undetected, he didn't know. With a jail cell having such sophisticated technology, no doubt his captors had him under surveillance and would know he'd escaped. Out here with the foliage, it would be easy to hide the cameras.

Schwat. The clear glass door opened. He hadn't moved. What triggered it?

He edged his upper body to the side to peek down the corridor again, but it was still empty. This was probably the best chance at recon he was going to get and know for certain his chances for escape.

One foot forward then another. Slow and steady. He kept his back against the curved wall, hunching forward to slide along it. At the end of the short corridor, he came to the opaque glass door. It slid open with the same *schwat* sound.

Pax's eyes grew wide before they narrowed.

Below him was a bowl-shaped, man-made valley. It stretched at least two football fields across and about as wide. The valley and surrounding high wall was covered in greenery, adding to the illusion that this interior space was part of nature, maybe a long-dormant volcano. Rising up the wall directly across from Pax were hundreds of balconies at multiple levels. A quick count revealed approximately fifteen stories. Cutting between the balconies was an open-air staircase leading to the field. He wondered if similar balconies and a staircase could be found below him on this side. He didn't want to lean over the rail to find out.

A crystal blue lagoon stood like a puddle of water against the center of the green valley, where a medium-sized yacht and two smaller fishing vessels were anchored. They bobbed around a large bronze statue of a woman, but he couldn't see any details. To the left, a channel cut out from the lagoon. It ran under a wide hill with tiered platforms where about ten people tended to rows of vegetables surrounding a shed and greenhouse.

Grassy fields enclosed by metal and glass barriers stretched around the center lagoon. In one field, women played soccer. On another, rows of women were lined up in a downward dog position with a female yogi leading them into the next pose. Farther away, Pax could make out even more women practicing what he recognized as kung fu and yet others on an archery range and, judging by the placement of the arrows on the target, they were damn good shots. Beside a shelf of archery equipment, there were fencing swords next to AK-47s—and was that a rocket launcher?

Pax stepped back, realizing he'd gotten too close to the railing facing the valley, a vulnerable position that would make him easy to spot. He certainly stood out. His bulk gave him away as one of the few men here.

The interior glass doors slid open behind him. He slipped inside the corridor then took off at a run toward the exterior glass doors and the balcony outside.

Schwat. The doors opened and he made it through.

A woman nearly Pax's height leapt onto the balcony and into his path.

He skidded to a stop.

Two more women swung over the balcony to flank the first. All were dressed in matching green and tan camouflage pants and sleeveless khaki shirts and combat boots. Holsters on their hips carried Glocks and small daggers. Judging by their muscular arms and wide-set shoulders, they were a force to be reckoned with.

"You've been a bad boy, Pax, breaking our toys," the tall woman said, a strict mother admonishing her son, not unlike Pax's mom when she was disappointed with him.

He recognized the leader's voice as the one from outside the limo. Same confident tone of a person used to giving orders. Straight black hair pulled back in a ponytail. Thick bangs hung low over her forehead. Her face was still painted with a grotesque yet compelling image of a skull with swirling lines sprouting flowers, but this time he also noticed there were words written around her mouth in an elegant script.

The two women, shorter and stockier than the speaker, stood close by her. Pax would have to knock them down to get to the hill. He'd need to disarm or incapacitate them before he could escape.

"Do you know what I used to do to my brother when he broke my toys?"

Pax barreled forward. He'd take the leader down with him, get her gun, and then—

She slammed her palm into Pax's chest. He flew backward through the exterior glass doors, through the metal corridor, through the interior glass doors. His back hit the railing, which bent under his force. His shirt disintegrated. The railing broke free. He fell backward into the valley. He flung out his arms and caught himself on the ledge below where he'd been standing.

An arrow grazed his ear and clanged off a metal wall in front of him.

A warning shot.

Chapter 10
Learning a New Tongue

You saw the video. You'll come to your own conclusions no matter what I say.

—Pax to reporters about the video showing Surefire and Raven vanishing from the warehouse lot after stealing an Aztec statue

---

Oracle lifted her behind into the air. Head down. Arms straight out pushing against the mat. Feet and legs shoulder width apart.

Breathe.

In and out.

In and out.

The plane vibrated and shook her out of the downward dog position. The flight to Mexico had been full of turbulence, not unlike her last few hours with Gloria, which is why she took solace in the yoga studio on this private plane.

Then there was Matthews's breakup, which didn't hurt as much as she thought it should. Maybe breaking up during a crisis was a good thing. She was too distracted by the crisis to care about the pain. Or maybe she knew Matthews was right and she needed to let go of him. It wasn't fair to either of them, especially to Matthews. Maybe there was no room to be sad when she was already drowning in guilt.

Oracle regained her balance and lowered into plank position. Her arms protested. Worn out. Stressed out. She cleared her mind.

She let out a long breath and took in a soothing one, letting the focused calm envelop her. This proved she didn't need the prescription pills. Her will alone could overcome her anxiety and control her power. She'd like to believe her resolve brought forth this serenity, but it could also be from separating herself from Gloria, who had told Oracle she needed quiet and space while she responded to emails and made a phone call. She didn't have to twist Oracle's arm.

The door yanked open to the yoga space. Heavy footsteps closed in. Flowery perfume overtook the calming lavender aroma piped into the room.

The hairs on the back of Oracle's neck stood on end.

"You need to straighten out more. Your rear is sticking up."

Oracle smelled the rubber soles mixed with the polished leather of Gloria's shoes as they halted next to the mat.

"Unless you're doing it the Cheetah way. Valerie Cheetah found a shortcut for everything even back in college. Looks like she found a way to make it pay out in the health industry to afford this jet. I'm seriously in the wrong business. No wonder my mom invested in her startup."

After flattening her backside, Oracle concentrated on holding the plank position. Unless Gloria was ready to talk about updates to the case, she'd rather keep her mind clear in anticipation of what was waiting for them in Mexico.

"I need to talk to you before we land." Gloria grunted as her clothes shifted over her skin. To Oracle's left came the sound of shoes scraping over carpet, then a pop as Gloria sat down next to her.

"And that was my knee. God, I hate getting older."

Oracle exhaled.

"Or maybe I could look into those new bio-upgrades that Dad has been testing on Sean?"

She inhaled, focusing on her lungs expanding and ignoring Gloria.

"Then again, Sean is dealing with his own issues, having to upgrade his internal operating system each month after every patch or enhancement tech makes."

Oracle dropped her knees onto the mat, lowered her head to the floor, and stretched out her back into a child's pose.

"It's important I say this now."

Oracle wondered if there was a kitchen on the plane. And if that kitchen had a frying pan, because Gloria wasn't picking up on her subtle hints and maybe a pan to the head might do it.

"What about?" She spoke into the mat so Gloria couldn't see the agitation pinching her face.

"I'm the reason Pax broke up with you."

The world stopped. But no, not the world around her. Oracle herself stopped. She stopped moving, stopped mid-exhale, stopped thinking. Silence pressed down against her ears, her back, her neck. For a moment, she feared this shock caused her to go deaf as well. But that was a momentary blip because she heard a voice. Gloria's voice speaking again. Her normal abrupt manner softened around the edges. As if Gloria recognized that she needed to dull her words or she'd cut too deep.

But it was too late for that.

"At the time, I thought it was for his own good. Sean and I both did. Some employees were getting jealous. Thought there was favoritism even though you were a contractor and not full-time. Then Pax became distracted. We were growing a company, and he didn't have time for the business. Sean wondered if you were just using Pax. I never thought that, by the way."

Oracle withdrew deep inside until Gloria's voice became a faint echo in the darkness. But no matter how much she tried to meditate away what Gloria was saying, a hot flare of rage surged up her spine, bringing her back to this room, this plane, this space with the woman who worked to take away what Oracle had loved the most.

"He lost his focus on assignments."

Ultimately, it was Pax who made the decision to end it. Not Gloria. Not Sean. Even if they planted the seeds and fertilized it with a truckload of manure.

"Then there was the Laser Killer. He found out about you. Pax's Achilles heel."

Oh, no she didn't.

"Pax couldn't put you in danger again."

Her arms, back, and legs shook. Oracle had worked with Pax to track down and arrest the Laser Killer. If she hadn't opened up and used her ability to find his hideout, U-Sec never would've solved that case.

"As an owner of U-Sec and former soldier with the ESP unit, he's been targeted in the past and will be again."

How did Pax fall for this? Oracle was far from a damsel in distress. He knew that, and she knew it was one of the reasons he loved her.

Had loved her.

"And we were afraid Pax would hurt you. Physically. He didn't know his own strength. He broke several desks from hitting them when frustrated. He ripped a police car door from its hinges. His laptop cracked from typing too hard, and a myriad of smartphones smashed into pieces."

"Just stop," Oracle muttered, wishing to bury herself deep into the mat and curl up into a ball, away from Gloria. On the heels of Matthews's breakup, this was too much to deal with.

"What if he hurt you during sex? Or just holding your hand? He was still learning his limits at the time you were dating. His strength had continued to grow."

"Stop."

They worked out his power in their lovemaking, which wasn't hard to do because he enjoyed her being in charge and being on top. They learned together. Their intimacy helped Pax master his growing strength. How dare Gloria assume and put these doubts in his mind?

"At the time, I didn't recognize I was sabotaging your relationship for personal reasons."

Red-hot anger grew in the pit of her stomach. It surged up her torso.

"I'm still in love with him," Gloria finished.

Oracle's power leapt from her body, poured from her skin, a hot lava flow toward Gloria.

A choked scream followed. In a blink, she was inside Gloria, sitting crossed-legged and staring at her own body still bent across the mat in a supplicant pose.

Gloria's hands clung to a fistful of her baggy black cargo pants.

You're stronger, Gloria said in her mind, not out loud, because Oracle had control of her lips, her limbs, everything.

"Why are you telling me this?" Oracle asked through Gloria's mouth, the words coming out strangled as she disjointedly controlled the jaw and tongue like speaking through a rubber Halloween mask.

I want to show you that I'm being honest with you. That when we get out of this, I will set things right. I'll do that for you, Oracle, and for Pax. He's my best friend and I want to see him happy.

Oracle filled every inch of Gloria with the pain her words inflicted. Gloria's white, slender limbs shook, and Oracle had the sense that if she wanted to, if she concentrated and focused hard enough, she could burst Gloria apart.

Oracle, stop. This hurts.

I know.

But there was one part of Gloria that she couldn't plug into. Far back in Gloria's brain. Her earliest memories whirled by Oracle's third eye on a roller coaster track—first dance, first kiss, first birthday, science awards, the day Victor and Valerie adopted her—and then Oracle's power slammed into a locked vault and sprung back. What was this woman hiding in there?

She pulled out of Gloria, or maybe she was pushed, or maybe her power just ran out. She wasn't sure, but suddenly she was back in her body, trying to catch her breath as if recovering from a sprint. She rolled out of the yoga pose. Her muscles throbbed. She lay on her back.

"Are we good now?" Gloria asked.

"No."

"I need you to trust me."

"I don't."

"I want you to know that whatever happens, it will work out for both of you. I promise you."

"What did you do, Gloria?" Oracle asked, raspy and tired.

"Just trust me."

"I can't," she whispered, barely getting the words out. She wanted to sleep, felt herself drifting.

"Suit yourself." Gloria's shoes scraped against the carpet. Palms rubbed across cotton. Joints popped in protest. Gloria's presence loomed over her.

"But I trust you even after what you just did," she stated.

Oracle swiped her hand across her moist brow. A hand she struggled to lift before it flopped down next to her head. A thick blanket of lethargy covered her from head to toe. A ghostly force pinned her to the mat. It took all her energy to fill her lungs with air.

Gloria stomped in a heavy gait that would impress an elephant. A door swung open and bottles clinked.

"When was the last time you took your pills?" Gloria's hand worked its way under her head, lifting up. A plastic lip of a bottle touched her lips. Cold water poured into her mouth. She swallowed.

"At my house. You saw me."

"I don't think you did. I think what I told you upset you too much or else this wouldn't have happened."

Oracle nodded or at least tried. Gloria's cold fingers pressed into the back of her head just under her bun.

Gloria gave her more to drink and told her just to sip it. She slowly eased Oracle's head back onto the mat, and the oppressive force started to lift but not enough that she felt safe standing. A slight lift of her head caused a teetering as if the plane were swinging back and forth on a string.

Please don't let me vomit. Of course, if it happened on Gloria, it may be worth it. She would've smiled at that image if she had any strength left.

Gloria's fingers slid over her neck and felt for her pulse.

"I'm going to make you a smoothie with the special TransGen protein mix Pax uses."

Oracle wished Gloria could make it silently. Drawers opened. Utensils rattled. *Plop, plop, plop.* Items dropped into what she assumed was a blender, which whirled and chugged a second later.

"Can you sit up?"

Oracle rolled onto her side. She curled her feet under her and pushed up into a sitting position, both hands flat on the floor.

"I'm good." She swallowed the remains of dinner threatening to come back up.

The warmth from Gloria's body tingled along her right side. Her nose became overwhelmed with a sweet bouquet of flowers mixed with bananas, strawberries, oranges, and vanilla.

"Here's a straw. I'm putting it to your lips."

Oracle sucked up the luscious juice, licked her lips, and drank more when her stomach rumbled with hunger.

"The energy you used to enter me burns through an incredible amount of calories. And I think it's even worse now that you have this power surge. Oh, and by the way, I blended your pills into this drink."

Oracle spat out the smoothie. Wiped away the sweet juice from her lips. "What? Why?"

"I'm being honest with you. I could've not told you."

"Yes, and you let me drink it first."

"True. But I did it for your own good. I need you to finish this shake. What you're experiencing is what happens when you push your power to its limits on an empty stomach. Missing a dose or two of the drug didn't help either. Whatever is in these pills has pumped up your ability like a powerful steroid. As I mentioned before, you need to be weaned off or you will crash or worse."

Oracle assumed she could push through it. But things had changed. She didn't know her own body—her own ability—anymore.

"You're angry with me. I know," Gloria sighed.

Anger doesn't hold a candle to how I feel.

"But I need you to be one hundred percent if you want to save Pax."

"And TimeTrap."

"Her as well."

"We both want the same thing, and we're going to have to work together so one of us can have it. And I can't have you dropping like a sad sack after you use your hyper power."

"What makes you so certain that I'll use my full power?"

"Because you're going to drink up and try again—on me—but this time without the almost-breaking-my-bones part."

"Can't make any promises."

"There you go. Feeling more yourself already."

Oracle pursed her lips.

"The more you practice, the stronger and more in control you become. Why do you think Sean does those inane things with his power like interfacing with phones or playing video games without a controller? It's making him stronger and keeping him active. Like doing sprints in preparation for a 10K."

When Oracle remained silent and unmoving, Gloria sighed again. "I need you to drink this. You're our only hope."

Didn't Matthews say those words to Oracle in the beginning of the case? Now two ex-boyfriends and a fellow UltraAgent had been harmed by Dama X. How many more people was this transcriminal going to hurt, kidnap, or kill unless they stopped her? Oracle needed to be in top shape to finish this operation, even if it meant taking on a power surge she feared and didn't understand.

"Fine." She put out her hand and Gloria handed the cold glass to her.

"When you're ready to try again, let me know." She patted Oracle's shoulder then left the room.

♥ ☠ ♥ ☠ ♥ ☠

Pax swung onto the level below and landed in front of a set of glass doors behind which two women stood, blocking the entrance. A residence? Office? He didn't have time to assess because another arrow flew past and grazed his bare shoulder.

He saw stairs leading down and sprinted for them.

Swish. Swish. Swish. The arrows kept sailing by as if the archers were using them to herd him, force him to move forward and down toward the grassy fields below. Pax didn't have time to think of where he would go to next. Move forward, away from the Sister soldiers and hope he'd find a way out.

He continued lower and lower through the levels, passing several women of various ethnicities. Some jumped out of his way or touched him as he ran by. Others put their arms protectively around their children and scurried away. More women shouted taunts, warnings, or pleas. He couldn't be sure. So many different languages, accents. Like he was moving down the stairs of the Tower of Babel.

"Tréximo choíron!"

"We're not violent like men. We don't do this."

"Bicho!"

"Love and compassion, ladies."

"Tosser!"

"Dama X won't stand for this."

"Basta esta locura!"

"Don't hurt him."

His feet landed on the turf. A throng had gathered on the fields, stopping their yoga and games and practice to stare at him. Pax spied three men in the crowd. Two looked away. One moved to help, but a woman next to him grabbed his arm and shook her head.

The arrows had stopped as the grass sloped toward the water. He slowed to a jog as he approached the crystal blue lagoon in the center of the valley. A statue of the goddess Artemis—or was it Diana?—stood tall in the middle of a wide bridge that led from the shore over the lagoon to a large platform in its center with markers of a helipad.

Ten archers lined the shore. Bows in hand.

Pax was surrounded. It would be a fool's errand to waste more energy trying to escape.

"Where's my agent?" he asked without turning around. The leader's presence loomed large at his back.

"She's safe at the moment. We don't harm our sisters, but that depends on you."

"Me?" Pax spun around to face her.

The leader nodded. The crowd parted. A woman in a long white dress and ebony hair streaked with white strands stepped from the crowd. She held out a box in her brown hands. A box just like the one Pax had found on his doorstep.

"We have a test that all men must pass before they can remain on our island."

The leader took the box from the woman, whose ethnicity Pax couldn't pinpoint. A mix of Native American, Spanish, and other. Her skin glowed as if dusted with gold. Her doe-like eyes stared at Pax and she mouthed, "Sorry."

The commanding soldier opened the lid, displaying two syringes inside. Both sparkled with turquoise flecks like what Oracle had described from the victims' memories.

"You know what this is, right? You heard what Dama X has done to her enemies?"

Pax met her eyes, unreadable and unwavering.

"I've heard the new serum works on transhumans especially well as you saw in Baltimore." She leaned closer, her hawk-like face impassive.

"I need you to choose, Pax." Her accent thickened the more her voice rose. Israeli, perhaps? It had been awhile since he'd been in that country.

In the distance, he heard a helicopter.

"I need you to prove that you respect women enough to be willing to become one." She pointed to the needle on the right.

"Or if you'd rather die than become that which so many men fear and hate." She then pointed to the needle on the left. "A fear and hatred that has caused women to suffer under man's control for far too long."

Pax blanked out his mind so he wouldn't think about what happened to those who were injected with the serum. It wasn't that he hated women. He loved women. He was raised by a strong woman who taught him to respect and love the opposite sex. His parents had an equal relationship. But he was a man. That was who he was. It wasn't a fear of becoming something he hated. It was losing his identity. This was his body. He was comfortable in his skin. He didn't want to change it.

"I warn you. Don't make the wrong choice. It won't be a pleasant death." She nodded behind him and the group parted to reveal a woman carrying a man's body covered by a white sheet. Through the fabric, he could make out Bruno's gray suit. His dark hair peeked out from the edge.

"He chose poorly," she tsked.

"What if I refuse to make any choice?" Pax asked.

The archers raised their bows and pulled back on their strings. The helicopter was closing in on their island. No one seemed concerned.

The shorter woman standing to the leader's left moved forward to Pax. She held out a phone with a video playing on the screen. She lifted it up to his face.

It showed TimeTrap strapped to a hospital bed. Groggy, she struggled to remove the IVs in her arms. Blood caked in the corners of her mouth.

"Your agent has broken ribs and a concussion. She needs medical help. You don't comply, then we will press this button"—the woman pointed to a neon red square on the bottom of the screen—"and a poison will release into her system. You choose the wrong vial, you die and so does she. What would you do to save your agent, Pax? Are you man enough to become a woman?"

She shoved the box into his hands.

Chapter 11
Friends from Your Enemies

The supernatural is the unexplained that hasn't been explained by science yet.

—Dr. Gloria Vivas in an interview for *Time* magazine about the crystal skull theories

---

"Oh, no, Pax." Oracle's arm flailed out. The back of her hand smacked against a cushion.

"Hey, that's my cheek," Gloria screeched.

Not a cushion, then.

Oracle shot up from the reclined chair, her forehead banging into another plusher object.

"Ow, and that was my breast."

"What are you doing?" Disoriented, Oracle edged back with a death grip on the thin blanket tangled around her legs.

"About to wake you up. We're landing soon."

"Oh." Oracle's tongue was dry as cotton. "Where's my water?"

"Here." A cold plastic bottle touched Oracle's fingers.

Underneath her, the seat back raised and the foot support lowered as the single bed transformed into a seat again. "Now tell me. What were you dreaming about?"

A needle pierced Pax's flesh. Acid coursed up his arm. His face clenched in pain. Skeletal women surrounded him. She rubbed her aching bicep as if she was the one who had been jabbed.

"I don't remember."

"Bullshit."

"What does it matter? It was only a dream." She took another drink.

"A dream about Pax?"

"Yes, about Pax. What are you insinuating?" Oracle flushed when the memory of an earlier, pleasant dream about Pax popped into her thoughts.

"It sounded like he was in danger."

"Of course he's in danger. He's missing, kidnapped by a transhuman cartel."

A lengthy sigh emanated from Gloria followed by the click of a seatbelt. Oracle felt around for her own and buckled herself in.

"How are you feeling?" Gloria prodded.

"Fine."

The plane shook as they hit turbulence before it tilted down into their descent.

"Are you up to this?"

"What do you think?" Oracle shot back.

Gloria was right. She was cranky when she first woke. She took another drink and winced at an odd metallic taste.

"I'm sorry, I don't mean to be—"

"Such a bitch?"

Oracle arched a brow. "—so rude."

"I'll tell you what I think since you so politely asked."

"This is going to be good," Oracle muttered into her bottle.

"You're ready. Sure you still need training in your new skill set . . . a few hours of practice doesn't make you an expert . . . but for what we need to do, you're ready. Because when you fully embraced your power, I've never been more afraid of another human being."

Gloria punctuated the statement with a motherly pat on Oracle's knee.

♥　☠　♥　☠　♥　☠

This time Reyes was not taking chances with his UltraSecurity guests. Armed bodyguards met Gloria and Oracle at the airport and ushered them into the back of a Ford Expedition, reinforced with bullet-proof windows and flanked by police on motorcycles.

Of course, Oracle didn't see any of this as they were escorted off the plane into the dry Mexican heat, hotter than she expected for this early morning. She took Gloria's word for it as she relayed the details down to the attractiveness or unattractiveness of the bodyguards. Oracle didn't understand the relevance of this information. How hot they were didn't impact their ability to keep Gloria and her safe.

Although it seemed more a ploy to engage Oracle or maybe lighten the mood after what had transpired on the plane. Admitting that she'd broken up Oracle and Pax was beyond upsetting. It was a theory she had considered but never verified and brushed off as too childish even for Gloria.

Then her boss confessed she feared Oracle—a confession that hit a nerve she wasn't aware was exposed and cut deeper than Gloria's scheming against her and Pax.

Her comment reopened the memory—along with the wound—of Oracle's family and friends pulling away, unable to handle her ability when it first manifested. A fact they didn't need to tell her. She'd read it in their minds.

But this past pain wasn't the only feeling that surfaced during their conversation. There was one so out of character that it spurred this much-needed introspection in the backseat of the SUV, while they sped down the highway to Reyes's home.

Merely thinking about Gloria's fear elevated her heartbeat. Her mouth watered, craving the bittersweet taste of it again. Her body hummed with desire, longing to feed on fear's potent energy.

Oracle rubbed her temples and tapped her foot.

Control it.

The power surged, pooling at the back of her neck, not as hot as before but warmer than normal. Enough to cause the skin along her hairline to perspire.

The power belongs to you. You do not belong to it.

A mantra that she and Pax used to say to one another when U-Sec first recruited her.

If Gloria noticed Oracle's growing distress from the other side of the wide backseat, she chose to ignore it and instead called Sean to report that they'd landed. To Oracle's relief, Gloria didn't mention the incident on the plane. She didn't want another person to fear her upgraded ability.

Her heartbeat quickened.

Or maybe I do?

Oracle's power poured down her right arm and inched across the seat toward Gloria.

"Hold on, Sean," Gloria said before directing the next question to Oracle. "Are you okay?"

"No," she whispered. She sucked in a breath along with the power.

"No?"

"Yes, I'm good." Oracle exhaled.

"Cause you look like you're about to get carsick."

"That's it," she lied. "But I'm fine now."

"If you say so. Just keep the vomit directed to your side." She resumed her phone call.

Oracle shook her head against the memory of her power surging into Gloria and chasing her boss's fear into every crevice of every appendage until her spirit wore Gloria's body like a spandex unitard.

She tried to push this image away but her mind kept replaying scenes from the plane. How Oracle stretched her metaphysical muscles to the limit. As

Gloria became tired from being used for these exercises, her fear subsided, causing Oracle's power to lose its juice and drain her own energy. Then Gloria made her drink another power-boosting smoothie until she could sit up without the room twirling around her like she had done several pirouettes en pointe.

Why can't I make this stop?

An odd theory occurred to her. One that was so odd it felt right. One that she'd absently considered and dismissed. This supercharged power fed on raw emotion—fear and anger. Hers as well as others. Revisiting the memory of hurting Gloria, and her fear of this pain, caused Oracle's power to spike again. Her rage over Gloria's betrayal boosted her ability. Then there was the dream about Pax being pricked with a needle. She sensed his pain, his dread, his outrage. Could his emotions have fed her ability, making her physically feel his trauma?

Her arm throbbed again, and she massaged it. The dream about Pax might be real. And he might be dead.

But where was he? Had the plane flown over where he was imprisoned? Because the farthest she'd ever opened up with her power was a few miles within a city, and she had to concentrate on seeking out the individual—sense their specific consciousness. To catch an image flash through a person who wasn't in the same room drained her more than doing eight hours of pointe work with Ms. Natalya, her childhood ballet teacher. She'd never experienced any physical trauma through someone else's body before. Was it another side effect of her enhanced pills?

Should she tell Gloria?

Or, to be certain, should she test it first by redirecting her amped up power to seek Pax out?

Oracle sat up straight and centered herself. Inhaling and exhaling, slow and controlled. She let the memory of his pain wash through her. Let the fear over his possible death grow her power until it expanded and pushed along the inside of her flesh like tiny fingers. Then she sent out her power, called out to Pax, and encountered . . . what was that noise? Snoring?

Gloria's conversation with Sean escalated, cutting into Oracle's concentration. She faltered, lost her grip, and found herself back inside her own skin listening to Gloria's words growing angrier and louder.

"Like I said thirty times before, we don't have enough samples from the skull to treat Dad now . . . he's safe in cryo, it won't progress as long as the temperature . . . Ron is supposed to be researching possible viral delivery systems . . . really, huh . . . well, if he says the effects are different on Dad than Cook then maybe it's not the same drug . . . I don't know, has Ron received confirmation from the lab that the two drugs are different? . . . Sean, don't you dare put her on . . . Hello, Mother . . . I did call Sean when we landed . . . Yes, I should have called you first . . . Yes, I know . . . Yes, thanks for reminding me my father's life is in my hands . . . No, I'm not being sarcastic . . . I need to go . . . we're here . . ."

"Well, I just hung up on my mother. I'll be paying for that one in the years to come," Gloria grumbled.

Oracle nodded. She'd been avoiding her mom's calls as well, trying to put off meeting with the media until she felt normal—and less likely to strike fear in the hearts of N-Ts. A hope that seemed less and less possible until she understood this recent power evolution.

"Still carsick?" Gloria asked.

Oracle took stock. She was no longer afraid or anxious. Her power softly hummed along her shoulders under control, docile, in line with the peace relaxing her limbs. So she could control her power, even if she still wasn't sure how she did it.

Oracle inhaled a deep, chest-expanding breath. "No."

"Glad to hear the car won't smell like vomit for the rest of the trip."

She pinched the bridge of her nose above her sunglasses. For a doctor, Gloria's bedside manner left much to be desired. Maybe that's why most transhumans preferred Dr. Smith to Gloria when they needed a checkup.

"Excuse me, Señor driver?" Gloria piped up as the truck slowed and bumped along.

"It's Ferdinand," he drawled.

"Sure, fine, Ferdinand, are we almost there?"

Oracle pressed into the armrest as the truck took a sharp turn.

"We have arrived en la casa de Señor Reyes."

Gloria gasped. "You should see this."

She jumped when chilled fingers wrapped around her hand, resting on the seat nearest Gloria. Her vision cleared from a gray-black haze to bright morning sun filtering through the SUV's tinted windows. Her control surprised her. Minutes ago, it took all her will to keep her energy from jumping into Gloria. Now it remained contained in Oracle, allowing the smallest tendril to enter her boss's mind and see through her eyes but nothing more. No reading of her thoughts. No possession. Just like Oracle could do before the pills.

Had she exhausted this power evolution when seeking Pax? Or was her fear extinguished when she encountered a peaceful slumber when reaching out to him?

"Stunning." Gloria whistled.

The SUV slowed down along a two-lane, straight road flanked by gated communities on the right and new construction on the left. Between the large homes, the sun's rays sparkled off the blue ocean stretching far out to the horizon.

"Not exactly the home of a serviceman," Gloria uttered.

"He is a general," Oracle said.

"Was a general. He was forced to retire," Gloria corrected her. "Unless generals make more money in Mexico, this doesn't seem right. These houses are at least in the several million range. My father considered investing in a home near here. Now I wish he had."

"It belonged to his uncle. Señor Reyes inherited it," Ferdinand explained.

They stopped momentarily at a wrought iron gate flanked by two guards, one man and one woman, wearing short-sleeved, button-up khaki shirts and matching shorts, not the uniform of the Mexican military.

Judging by the security and the manicured tropical gardens surrounding the long driveway, Reyes's uncle had been part of Mexico's one percent.

"Who was his uncle again?" Oracle asked as the truck turned onto a stone drive. She couldn't recall if he was mentioned during their initial meeting.

"Antonio Suarez," Gloria and Ferdinand both answered.

"Suarez owned the largest tech company in Mexico. Got his start in Silicon Valley with a robotics firm he sold to DERST Industries—a tech giant that beat out Boeing to sign a lucrative contract with the DoD."

"I know DERST. They sponsored my brother's fundraising dinner." *That I missed.*

"Huh . . . I didn't realize that."

Oracle shrugged at the surprise in Gloria's voice. Lots of Beltway Bandits contributed to political races through fundraising organizations. Even TransGen had given money to her brother's campaign.

"After he sold his company, Suarez moved back home to Mexico," Gloria said. "Presumably to start a new business venture and create jobs in his home country, but, if you ask me, it was for a tax break and making his money go farther here."

The brick driveway circled around a stone obelisk topped with a gold platter, standing on its edge, which could serve a roast to a giant—Gloria's thought not Oracle's. She dropped Gloria's hand. She considered retrieving her gloves from her suitcase.

Focus. No thoughts. Just her vision.

"What's wrong?" Gloria asked.

"Nothing." She put out her hand for Gloria to touch once more.

"What do you think this represents?" Gloria stared at the platter with its thin edge wedged into the apex of the obelisk.

She squinted, and Oracle noticed an etching in the center of the plate with a bold black spiral overlaying a stacked cross-like shape.

"It looks like an Aztec symbol," Oracle said, recalling the research into Pre-Columbian art she'd done during Surefire's case.

"That's what I thought."

Their SUV pulled behind a black limousine. Gloria dropped Oracle's hand, leaving her in the dark once more.

The passenger door opened and the oppressive heat smothered the cool air-conditioned interior. Moisture beaded on Oracle's forehead, still wet from battling her hyperactive power. Perspiration built under her arms.

Why did I bother showering on the plane?

Thankfully, she'd left off her U-Sec blazer, opting for a linen dress shirt and pants and flat sandals. Her outfit at odds with Gloria's cargo pants, black U-Sec T-shirt, and combat boots—the opposite from her executive boardroom style—which she'd seen from Gloria's eyes on the plane. She didn't tell Oracle that they were directly engaging the target, which is something her boss had never done. Even though she was a partner in U-Sec, Gloria oversaw the health of the agents—she didn't do fieldwork.

Oracle unfolded her cane and slung her purse over her shoulder. As she slid off the seat and her feet touched the ground, a woman spoke, "Buenos días, señorita."

Judging by the greeter's voice, she stood about a foot in front of Oracle. Possibly the one who had opened the door. She touched the door's edge and received a static shock. The hairs on her arms stood on end.

"Buenos días." Oracle's accent was not as good as it used to be but apparently good enough that she didn't sound like a total gringo.

The woman continued speaking in Spanish, which she understood to mean, "May I guide you into the house?"

"I got her." Gloria wedged herself between the woman, drenched in a spicy cologne, and Oracle.

"As you wish," came the reply in accented English with a shot of spite. "I am Alessandra. I'm working with Felix, who will join you momentarily. If you would please follow me, I will show you inside."

Gloria took her hand. She received an image flash of a woman taller than her with broad shoulders, athletic arms sprouting from a silk tank top over black slacks, and stilettos with points that qualified as deadly weapons. Her straight brown hair was pulled back in a ponytail, swishing in time with her steps and revealing a stylized tattoo of a name—Micah? Miguel?—on the base of her neck. The delicate fabric of the tank top contrasted with the strength she emanated—and not just physically. She motioned them to follow with an authority Oracle had seen from foreign dignitaries her parents often hosted at their home. When Gloria let go of Oracle's hand, the image dissipated. She guided it onto her sleeved arm and led the way forward.

The static electricity Oracle encountered at the car door trailed behind her. It lingered along the backs of her legs, causing goosebumps to spread down her shins.

"Do you feel that?" she whispered to Gloria.

"Like someone rubbed a balloon against the carpet and then stuck it to your hair?"

"Yes. What is it?"

"I don't know. But we'll find out."

Oracle took a breath of the hot, sticky air. She smelled the ocean and sweet flowers. To the right, their footsteps echoed off brick. Gloria continued forward, leading Oracle toward a blast of cool air she assumed was from the A/C inside the home. She counted her steps from the truck until her shoes left the pavers: forty steps. Then she started counting again when they stepped over a threshold and her shoes tapped against tile. Somewhere in front of her, a salt-laced breeze blew in from an open door, bringing the sound of waves pounding and then spraying against rocks. A delicious whiff of chocolate made her stomach growl. Baked scones or brownies?

"Would you like a beverage? Coffee, water, or tea, maybe? He can ask the staff to make you breakfast. Also, Felix's guest has graciously made chocolate scones. A favorite of Felix's and mine," Alessandra said.

Gloria stopped; her rubber soles squeaked against tile. Oracle halted at twenty-one paces. The air was cooler. The tiles were slightly uneven under her feet compared to the brick pavers.

"Water with lemon," Gloria replied.

"Nothing for me, thank you," Oracle said, facing in the direction she assumed Alessandra stood. She was still full from the power smoothies Gloria had given her.

"I'll let them know you have arrived." Stilettos clicked against the tile, echoing across the room.

When the heavy clicks faded, Gloria said, "I don't trust her. Reyes didn't mention that this Alessandra was working with him. But here—" she took Oracle's hand—"I want you to see this room."

They stood in a spacious foyer that led into a living room. Vaulted ceilings soared at least thirty feet in height. Flanking both rooms, tree trunks wider than Pax were used as columns, meeting dark wood beams spanning the width of the ceiling. Terra cotta floor tiles contrasted with white walls adorned with vibrant oil paintings, tapestries, and rugs.

Gloria held Oracle's hand and led her into the great room from the foyer. "I swear this place was on a *Real Life Reality Channel's* cartel wives special."

Oracle shushed her, afraid Reyes or Alessandra may hear her.

Gloria's gaze swept to a wall of windows opposite them. It opened up to a large veranda that overlooked the ocean where Oracle had first sensed the calming breeze, which again blew through the room, bringing with it the sound and smells of the ocean.

"It's beautiful," Oracle said.

"Thank you." A slight man appeared on the oceanfront patio, silhouetted by the blue sky behind him. "When my uncle passed away, he willed it to me. A soldier's salary wouldn't afford me this luxury."

"Señor Reyes, I presume," Oracle said, but she was no longer seeing their host. Gloria, with her hand tightening around Oracle's fingers, was leaning forward, staring at an odd collection of art and artifacts that spanned cultures from Indian to Egyptian to Aztec, along with a few styles Oracle didn't recognize.

"What's his story?" Gloria pointed to a statue of a cross-legged man, hunched over with the weight of a flying-saucer-shaped object lined with crosses on top of his head. The same symbol from the gold plate outside appeared on the cloth underneath him.

"Ometeotl. One of the oldest deities the Aztecs worshiped. Represents order and chaos. Male and female. The duality of nature."

Gloria's gaze shifted to Reyes, who had sauntered toward them, wearing a silk floral shirt and khaki pants. He appeared delicate, too fine-boned compared to the military men Oracle knew. She had to remind herself that he was a transhuman—a deceptively strong transhuman, according to Pax, who wasn't prone to exaggeration.

"Dr. Vivas. UltraAgent Oracle." Reyes nodded to each of them, hands clasped behind his back, making no move to shake their hands.

"Any developments?" Gloria asked, dispensing with a greeting.

Oracle gently nudged Gloria with her power, attempting to read her thoughts. As if sensing her attempts, Gloria dropped her hand.

"I believe we found one of your agents," Reyes replied.

Oracle's heart leapt with hope. "Pax?"

As his name left her lips, an image flashed before her—a dark-haired woman with delicate, doll-like features leaning over and looking at Oracle.

No, not Oracle, she was looking at Pax.

An icy cold blast slammed against Oracle's energy. She reeled as her power bounced around her body. She reached out to catch herself from falling. A metal object clanged to the floor.

"Oracle?" Gloria ventured.

A static shock buzzed between her shoulders as two hands gripped either side of her. The spicy scent told her it was Alessandra. She didn't glimpse the room because Alessandra placed her hands over Oracle's shirt.

"Thank you." She gave the woman what she hoped was a confident look.

Alessandra let her go. Her heels snapped away in a quick retreat.

"What did you see?" Gloria demanded.

"I'm sorry. Did I break anything?" *How did Gloria know I saw something?*

"You displaced a satanic altar, but otherwise . . ." Gloria touched Oracle's wrist. A vision flashed in her mind of a rustic wooden table, draped in a cloth sewn with a squarish shape and a circle with a triangle in the center. Set along the circle were small bowls and three objects placed in the corners opposite a statue of a blue woman lying on her back. One item appeared to be a small silver dagger. Around the objects was strewn a necklace of small white crystal skulls.

"That is a tantric altar. It belonged to my uncle, who traveled the world after he retired to study witchcraft and magic of various cultures. The statue is Kali, the goddess of death and destruction." Reyes bent over to set the objects right.

"And also time, don't forget that one." A familiar female voice resounded from the foyer. "That is, if you're talking about the Hindu goddess."

"Kali—TimeTrap, you're . . ." Oracle's tongue tied at seeing her fellow agent being carried into the foyer.

"You're alive." Gloria tugged Oracle into a trot toward TimeTrap and the tall drink of cerveza holding her.

She shook her head as Gloria's description seeped into her thoughts. But the man gripping TimeTrap to his wide chest clad in a dress shirt did cause a flutter in Oracle's stomach . . . no . . . actually, Gloria's stomach, followed by a few other . . . seriously, now?

She needed to get a handle on this power before she heard or felt anything she'd regret.

Oracle wrenched herself out of Gloria's grip. From what she could tell before Gloria started drooling, TimeTrap had a knot on her head and yellow-purplish bruises on her fair arms.

"I'm so happy you're alive." Oracle blinked back the tears of relief.

"Me too," the UltraAgent said.

Oracle reached out to touch her fellow agent and make sure she was real but then pulled back. "Can you walk?"

"I'm a little shaken and stirred. My knees buckled when I got out of the car, so Roberto offered to carry me," she replied, rolling her savior's name on her tongue.

"Where should I put her?" Roberto asked.

"In your arms, my head feels much better," TimeTrap exclaimed. "I should probably stay here all night to properly heal."

"Reyes, do you have a place where I can examine her?" Gloria said.

"Roberto, here on the couch," Reyes replied.

"Where's Pax?" Oracle asked as they breezed by, leaving scents of patchouli oil, men's cologne, and a hospital-like antiseptic mingling in their wake.

Gloria guided Oracle's hand onto her arm.

"Sorry about that," Gloria whispered to her. "I told you it's been a long time and when I get stressed . . . it makes me . . . well, you heard."

Oracle ignored her and continued toward the sound of TimeTrap's voice, as she complained about Reyes dismissing Roberto.

When the couch's corner bumped into Oracle's leg, she asked again—no demanded—"Where's Pax?"

There was a pause, and Oracle had the distinct feeling that TimeTrap was fidgeting, buying time.

"I don't know," she finally answered.

Oracle swore the weight of the ocean just crashed over her shoulders. She stared unblinking at TimeTrap, and even through her sunglasses, the agent must've felt the intensity of Oracle's gaze because she started to talk.

"I woke up on a bed by myself in an aquarium. Well . . . it looked like an aquarium, like the one at the Inner Harbor in Baltimore. You know, the area where you walk between the tanks that tower above you with sharks and turtles and . . ."

"We got the visual. What else?" Gloria interjected.

"It wasn't real."

"Who do you mean?" Oracle chimed in.

"The tank, the fish, the sharks, and even a sea lion. I mean they would never put a sea lion with a Great White. That was on the Science Channel just last week. Duh."

"Unless Pax was floating in this tank—" Gloria started.

"Fake tank," TimeTrap corrected. "More like large TV monitors playing a fish video."

"Did you see anyone?" Oracle didn't bother to hide her frustration.

"Just the fish or rather fake fish, although it was serene with the floor, ceiling, and walls all sparkly blue like the Caribbean."

"What about a way out?" Oracle clasped her hands together to keep from shaking the UltraAgent to get the information she wanted.

"A door must've been hidden behind the screens. I had to get in there somehow."

"How do you feel? Any pain?" Gloria asked.

"A little nauseated and a bit lightheaded like I can feel after QT-ing on an empty stomach."

The bangles jangled on TimeTrap's wrist.

"Does it hurt when I press here or here?" Gloria asked.

"Not much. Just sore. I think it looks a lot worse than it is. My fifty shades of paleness bruises easier than a peach. I did wake up with an IV in this arm. I pulled it out before I jumped."

"Looks like they treated you for a concussion and sutured you up with a strong tissue adhesive that seems to have sped up your healing as well. From the photos Reyes sent of that wreck, I'm surprised it's not much worse."

"What do you remember of the accident?" Oracle left unspoken about wanting any clues to Pax having survived it.

"We were on this steep road. Stuff was sliding off the bar—oh, and thanks for the snacks, Reyes, although Pax wouldn't let me imbibe—and then the car shook and skidded, and the ceiling cracked against my head, and then I was in an aquarium that wasn't an aquarium. When I couldn't find a way out, I popped back to the road we were on and that's when Roberto found me."

Oracle twisted her hands tighter until her fingertips lost feeling.

"I think they administered a numbing agent similar to the Happy Pills our UltraAgents are given in the field to dull the pain until they reach a hospital. And these bruises around her ribs indicate a fracture, but it's not hurting when I press it," Gloria stated.

"Nope," TimeTrap said.

"The way this skin has sutured together, it's like nothing I've seen before," Gloria continued.

"The Sisterhood took care of her," Reyes said.

"They healed her. Judging by how these bones feel in her shoulder, there were other fractures that are mending quickly," Gloria noted.

"That's good. That means they took care of Pax, right?" TimeTrap asked.

"Possibly," Gloria said with hesitation.

"No, they didn't." Oracle shook her head.

Their silence indicated they were waiting for her to elaborate. Her words conveyed too much confidence and certainty for someone who hadn't been kidnapped with Pax.

"What do you know, Oracle? What did you see?" Gloria spoke.

She opened her mouth to explain then clamped her lips shut. The energy in the room changed. It became heavier, charged with a frenetic buzzing stronger than what she'd experienced when meeting Alessandra.

"See?" Reyes asked, incredulous. "I thought Oracle needed to touch someone to see through their eyes."

"Bravo! You are certainly the perfect subject." A woman applauded from across the room.

Oracle spun toward the new voice's direction. No, it couldn't be.

"Lucy?"

Pax grabbed the vial on the right—Diosa de la Venganza. He jabbed the needle into his arm. The liquid burned up through his veins. A hot poker pierced his heart and talons twisted his guts. Tiny fingers massaged along the inside of his skin, growing stronger and harder until he swore his flesh would rip open. He dropped to his knees. Behind him, he heard a helicopter land on the helipad.

"It's Dama X." The name rippled through the crowd.

"Magda, she doesn't look pleased," one of the women said.

"He needed to pass the test before he could stay. We had to see where his loyalties are," their leader replied.

The searing, twisting heat traveled to his groin. Pax's fingers dug into the grass, grabbing fistfuls of dirt.

Oh, no, Pax.

He could almost hear Oracle's voice. Feel her breath cooling his feverish skin.

"Magda!" A woman with a Hispanic accent shouted. Pax couldn't make out anything else over the chopper blades and the ringing in his ears.

Bare arms wrapped around his shoulder. His vision blurred. Magda and her cronies blinked in and out from his line of sight.

"What did you do?" The woman clutched Pax to her body. Soft cotton lay against his cheek.

"We administered the test."

"Not on him. He was mine to decide," the woman said.

"He was a threat, trying to escape. We learned who he is working with. He was to meet with our enemy in Mexico. We had to know if we could trust him."

"There is always a choice." Her hands massaged his temples. Pax found himself sinking down onto her lap.

"Not when it comes to men working with our enemies."

"Magda, he saved my life. We wouldn't be here if it wasn't for him. I don't believe he knew what they wanted of him."

"With respect, Dama X, you give the man too much credit. The problem and downfall of our sex."

"Hold on, mi amor. It will pass," Dama X said, but her words overlapped Oracle's comforting ones, which seemed to come from dreams he drifted in and out of until he wasn't sure what was reality any more.

"Shit. The other agent's gone." The gray cleared from Pax's vision, and he saw Magda and her sidekick staring down at a phone screen.

"UltraAgent TimeTrap? Is that who you mean, Kristina?" Dama X inquired.

"Yes."

She laughed bitterly. "You left a woman who can travel through space in a cell by herself?"

"She was injured."

"Not injured enough to stop her power," Dama X said.

"Naomi was watching her. She was supposed to keep her unconscious," Lisa said.

Dama X laid Pax onto the grass. He couldn't move his limbs or feel his lower body. The numbness rose across his stomach to overtake his chest. He struggled to breathe.

"You two, take Pax to my room. Magda, secure Naomi as a precaution. I was suspicious of her loyalties anyway after what just occurred in Baltimore. Alert the Sisters. Put them on standby. It won't be long before they come for him now."

Chapter 12
Bold Entrance

Yes, TransGen's patients encountered side effects that ran the gamut from mental illness to deformities to death. However, these subjects knew the risks before they signed on. In these cases, we were their last hope. During TransGen's early stages, we struggled to understand why our brand of gene therapy worked on some but not others. Now we are close to finding an explanation and developing a screening process to know who will qualify for treatment.

—Dr. Victor Vivas on a never-released documentary

"I go by Lucinda now. I left Lucy behind when I left the states," the woman corrected Oracle in a pleasant way, as if they were old friends reuniting after a long absence—that couldn't be farther from the truth.

"Lucinda's flight arrived earlier than expected," Reyes explained.

"Lucy . . . I mean, Lucinda, why are you—?" Oracle started but couldn't finish. It was more than the shock of Lucinda's presence. The buzzing energy returned with a distracting tingle along her skin.

"Didn't Glor tell you?" An intake of breath followed by hard-soled flats smacking against the tile floor. "Oh, I see, judging by Gloria's resting guilt face she didn't. We've been discussing your situation for the last few months."

Was that the secret Gloria kept hidden from me in her mind?

She managed to move her clenched jaw enough to ask her boss, "What is she talking about?"

"Lucinda, Oracle doesn't know—"

"Know what?" She was not letting Gloria off about this.

"I think she deserves to be told. We're practically partners," Lucinda said.

"Practically," Gloria muttered.

"Tell me," Oracle ordered.

"Fine but let me tell Pax because he doesn't know, and he'll go all Angry Pax for being kept in the dark." Gloria paused as if collecting her thoughts before saying, "Back in May, when you were dealing with Surefire's case, I was away on a classified mission to meet with Lucinda. TransGen contracted with her transgenetic lab to give us additional support for research and whatnot."

"Like the pills prescribed to me?"

"I knew that her pharmacy had begun supplying us with certain medications, but I didn't know *your pills* came from her lab. I swear. Cross my heart and all that jazz." The certainty in Gloria's words convinced Oracle that she told the truth. Regarding her explanation of the partnership, not so much. Gloria was leaving out details. Important ones.

"In June, Gloria contacted me about your anxiety issues when your situation deteriorated. I promised to find a solution based on research my company has been doing for the past few years."

"You promised, but I was still waiting for it. You said it would take your lab until this month," Gloria said.

"I did?" Lucinda's words dripped with sarcasm, a faux display of ignorance. "Sorry about that. It must've slipped my mind to inform you about the prescription I gave to Oracle's psychiatrist."

"Don't pull that act in front of Oracle. She knows that you're lying."

"My actions appear to have helped Oracle immensely. She's certainly improved since you called me from the plane. That is if she can truly link her mind with Pax's, as you believe, based on what transpired." Lucinda's blasé explanation grated Oracle more than her presence.

"Whoa, whoa, whoa. Let's rewind this scene." TimeTrap made the sound of an old tape deck rewinding. "You're that crazy chick, Lucy?"

"Misunderstood, not crazy. Don't ever call me crazy. Men call women crazy or stupid when they want to diminish what they've done. You get one pass and then—"

"You'll kill me like you did your father?" TimeTrap finished.

"Who told you that?"

"I . . . um . . . Sean probably."

"Sean? And after all I did for him?" Lucinda sighed. "My father is chilling out with the money I paid for his shares in Circe."

"No, she's not crazy, TimeTrap, she's dangerous," Oracle said. "Lucinda left the country after the transhuman police sergeant under her care lost control and electrocuted a suspect he was pursuing. Or possibly she ran because of the other transhumans who were institutionalized after her so-called treatment, unable to function in society."

"Unlike Gloria, I wasn't afraid to break a few eggs. We learn from mistakes more so than triumphs. I was missing an essential protein in the cocktail used to treat that sergeant, which I've since discovered in the skulls. That incident—and a few others of which I'm not proud—pinpointed an issue with my treatment."

"This doesn't explain why TransGen would work with you again."

"Because they realized their mistake in not defending me against those small-minded allegations. Victor, especially, regretted letting me go, even if he's too pigheaded to admit it. I'm thinking outside the chromosomes, finding alternative solutions to enhance and help transhumans. I had a theory that all transhumans have the same gene in their DNA that allowed their abilities to be turned on, which I shared with Gloria back in our ESP days. I was right. And when I studied shavings from the skulls, I found they contain a protein that can bind with this gene in transhumans but not in N-Ts. I call it the Lucinda Protein."

"That's not narcissistic at all," Gloria said.

"Like you wouldn't do that," Lucinda returned.

"Maybe," she conceded. "Doesn't make it *not* narcissistic."

Lucinda dismissed her with a sniff. "When I first arrived in Mexico, a client of mine tasked me with studying her crystal skull collection. She wanted to see if their purported preternatural properties had any basis in science and were related to theories she had regarding transhumans. These were the skulls Ari had stolen from a private collection. Fortunately, I acquired enough crystal scrapings before the theft for my research. Analysis showed that each skull's unique proteins create different results in transhumans. Yet I couldn't *fully* activate these proteins until I discovered an outside element that acts as a binding agent."

"Is that how Diosa de la Venganza was created?" Oracle tried and failed to keep the accusation out of her voice.

"That drug was created by mixing one of the skulls with the special element. My skull research—along with my most recent breakthrough—enabled me to create a cellular restructuring serum. Dama X stole my research and found a way to reproduce it in Diosa de la Venganza, which is why I'm here to help find her. But she also used this special element combined with a *different* skull to quickly heal TimeTrap from the car accident just like I healed Felix. I have a patent pending on that treatment, and the bitch stole it too."

"Like she stole the crystal skull from TransGen," Oracle stated.

"You'll need to be more specific. She's taken several of the thirteen skulls from secret facilities in both the U.S. and Mexico."

"What?" Oracle was certain she'd heard Lucinda incorrectly.

"We weren't aware that any others had been taken," Gloria said.

"The Mexican government launched an investigation into the thefts and didn't want to involve outside agents until necessary," Reyes explained.

"You should've told us. Warned us, so we could've tightened security," Gloria argued.

"It happened a week ago. There was one taken from another location in the U.S. as well. St. John was conducting an investigation himself," Reyes said.

"And didn't share the details with us? Typical," Gloria spat.

Pax's memory of Ari—the man who nearly destroyed the world—and the crystal skulls flashed through Oracle's mind. One that stuck with her and gave her nightmares right as the anxiety took hold. He'd warned her not to read his mind, but she wanted to see what he saw, because what he described when he returned from Mexico seemed so far-fetched. Surefire covered in Ari's blood, standing in the middle of the skull circle and glowing with a purple light, while the goddess's power filled her, claiming the UltraAgent as her vessel.

"Does Dama X plan to raise a god like Ari had done?" Oracle asked.

"I think she has a better plan," Lucinda replied. "One of the skulls she has stolen contains a protein that can boost a transhuman's ability. The Sisters in her inner circle have increased strength similar to Pax's. Several were part of their respective countries' ESP agencies. She could use the skull to enhance them and create a superhuman army."

"Dama X's island has the technology and resources to do it," Alessandra added.

"That isn't scary at all," TimeTrap said.

"Alessandra, how would you know this?" Gloria asked.

"I helped Suarez design this island."

"Huh, I thought you were the housekeeper. You said you work for Felix—"

"*With* Felix."

Oracle considered offering Gloria her U-Sec blazer. The woman's frigid tone cooled the room by a few degrees. Unfortunately, she'd left it in the truck.

"Alessandra has a dual degree in electrical and computer engineering," Lucinda explained. "She worked at Suarez Tech after college before moving on to better things. She has graciously volunteered to help us find the skulls, which we believe were taken to this island."

Gloria was right. Oracle sensed Lucinda wasn't telling the whole truth. The woman had a slight tremor, a hesitation in her speech pattern, so Oracle asked point blank, "Which skulls has Dama X stolen?"

From what she'd learned from Surefire's case, each skull contained a different preternatural energy—some positive and others that made the devil seem like a misunderstood tween—which explained why the proteins and effects would vary.

"Based on Gloria and my findings, the skull Xalvadora—Dama X—took from TransGen contains one of the two active ingredients in Diosa de la

Venganza. We need this skull to cure Victor and your other victim. Although maybe cure isn't the best word. Being a woman isn't a disease. Right, Reyes?"

"No, it's not," he replied softly.

Oracle frowned in the direction of his voice, not sure what this exchange meant and not caring at this moment because she had more important concerns. Lucinda couldn't stop lying through her perfect teeth.

"Which skull did you mix into my pills?" A warm, gooey energy prickled along the base of her neck.

"You surmised that I used a skull protein? Well, you're smarter than I thought. Or maybe Gloria told you?"

"Which one?" Her energy flared out then whipped back inside. A misfire.

"Can't you tell?"

Outrage burned like sour milk in her gut. It fueled her ability—not as potent as fear, but enough to blast it toward her target, Lucinda.

But the psychic burst never made it to her target. Instead of seeing through Lucinda's eyes, tearing apart her memories, filling every crevice with Oracle's spirit, her power ricocheted off a metaphysical wall and bounced into Gloria.

Her boss cursed. Oracle received an image flash of the room. TimeTrap struggling to sit up on the couch. Alessandra glancing over her shoulder from near the windows where she was talking on her phone. Reyes standing with arms crossed, eyes darting from Oracle to Lucinda.

In a black pantsuit and flats, Lucinda looked the part of the corporate power broker instead of conniving doctor. Her white blouse was unbuttoned to reveal a necklace with a tiny bottle containing a sparkling dust.

Oracle sucked her consciousness back into her body.

"This vial around my neck contains crystal dust from the Ometeotl skull that Dama X stole from your offices. It repels the power from the other skulls, including Tezcatlipoca's—and he's the one fueling your upgraded power." Lucinda's flats clack, clack, clacked closer until Oracle felt the woman's warmth within arm's length. Smelled the soap used on her clean, slicked back hair.

"Will it repel this?" Oracle pulled back her fist. A hand seized her arm, followed by a static shock that made her knees wobble.

"Don't," Alessandra spoke close to her ear. "And if you pry into my mind or Felix's, you'll regret it."

Electricity snapped against her cheek. Oracle flinched and Alessandra released her.

Two things she learned in that moment: Alessandra was definitely a transhuman. And Oracle didn't know herself anymore. She'd never raised a hand, let alone a fist, to a person out of anger. Defense, yes. Anger, never.

"Tezcatlipoca is a god of rage," Lucinda said as if she'd read Oracle's mind. "And rage is one of the side effects of using his skull to help you. Oh, yes, and fear. He savored humans' fear as a Marylander savors steamed crabs. The only thing I miss from Baltimore. Oh, the sacrifices we make for science."

She circled Oracle, her shoes scraping against the tile floor. She hugged herself so Lucinda wouldn't notice her shaking.

"A bit of Tezcatlipoca remained inside you after your encounter with him. It made you sick and anxious. Just like a virus," Lucinda continued. "I treated the illness with a genetically watered down version, a vaccine, to help you fight it off. I theorized your power would grow as a side effect and it did. It also ate away at your fear, boosting your confidence. A win-win if I ever saw one."

"He's inside me?" Oracle dug her nails into her arms. She wanted to rip the flesh off. Tear into her veins to remove each granule of this wicked god infused in her blood.

"Hold on for a second," TimeTrap spoke up. "You're saying the Aztec god that Ari—the dick-villain-of-the-year—tried to raise is inside of Oracle? This same ancient god who wanted to destroy our world? Because I thought you were supposed to be smart but you're now seeming a little . . ."

Lucinda must've shot TimeTrap a vicious look because she quickly added, "I didn't say it."

"When Ari died, the god passed back over into his world and into that in-between, Eden-like place Surefire mentioned in her report," Lucinda explained.

"How did you see that report?" Oracle asked.

Reyes cleared his throat. "I gave it to her."

Oracle struggled to take a breath into her ever-tightening chest. "How is this possible? Surefire had removed Tezcatlipoca's skull from our world. Supposedly, she left it in the past."

"It appeared back inside the safe in my lab from where Ari had stolen it a year prior," Lucinda said.

"Possibly a self-existing object. Trippy." TimeTrap whistled the theme music to *The Twilight Zone.*

"She handed over the skull to my government, and we thought she could help," Reyes replied. Without reading his mind, Oracle believed him, but it didn't make it right.

"Those skulls were to be locked away, protected from people like her who will abuse their power," Oracle said.

"Really?" Lucinda nearly choked with indignation. "Given my experience, I was placed on an advisory board by the President of Mexico to study the properties of those skulls."

"And that included testing samples on unsuspecting human guinea pigs?"

"Transhuman," Lucinda corrected Oracle.

She swore her blood was actually boiling. Oracle hugged her arms tighter around her chest. Her nails dug deeper into her triceps to stop herself from launching at this woman.

"Let's take a breather," Gloria interjected. Rubber soles squeaked against the tile. A light floral scent filled the air as her boss wedged between them.

"I recommend you getting as far from me as possible. Lucinda may have poisoned me, but I trusted you, and you don't have a trinket around your neck to protect you," Oracle said.

"Fair enough. But I was—scratch that—am under a contractual obligation not to divulge Lucinda's arrangement with TransGen." Gloria's shoes squeaked against the floor, her scent retreating as she did.

"I don't care if God told you to lie to me. I have a demon's power inside of me, and who knows if he'll decide to possess me like he did Ari."

"He can't possess you. There's not enough of him in you. Besides, Ari made a blood sacrifice to be the god's vessel, which we're still trying to understand," Lucinda said.

Oracle relaxed her hands. The flesh along her upper arms throbbed from where her nails had dug in. She turned her head to where she last felt Gloria's presence. "Is this what you meant by trusting you?"

"I confronted Lucinda from the plane. She knows it isn't acceptable that she gave you these pills. At that time, she admitted to using a skull protein in them. I didn't know the proteins were from Tezcatlipoca's skull," Gloria said.

"You didn't know what any of those skulls could've done to me. You shouldn't have allowed this to happen even if Lucinda was using the goddess of rainbows and unicorns. You should've told me and allowed me to make the choice instead of mixing those pills into my drink." Oracle's voice rose with every word as the implication of what Gloria kept from her became clearer.

"You're right. I should've told you when I found out." She strained to hear Gloria's semi-apology.

"That is seriously effed-up," TimeTrap murmured.

"No, it's science," Lucinda replied.

"You weren't there. You didn't see him or feel his power. He is pure asshat evil." TimeTrap paused then said, "Sorry, Oracle."

"No, don't be. You're right." Bile pooled in the back of her throat. If only it would be as simple as vomiting to expel his presence from her.

"If it's any consolation," Reyes spoke up. "In Aztec mythology, he is a creator god, patron of the nobility. He saw into the hearts of man and was capable of dispensing good fortune."

"See, it's not all bad," Lucinda said punctuated with a hand clap.

Oracle was about to dispense anything but good fortune on this woman.

"What's going to happen if I don't take those pills?"

"I don't know. In fact, I didn't know that you would react so well to the treatment."

"So I was your lab rat?" Oracle rubbed her sweating palms over her pants.

"Your psychiatrist kept me apprised of your condition. You were no good before you started taking the pills. Unable to work. Wallowing in a pity party because a preternatural energy gave you a brain freeze. I did you a favor."

"I didn't ask for that kind of help."

"No, but you needed it."

"Oracle," Reyes said gently. Shoes scuffed against the tile toward her. To her right, she sensed his warm presence and smelled his musky aftershave. "We need to save Pax, and we need to retrieve the skull to stop any future attacks. Our samples are not enough to create a cure for Gloria's father and your other victim. With this skull, Xalvadora can create larger batches of Diosa de la Venganza."

"While you were en route here, we received confirmation from a spy inside her island compound that Dama X has acquired a powerful weapon," Alessandra said.

"What kind of weapon?" TimeTrap asked.

"World-destroying kind."

"Oh, that clears things up," the UltraAgent quipped.

"Then why isn't the military responding? Get St. John's Special Forces unit involved. The team that assisted Pax with Surefire's extraction," Oracle said.

"Any backup we call in needs our help to scout and determine the threat and create the best plan to ensure no civilian casualties. They can't find my uncle's island without us," Reyes said.

"I was one of the chief engineers on the island project before Suarez let me go. Once we find it, I can disable the cloaking features, enabling them to help," Alessandra said.

"What do you mean by 'find it?'" Oracle recalled Reyes mentioning this during their phone meeting, but she dismissed it at the time, believing she'd misheard him.

"My uncle built this island and planned to lease it to the U.S., Mexico, and other military powers. Then he had a changed of heart and decided to keep it for himself. It's a floating research facility, containing residences, fully sustainable for scientists and engineers to live and work to test theories and ideas hidden from the public's eyes."

"And away from governing laws, which is why he created a cloaking system that makes the island invisible and untraceable to radar and sonar," Alessandra said. "The cloaking system also distorts the atmosphere around it, making it impossible for anyone on the inside to send even star-based coordinates to us."

"Then how are we supposed to find it?" Oracle balked.

"With your supercharged transability," Lucinda said. "You reach out to Pax, see through his eyes, and find out where he is. You feed that image to TimeTrap and . . . viola! She takes a few of us via quantum transference to Dama X's compound. We return with Pax, the skull, and Dama X. Alessandra disables the cloaking so our military can safely remove those living there."

"It sounds easy when you're not the one doing it," TimeTrap replied.

"Too bad you can't travel back in time in this universe," Lucinda said.

TimeTrap could travel back in time but only in an alternate universe that followed a similar history and somehow touched theirs. She'd offered to take Oracle on one of her jumps to the sixties, where she enjoyed hanging out with other free spirits. But Oracle declined. The present time period in her own universe offered enough prejudices and challenges for her.

"Even if I could, there would be too many paradoxes. I might reset our universe and possibly destroy it, which you know, would be bad," TimeTrap said.

She felt TimeTrap's frustration at having to constantly explain the parameters of her power.

"I don't even know if what I'm seeing is real. If I'm connecting to Pax. TimeTrap traveled from the island. Can't she pop everyone back there?" Oracle didn't need to add how she'd be working with people whom she didn't trust feeding her dog let alone saving her friend and boss.

"She has a point. I could take us to the jail-cell-slash-trippy-fake aquarium," the agent said.

"That isn't an option. Our insider sent us a message before the Sisters discovered her in the comm room and we could get a location read. Dama X is keeping Pax hostage in her room. TimeTrap's cell is on the opposite end of the island. We'd never get there without being detected," Alessandra said. "We need to get to Dama X before we can secure the island. We cut off the head and La Hermandad de Diana falls. They are nothing without Dama X."

"My sister is not to be hurt let alone cut off. That was our deal." Reyes's voice resounded through the room with an authority that no reasonable person would question.

"Felix, I assure you," Lucinda purred in an agreeable tone Oracle was growing to loathe, "we will we do everything in our power so no harm comes to your sister. However—"

"There is no 'however.' You want my help, then you promise that my sister will not be hurt or killed."

Alessandra swore under her breath.

"Don't worry, Alessandra," Lucinda said.

"I never worry."

The hairs on Oracle's arms stood on end from a low current passing through the room.

"I can't promise Dama X won't be harmed. None of you know what that bitch is capable of. I've seen it. Firsthand."

"How do you know?" Gloria asked. Neither woman acknowledged her question.

Lucinda continued speaking to Alessandra in a soothing tone Oracle found condescending because it sounded forced. "The tranquilizer I created will be sufficient to disable her. Are we in agreement?"

"Yes," Alessandra replied, leaving no doubt she wasn't happy to comply. There was more to this exchange. Oracle longed to pry open their minds for the truth but the vial and Alessandra's threat kept her power corralled.

"We will use tranquilizer darts on Dama X if necessary. One problem solved. Next up, Oracle. We need your help—now."

"I don't know if I can do it," she replied.

"Do you want to save Pax?" Lucinda countered.

She had to go for the heart, didn't she? As if saving the world wasn't motivation enough. But how could she trust any of them after they manipulated and lied to her? She started to wonder if Dama X was the real villain here.

"It won't hurt to try, would it? Sit down." Lucinda moved in front of Oracle.

Fingers touched her shoulder. Oracle jerked away.

"Fine, don't sit, but it might be easier than potentially getting disoriented and cracking your head on the tile."

She wanted to save Pax. At the moment, working with them was the only option to help him no matter how wrong it felt to do so. Oracle reviewed the last image flash of Reyes's home she'd received from Gloria. She took an awkward step toward the couch where she'd last seen TimeTrap lying.

"Here, babe." TimeTrap touched Oracle's thigh. She stooped to feel for the cushion. The other UltraAgent rubbed Oracle's back in support before bouncing further down the cushions to make room.

"Focus on Pax." Lucinda tried her mothering tone on Oracle.

"I know how my power works," she snapped back.

"Then show us."

Another deep inhale and then an exhale as she recalled the last time she saw Pax outside her apartment in his truck. Their argument and how she didn't say goodbye, and may never have the chance again. Her eyes watered, as they closed, causing her to sniffle. She smelled lavender and coconut. Heard waves slapping against a shore. Felt the sun's heat warm her left arm.

Pax.

Her eyes squinted against bright sunlight pouring through a floor-to-ceiling window that made up one wall in a white room. Bed sheets tangled around thick, muscular legs with fine blond hairs, which she remembered being soft to the touch. In the corner, a shapely blur walked slowly toward the bed. Eyes remained unfocused, vision hazy, body numb. The shape leaned close enough to kiss, and Oracle made out a face with large green eyes, soft pink lips. Delicate bones like Reyes. The woman reached a hand down and—

Oh, hell, no.

Oracle's eyes popped open. The vision faded to black. Her pounding heart and erratic breath drowned out the movements around her.

Fingers touched her shoulder and then retreated. "Oracle?" TimeTrap ventured.

"Fine," she croaked then cleared her throat and stated with more authority, "It's fine."

"What did you see?" Gloria sat on the arm of the couch next to Oracle, who scooted away until her leg hit TimeTrap's.

"Pax was on a bed in a room with windows to his left. His vision was foggy like he had been drugged."

"And Dama X?" Lucinda asked.

"She was there with him."

"We need to act now," Lucinda said.

"Hold on. No one has asked me if I could do this," TimeTrap said.

"Can you do this?" Lucinda asked.

"Yes . . . maybe . . . I don't know," she replied reluctantly.

"You could've mentioned this earlier," Alessandra huffed.

"I was a bit distracted with asshat Aztec gods and vague references to weapons of mass destruction to consider if I can do what you're asking me to do."

"What's the problem?" Lucinda punctuated the question with a long sigh.

"The problem is that my power doesn't work like fictional superheroes. I need to rest between travels, especially when I'm still not quite healed from . . . oh, let's see . . . a car accident. No matter how well your serum worked in healing me, I just traveled from Dama X's island and am still drained. I can't just pop over there with everyone and pop back out, toting one more person and a transhuman with a body three times my size without repercussions. Then there's that skull."

"What about it?"

"Last time I was near those skulls, it screwed with my mojo. In fact, I sensed a draining buzz just from your necklace. I can't guarantee my power will work properly when around the real deal."

"I didn't see or sense the skulls in the room with Pax," Oracle said.

"I'm hearing excuses and not solutions," Lucinda said, singsong.

"We could travel closer to the area so you don't have to jump far," Alessandra offered. "When our spy flew to the island, she turned on her tracking device. The final signal I received from her was twenty miles southwest of our current location in international waters." From across the room, keys clicked on a laptop.

"But the satellite images we took of that location were unclear. The objects large enough to be the island disappeared in the next frame and never reappeared," Reyes said. "Plus, its cloaking technology makes it completely invisible to anyone flying over."

"Will it be easier for you to travel there if we are closer?" Alessandra said followed by a few more taps.

"If I only take one of you. Preferably someone smaller and not as staticky as a certain person in this room."

Alessandra muttered a few words in Spanish. One word Oracle recognized. *Puta.*

"I'll go with her," Reyes stated.

"No, I'm going. TimeTrap's my agent and Pax is my partner," Gloria argued.

"Dama X is my sister."

"You wore your shit-kickers, Gloria, but Reyes is a trained soldier. He should go. Dama X will be less likely to attack him over Alessandra or myself or even you, someone she doesn't know," Lucinda said.

"If he's going instead of me, I'll give TimeTrap this." Gloria leaned across Oracle, who pressed herself as far from that woman's body as the seat cushion allowed.

"A pebble?" TimeTrap exclaimed.

"A necklace with a stone that transmits your location."

"Doesn't match my outfit."

"Is she joking?" Alessandra jeered.

"Debatable." Gloria blew out a breath. "When you were missing after the accident, we couldn't reach the signal on your watch."

"My watch! They must've taken it. Sean is going to be ticked. He's going to totally make me pay—"

"It was an accident. You don't have to pay for it. Shut up and listen."

"I'm zipping it."

"This stone contains a modified locator from U-Sec's master of tech. Oliver's been developing it for the military and received permission for me to test the prototype on this mission. It can't be blocked by conventional scramblers used by our enemy combatants. However, there's no guarantee it will work from Dama X's island. It's only for backup."

"Backup, schmackup. It's worth a go, and hopefully, I won't lose this one." TimeTrap settled closer to Oracle.

Gloria retreated to the other side of the sofa. Oracle relaxed in her seat.

"Then it's settled. Reyes has a helicopter in his backyard," Alessandra said.

"And who doesn't?" TimeTrap commented under her breath.

"We will fly your helicopter to the area where we last received signal. Oracle may get a stronger lock on Pax with a closer proximity. It should shorten TimeTrap's transference and use less energy."

"And if something goes wrong, we'll be close enough to react quickly and hopefully pick up the signal from the locator," Gloria added.

"Alessandra, you are my solutioner." Lucinda made an exaggerated kiss smacking sound. "Felix, is the helicopter prepped?"

"It's fueled and ready to go," Reyes responded.

"Gloria, are you still comfortable flying one?" Lucinda asked.

Oracle stood. "Gloria can fly a helicopter?"

"I'm full of mysteries, aren't I?" Gloria chided.

Oracle shook her head, not wanting to engage Gloria in a friendly conversation, but her boss didn't take the hint.

"Our father challenged us to master a unique skill. Sean learned to fly planes and I went for the helicopter. Heard it was a lot harder to learn than flying a plane."

"And was it?" Alessandra asked, her voice floating closer as she stepped further into the room.

"Not for me."

Oracle let out a snarky laugh. If Gloria noticed, she kept it to herself.

"I still need to refuel after my last jump . . . Do I smell something sweet?" TimeTrap asked.

"Alessandra, get TimeTrap a few scones and see what else we can feed her to get her mojo—or whatever—up to transference levels," Lucinda said.

"Oh, and I still have the banana in my bag. My phone had fallen out in the car during the accident and Roberto had found it, sweet thing that he is. Fortunately, the Sisters left the other essentials in here." Oracle heard rustling next to her with keys and other things jingling and shifting.

A plate slid onto the table. The scent of chocolate chip scones filled the air in front of her. She could almost taste the bittersweet treats.

"As much as this appears to be a semi-solid plan on hypothetical paper, I'm not getting the good feels from it," TimeTrap said between chews of what smelled like a banana.

"It's our only plan, since we have no idea where this mystery isle of X lies," Gloria said.

"I guess X doesn't mark the spot," TimeTrap said with a full mouth.

"We're not even sure if what I saw was legitimate. TimeTrap's right, this is a bad plan," Oracle argued.

"And a worse plan would be doing nothing while X does what she wants with Pax." Gloria tapped her arm.

Pricks of heated energy danced along Oracle's neck caused by fear or jealousy or both.

"And wait for her to attack a world leader with the Diosa de la Venganza? Or even hold a country hostage with the weapon she's keeping?" Lucinda said.

"We don't know her plans for certain. This is speculation," Reyes said in a weak defense of his sister.

"What use does she have for Suarez's high-tech island and cloaking ability? Why would an island sheltering women and children need a high-powered weapon?" Lucinda argued in a rational, calm tone.

"I'd rather not condemn her before I know for certain." Reyes's voice raised, his anger carrying it across the room.

"Don't let sisterly love cloud your vision," Lucinda admonished.

"Xalvadora wouldn't endanger people under her care," Reyes stated.

"Why not? What a fantastic cover to dissuade any attacks. No military wants the bad PR of destroying an island full of women and children. That's why your military let you call Pax in, to negotiate with Dama X first before invading the island. It's brilliant, really." Lucinda's nonchalant comment gave Oracle pause, as if this woman resented not thinking of it first.

Reyes excused himself to dress for the mission, his outrage at the group's judgment of his sister loud and clear in his heavy steps as he left the room.

"What is this weapon you keep alluding to?" Gloria asked the question that had been on Oracle's mind since they first mentioned it.

"If and when I'm cleared to discuss it with you, I will. I don't want to lose my biggest client by leaking classified secrets. You understand, don't you?"

"Did you design this weapon?" Gloria cut to the core of what Oracle suspected.

"Design it? No, it wasn't my creation. My team was studying it for my client before it was stolen from their facility by Dama X. Don't worry, it shouldn't hurt you."

"Shouldn't?" TimeTrap croaked.

"As long as it's kept on ice, everything will be fine."

Reyes returned, giving Lucinda an out to stop further inquiries about the weapon. She hustled everyone onto the back patio. The salty sea air blew across Oracle's face, but the sun's heat felt as oppressive as the vast space she sensed to her left where the land dropped off into the Pacific, thundering and crashing below them.

To focus on the task at hand and not the knots in her belly, Oracle counted over a hundred steps from the tiled patio to the turf helipad. Lucinda directed TimeTrap to sit between Oracle and Reyes. She smelled Alessandra's cologne as she bumped the back of Oracle's seat.

"Put this on," Alessandra said as a helicopter headset dropped into Oracle's lap.

She adjusted it to fit over her head and cover her ears and ensured the microphone was near her mouth. Once settled, she reached out her power and touched Gloria's mind, receiving an image flash of her boss strapping into the pilot's seat and Lucinda riding shotgun. The helicopter was wider and larger than Oracle expected for a private owner. Gloria turned in her seat and let her eyes trail over the large area behind Oracle that should've been the cargo space. Instead, she found furniture and a computer console and a narrow hallway leading to two doors, giving the appearance of a sailboat's interior cabin.

Within minutes of the propellers starting, the helicopter rose—teetering at first with some hesitation, enough that Reyes asked Gloria if she still wanted to do this.

"Roger that," Gloria's voice crackled over the headset. The chopper proceeded forward at a fast clip.

With Alessandra behind her unable to see her face or Reyes's, Oracle tried entering his mind to find out if she could trust him to help Pax. But her power was repelled as when she attempted to read Lucinda, who must've given him a crystal-filled vial as well. Oracle felt helpless, which led to anger, which led to her wanting to control the situation the best way she knew how.

Get answers. Verify it is Pax's eyes she's seeing through, his ears she is hearing through. She had to learn the truth herself. Test out her power. Learn her new limitations. If she knew without a doubt it was Pax and not some memory or dream or telepath feeding her this image, then maybe she could find out Dama X's plans. Listen through his ears. Was she as nefarious as Lucinda suggested? Or was Reyes right? Were they rushing to judgment? Oracle couldn't shake the feeling that she wasn't here to help with this mission, to be part of the team with Lucinda and Alessandra. She was being used for this mission. Would she be tossed aside once they were finished?

Oracle closed her eyes and retreated inside her mind until the helicopter's vibrations around her faded.

Pax, I need to know this is you.

Oracle was learning. She tapped into the power easier and without needing strong emotion to fuel it.

From a distance, she heard Reyes over the headset give pointers to Gloria, who insisted she had everything under control after the copter dropped along with Oracle's stomach.

She refocused.

Pax.

His name was a prayer from her heart to her mind. Centering herself, she pushed out her power, chanting his name until his eyes blinked open and then squinted against the bright room.

She concentrated. Poured herself into him.

Look around.

His head moved from side to side. Oracle felt the soft feather pillow as if her head rested on it.

From far away, Gloria shushed TimeTrap, who was asking Oracle what she was doing.

In the corner of the room, near the window, was a space large enough for TimeTrap and Reyes to transfer into without disturbing anything.

"Qué estás haciendo? Don't worry. You're safe here with Dama."

A smooth hand slid along the right side of his face and another on his left. She saw Pax's torso buck, but his body was numb. Oracle didn't know if it was the drugs or if she wasn't strong enough to feel all of him. But as the sheet dipped lower, she was relieved to see he was still all Pax.

And that meant Dama X saw him too.

"Oracle," Pax whispered out loud.

Fingers pressed into his temples. A heart-shaped face framed by curly dark hair filled his vision.

"Are you in there, chica?" she growled.

Oracle gasped and Pax did the same.

"Let's force her out, papi chulo."

A blast from a hurricane's winds would be less severe than the gust that knocked Oracle's spirit out. Pax's vision narrowed to a pinprick of light until the darkness consumed it. She felt the helicopter's seat under her bottom, and the straps securing her, and TimeTrap's hand at her right, rubbing her leg.

"I think Dama X is in Pax's head." Oracle spoke into the headset.

"But she can't affect transhumans," Reyes said.

"You were wrong."

And what else was he wrong about?

"You need to go," Lucinda ordered.

"It's just Pax and Dama X in a room, yes?" Reyes asked.

"If what I saw was real," Oracle replied, still finding it hard to believe that she could see so clearly from eyes that weren't near her.

"If you go now, there's a chance you'll catch them alone," Lucinda said. "You'll have the element of surprise. Secure the room, secure X, and Reyes can find the skull while you recoup. Hopefully, we can track your signal."

"We're within the range of the signal Alessandra picked up from her spy. I'd say it's safe to pop out here," Gloria said.

Oracle took TimeTrap's hand. She pushed the image of Dama X's room into the agent's mind.

"Got it." TimeTrap released her. "Give me your hands, Reyes, and don't let go."

With that, their scents—one of patchouli and antiseptic and the other of musk and gun oil—disappeared from the helicopter. They popped out, as TimeTrap liked to call it, and left Oracle in a helicopter, miles away from land, with three people she trusted less than that crazy Aztec god floating in her veins.

Chapter 13
I Must Be Dreaming

I didn't ask for any of this. No one in their right mind would.

—UltraAgent Surefire in a classified report to the DoD

Pax was a floating head detached from his body. At least, that's what he surmised in his high-as-a-balloon state where he couldn't feel anything below his neck. He tried not to think what that could mean.

He wriggled his head deeper into what felt like a fluffy feather pillow—a big difference from what he last woke to.

Pax.

He cracked open his eyes and squinted against the bright sunlight streaming in from a wall of windows to his left. It ricocheted around white-walls, making the room glow a warm yellow.

He wanted to close his eyes again, which ached in protest against the brightness. But he couldn't shut them. Invisible toothpicks held them open.

He was in a big bed covered in gray sheets, overlaid by a white comforter. He felt a familiar, soothing warmth envelop him, like a heated towel at a barber's shop. The same sensation of Oracle's power whenever she entered him. But when movement caught his eyes, he saw a petite, shapely woman walking around the bed, not Oracle's tall, dancer's body.

The not-Oracle woman leaned over him. Large green eyes with flecks of brown gazed at him from delicate features he was sure would break if he touched them.

A small, lovely hand traveled to the sheet at his waist and held it up.

"See, your body is all man."

Dama X? He opened his mouth to speak but couldn't make a sound.

A cold breeze drifted across his face and the warm sensation, he thought was Oracle, retreated and disappeared.

"Don't you worry. Your man Bruno is alive, even if he didn't choose correctly. He'll be picked up by the Armada de Mexico safe inside a disabled fishing vessel. His memory wiped."

Pax furrowed his brow and moved his lips, but his vocal chords refused to work.

"I'm not going to hurt you, Pax. I would never hurt you." Her accented words rolled off her tongue with authority.

"You are my salvador. Without you, this,"—she pulled away from him and flapped her hands toward the walls, the ceiling, the window—"would never have happened."

Pax tried to move his right arm to rub the sleep from his eyes. He managed to slide it across the bed but not lift it. He blinked to refocus the room. His eyes were drawn again to the wall to his right where images of women faded from one into another. Some were photographs, some paintings, others were images of statues.

"They're important women from history. Saviors and leaders to remind me of the high bar I've set for myself. Goddesses from across cultures who protected women and advanced society."

Pax opened his mouth again to speak but only managed a strangled breath.

"Here." She put a straw to his lips. He sucked in the cold, refreshing water.

"Don't worry, you won't change. I would never let an inch of you change." She dabbed the corners of his eyes with a tissue then sat on the bed to his left. "The injection was a ruse. A fake version of the serum. One we use to test the loyalties of men, the questionable ones, wanting to join our sisterhood. And you passed the test to save your female agent. I knew you would."

Pax tried to scoot away. He wasn't comfortable being naked around a stranger, unable to lift a finger in defense. Not a sexy fantasy, no matter how beautiful the woman.

Dama X laughed. "I won't take advantage of you in this state, you can trust me. That's not how we operate on the new Tamoanchan. We are building a better society here. One where people can feel safe to be themselves, pursue their own paths without conforming to roles a patriarchal society has laid out for them. I always wondered what the world would've been like if women had built governments and created the rules—and here we will find out. I consider it the greatest social experiment womankind has ever attempted."

She stood and smoothed her hands down the front of her black leggings. A V-neck purple T-shirt dipped low on her chest, revealing a stone pendant necklace. The black wing of a butterfly tattoo peeked out from between her breasts. Pax watched her walk across the room to the far corner, away from the windows. His blurry vision returned, making her look like a ghostly fog flitting around the room.

"In the Aztec world, Ometeotl, the creator god had both a female and male identity, as did many creator deities throughout many different cultures." A refrigerator door opened and closed. A lid from a can popped open.

"But over the millennia, men in power confiscated religion and mythos, rewriting the rules and tipping the balance to them. I plan to set the balance straight. Our goal isn't to hurt men. I love men. Their bodies"—she fluttered a blurry hand in his direction—"their spirits. But sometimes a woman needs her space to find herself without rules imposed by men in power that often only benefits their sex."

Pax tried once more to move his lips, find his voice. He wanted to ask her why the attack on men and changing them into women. What did she hope to accomplish? But the best that came out was a weak grunt.

"I didn't poison your victims with Diosa de la Venganza, if that's what you're trying to ask. Ah, there are many men I would relish doing it to. But I only used it once—the less-potent version—and that was enough." A drawer opened, silverware clanged together.

Less-potent version? There is more than one?

"I would love to transform those oppressors into women," she continued. "Those men who force women to endure second class treatment. Women who have no access to education and no rights while wearing stifling, oppressive clothing and being blamed for any ills that fall upon them. Oppressing these women make the men who are not in power feel powerful by having someone to control." Dama X carried a tray over to him and placed it on a stand next to the bed.

"Those men resent having been born from a woman. Resent they are only alive because a woman let it happen. We hold the power of life in our hands, in our wombs." She touched her stomach. "And they despise this power we possess over them, so they want to control everything else."

Dama X pressed a spoon to Pax's lips.

"This will help you heal," she explained when Pax turned his head and pressed his lips together.

"Ay dios mío, it's only pudding." She smeared it on his lips.

Vanilla pudding, cool and sweet seeped through his sealed lips. He swallowed, savoring how it coated his dry throat. His stomach growled. He relented and let her feed him the rest. He'd need his strength any way he could get it.

"I was married to one of those oppressors. A true pot-bellied chauvinist pig." Dama X pulled a face as if she'd tasted something sour. "So proud of his male superiority, he didn't see me coming. Most men like him underestimate women. Marrying him was a sacrifice I was willing to make. As Americans say, 'if you can't beat them, join them.' And now his money is used for good, supporting this haven for my Sisters, our Tamoanchan, which was safely off the radar until my Sisters brought you and that woman here."

"Ti-i-i . . ." was all Pax could say.

"She left." Dama X put the empty pudding cup on the tray with the spoon. "Now Felicia and Lucinda know where we are. So I need you to rest so you can help us defend our Tamoanchan."

"Who . . . who . . . ooo—" Pax tried to ask who Felicia and Lucinda were, but his lips wouldn't form the letters. He sounded like an owl with a stutter.

She held the straw to his lips again.

"I have the crystal skulls, and Lucinda can't get them. She will destroy the world if she does. "

Pax spit out the straw. "Whaaaa . . ."

This having no voice was bullshit. What was she talking about?

"Lucinda, who used to work for TransGen, who worked on you at ESP. She's seeking the skulls my Sisters and I have reclaimed. She specifically wants the skull I took from TransGen the day you almost caught me. Among other things that I reclaimed from her," she added softly.

Pax was delusional. The only explanation for having the transhuman leader of a drug cartel feed him vanilla pudding in bed, while going off about Lucinda Troy. A name he hadn't thought of until Jaybird mentioned her a few days ago.

That had to be it. This was why Lucinda's name popped into his insane dream.

"Lucinda only cares about power and changing the world as it fits into her narrow view."

That does sound like Lucy.

Dama X sucked in a breath. "She's taking a page from man's history. I only wish I saw it before I gave her so much control."

This was going on far too long. He needed to find out if this was a hallucination. Did he have the strength to pinch himself?

"And now Felicia is helping her, backed by the military and UltraSecurity," Dama X went on.

"Who?" Pax finally choked out. He wished he could reach the cold water set somewhere off to his side but he could no longer see, the room turning a darkish-gray.

"Who, you ask? Why, a traitor to my sex, who believed that becoming a man was the only way to survive in the world."

Dama X smoothed a hand along the top of his head. "Ah, I see our conversation has exhausted you. We'll talk more later. Once the drug is out of your system. Rest, mi amor."

She kissed his forehead. A blast of cool air followed, streaming along Pax's face. He drifted into a deep sleep, and hopefully into a peaceful dream that wasn't as weird and stressful as reality appeared to be.

He again woke up to a familiar, soothing warmth covering his head and chest. An electric blanket floating inches above him. He wanted to reach out and curl into it, but his limbs weren't listening.

Then the blanket whispered. *Pax, I need to know this is you.*

Pax moaned. His head thrashed to the side.

Pax.

The barest of whispers before the blanket hovering above wrapped around him tight enough to be a straitjacket.

His eyes opened then blinked against the light.

Look around.

The blanket melted through his skin, twisting up his throat and burying into his brain. He tried to form words but a gurgle came out instead.

His head jerked from one side to the other while he remained in the passenger seat, unable to take the wheel of his body.

Feet padded across the floor. A shadow crossed his line of sight as his eyes stared at the corner of the room.

"Qué estás haciendo? Don't worry. You're safe here with Dama."

Dama X's hands cupped his face. His back arched, driving his head into the pillow. He hazarded a glance down and saw his legs tangled in the sheets that had dipped well past his waist.

Pax's ears perked at a surprised intake of breath that didn't come from Dama X.

"Oracle," Pax whispered.

Fingers pressed into his temples. Dama X filled his vision.

"Are you in there, chica?" she growled.

Pax gasped at the pain shooting down his torso. Electric shocks lit up his nerves like a circuit board with a power surge.

"Let's force her out, papi chulo."

Cold wind blew over and into Pax's body. It wasn't from a vent, and Pax couldn't tell where it was emanating from with Dama X leaning over him, obscuring his vision and blocking his view of the room.

His breath hitched, taking in a bittersweet scent as the press of energy clouding his brain left a frosty gap in its wake. Pins and needles danced up and down his limbs as his nerves woke from their slumber.

Dama X stood at the side of the bed. A string of curses both in Spanish and English poured from her mouth.

"Lucinda, that puta! She did that to Oracle. She powered her up. Oracle couldn't do that before, could she, Pax?"

Pax shook his head. He wouldn't have believed it was Oracle prodding his brain had he not recognized her voice. Knew her power intimately after all those years she'd practiced on him. But this time was different. Stronger.

Dama X ran to a control panel on the far wall near the kitchenette. Six separate screens filled the right wall, replacing the female images with security camera footage of the island.

Pax wriggled his fingers and his toes. Okay, so that was progress.

"Magda, they're coming," Dama X spoke while staring at the live feed of the water surrounding the island. "Station someone at TimeTrap's room in case she transfers there. Be on alert. I want backup here as well."

Pax scooted to a sitting position. Almost there.

"You got it, Dama." Magda's reply filled the room from hidden speakers.

"I need your help." Dama X spun to face him. A cold blast of air streamed along his face and chest.

I'm sorry, Pax, but this is the only way.

Dama X didn't say the words out loud, but in his mind, as Oracle would speak to him when she didn't want others to hear. He wanted to look at Dama X. Demand what she meant. But then his torso twisted. His legs followed suit. His feet hit the floor and he stood.

And he didn't know how he did that.

He couldn't feel the floor under his feet or the temperature of the room. He was far inside his body with someone else steering the rig.

Pax concentrated on standing still, but his commands were overridden. In jerky steps, he made his way to the corner of the bed.

Then he came face to face with TimeTrap holding Reyes's hand.

"Ugh, Pax." Her eyes widened as she gazed down. "You want to cover that thing?"

Pax couldn't look down, couldn't respond.

"I knew Lucinda would send you to do her dirty work," Dama X sniped.

"Xalvadora, we need to talk." Reyes let go of TimeTrap's hand and held up his arms in a gesture of surrender.

"You had your chance to talk, Felicia," Dama X spat.

A cold current surged through Pax's arms, down his spine, and along his legs. In three steps, he was behind Reyes. One hand locked around Reyes's neck.

"Pax, stop!" TimeTrap knocked over a chair and flattened herself against the fridge.

It killed him to see his agent so afraid of him. But he couldn't control himself. He lifted Reyes by his neck and flattened his palm under his lower back. Hoisting the small man above his head, Pax turned and threw him through the window. Glass sprayed out. TimeTrap screamed. He looked out the opening to find Reyes hanging onto a palm tree on the side of the slope.

"I told you this was a bad idea," TimeTrap shrieked before she disappeared.

"Finish him," Dama X ordered.

Pax vaulted through the window.

Chapter 14
Expect You to Die

---

*I only want what's best for the human race—exponential evolution.
Unfortunately, I am the only one willing to try it.*

—Dr. Lucinda Troy in a note to Dr. Gloria Vivas before Troy left the United States

---

"I can't reach Pax. There's no response. It's like he's disconnected, offline." Oracle stopped herself from saying "dead."

She stretched and popped her back after sitting for what seemed like hours—but was only minutes—buckled in the helicopter's seat.

"The locator worked. Oliver sent the coordinates to my phone. It's about fifty miles west of our current location," Gloria's voice cracked over the headset.

"How are we going to land? I'm assuming Dama X won't be lighting up a helipad for us," Oracle said.

"That's not your job, therefore, not your concern," Lucinda returned. "I need you to concentrate on your task."

"Not my concern?" Oracle raised her brows. "Considering I am on this helicopter, which you are landing at a dangerous transhuman's compound, I believe it is my concern."

"Your concern is your job," Lucinda said simply.

"And what would that be?"

"Dama X might be blocking you from Pax, so I need you to focus on TimeTrap and get the lay of the land through her eyes."

"How?"

"Do what you did to find Pax."

"That was different. I don't even know how I did it. It's like there's a connection between us."

"It was stronger with Pax because of your feelings for him, but you can do it with anyone. I have faith in you."

Alessandra grabbed Oracle's shoulders from behind. She smelled the woman's cologne, felt the heat of a body alongside her own and a small shock, before a needle jabbed into her neck.

"Ow!" A slow burn flowed down her shoulder.

"What was that?" Gloria exclaimed as the helicopter listed to the side.

Oracle clutched her neck.

"But I have more faith in my serum," Lucinda continued. "You needed a boost, which Alessandra just administered. I upped the dosage Gloria gave you on the plane to help you concentrate."

Oracle pressed back into her seat. A hot gooey liquid spread out across the base of her neck, under her skin, and through her veins.

The injection must've contained ten espressos. Her arms and legs spasmed. Her torso bucked against the restraints. This spastic energy twitched inside her, eager to escape. Oracle feared it would tear her skin off, so she gave it a mission. She pictured TimeTrap. Concentrated on her given name, Kali. Thought about the UltraAgent's laugh, her voice, her ability. Oracle's energy flew past a blurry collage of images until she saw sunlight and heard screams and branches snapping as a naked Pax climbed down a hill toward a panicked TimeTrap and Reyes.

"Pax, stop!" Oracle screamed and TimeTrap followed suit. Pax paused with his hand on a large leaf. He blinked and shook his head and squinted at TimeTrap as if he saw through Kali's face to Oracle.

She pulled back into her own body where it was dark and vibrating and cold and loud, and she was still belted into a chair.

"Pax is about to . . ." She trailed off as she got her bearings.

"Pax is about to what?" Lucinda's voice cut over the static in the headset.

"How long was I out?" Oracle rotated her neck and it popped.

"About ten minutes. What did you see?" Lucinda asked.

"Pax is about to kill Reyes."

"That's not good," Lucinda said. "I hope we don't have to kill him. I know how much he means to you and Gloria, but if Dama X is possessing him . . . we may not have a choice."

Oracle's power shot out and careened into the person in front of her. Gloria.

The helicopter dipped. She received an image flash through a pair of dark sunglasses of a blue ocean and horizon line.

"What's wrong?" Lucinda asked. Gloria glanced at her. Oracle remained inside her boss's mind but pulled back before she took over completely.

"Nothing." Gloria gave a nonchalant wave of her hand. "Had an itch, that's all."

Lucinda nodded.

How are you in my mind? Gloria looked down at the vial hanging around her neck. Oracle received a memory flash of Lucinda handing a necklace to Gloria after they took off.

Lucinda's drug must've made me stronger.

I didn't know Lucinda was planning to inject you with that drug.

Even though Oracle knew Gloria told the truth, she responded, *I don't believe you.*

I knew Lucy was going to meet us at Reyes's place. I learned on the plane that she was involved in amping up your medicine, but that's all.

You should've told me everything. Been honest with me from the start.

I couldn't. TransGen's arrangement with Lucy's lab wasn't made public. I could've been sued. Besides, I needed your help. I was afraid if you knew the whole truth, you'd be too angry to even go. I needed Lucy to believe I was here to help her so I can save my father. I want her to trust me enough to tell me how she increased your power, so I can help you.

You can't trust her to tell you anything.

It was hard to argue with someone when they were open like a book. There was no way for Gloria to hide her emotions behind a blank expression when Oracle wasn't looking at her face but peering into her mind. But that didn't stop Oracle from being angry.

You had no right to not tell me on the plane.

I know.

Gloria's heart beat heavy with guilt.

Good.

Gloria adjusted the controls to stay in line with the coordinates. *Lucy hasn't been straight with me since we arrived. She's holding back. St. John won't like the idea of her having studied this supposed WMD.*

She recalled the locked area deep inside Gloria's mind and wondered if her boss kept other secrets hidden there. Was Oracle now strong enough to break into it?

Lucinda never told you her plans?

We each have a task. She doesn't want you or me to know everything in case Dama X gets into our minds.

Can't Dama X get into her mind if she removes that trinket?

Gloria shrugged. Lucinda gave her a suspicious side-eyed scan. Gloria played it off as rotating her shoulders. *Can you get inside Lucinda without her knowing?*

I can try.

With a deep inhale, Oracle sucked her power out of Gloria and back into herself. She shifted her target to Lucinda. Instead of launching her power at that woman, she practiced control. Inch by inch she eased out the energy, until she felt resistance. A plastic membrane wrapped around Lucinda. She pushed lightly then harder, picturing a safety pin puncturing a balloon.

Lucinda wriggled in her seat. Oracle felt Lucinda's arms resting on her thighs. She glanced at Oracle over her shoulder and she saw herself through the other woman's eyes. From behind dark glasses, Oracle stared forward at the back of Gloria's chair. She sensed Lucinda's suspicions, so she split her power, flowing part of it back into her form. She made herself yawn and crack her knuckles. That seemed to satisfy Lucinda, who went back to staring out at the bright horizon.

Then Lucinda's next thought sent Oracle fleeing into her body.

Oracle didn't realize she let out a loud gasp until Lucinda asked, "What is it?"

"Nothing, I was just . . ." Lucinda wasn't going to do what Oracle just saw. No, it wasn't possible. "Having trouble making contact again."

"We're almost there. It won't matter anymore."

Yes, it will.

Oracle's spirit blasted out of her body. Her power flew through the dark void until she sensed the body she sought and poured every ounce of her power into that vessel.

Chapter 15
Going Off Half-Cocked

How can we trust someone with the power to read minds or bend steel?
How do we know they have our country's best interest at heart?

—Former Senator Janet Donovan criticizing Alex Cross for his law office's defense
of transhuman suspects in a *Newsweek* interview

Pax stalked after his prey. Still holding onto the palm tree that broke his fall, Reyes shimmied down its trunk to the ground. He shook debris from his arms and pulled leaves from his hair. When he finally noticed Pax closing in, he jogged backward down the hill along a dirt path before turning to sprint.

Pax's feet sunk into the dirt. Roots cut into heels already sore from stepping on broken glass from the shattered window. Leaves and branches from tropical trees and bushes scraped along his stomach, chest, and groin. The cuts stung but not as badly as they should have, as if Dama X's energy included a numbing agent that covered his skin. He wanted to stop pursuing Reyes. He wanted to cover up his nakedness. But he struggled against Dama X's energy. For the first time since he could remember, he was powerless.

TimeTrap appeared in front of Reyes as he ran down the hill and cut through the foliage. He slid onto the ground to avoid colliding with her.

"Let's go." She grabbed Reyes's hand.

Pax's legs leapt over a small bush, bridging the distance.

I won't hurt them. Pax summoned all his will to push against Dama X's power. His legs slowed their pace.

TimeTrap helped Reyes to his feet, but instead of popping them away, she shoved him behind her and faced Pax.

A warm gush of air streamed across Pax's face. His feet stopped moving. Dama X's power wavered, enough for Pax to gain control and step a safe distance away from his agent and Reyes. He shoved a giant leaf in front of his exposed bits.

"Oracle?" Pax narrowed his gaze.

No, not Oracle. It was TimeTrap, who was changing into . . . Oracle?

TimeTrap's tall frame angled in front of Reyes's shorter one. Her long arms stuck out. One behind her to stop Reyes and the other in front to stop Pax. Her dark eyes grayed out. Her irises disappeared. The corners of her oval eyes transformed, dipping down like Oracle's. Her nose flared, forehead became more pronounced, cheekbones rose.

"Pax, stop!" she screamed.

He shook his head and the world came back to him. Like his ears had popped during a flight, allowing him to hear every sound with clarity. He took a deep breath, flexed his arms, stretched his back. He was in control again. Dama X's energy no longer filled out his limbs.

TimeTrap slumped against a small palm tree. She rubbed her temples. The vision of Oracle's face overlaid on hers flickered away.

"What was that?" She looked from Reyes to Pax.

Instead of answering her question, Reyes walked past her toward Pax, but his attention was focused beyond his pursuer when he shouted, "Xalvadora, you don't have to do this."

Despite having been thrown through the window and careening into a tree, Reyes only had a few cuts and walked up the hill toward Pax without so much as a limp or a wince.

Pax followed Reyes's gaze to where Dama X stood on the other side of the broken window in her room. A breeze kicked up and lifted her hair. She squinted against the sunlight that burned down upon Pax's shoulders.

"You come to my house without permission," she yelled down to him. "You force your way into my home. I see you're wearing a man's skin well, sister."

Sister? Pax spun back to Reyes. He was a slight man, but Pax would never have guessed he was transgendered.

"I'm here to protect you, not harm you," Reyes stated.

She laughed bitterly. "I don't need your protection."

Dama X spread out her arms. Along the top of the hill, a line of women stood with semi-automatics slung over their shoulders. Others with bows and arrows fitted with high-end scopes and lasers. Three of Dama X's guards with Day of the Dead faces, the Sisters who had administered the test to Pax, stood in front of the women and crossed their arms. The leader, Magda, grinned as her gaze dipped below Pax's waist.

He edged farther behind the leafy plant.

"You don't understand," Reyes pleaded.

"No, you don't. Not anymore."

Bring him to me. Dama X's words were a whisper in Pax's mind, but her power ripped through his muscles like a banshee's scream. His body strode down the hill. In three paces, Pax reached Reyes and gripped his shoulders. Reyes's arms shot in between their chests and swung outward, knocking Pax's hands off him. He kneed Pax in the stomach then slammed a fist into his jaw. The force whipped Pax sideways into the trunk of a palm tree, which splintered.

From above, Dama X screeched. Her power dulled the pain for him, but judging by her cries, she felt the hit. Maybe not the full force, but it affected her, because her power ebbed before streaming back into him. Pax struggled against the freezing energy, paddling frantically against the current that washed over him.

"Pax, fight her power!" TimeTrap crouched behind a small tree.

"Listen to her, Pax. I know you're in there. Don't be her pawn." Reyes bent his legs. Arms out to his side. Ready for Pax's next attack.

His body launched itself at Reyes. His arms wrapped around the man's small frame, and they rolled down the hill. Branches and leaves snapped and cracked underneath them. Pax took the brunt of the fall, landing with Reyes on top.

Pax squeezed him in a bear hug.

Reyes sputtered, "You're in danger."

There was a crack, possibly a rib. Pax wasn't sure. His arms loosened their grip as if Dama X had second thoughts.

Reyes flexed his arms and managed to pull free.

"Sorry, mi amigo." Reyes angled his lower body and thrust his knee into Pax's testicles.

Dama X retreated from the pain of Reyes's low blow. Pax's last meal shot up to his throat. He swallowed, trying not to vomit.

He shoved Reyes off and curled into a ball, cupping his hands over his privates. "Son of a bitch!" He slammed his fist into the ground.

Fingertips touched Pax's shoulder. He jerked against the heated sensation, hotter than the sun's rays.

Pax.

"Oracle?" He rolled onto his back and stared up at TimeTrap.

His agent nodded stiffly. Her dark eyes were wide open but someone else was home.

This time Pax didn't see the outline of Oracle's face, but the warm caress of energy belonged to his ex-girlfriend.

"How?" he asked.

Her mouth opened slightly. A strangled sound came out.

"What's going on?" Reyes crawled over to Pax. "What's happened to her?"

"Oracle has taken over her body," he replied.

Reyes looked out to the sea then back at Pax. "Where is she?"

TimeTrap squatted and cupped Pax's cheek, which twitched as a current traveled from her fingers into his brain, carrying her words along with it.

"She said they're in your helicopter a few minutes out." Branches snapped behind them. Without looking, he knew Dama X's guards were closing in.

"They won't land here. They'll do it a few miles out of range and then motor closer," Reyes said.

"Motor?"

"It's a prototype helicopter-boat my uncle's company developed with DERST. It has cloaking technology similar to this island, so we won't see it coming."

"Sure it does," Pax replied, too confused to be surprised.

Oracle continued on, talking nearly as fast as TimeTrap. It wasn't until Pax relayed the words out loud that he understood their meaning.

"Lucinda is going to take the island for herself. Move her company's research facility here. She plans to keep Dama X, her Sisters, and any transhumans on the island as test subjects—with or without their consent. Did you know about this, Reyes?"

"We had a deal. Dama X would be protected along with La Hermandad de Diana. Lucinda, aided by the Mexican military, would take over the island peacefully once we subdued my sister. They were to hurt no one. Only remove the weapon Dama X is harboring." Reyes held his head in his hand. "What have I done?"

"How is she going to do this?" Pax addressed Oracle out loud.

She has backup from one of her clients funding Circe. Couldn't get the name. But I'll find out. Stay safe. And please put some clothes on.

TimeTrap exhaled. Her head rolled back along with her eyes. Her hand dropped from his face.

"What the freak just happened?" TimeTrap shivered despite the intense heat.

"Oracle was inside you."

"That is a sentence I never thought I'd hear. Ever." She shook out her limbs and scrunched up her shoulders as if she'd touched something slimy. "Not that she isn't hot, but I don't get off on body possession."

TimeTrap's gaze trailed down Pax's stomach, her eyes widening the lower she looked.

"Here." She broke off a leaf as wide as her. "Make like Adam and fig it."

Dama X's three guards closed in, a weapon pointed at each of them. Still sensitive from Reyes's low blow, Pax remained doubled over, trying to will the discomfort away.

"I don't have enough mojo left to pop all of us out," TimeTrap whispered.

"You leave, Pax gets shot. Your choice." Magda aimed her gun at him.

"I'll stay." She raised her hands.

"Good choice. It would be a waste to put a hole in such a body." Her eyes flicked to Pax, pressing the leaf between his legs.

"Don't know about all that, but he's the one who signs my checks so I prefer him alive." TimeTrap gave a jittery laugh that stopped when she saw Pax's expression, "I say stupid things when I'm nervous."

"I got that." Pax rose to his feet with one hand up, the other grasping the leaf over his nether region—not that modesty mattered since he had been on full display for the Sisterhood during his fight, but it made him feel vulnerable without it. He stepped back when Dama X strode into the semicircle. He wondered if he could take her out before she controlled him again or one of the guards put a bullet in his head. Then again, the guards had increased strength as well. With Reyes's help, he could take them, but Pax feared TimeTrap may get caught up in the fight.

Reyes put up his hands. "Xalvadora, you don't have to do this."

"Sí, tengo que hacerlo." Dama X's purple tennis shoes sunk into the dirt as she pivoted and waved her hand. The island rumbled under their feet.

Several large squares slid open on the side of the hill near the apex. Mounted laser cannons rose from the holes aimed out to sea.

"Uncle thought of everything, no?" Dama X put her hands on her hips.

"He was a paranoid genius but a genius nonetheless." Reyes rose to his feet.

Pax took in the cannons. "Your uncle needed this much protection?"

"More." Dama X smiled.

The cannons blinked out and faded away. The island shimmered and disappeared from under their feet, and they seemed to float in the air above the churning water below. But the dirt and roots still cut into the soles of Pax's feet. The leaves and branches brushed his legs and torso.

Pax's mind raced with possible escape plans. But it was a futile exercise. The cannons, invisibility cloak, and transhuman soldiers flipped the entire board in La Hermandad de Diana's favor.

"You're in danger, Xalvadora. Lucinda will use you for her own means if you don't leave now," Reyes said.

"Psh. She can try." She batted her hand. "I heard everything, mi hermana. A small part of me remained in Pax's mind when Oracle told him."

Pax clenched his fist, wondering if she was still reading his mind. And if so, how would he know? How could he stop her?

Dama X tilted her head. "Do you think I'm as dangerous as they say?"

"Yes," Pax replied before Reyes could.

She quirked a brow at him.

"No one wants to be possessed. Unable to control their own body. Forced to do someone else's dirty work. So, yeah, you're dangerous." Pax set his jaw, waiting for a blast of cold power to enter him again. Instead, she sucked in her bottom lip and bowed her head.

"I'm sorry I used you. But it had to be done. I will do whatever it takes to protect our home and La Hermandad de Diana."

He hadn't expected an apology—a sincere one at that—and wasn't sure how to reply.

As Pax considered her words, Reyes said, "Then why attack those people with Diosa de la Venganza? How does that protect the Sisterhood? Why steal a powerful weapon from Circe's client?"

"Mentiras," Dama X spat.

"Then it is a lie that you are housing a weapon of mass destruction?" Reyes folded his arms.

"Do you even know what the weapon is?" Dama X squared her shoulders.

"What weapon?" Pax asked. "I thought we were here for the skull she'd stolen."

"A weapon Lucinda's team was studying was taken last night from Mexico's military defense facility. I don't have clearance for the Top Secret details, but my sources confirmed it is indeed as hazardous as she has described." Reyes stepped closer to Dama X. "You don't dispute that you have it?"

"I don't dispute it." She stood her ground.

"Then you are as dangerous as Lucinda said." Reyes shook his head in disappointment.

"Why would you steal this weapon?" Pax asked.

"I'll show you why." Dama X nodded to Magda and Kristina, who flanked Pax, TimeTrap, and Reyes. The other guard, Pax hadn't yet heard her name, trailed behind them.

Dama X led them up the invisible hill to the broken window of her room, which floated above them.

"Replace this window," Dama X ordered several women standing above them on the edge. A shard of glass pricked Pax's heels. He stopped to pull it out.

"Magda, have Andrea bring Pax's jeans and shoes to my room." Dama X waited for Pax as he struggled to balance on one foot while holding the fig leaf in place.

"Andrea washed your jeans and underwear. Unfortunately, your shirt . . ." Magda's lips twitched as her gaze wandered over his chest and shoulders. "Was destroyed and you're a bit wider than the men currently living here."

Pax blushed and pretended to inspect his foot, trying to avoid her pointed appraisal.

"No need to be ashamed. I respect men of your stature. You gave me a good tussle. I like it when a man can take what I dish out." Magda slapped his arm before jogging ahead of them to carry out Dama X's orders.

They climbed back through the broken window and into Dama X's chambers, where she led them through a set of doors and into a meeting space with a glass wall that overlooked the valley below. Pax watched the frenetic activity of a base prepping for battle.

"Who are you expecting to fight? The Galactic Empire?" TimeTrap exclaimed.

"I only wish," Dama X replied.

Chapter 16
Knowing Who to Trust

———————————

I'm not ashamed or embarrassed to tell you my sister is a transhuman. I'm proud to say that she's an UltraAgent. She's used her ability to save our city, our state, our nation from countless threats.

—Alex Cross during his campaign fundraising dinner

———————————

The helicopter bobbed. Water splashed against the window where Oracle's head rested, jolting her awake. She rubbed the back of her neck. Her headset pressed down and irritated her scalp. She slid it off and let it drop to the floor.

"Hello," Oracle called out.

Waves slapped against the metal hull. But otherwise, the cockpit was silent.

She leaned forward to run her hands over the pilot's seat in front of her.

Empty.

Had they crashed? If so, where was everyone? The rocking continued followed by a harder spray of water hitting the sides.

"Hello," she called out again.

Nothing.

Frantic, she unfastened her seatbelt and climbed over the passenger seats next to her where TimeTrap and Reyes had been sitting.

She felt along the interior. Smooth and warm. A glass window heated by the sun.

She lowered her hands until she came across a ridge between the window and the metal support. There had to be a latch. But should she open it? Would she spill out into the ocean or flood the compartment?

She perched on the seat's arm. Sweat moistened her forehead and a few drops trickled between her breasts. Oracle heard no whirring of an engine, which meant the controls were off. And with the controls off there was no air circulating inside. No wonder the cabin was as hot as a sauna.

Oracle climbed into the front. Could she tell what controlled what? Did they have Braille underneath the switches?

Don't be ridiculous.

She could send out her power to search for them, for anyone. Her head throbbed in protest to this idea. She sniffed and then rubbed a finger under her nose when it started to run.

The side door unlatched with a loud snap then creaked open. Oracle gulped at the fresh humid air.

"It's not a good idea for a blind person to touch the controls," Gloria said.

"Where are we?" Oracle ignored her playful tone.

"We're floating in the Pacific less than a mile away from Dama X's island. The helicopter transformed into a boat just before we landed. Definitely a bucket list item I didn't realize I wanted to experience. We have a shield up, as well as a radar blocker, which is one reason I didn't want you to touch anything. If they see us, they'll use their lasers to burn us out of the water."

"I saw their cannons."

"You were in Pax's head again?"

"TimeTrap's." Oracle threaded her way over the midsection controls to the front passenger seat. She slid across the seat to the exit.

"Your nose is bleeding. Pinch it and lean forward. Don't want the blood going to your stomach."

Oracle felt her nose again. It wasn't mucus but blood. She licked her top lip, tasted iron.

"Here." Gloria dabbed her nose with a tissue. She placed her hand behind Oracle's head while the other pinched the cloth over her nose and forced her to bend over.

"How long was I out?" Oracle asked.

"Not long. But I'm concerned that you pushed too hard this time. Have you experienced a nose bleed before?"

"Not since my power first manifested."

"Did you do anything different this time?"

Oracle replayed how she fully possessed TimeTrap to touch Pax. She remembered pushing through a membrane of invisible cold jelly when she touched Pax's shoulder. Then she summoned her last bit of energy to force a warning into his mind.

Oracle didn't know if Lucinda or Alessandra were listening. She didn't want that crazy woman to know what she knew about her plans.

"Dama X was using Pax to attack Reyes. I stopped him. Maybe it hurt me to do that."

Gloria took the tissue from her hand. "Looks like it stopped bleeding. I think you need to relax. No more using your ability until we know why this occurred."

And if there's any damage. Gloria left that bit unspoken but her worried tone conveyed it.

"Can you stand? There's a platform outside the door. You have a half-foot step down." Gloria reached to help her up and onto the platform.

Oracle lifted her face to the sun. Inhaled the salty air. Water hit the platform sending a light spray onto her face. She reached for the door when the deck pitched from the choppy ocean.

"It disappeared," Alessandra spoke from their right.

"Except for that floating rectangle," Lucinda noted. "Looks like it's a broken window . . . now it's gone."

"They must know we're out here," Alessandra said.

A large hand wrapped around Oracle's bicep and yanked her from the cabin's entrance. She tripped at the sudden jolt before regaining her balance on the metal deck.

Water lapped to her right. Softly at first, then a louder splash that sent up a spray wetting the side of her body.

"Easy now." Gloria's shoulder hit against Oracle's arm, the one not losing feeling from fingers squeezing her bicep. A static current pricked along the right side of her body.

"Why would you tell her?" Alessandra shook her. Fingers dug deeper. Oracle refused to flinch no matter how much the electric zaps of energy burned.

"Because I know what both of you are doing," Oracle confessed.

"Gloria?" Lucinda demanded.

"I have no idea what any of you are talking about," Gloria replied.

"I saw into your mind. Past your little crystal thanks to the booster shot you gave me." Oracle couldn't help but gloat at the irony of Lucinda's serum working against her.

"And what did my mind reveal to you?" Lucinda's words were calm, controlled but Oracle heard past her contrived tone.

"You want this island for yourself. And you'll do whatever it takes to get it. Lucinda wants every transhuman on that island, including our agents, for her sick experiments."

"The Isle of Dr. Lucinda? Does have a nice ring to it," Lucinda singsonged.

"Is this true?" Gloria asked.

"It's situated in international waters. Has its own power source. It's hidden from any detection. It has a state-of-the-art laboratory that Dama X has no use for," Lucinda replied.

"Is the *other* part true?" Gloria clarified.

"Dama X is dangerous. We need to understand how her power works to defend ourselves."

"From transhumans?" Oracle had a sense of déjà vu. She'd heard this same argument from politicians and Surefire's father.

"From those who do not have the world's best interests in mind." Lucinda continued to patronize Oracle as if she had no clue how the world worked. "Dama X doesn't care about any of us. Why would she threaten the security of mankind by stealing a weapon that could potentially cause mass destruction? Why would she need it, if her goals were peaceful?"

"What do you plan to do with this island?" Gloria asked.

"What do you think, Glor? What we always talked about. Total freedom and autonomy to practice without oversight."

"That was a drunken fantasy when we were in med school. I wasn't serious," Gloria said.

"And here I thought my old partner in crime would be the one person who would understand."

Alessandra's hand loosened around Oracle's bicep. She tugged her arm away and stepped toward the sound of Gloria's voice.

"Oh, I understand all right. And who in the hell is going to fund your secret lair?" Gloria challenged.

The deck lifted at a steep angle. Oracle widened her stance to keep her balance. To her right, she heard the deafening rumble of an engine. A loud splash was followed by copious amounts of water pouring off an object. The sun's heat no longer warmed her face. Something blocked its rays, putting her in the shade.

"You've got to be kidding me." Gloria's fingers touched Oracle's, and she received an image flash of a submarine dwarfing their helicopter-boat where the four of them stood on deck. A series of numbers and the name Leviathan IV were painted on the sub's side near the nose.

The hatch opened and three men climbed out. They wore black uniforms and black berets with silver insignias Oracle couldn't make out and didn't recognize as belonging to a U.S. military branch. Then Stephen St. John—UltraAgent Surefire's father and head of a special DoD transhuman committee, U-Sec's main client—ascended to the deck. He walked stiffly to the railing, his back straight under his starched black shirt pinned with a hodgepodge of medals. From behind mirrored sunglasses, he surveyed them.

"Do we have eyes on Surefire?" St. John yelled to them.

Oracle's stomach clenched at the mention of their agent.

What is he talking about? She sent the question into Gloria's mind.

"Oh my God," Gloria whispered. "Our Surefire can't be the—"

"The weapon hasn't been located yet, sir. From what we can tell, Dama X hasn't activated the asset," Lucinda shouted to him.

"I'll ready my team," he replied.

♥ ☠ ♥ ☠ ♥ ☠

The interior hallway ran deep inside the island's hill. Stainless steel railings lined either side in front of glass walls that showed office spaces and labs. Some lit up with busy lab techs, IT crews working on servers, and classrooms filled with female students. Most rooms were dark and empty. Large HVAC pipes ran along the ceiling above them. The fluorescent lighting and cold, stark surroundings of these interior corridors contrasted with the lush tropical foliage growing on the outside of the structure.

"Where are you taking us?" The cold metal tip of an AK-47 jabbed into Pax's rear either to make him walk faster or out of annoyance over the question he, Reyes, and TimeTrap had repeated since they left the hillside and climbed inside the structure.

"A surprise." Dama X passed her hand over a control panel.

"Did you think her answer would be any different from the other times it was asked?" Magda butted him again with the gun.

"Worth a try." Pax shrugged.

Magda and Kristina shared a conspiratorial chuckle behind him. The third guard, Penny—he'd finally heard her name—stood at his side and shook her head at the two women.

A door slid open to reveal a circular elevator. They filed in, the door closed, and the compartment and Pax's stomach dropped. He grabbed the railing, TimeTrap let out a "whoa," and Reyes pressed back against the wall.

Dama X and the Sisters laughed at them.

"At thirty meters per second, it's like that ride we rode in Vegas when we were children," Dama X said. "I believe you were sick after, or was it during?"

Pax glanced at Reyes, who had turned a shade of green.

The elevator slowed to a stop and they were led into another hallway—wider and colder. Goosebumps broke out along Pax's exposed torso. At least he had his jeans and shoes back on. He'd never been so grateful for clothing.

"This isn't a video screen," TimeTrap said in awe.

The elevator had taken them into a structure below the surface, inside what looked like a caldera. How many feet, Pax couldn't tell. The lights from the corridor shown through the floor-to-ceiling windows that bowed out from the walkway. They lit up the sea outside where fish and an occasional squid swam along the rocky wall surrounding them. Every twenty feet or so, angled steel beams anchored to the caldera rose out of view. Based on their angle, he assumed they attached to the island somewhere above his head.

"How was the island moving earlier if it's anchored to the caldera?" Pax ran his hands along the railing, unable to take his eyes off the engineering feat outside the windows.

"Two separate structures. The island above is essentially a large ship. It detaches and reattaches from the caldera, which serves as its dock. You're walking inside a funnel-shaped building that is affixed to the caldera's walls surrounding us."

"I didn't know about this island lab until after the funeral when my uncle's lawyers read the will. I later found the schematics and contracts on his hard drive. I can't believe he kept this a secret," Reyes said.

"Not from me. A change of heart, maybe? Facing death will have that effect," Dama X said, and Pax turned to see Reyes's reaction.

"He did resign himself to certain truths about the world before he died." Reyes stared at a turtle swimming by.

They stopped when they reached a glass door leading to the lab they had been circling.

"And one of those truths included his distrust in the society that *men* created," Dama X added. "He thought maybe I could do better once he heard my plans."

The doors slid open to a lab containing two cryochambers like the ones in which Dr. Vivas and Andrew Cook had been placed at TransGen.

Once inside the room, Dama X moved to the side. She swung out her arm to indicate they should walk ahead of her. Pax halted when the idea of Dama X leading them to cryochambers sunk into his thick skull. TimeTrap and Reyes followed his lead and stopped as well. Judging by the worry cinching their faces, they had the same concern as Pax. Were those chambers to house them? If so, then there were only two chambers and three of them.

Pax noted where each person stood in the room. Reyes and TimeTrap at his back. Dama X a foot to his left. The three guards spread out behind them blocking the exit.

A woman with dark skin creased with age and a halo of gray hair looked up from her laptop on the far side of the room. A few strands of hair escaped from her bun and fell over her forehead. She was so small, Pax didn't see her until she lifted her head.

"I didn't realize it was time." She pushed back from the desk and walked over to the two chambers.

"I don't want to become a human popsicle," TimeTrap whispered to him.

"We won't." At five, six, and eight o'clock, the guards remained at their posts. Dama X, he needed to take out first. Knock her out quickly before he could deal with the others. His eyes met Reyes's gaze. He nodded as if he'd read Pax's thoughts.

"Thank you for accommodating us, Dr. Banerji."

Banerji? Why did that name sound familiar?

"Never a problem for you, my dear. I'm reconditioning them now. Doing a slow thaw. They may be disoriented at first," the doctor responded.

Pax studied the chambers but couldn't see what or who was in them. He'd assumed they were empty.

"They?" he asked.

"UltraAgent Surefire and Raven, who else would it be?" Dama X asked incredulously.

He stalked past Dama X. TimeTrap followed close behind and laid her hand on his shoulder. "Pax, what is she talking about? I spoke with Surefire two months . . . ago . . . oh, shit."

"Language, missy," Dr. Banerji admonished.

Pax had the same thought as his agent, which he didn't voice. The glass chamber became increasingly clearer as it thawed to reveal Surefire. Blond hair longer than when he'd last seen her. Eyes closed. Lips a pale blue. Fair skin the eerie color of the walking dead. His eyes dipped down to find her breasts bare. He turned away.

"Who did this to her . . . ?" Pax pivoted toward the second chamber and found Raven, frost melting from his black hair, tattoos standing out against his ashy skin. ". . . to them?"

His hand fisted and unfisted, wanting to smash the glass, get them out, and take them far away from here. Then he was going to deal with Dama X.

"I didn't put them in cryo. Lucinda did. Dr. Banerji and I saved them from her." Dama X crossed her arms and met and held Pax's glare.

"What did she want with them?" In horror, Reyes gazed down at Surefire while he rubbed his hand along her chamber.

"You weren't privy to her plans, Felicia? After she used you to gain access to your military contacts?" Dama X cocked her head.

"I would never have allowed this to happen. She told me you—"

"She told you I was a terrorist, plotting to execute men. Turn them into women. And you believed her—rather than asking me, your own flesh and blood."

"You stopped talking to me."

"To Felix, yes."

"I have always been Felix even if my body didn't match who I was on the inside."

"You became Felix because it's easier to be a man than a woman in this world, and it worked. No woman would've risen to your position in our military."

"That isn't why."

Pax put his hands out between them. "Can we have this family chat later? My agent and her . . ." *boyfriend?* ". . . partner . . . are about to be thawed out, and I have no idea why or how they got here."

"Lucinda tricked her. Said she would help her. Captured them both to study their powers. Raven doesn't even have a normal heartbeat. He shouldn't be alive. In fact, when they were too far apart, he started to die so we had to keep them in the same room," Dr. Banerji explained.

Pax hung his head, fighting back the nausea pooling in his gut. This was what Surefire was trying to avoid. Why she'd gone into hiding because she believed the government—or a terrorist group or someone worse—would want to weaponize her. Pax blew it off as paranoia.

If he would've believed her, she wouldn't be in this predicament.

"Don't worry your big heart." Dr. Banerji patted her small hand against his chest. "This girl will be fine. Plus, she's surrounded by people she knows, which will be a big help since I have no idea how she's going to react when she wakes up."

"What do you mean?" TimeTrap's eyes darted from one chamber to the other before landing on the doctor.

"Usually, a person coming out of cryo will flail and kick whatever is nearby when they wake, especially in strange surroundings. We usually have to sedate them. But this one, with the power of a goddess, who knows?" Dr. Banerji made a mini-explosion sound and mimed it with her hands.

The doctor laughed. The others didn't.

Chapter 17
Someone Usually Dies

I don't trust anyone, especially someone with special abilities. You never know when it will go to their heads.

—Stephen St. John during a phone call with Pax on why he insisted on monitoring U-Sec agents

---

Oracle's anger flared. She had been Surefire's mentor, responsible for the UltraAgent as if Surefire were her own flesh and blood. Was this the secret Gloria kept stowed away in her mind where Oracle couldn't reach? If only she had pressed further into Lucinda while they were flying in the helicopter when her power was at its height, then she might've seen this coming.

"Dama X has Surefire? Gloria, did you know about this?" Oracle's word shook with outrage she couldn't hide.

"No, I didn't. I thought we were talking about the skulls and their potential for weaponization—not our Surefire."

Gloria tried to wrench her hand from Oracle's but she wasn't letting go. Her power flooded Gloria's mind, forcing it to replay every conversation with Lucinda, fast forwarding through them like a bad movie.

But Gloria told the truth. She didn't know any more than she'd revealed and hadn't seen Surefire since July 1st, when she ran blood work on her. Surefire was supposed to return for a follow up two weeks ago but never showed.

Oracle hadn't spoken with Surefire since the UltraAgent stopped by Oracle's apartment after she became a vessel for the goddess, Xochiquetzal. She'd never forgive herself for letting Surefire down. Oracle's power had failed her when the agent needed her. She couldn't save Surefire from that fate, and now Dama X had her.

"How did Dama X get her?" Oracle spoke through her own lips but forced Gloria to face Lucinda so she could gauge her reaction.

"Dama X stole Surefire from my client's secure research facility where I assumed she'd be safe." Lucinda stared into Gloria's eyes, her face impassive. "Surefire came to me seeking help. She wanted more information about her condition. She'd read my transhuman theories related to the Enhanced Soldier Program that Gloria and I had worked on with St. John's team. She tracked me down when she learned that I'd been studying the properties of the crystal skulls and a possible connection to transhumans. She thought I could provide her with answers regarding her condition."

"And did you?" Gloria focused on Lucinda's hazel eyes, one slightly larger than the other.

"Her power was out of control. I had to contain her and Raven in a cryo state for their own safety and ours."

Liar! The accusation popped into Gloria's mind at the same time she dove at Lucinda. Oracle's body jerked forward as Gloria tugged her along.

"You're lying." Gloria stopped inches from Lucinda's face. "I can tell. Your left eye squints ever so slightly when you're bluffing, just like you did when we played poker."

"Ridiculous." Lucinda rubbed at her left eye.

"Step back." Alessandra yanked on Gloria's shoulder. A static shock shot across Gloria's back. Oracle winced but kept hold of her boss's hand.

"What are you doing with her, St. John? Why didn't you tell us about Surefire?" Gloria yelled at him.

He didn't acknowledge Gloria's question. Instead, he crossed his arms and said, "Have you received further Intel, Dr. Troy?"

"Both transhumans are being kept in a secure area ten stories under the water. It has a lab capable of housing two cryochambers," Lucinda replied.

"You were able to confirm this?" St. John asked over the water lapping between both vessels.

"Alessandra worked on the team that drafted the original designs with Suarez. If he hadn't changed anything since she left, then there are four labs that could support the cryochambers. They're located in the underwater lab connected to a caldera, upon which the island-ship has docked. TimeTrap's locator indicated they are on the tenth floor below the surface," Lucinda explained.

"And we'll get in, how?" The sun glinted off St. John's mirrored sunglasses.

"There's a hatch with an airlock twenty feet under the water. It's several levels above the one holding the chambers. Once inside, we can disable the island's security and take the stairs to the cryo room. We'll open this airlock with Alessandra's help."

"And how will she do that?" Gloria interjected.

"We each have our task," Lucinda answered.

Oracle frowned at her cryptic response.

"Reyes will secure the room before we get there. Once we have the all-clear, you can send the rest of your soldiers through the airlock. Alessandra will cut the power and security streams. With most guards stationed on the topside of the island, we shouldn't run into any interference we can't handle."

"Two of my men are going with you. Keep an open comm link. If I don't hear from your team within thirty, we do it my way."

"And how would that be?" Oracle shouted.

St. John turned on his heel.

"But your daughter . . . Surefire . . . and children are on that island," Oracle screamed, not checking her anger but letting it infuse each word.

St. John kept walking.

"No, you don't." Oracle channeled her power into the back of his head as he headed for the hatch.

Through his eyes, Oracle saw the metal door. The two soldiers next to him. And . . . nothing. His mind was an empty stage.

"Get out of him." Alessandra pressed a finger to her temple. A zap of electricity followed. Stars exploded in her vision, killing the connection with St. John.

Oracle pulled her power back into her body and released Gloria's hand.

"I sensed it this time. Keep it in your head." Her finger fell away.

"He can't be trusted."

"None of us can. Especially telepaths like you." Alessandra bumped hard into Oracle's shoulder as she walked past.

"Suit up, ladies," Lucinda announced.

"For what?" Gloria squawked.

"We're going diving. It's the best way in."

"I haven't been diving since I was thirteen . . . and could see," Oracle added the latter to herself.

"At least you've been diving," Gloria said.

"We're not going too deep. Alessandra has special breathing apparatuses for us. Otherwise, it's sink or swim, Gloria. What will it be?" Lucinda taunted.

"I'd rather see you sink, Lucinda. I should've guessed St. John was your biggest client. His DoD committee members were there when TransGen signed the contract with Circe. They used TransGen as a front to work with you and your company, didn't they?"

"I don't understand how St. John can support you in this." Oracle shook her head.

"He wants his daughter, this weapon, in hands he believes he can control. He wants a transgeneticist who is familiar with this type of power and understands the skulls' makeup. So he made a deal. Just like you have no choice but to work with me to help those you care about."

"He knew about Surefire and Raven being kept at your client's facility. He funded your research, didn't he?" When Lucinda didn't respond to Gloria's accusation, she said louder, "Didn't he?"

A helicopter door opened and hard flats clacked against the floor inside as Lucinda walked away from them.

"Move." Alessandra shoved Oracle and Gloria forward.

Moments later, Oracle was stripping down to her underwear in the cargo space of the helicopter. After a few tries, she managed to pull up the wetsuit Alessandra had provided. She sent out her psychic feelers, but either she was weaker or Lucinda anticipated her invasion because she hit a solid wall. Her energy bounced back. She tried with Alessandra and received resistance as well. She was afraid to force her power and expend more energy. What if the power booster was wearing off? Besides, Alessandra didn't shy away from whipping her electric fingers when threatened. If she knew Oracle was inside her, then she wouldn't hesitate to retaliate.

Oracle heard two men speaking from the deck as they reviewed old schematics of the underwater lab Reyes had found on his uncle's hard drive. They were soldiers whom St. John had issued to escort them to the airlock.

"Are you good with this?" Gloria's shoulder brushed Oracle's bicep.

"No." She shook her head before stretching the wetsuit's hood into place.

"Me neither."

Oracle considered the soldiers talking strategy. Could she get inside their heads, control them, and overtake Lucinda and Alessandra? It was an option. But not here with the submarine at their side and St. John watching over them.

"Are you still angry with me?" Gloria asked.

"Yes, but that's irrelevant at this second."

"I need you to trust me."

"I trust you more than those four out there and St. John."

"That'll have to do." Gloria pressed a diving mask into Oracle's chest.

She adjusted it over her face. The rubber created a seal around her eyes and nose. She took several deep breaths through her mouth, prepping herself for what she was about to do.

Gloria led her outside to the deck where the four conspirators waited.

"Are you ready?" Alessandra's feet padded across the deck to them.

Oracle nodded.

"Excellent." Fingers dug into Oracle's left forearm. Instinctively, she tugged back but couldn't pull free before a metal cuff wrapped around her wrist with a click.

"What are you . . . ? Get off!" Gloria shouted. Feet scuffed against the deck, which vibrated under Oracle with the struggle. Gloria banged into her and she toppled over, catching herself before she hit the deck.

Oracle's left arm was jerked up and she heard another click. Alessandra had handcuffed her to Gloria.

"You need to lead Oracle through the water. I thought the handcuffs would make it easier," Alessandra said. Based on her chiding tone, Oracle surmised she enjoyed this.

"I always wanted to try synchronized swimming. How about you?"

Oracle ignored Gloria's attempt to lighten the mood but couldn't ignore her panicked thoughts about swimming blind in waters she didn't know, and with a guide who a crossroads demon wouldn't strike a deal with.

Her only solace was that diving into unknown waters was worth getting her closer to Pax and out of this situation—before St. John did it his way.

She shivered, recalling the void she encountered in St. John's mind.

"Oracle and Gloria, these men are Sergeants Smith and Jones, who will be escorting us," Lucinda said.

Neither men shook their hands or offered a greeting. Smith launched into their next steps, "Sergeant Jones and Lucinda will lead. Alessandra and I will take up the rear. We each will get an underwater scooter with Gloria and Oracle sharing. Keep up. We've triangulated the location accounting for any drift on our end, so conserve your oxygen."

"What about tanks?" Gloria asked.

"No tanks. Breathing vials. They'll last sixty minutes."

Gloria turned over Oracle's hand and pressed a small metal cylinder into her palm. On one side was an opening with a piece that fit inside her mouth. Oracle tested it out. Then they lowered themselves into the cool water off the back of the vessel.

Gloria took her ungloved hand and guided it to the propulsion device. They gripped it together with Gloria touching her skin, allowing Oracle to see through her eyes. Once everyone was submerged, they headed out. Slowly they started diving downward, the hum of the submarine and the pressure of the water increasing. A school of fish parted to let them by. Below, the ocean dropped into a dark oblivion.

Soon, something rose from the darkness. Oracle sensed its mass before it came into view. A wall, covered in rock and coral and aquatic plants. But no, it wasn't a wall; it was the side of a caldera. Gloria's eyes tracked the metal beams that stuck out of the surface to connect the fabricated island with the sleeping volcano below. They glided along the surface to a cave-like entrance.

Lucinda and Jones swam through the opening and Gloria and Oracle followed.

Wow. Gloria's eyes scanned the glass structure that funneled down like an icicle hanging from an awning, sparkling in the winter sun. It cut through the darkness below, but Oracle couldn't see where it ended. Walkways circled the structure inside and reminded her of a layered popsicle. One, then two shadows flickered past on a lower walkway, but otherwise the floors appeared empty of life.

Pax. Oracle let his name vibrate through her thoughts. She shook in her suit down to her toes covered by dive boots and flippers. Her knuckles and fingers ached from the cold water. She opted to hold Gloria's hand to conserve the extra energy it would take to see through her eyes without touching.

Levi.

She whispered his first name, his given name, not the nickname that everyone else called him. One she only said when they were intimate.

Pain rose in her groin area. Sore legs, feet, and back. Next, she received an image flash of a lab. Of Surefire in a cryochamber. Her skin pale. Her eyes fluttering open. Oracle jerked at the panic twisting in her gut.

Cassandra.

Pax said her name. He felt her. Knew she was there. She could smell his salty skin. Feel it itching from a sunburn.

We're coming. She pushed the words across the distance.

Don't. It's not safe. His eyes flicked up to two women flanking the doorway with guns.

We have backup.

You don't have the backup you need. Pax's gaze landed on Surefire again, and this time Oracle noticed two IVs sticking in her arm connected to bags hanging on the outside of the chamber, either collecting or giving her blood.

Go! He shoved her out. She snapped back into her own skin. The jarring forced pulled her hand free from Gloria's, but the chain kept her from floating away.

Gloria grabbed her hand again. The darkness cleared. She watched Alessandra swim up to an airlock—a glass box jutting from one of the floors. In the side facing them, a rectangular shape—a door to the airlock?—had been cut into the glass.

What did you see? Gloria asked.

Pax. Surefire in cryo waking up.

Alessandra pressed both hands against the door.

That's good. She can help us escape.

Pax didn't think so. He told me to go. Said it wasn't safe.

Typical Pax, thinking we can't handle ourselves. Oracle felt Gloria rolling her eyes.

Surefire had IVs hooked up to her. One was draining her blood.

Gloria turned her head to look at Oracle, and she saw her own body floating next to the other woman, face and eyes focused forward. She looked to be sleeping or dead. But she could still feel her toes and legs encased in the suit, the mask pressed against her face, the breathing apparatus stretching out her lips, cutting into her gums. But she could feel what Gloria experienced as well. Like she was straddling two different spaces.

Then a sonic boom vibrated the water and whipped them backward.

♥ 🕱 ♥ 🕱 ♥ 🕱

Pax scowled at Dr. Banerji and her cavalier description of Surefire waking from cryo and exploding the room. The proper words for this situation eluded him. Improper words he had in spades.

"That's not funny. You didn't see what Surefire could do with her goddessy powers. I'm waiting outside—way outside." TimeTrap strode to the exit then scurried back with her hands up when the guards lifted their guns at her. "Or not."

Pax squirmed. He stretched an arm around his back to scratch an itch. But the itch grew to a tickle before warm fingertips pressed up his spine ending at the base of his neck. His heart caught in his throat.

Cassandra.

Pax braced himself for what happened earlier, when Dama X possessed him and Oracle possessed TimeTrap. Instead, her words whispered through his mind. So loud and clear, he swore she stood over his shoulder. In his thoughts, he sent out a warning that she should leave. His gaze circled the room, hoping she could see the danger awaiting them. Oracle said she had backup, but he wasn't sure what that meant. Whatever or whoever it was wouldn't be enough, especially if Lucinda was with them. Facing the person who betrayed her may send Surefire into further shock and further destruction, testing her control. Hell, even Pax's temper flared at the mention of Lucinda's name. His muscles twitched, wishing for release and revenge.

Pax noticed blood dripping into a bag at the back of the cryo machine. As the frost cleared along the chamber's sides, he saw two needles sticking into Surefire's arms. One appeared to give her fluids, but another IV drained her blood.

With every fiber of his being, Pax shoved Oracle out with a final plea, *Go!*

"What is this?" He motioned to the blood bag and IV.

"Lucinda was drawing her blood and synthesizing it. It began when TransGen sent samples of Surefire's blood to Circe for testing. That's how she developed the cure for Felicia after the attack by Tezcatlipoca." Dama X waved her hand toward Reyes.

"TransGen's working with Lucinda's lab?" Pax recalled Gloria mentioning Circe but not any relationship between them and TransGen.

"After I cut ties with Lucinda, she sought funding elsewhere," she replied.

"How did Lucinda create this cure with Surefire's blood?" Pax demanded.

"I believe the Aztec goddess embedded her DNA in Surefire's code. It's how Xochiquetzal can use Surefire as a vessel. But it also acts similarly to O negative blood on a chromosomal level. In this case, instead of a universal donor, her blood is what enables any skull's proteins to bond with the transhuman gene. The effects are dependent on each skull's unique properties, or rather, each god or goddess's unique domain. Ometeotl is the god of male and female identity, so when this skull's proteins are added to Diosa de la Venganza along with Surefire's blood, the result in a transhuman is complete gender modification. Without her blood in the mix, this deity's proteins don't alter the drug."

"You used my agent's blood to create that poison?" Pax glared at Dama X.

"Me?" she exclaimed, offended. "That was Lucinda, who created Diosa de la Venganza and poisoned your two victims. She set me up. Let me take the fall for it. When you were unconscious and I read your mind . . . ah, papi don't worry—" she stroked his cheek when his brow furrowed—"I only did it to verify you meant us no harm. I didn't go deep into your private thoughts, only far enough to see the memory of you finding my box at your home—a gift I had given Lucinda when we first partnered."

Pax removed her hand from his cheek, knowing the outrage he felt over this violation showed on his face. Her eyes searched his as if looking for forgiveness he wasn't willing to give. Her shoulders slumped, and she dropped her gaze to the floor. Later, he'd address what else she'd seen in his mind, but now he wanted to know. "You mentioned two victims but there were three."

"Only two were injected with the *potent* version of Diosa de la Venganza. The last batch Lucinda had created, I'd accidentally contaminated." Dr. Banerji fluttered her eyelashes in exaggerated innocence. "I need better glasses, you see, and I made a mistake by mixing the anti-viral solution with the viral one. Alas, Lucinda had already shipped the skull to TransGen to get it far from Xalvadora and hasn't had time to create a new batch."

"Dr. Banerji worked for Circe. She was on Lucinda's team, which I'd hired several years ago to study proteins from the skulls in my collection." Dama X placed a gentle hand on the doctor's arm. "When she learned about Lucinda harboring Surefire and Raven, she contacted me and we arranged for their escape. Now she works for the Sisters."

"You used to work for TransGen." Pax finally recalled how he knew her. She'd overseen ESP. One of the higher-level doctors who occasionally ran tests on the soldiers. He'd met her only once or twice. She'd headed up an R&D department at TransGen until she left five years ago. They'd even dedicated a wing after her, making Pax assume she'd died or retired.

The doctor clasped her hands together. "So you do remember me. You just made this old girl's heart flutter."

"I . . . uh . . ." His face flushed when she rubbed his bicep and winked at him. "Let's get back to the topic. If Lucinda didn't have the real drug, what did she use instead on the third victim?"

"I assume she used the version Magda administered to you. It was made to resemble the original drug to fool our enemies. It causes severe pain and induces unconsciousness but doesn't cause genetic restructuring," Dama X said.

It was a matter of time before Pax's head exploded with this information overload. "But Reyes told me that you used this drug on your enemies and threatened politicians."

"I can no longer stand these lies being told by my flesh and blood." Dama X spun her heel and shook her hands at Reyes standing across the cryochambers.

"I'm sorry, Xalvadora. I didn't—" Reyes began but Dama X kept yelling.

"I never threatened any politicians nor President Diaz. I'm not stupid. I did use a lesser version—made *without* Surefire's blood—of Diosa de la Venganza to scare off my enemies. It damaged their genitals through traditional gene manipulation, regardless of whether the man was a transhuman. And those who suffered and died under it deserved it. The world is a safer place without them."

Dama X took a steadying breath. When she regained her composure, she rested her forearms on the chamber and gazed down at Surefire, whose muscles twitched as her body thawed. "Lucinda took the drug to the next level when she used proteins from Ometeotl's skull mixed with Surefire's blood. Baltimore was the testing ground and where she could scare U-Sec to come to her aid against me. She proved that while the new cocktail could cause complete gender modification in transhumans, it could also be used to cause horrific death in non-transhumans. Since she proved it works, her next step is to weaponize it. Sell the serum to the highest bidder. Just one of the reasons I took the skull before she could extract more of the proteins."

She raised her head and eyed Pax. "Lucinda may claim she created the serum for the greater good, to help transhumans with gender dysphoria, but she only cared about money and building a TransGen of her own. When I learned about the final potent ingredient in Diosa de la Venganza . . ." She ran her fingers over the glass.

"I swear I didn't—" Reyes began.

"I believe you," Dama X interrupted him, "but what hurts me is how you believed your sister would be capable of this. You grow a pair of balls, and you lose touch with who I am?"

"It wasn't like that," Reyes said.

"Take these out now." Pax jabbed a finger toward the IVs.

"I can't. Not until she wakes," Dr. Banerji replied.

The floor vibrated, making Pax jump. The power cut out. Machines running in the background wound to a low murmur before shutting down completely. Air stopped blowing through the vents above their heads. Outside the glass wall and doors, green emergency lights flicked on in the corridor. Within the room, similar lights blinked to life in the corners.

Pax's eyes adjusted to the dark. He searched out Reyes and TimeTrap. Kristina and Penny, who guarded the door, appeared distracted by the sudden darkness.

If Pax acted now, he might have a chance to disarm the guards.

A purple light reflected against the glass door and walls. As it grew, the light bathed the two guards in a violet hue. Pax spun around to find Surefire standing in the middle of the room. He shielded his eyes from her skin, illuminated in a neon purple light. IV lines dangled from her arms. Her eyes shown like glow sticks.

Kristina back-stepped until she banged against the glass. Magda raised her gun. Surefire swung her head toward the click of a round being chambered.

"No! Don't shoot!" Dama X leapt in front of the barrel.

"What is that?" Magda lowered the gun and peered around Dama X.

Surefire cocked her head and eyed the guard. Kristina wedged open the glass door and ran from the room. The third guard, Penny, crouched in the dark at the edge of a counter, her gun aimed and ready.

"Where am I?" Surefire asked, but it wasn't her voice. It was deeper, sensual.

"You are off the coast of Mexico. In the Pacific Ocean on a manmade island." Dama X put out her arms in a welcoming gesture.

Hips swaying, Surefire sauntered toward Dama X. She reached out and caressed her cheek. Dama X closed her eyes and groaned. Warm air brushed across Pax's chest and down his stomach to his groin. A lavender scent filled the room.

"That's not Surefire," Pax said.

The young woman's body slipped away from Dama X. She turned her eerie eyes on him. Her lips parted. She ran her hands over her bare breasts and down her stomach to rest on her hips. At her feet, small white flowers sprouted along the floor as she strutted toward him with cat-like sensuality.

"Pax," she breathed his name. "I remember how much I wanted to touch you at the temple where you saved us." Her palms smoothed across his chest. Her fingers played with his fine hairs.

In spite of everything, Pax's body reacted to her touch. His jeans tightened. *Damn Xochi's power.* He slid back but she pressed against him, grinding her bare chest against his stomach. This wasn't right. Surefire was not only his employee, she was like a little sister. He snatched her hands.

"Xochi, stop this," he said.

"Ah, you know my name. How I love hearing it on your lips. Say it again."

"Where is Synthia?" He used his agent's given name.

She stuck out her bottom lip in an exaggerated pout.

"Your heart belongs to another. Too bad." Her sharp nails scraped across his chest.

Pax winced at the four red scratches burning his skin.

"Surefire—Xochi, whatever—can you help us? It's a bit awkward holding up your naked boyfriend," TimeTrap uttered.

Pax looked over Surefire's head to find TimeTrap and Dr. Banerji bent under the weight of Raven. Both his arms were slung around their shoulders. His head wobbled and legs dragged under him. Half his face drooped to the side.

Surefire ran to him and wrapped her arms around his waist. TimeTrap and Dr. Banerji let go. Surefire lowered him to the floor as if he were light as a toddler and not a six-foot-tall athletic man. Her purple aura wavered. She cradled his face and kissed his lips.

Raven's back arched and limbs tensed, then his body relaxed. He lifted his arm and his fingers tangled in her hair. He pulled her closer and deepened the kiss.

Pax averted his eyes, as did TimeTrap and the doctor.

"Synthia." TimeTrap called Surefire by her real name.

"Syn," TimeTrap repeated, still facing the other way. "You can rent a room later for this reunion."

"Oh, God!" Surefire squealed in a voice Pax recognized as her own.

"Oh, shit . . . Pax and strangers who are watching us . . . I, umm . . ." Raven stammered. He cupped his hands between his legs and jumped to his feet.

Surefire bent her legs to her chest and wrapped her arms around her knees.

"Here, babes. Cover up your naughty bits." TimeTrap tossed lab coats to the two lovebirds.

Surefire buttoned up the jacket and stood. Raven turned from the group and slipped on the lab coat.

"Pax, yeah, that was just—" Raven began, and Pax held up his hand to stop him.

"That's how Raven heals." Surefire grabbed her lover's hand and squeezed it.

"Xochi's power keeps me alive, and Surefire is her conduit—for those who are new to this story." Raven shifted on his feet.

"That was extraordinary," Dama X murmured.

"I'd say. So glad I was wrong about the explosion part. The goddess's will must be strong," Dr. Banerji said with a wag of her head.

"Speaking of Xochi," Surefire began. "When she was playing puppeteer, you said we're on an island?"

From the corner of his eye, Pax noticed Reyes slinking into the shadows.

"Remember Dr. No's lair from that James Bond movie?" TimeTrap chimed in.

"I'd like to think it's more spectacular—and functional—than that. We're a society of women—and a few men—who want to build a better and safer space for us to live the lives we want without patriarchy's rules," Dama X said.

"Are we safe here?" Surefire's eyes darted to the cryochambers before seeking out Pax.

"I don't know." Pax cut Dama X a look.

She lifted her chin at Pax. "You are safe and can remain here under the Sisterhood's protection for as long as you need."

"Do you work for Lucinda?" Raven pulled Surefire closer to his side.

Dama X spat on the floor. "Puta."

"Guess not." Raven raised his brows.

Pax peered over his shoulder, searching for Reyes, but he was gone. His eyes landed on the sliding glass door fully open to find Kristina, who had run off, entering the room.

"Lucinda's here," she announced out of breath.

A flash of purple lit up Surefire's skin.

"Where?" Raven stepped forward.

"She's broken though the airlock above us. I ran into one of the security details in the stairwell. They tried to alert you but the comm systems are down."

"We need to get our guests somewhere safe," Dama X said.

"No," Raven and Surefire said in unison.

"We'll take care of Lucinda," Raven added.

The hairs on Pax's arm stood on end. Emergency lights in the room flicked on and off. A static charge danced along his skin.

Pax tensed as the air in the room became heavier. He wanted to ask Raven what he meant, but Kristina spoke, "Wait."

She stuck out her hand but kept her distance from Raven and Surefire.

"There are people with Lucinda. Alessandra is one of them."

"Which is how they broke through our barrier." Dama X nodded.

"And two men. Soldiers or something else . . . couldn't tell what branch of the military, but they're Americans. UltraAgent Oracle and a woman they didn't recognize were also with them."

"Oracle is with her?" Surefire's eyes found Pax's across the darkened room.

"Not by choice," Pax said.

"We have to get Oracle away from them," TimeTrap stated.

"And Gloria. The other woman is probably Gloria," Pax added.

"Meh, if we have to help her too," TimeTrap muttered.

"Why is Gloria here?" Surefire asked.

Pax started to reply when Kristina continued speaking. "That's not all. There's at least one submarine that we've detected off our shore. That appears to be American as well."

All attention turned to Pax. "I didn't notify the military unless Gloria did. I don't know why they'd be here."

"For her." Dr. Banerji pointed at Surefire.

"It's my father," the agent said with a certainty that Pax felt as well.

"I need to get to my room and organize our defense and gather weapons. I have something in my chambers that can help us." The guards filed into the corridor. Dama X motioned for Surefire and Raven to go ahead of her.

"We don't need any weapons. My father believes I am one, so I'm going to show him what I can really do," Surefire announced before she disappeared with Raven.

Chapter 18

Into Some Deep Water

Crimes committed by transhumans rose enough in several major cities during the last few years that police added new departments to handle it. Do you still believe transhumans don't pose a threat to Americans?

—Former Senator Janet Donovan interviewing Alex Cross on her talk radio station

---

Oracle's hand slipped from Gloria's, but the handcuff kept them tethered. She somersaulted backward in the water until she couldn't tell which way was up or down. Her tethered arm jerked and twisted out to her side as Gloria's wrist yanked against the chain. Rough rocks stopped Oracle's descent. Seagrass slid across her cheek. Her teeth chomped down on the breathing device to keep it in place.

She steadied her breath. Panting would deplete her oxygen fast. A hand wrapped around her bicep—too big to be Gloria's. She let herself be pulled forward. The water churned to her side as Gloria paddled to keep up. With her ears ringing and head disoriented, she didn't want to open up to find out who was tugging her.

She felt a smooth surface before her arm scraped against the edge of an opening. A different hand, leaner but strong as well, grabbed her and yanked her forward. She banged into a soft body and a small hand felt for hers.

Gloria.

Through her boss's eyes, she received an image flash of a glass cube about the size of a large walk-in closet where all of them were crammed. Jones popped the exterior glass door into place, locking them inside the space, which became tighter as they bumped into one another. On the opposite end, Oracle noticed the cube was attached to the structure where a walkway lit by dull green lights wrapped around a metal and glass wall. The ocean vibrated. A loud click made her jump. Water drained out of the room, and soon she wasn't floating but standing inside the cube on a glass floor hanging over the dark depths.

Gloria continued to hold her hand, giving her a view of the group taking out their mouthpieces and removing their wetsuit hoods and flippers. Her ears popped. The scooters rested on the floor.

"Decompression chamber," Alessandra explained. She nudged Gloria and Oracle toward the keypad on the wall.

"How did you unlock it?" Gloria asked.

"Like this." Alessandra covered the keypad with her long fingers. The digital output sped through hundreds of number combinations before it started to smoke.

"And how did you not electrocute us in the water?" Oracle covered her nose against the odor of seared plastic. Gloria and Smith coughed as smoke filled the confined space. The lock popped and the interior door swung open.

"I concentrated my power into the airlock and allowed it to follow the grounding wire."

"You're a high voltage human." Gloria clung to Oracle's hand and pulled her into the hallway after Alessandra.

"*Enhanced* high-voltage human, no thanks to Suarez." Alessandra stalked down the hall illuminated by dull green emergency lights along the floor.

"How?" Gloria asked.

"None of your business."

They stopped outside a glass door leading into a dim room lit only by computer monitors. Alessandra wrenched down a red emergency lever on the wall. The door opened a foot. She stepped aside to let Smith pry it open.

"This is the main control room, self-contained with its own generator and runs with minimal oversight, which is why the computers in here are still lit up." Alessandra stopped to gaze at a glass screen dotted with red and a few green lights. "When I fried the airlock, I sent out a charge to the main electrical lines. Everything is down—weapons, cloaking, security. It'll take at least an hour for the system to be up again once someone arrives to override the shutdown."

Alessandra sat down in front of the electronic glass and put her feet on the desk below it. "And when someone does come, we will take care of them."

"What about oxygen?" Oracle asked. The room was stuffy. No air blew from the vents.

"They have twenty-four hours of reserve pumping through here. It may get warm but you can breathe."

"And that's how women get it done." Lucinda wrapped her arm around Alessandra's shoulders and squeezed. "Fabulous work."

Smith and Jones gave each other a side look.

"Where's the package?" Jones asked.

"And there he is." Lucinda clapped her hands.

Smith turned, and Gloria followed his gaze to where Reyes stood.

"Did Xalvadora take you to the weapon as predicted?" Lucinda asked.

Reyes nodded and walked stiffly into the room.

"I knew she'd want to show it off. Did you secure the room for us?" Lucinda asked.

Reyes stopped an arm's length from Lucinda. "You told me Dama X has a powerful weapon."

"She does, didn't she show it to you?"

"Surefire and Raven are not weapons, and my sister certainly doesn't plan to use them as such. I can't say the same about you."

Lucinda responded with a dismissive laugh. "Did your sister get in your head? Did you lose your pendant?"

"The only thing I've lost is respect for you," Reyes said.

Alessandra bolted to her feet. In unison, the soldiers rested their hands on the guns holstered at their waists. Gloria squeezed Oracle's hand.

We run at the first chance, Gloria pushed the thought into Oracle's mind.

We take one of the soldiers with us, she responded. A bold move, but they needed a weapon and a fighter Oracle could control.

Gloria cut her a look as if Oracle's face would reveal she was kidding.

"You lost respect for me?" Lucinda pressed her hand over her chest. "I'm risking my life to save them."

"You're risking your life to save them for yourself."

"Ha! She did get in your head." Lucinda tapped a finger against his forehead.

He stood his ground, unflinching. "She woke them up."

Lucinda's face crumbled. "What did you say?"

"Xalvadora woke them from cryosleep, and I know what you did to them—and what you truly did to me. You used all of us." He swept his arm out to the room.

"What's he talking about?" Smith held his post.

"Lucinda lied to me about what the weapon was. We need to secure her and Alessandra. Take them to Dama X to show we mean them no harm. Lucinda needs to pay for her crimes against transhumans," Reyes replied.

Alessandra moved to Lucinda's side holding a gun in her left hand that Oracle hadn't seen her take out.

"Don't listen to him," Lucinda said.

Jones unholstered his pistol then hesitated. His attention split between Reyes and Alessandra.

"Contact St. John." Reyes pointed to a watch-sized device on Jones's wrist. "Tell him to stand down. His daughter is alive and safe and Dama X has no intentions to fight unless she has to."

"Don't do anything," Lucinda said between gritted teeth. "Dama X is controlling him. She sent him here to confuse us, disarm us."

"I came here on my own to request that you and these men stand down to avoid a fight," Reyes said.

Smith lifted his wrist and spoke into the small square screen strapped around it. "Leviathan IV this is Atlantis One."

"What are you doing?" Lucinda demanded.

"Contacting *my* superior for orders." Smith tried again. "Leviathan, do you copy?"

From the small speaker came a chorus of screams followed by gunshots before the sound cut out. Smith pulled out his gun and aimed it at Reyes. "Is La Hermandad de Diana attacking our ship?"

"Whatever is happening, it's Lucinda's fault." Reyes pressed forward, forcing Lucinda back into a table. "She tricked Surefire and framed my sister. Tell them, Xalvadora is innocent. Tell them—" Reyes grabbed her throat. Held her aloft.

Pop. Oracle and Gloria jumped in unison at the deafening sound. Reyes dropped Lucinda. He collapsed on the floor. Knee shattered by the gunshot. Blood spattered over the floor and servers.

Smith lowered his gun. "Try it again."

"I thought you had tranquilizers." Gloria moved to help Reyes, howling in pain, but Alessandra blocked her.

"I do, but they don't." Alessandra smirked.

Leaning over a desk, Lucinda coughed, rubbed her neck. When she managed to breathe normally again, she knelt next to Reyes, as he rolled on the floor, cradling his leg. "Who opened the cryochambers for her? She couldn't thaw them on her own."

Reyes's screams kickstarted Oracle's adrenaline, igniting her power, which traveled down her arm and through Gloria and landed into Smith who trembled before she filled his body.

"Who was it?" Lucinda shouted over Reyes's cries.

"Dr. Banerji," he said, sucking in a breath.

"I should've known she would turn tail. What about the skulls? Where are they?" Lucinda kicked his shoulder.

"I don't know."

Oracle sensed Smith's wetsuit hugging his body. She wriggled his toes inside his water shoes. Memories flooded her vision. Jones and Smith belonged to a black ops transhuman unit, an offshoot of the squad sent to retrieve the UltraAgents in Mexico—a black books operation not even Pax knew about. Smith wasn't a transhuman but trained to monitor, capture, and kill them. She glimpsed a conversation he'd had with St. John. A snippet but enough to understand.

St. John had given the order to freeze Surefire and Raven.

She raised Smith's hand to aim his gun at Alessandra. His consciousness was relegated to the recesses of his mind, but she could feel his energy shove against hers. But the soldier didn't know how to fight this power. She turned his head to look at Gloria who quickly morphed her surprised expression into a neutral one.

"Drop the weapon." Oracle forced the words from Smith's mouth. The order came out slow, off-pitched. Jones followed his lead and aimed his weapon at Alessandra as well.

Oracle slipped Smith's finger onto the trigger.

Lucinda glanced from Reyes to Smith to Gloria. A smiled played upon her lips in contrast to the tense scene unfolding around her.

"Oracle is controlling your friend." Lucinda pointed to the UltraAgent.

"Smith?" Jones kept his weapon pointed at Alessandra as he hazarded a glance at his battle buddy. "Smith, is this true?"

The sergeant pushed back against Oracle, keeping his lips sealed against her attempts to make him talk. Her power waned. She made him nod, disjointed like a child trying to work a complicated marionette.

Jones swung his weapon to Oracle.

"We need her." Lucinda stepped in front of his gun. "But Gloria's task is not necessary anymore."

Her attention fractured, she didn't see Alessandra raise her gun until it was too late. *Pop.* She shot Gloria in the chest.

The momentum of Gloria falling yanked Oracle's wrist, sending her to the ground, and her spirit slammed back into her own body when Gloria squeezed her hand. She doubled over at the sharp pain that took her breath away before wresting her fingers out of Gloria's grip. She welcomed the gray-black void as the pain in her chest faded.

"Shit," Gloria wheezed.

Oracle felt across her boss's torso and found the hole in the wetsuit. Warm blood pulsating out. She pressed both hands over the wound, applying pressure.

"What did that bitch to do me?" Smith stomped across the floor. A cold, round barrel pressed into Oracle's scalp.

"Don't use the b-word. It makes me twitchy," Alessandra said followed by the pop of joints, and Oracle imagined her cracking her neck.

"St. John is right. These freaks need to be locked up." Smith shoved her head with the gun.

"Freaks?" Alessandra quipped. "Jones, please check your boy over there."

"I'm not your boy," Smith spat.

"Smith, are you okay?" Jones asked.

"Peachy."

"What next?" From reading Smith's mind, Oracle knew Jones wasn't in the meeting with St. John. He didn't know the contingency plans.

Smith's heavy breathing upped Oracle's nervousness. It was not from exertion but anger directed at her. He continued to hold the gun to her head. She kept her face averted. Hands still pressing down on Gloria's wound seeping out blood.

"We retrieve the package if it's still retrievable," he replied to Jones. "Secure the island and remove anyone who stands in our way. We contact our base if our sub's been compromised."

"And them?" His partner stepped closer and Smith's gun lowered, but Oracle wasn't out of the clear yet.

"We're on the same side," Lucinda spoke softly, trying to reclaim the situation. "Except those three, but they won't stand in our way now, will they?"

Without seeing her, Oracle knew Lucinda stared at her, waiting for an answer. She shook her head.

"Oracle's task is not finished. We need her, Smith, and I doubt she can do her job well with a bullet wound and certainly not with one in her head," Lucinda said.

"If she does it again . . ." Smith grunted. His feet scuffed against the smooth floor as he moved away from her.

"If she does it again, then shoot her in a place that doesn't kill her. I recall St. John making the request that UltraAgents are not to be killed."

Gloria gulped at the air, fighting for each breath. Her bowed back banged against Oracle's thigh. Alessandra unlocked the cuffs that tethered them and wrenched Oracle to her feet.

"I must've hit her lung. My aim is off," Alessandra noted.

"You weren't using tranquilizers." Oracle tried and failed to pull out of the woman's grip.

"Must've taken the wrong gun then. My mistake."

"That works out better. If she would've used the transhuman tranquilizer it would've killed Gloria," Lucinda said.

"No hay mal que por bien no venga," Alessandra whispered in Oracle's ear. "A positive to every action, even if I didn't mean for it."

"Gloria won't die from her wounds yet. But she will, if you don't cooperate, and St. John won't be pleased to lose one of his best transgeneticists." Alessandra held Oracle steady as Lucinda closed in with every word.

Oracle's power flared, but she pulled it back before it touched anyone.

"I need you to seek out Pax." Lucinda's breath smelled of chocolate scones, which Oracle didn't think she could eat again without thinking of this woman. "I'm sure you already notified him we were coming. I want their current location, current plans. Dama X is housing more than one skull on this island. I need those skulls to control Surefire."

Alessandra handed Oracle over to Lucinda, who jerked on her arm, forcing her to walk in front.

"Despite what you believe about your young agent, Surefire is dangerous. A ticking bomb and no one knows when it'll go off, not even her. If we don't find her and the skulls, then St. John's enemies will. Smith's unit has orders to destroy this island, with your precious Pax on it too, if the mission fails. The ship's crew no doubt sent out a distress signal."

"Our base unit will be here within thirty unless I contact them to stand down. I will only give that order if we have the targets in our possession. I will not hesitate to allow everyone to die on this island to protect our world," Smith said.

Oracle squared her shoulders. She didn't know what to believe and didn't have the luxury to find out.

"Locate them, and if we find out you revealed our plans to him, well . . ."

"No," Gloria wheezed.

"So, what's it going to be?" Lucinda asked quietly. In the background, Reyes cursed them. His voice hoarse from screaming.

Oracle took a deep breath and with an exhale pushed out her power.

♥ ☠ ♥ ☠ ♥ ☠

Pax locked his gaze with TimeTrap. With the Sisters and Dama X caught off guard by Surefire's and Raven's disappearance, now was their time to go. She nodded in understanding, and he lunged. His arm extended to meet her outstretched hand.

Then he froze. It was as though his body was covered in glue, cementing him to the floor with his arm out and fingers extended toward TimeTrap. Her large brown eyes bounced frantically back and forth, her face frozen in a shocked expression. A high-pitched wail, like air deflating from a balloon, whistled between her lips.

"No, you don't." Dama X clucked her tongue. The Sisters swung their weapons toward them, although Pax had no idea why, considering they couldn't move except to blink and breathe.

"Where's Felicia?" she demanded.

Magda glanced around the room then peered into the hall. "Gone."

"Always a sneaky puta." Dama X spun on Pax and TimeTrap.

"What do I have to do to convince you that I'm not the bad woman here? Hmm?" Dama X stood on her tiptoes. Sharp green eyes bored into his.

Pax's muscles tensed. Summoning every ounce of strength, he shoved against her power, wrapped around him like a cocoon. His forehead broke out in a sweat. He extended his arm an inch at best. He might as well be trying to push through a steel wall. Only a simpering sound came out when he attempted to speak.

"Are you trying to apologize?" Dama X snapped her fingers.

Pax's jaw loosened enough for him to say, "My agents need me. They're in danger."

"And what were you going to do? Where were you going to go? Do you know this island as well as I do?" She fluttered her hands in his face.

"She has a point," TimeTrap somehow uttered with a semi-closed mouth.

Pax tried to frown at her but couldn't change his expression.

"Always the men think they know what's best, think only they can save us." Dama X rested her forearm on TimeTrap's stiff shoulder.

"Show him." She beckoned her guards closer. Magda and Kristina lowered their weapons and stepped into Pax's line of sight.

"You see this." Dama X ran her index finger over the skull artwork adorning their faces. Specifically she pointed to names woven into the floral designs around their eyes and mouth. "These are names of women and men—family and friends and lovers—they've lost to violence perpetrated by the patriarchy's rules, religions, and wars."

She caressed his cheek. "No, not all men are bad. I can hear it in your mind that's what you want to say. And we know. You aren't. But the world is full of the bad ones in power. But here on my island, the women rule, and we don't harm other women. Except for one."

"Lucinda," Kristina sneered.

"I have a plan to save your agents. We need both of you to help. Can we rely on you or should I get Dr. Banerji to prep these cryochambers?" Dama X asked, her voice as cold as the chambers behind her that the doctor was cleaning.

"Yes," he hissed.

"Does that mean 'yes' to help or to the cryochambers? I should've phrased that better." Dama X pursed her lips.

Pax tried to say help but could only manage a *hee* sound.

Immediately, his muscles relaxed. His arm fell. He staggered and caught himself before he tipped over. Pins and needles exploded along his arm from holding it outstretched. TimeTrap shook out her hand, stretched, and cracked her back.

"That sucked big time." TimeTrap shuddered.

"Not as much as it does to me." Dama X wiped away the sweat beading her forehead. "Takes too much strength to hold two people—particularly transhumans—for too long."

"I need to get us out of here and to my room so I can recharge," she addressed TimeTrap.

"We need to find Surefire and Raven," Pax stated.

"They'll find us of that I'm certain," she replied.

"Not sure if I have enough juice to pop all of you there," TimeTrap said.

"Dr. Banerji can help," Dama X offered.

"Oh, yes, I have a power booster solution I've been excited to test out." Dr. Banerji opened a small fridge and took out a needle large enough to pierce a rhino's flesh.

"Test out? That?" TimeTrap gulped. "A big N-O."

She scuttled back and banged into Magda, who rolled her eyes. TimeTrap reached into her shirt and foraged in her tank top and pulled out a protein bar.

"Found this in my purse back at Reyes's house. Courtesy of the bio-brains at TransGen, in case I lose any mojo. It works pretty fast," she said between bites.

TimeTrap swallowed the last piece and placed a hand on her hip as everyone in the room watched and waited. She stared at the ceiling and narrowed her eyes as if taking stock. "Okay, based on this energy boost, I can pop out all the women in this room . . . or I can take Pax and one gal."

TimeTrap held out her hands. Dama X grabbed it and motioned to Pax to take the other.

"The three of you go up the emergency stairs and notify anyone you meet of the breech. Secure the floors. If you see my sister or Lucinda, do what you feel is necessary," Dama X said.

They nodded in unison before leaving.

"Will you be safe here?" Dama X asked Dr. Banerji.

"I have enough chemicals in this room to knock out a Grateful Dead audience. I'll be fine." She held up the needle.

"Wasn't that the same shot you were going to use on me?" TimeTrap arched a brow.

"Oh, no . . . well . . . oh, my . . . you're right . . . it's this one. My eyesight is horrible in this dim light. That would've been awkward." Dr. Banerji took out another syringe from a small refrigerator.

"And I dodged that bullet," TimeTrap murmured.

"Take us to my room where you first entered and found Pax," Dama X said.

"You mean where my naked boss attacked me?" TimeTrap quipped.

Pax blushed in spite of his frustration. He didn't want his agent to fear him, let alone know what his private parts looked like.

TimeTrap's brow furrowed when she caught his eye. "Errr . . . I mean when this chick attacked me. Sorry, Pax, all this is very confusing. You weren't yourself at the time. And your ding-a-ling is totally erased from my memory."

They popped out of the room.

Chapter 19

Equal Temper of Heroic Hearts

———————————

I prefer working with women. Their minds are the world's most neglected resource, filled with untapped knowledge and perspective.

—Dr. Banerji to her colleagues at TransGen

———————————

Pax's voice echoed in the dark void. Oracle's power surged forward, honing into the sound until she sensed his large body as if he stood in front of her. She zeroed in and dipped the edge of her power into his mind, not going too deep, afraid to give away their plans or position and cause Lucinda to make good on her threat.

"Let me in, so I may see," Lucinda spoke in her ear. A cold hand clamped around the base of Oracle's skull. Nails dug into her neck.

She opened a connection for Lucinda as she'd done with TimeTrap back in the helicopter. Oracle tempered her thoughts, pushed back memories, and stamped down any feelings that this woman could use against her. She emptied her mind to focus solely on Pax standing inside the same bright room where he'd been lying hours before. Through his eyes, she observed Dama X placing her hand over a touchpad on a kitchen backsplash. A grinding of gears, then the cabinets slid aside to reveal a circular room.

After a few paces into the chamber, Pax halted. His mouth went dry. Crystal skulls set in glass cases formed a semicircle around him. A single light shone on each one, illuminating their colors—purple, pink, blue, black, turquoise, and several that were clear, reflecting rainbow prisms behind the empty, chiseled eye sockets. He counted eight crystal skulls.

"She will be invincible," Lucinda said out loud.

"What's going on?" The heat from Smith's body closed in on Oracle's backside.

No freakin' way, man. TimeTrap backed out of the room. *I'm not doing this again.*

"That's all. Stop." Lucinda didn't let go of Oracle until the transhuman withdrew fully back into her body and the room faded into grayish black.

"They're in Dama X's room. And she has a secret chamber where she's housing the crystal skulls. I counted eight of them," Lucinda said.

"Why does she have them?" Oracle asked.

"Why do you think?" Lucinda shot back. "To gain the power of the gods. Create an army of Surefires. That's why she took Surefire and Raven."

Lucinda didn't need to keep up her ruse that Dama X's goals were any different than hers—or St. John's, who Oracle surmised was Circe's secret client. Black book jobs tended to have unlimited funding with no oversight from Congress or the public. From Oracle's perspective, neither woman could be trusted even if a small trickle of trust ran through Pax's veins where Dama X was concerned. Why would Pax trust her? What had he seen that Oracle hadn't? Although right now, trust didn't matter. She needed to cooperate. Keep her and Gloria alive long enough to get to Pax and get them to safety.

"Bull . . . shit," Gloria managed to say.

"Do you want me to collapse your other lung?" Lucinda said.

"No."

"Then shut your mouth." Lucinda's hand clamped around Oracle's bicep.

"We'll use the emergency stairwell on the other side of this corridor. It's a hike, but there's a hidden door that leads to Xalvadora's room," Alessandra said. "We should go. So far, the security cameras are offline but they will be back up in twenty minutes."

Lucinda shoved Oracle ahead of her. "This one's coming with us. The rest—"

"She'll stop you," Reyes ground out.

"Shut this traitor up," Lucinda ordered.

Electricity snapped over Oracle's exposed skin. She heard a crack. Then Reyes screamed then fell silent. The smell of burning flesh turned her stomach.

"Is he dead?" Oracle spun toward the sound of Reyes's cry and ran into Lucinda.

"Just stunned. I'm conserving my power for Dama X." Alessandra breezed past her.

"It's safe to leave them. They can't go anywhere," Lucinda said to one of the soldiers behind Oracle. "Besides, we may still need them."

"Gloria?" Oracle called over her shoulder as Lucinda pushed her forward.

"Fine . . . just pain . . . Go." Gloria's wheezing worsened with every word. She feared Gloria wouldn't be alive when they returned.

Oracle tried to dig her heels in to slow Lucinda, only to have a metal object butt into her lower back.

"Keep moving. And you get in my head again, I put a bullet in yours." Smith's gun lowered from her back. She had no doubt he'd make good on his promise.

Oracle considered the other soldier, Jones, and wondered where he was. Did Lucinda carry a weapon as well?

"Don't think about it." Lucinda squeezed Oracle's arm. "I can tell when you're making a connection. Your blank face is a dead giveaway."

Fifty. Oracle counted her steps from the control room to the stairwell. She'd find her way back to that room and to Gloria when the time came.

They stopped. Body heat surrounded her on all sides. A dull creak of hinges. An echo of a door slamming open. Then a blast of stuffy air.

Someone left their group, leaving a cool spot in front of Oracle.

"It's clear and mostly dark. Only a few emergency lights are lit," Jones said.

"We won't use any lights to give away our position. Everyone stay close and pay attention to where you're stepping," Smith ordered from behind Oracle.

Rubber water shoes squeaked against the floor as they filed into the stairwell.

"No words." Lucinda dug her nails into Oracle's arm.

They continued down. Twelve steps. A landing five paces wide. Another twelve steps. The next landing and five more paces. She longed to unzip her wetsuit and let her overheated skin breathe. Lucinda panted next to her, apparently not used to cardio.

"Try to keep up, Lucinda. I told you the Cheetah workout was mierda," Alessandra said.

"Qué cabrón," Lucinda whispered.

Alessandra softly chuckled.

"It's my bad ankle. It's gone stiff. I need to rub it." Lucinda and Oracle paused on the sixth step of the fifth stairway. Her ponytail hit Oracle's face.

Alessandra said in a hushed tone, "There's a dumbwaiter here that drops down the center of the stairs. I was going to use it to tote a few of us down at a time, but someone must've lifted it up."

A gun clicked as a round was loaded. Above or below?

A shot of air breezed by Oracle's cheek, followed by a pop of gunfire. The bullet hit the wall next to her.

"Get down!" Smith shouted.

Lucinda's hand dropped from her arm. Oracle crouched on the stairs, making herself as small as possible as she felt her way toward the wall. Smith's foot kicked her side when he jumped over her. She pressed her palms against her ears to dampen the loud blast of his pistol. He stood two steps from her, returning the fire.

His feet padded further down the stairs, away from her. Oracle slipped three steps up. When no one stopped her, she took three more to the landing above.

A bullet struck the step near her foot.

"I'm hit," Lucinda yelled, followed by feet scraping against the metal stairs.

A loud shot resounded from a handgun in the direction of Lucinda's voice. Six more steps up.

Twelve.

No one appeared to notice Oracle moving farther above, farther away from the group.

"Should we retreat?" Lucinda shouted.

"No. There's only three, and we hit one of them. I think they're running out of ammo. We can take them before backup arrives." Smith's booming voice echoed down to her.

Another bullet struck the wall several feet below Oracle before a person from their group fired three more rounds.

"Communications are down. That'll slow backup, but someone may have heard the shots," Alessandra replied.

Oracle reached the next landing then made it six steps up.

"How bad are you hurt?" Alessandra's voice called to Lucinda in between shots.

"Mostly my pride," Lucinda said. Another bang resounded. "Can you kill those women, please?"

Five more paces. One more landing. Three more steps.

"Where's Oracle?" Alessandra asked between the intermitted shots.

Nine more stairs. One more landing.

"She's gone," Lucinda exclaimed.

Heavy steps hurried up the stairs. The railing vibrated under Oracle's palm after several thumps of what she assumed was Smith or Jones running toward her.

She hurried her pace. Legs burning, muscles protesting the steep stairs. Chains rattled at Oracle's right, followed by the sound of gears grinding and banging against the metal rails like a platform was being lowered.

"What's that?" Smith asked, as the heavy steps pursuing Oracle slowed to a stop.

She kept moving. Twelve more stairs.

"Grenade. Everyone out!" Jones screamed.

Doors banged below her just as Oracle reached the exit to the hallway leading to the control room. She slammed into the door as the blast went off. She dove onto the floor and slid along the slick surface, covering her head with her arms.

A hot blast hit against her back. Debris clattered and fell around her. Smoke clogged her nose. She coughed and lay still as a sleeping baby. She strained her ears, listening for footsteps or shouts from the stairwell.

Nothing. The ringing in her ears drowned out all sounds.

"Coming through. Stay down." Oracle jumped as a female voice spoke next to her ear. Her words were accented. Middle Eastern? Indian?

The ringing subsided enough for her to hear the woman shout, "Don't worry. A control box caught fire."

Whoosh went a fire extinguisher.

Oracle pulled herself up. Her knees ached and elbows throbbed, but otherwise she didn't have any major cuts or broken bones. She hurried down the hall, counting her steps. When she reached the glass wall, she ran her hands over the surface until she felt a break. The door was open.

"Gloria." Oracle tiptoed into the room and pushed out her energy.

Over here. Gloria sent the words into her mind when she made contact and saw an image flash of the room. Dark with dull green and red emergency lights along the floor and ceiling. The blast had taken out the power in the room. She pulled out when her chest ached from echoing Gloria's pain.

"Reyes, are you still with us?" Oracle asked then realized she could barely hear own voice let alone Reyes's response. She managed to feel her way across the room to where she saw Reyes collapse. Her foot slid on the slick floor and kicked into his shoulder. She grabbed onto a table to keep from falling, lowered herself to Reyes, and felt for a pulse. He had one, but it was weak.

She returned to Gloria. Her hearing slowing returning to normal. Her boss struggled to breathe as she struggled to say something to her.

"You shouldn't speak."

"Enjoy it . . ." Gloria tried to joke but the wheezing made it hard.

"Dama X's guards tossed a grenade down the stairwell. In the confusion, I was able to lose everyone."

"Blind . . . losing . . . spec ops . . . classic." Her words were fading. Oracle smoothed her hair back, laying a comforting hand on her too warm forehead, reaching inside Gloria, making sure she wasn't about to die.

"And there you are! You are quick." That same voice from outside the hall chirped inside the room.

Oracle froze and watched the woman approach through Gloria's foggy vision. Her graying hair was pulled back in a loose bun. Glasses over sharp eyes that glinted even in the shadowy room. Her hands were stuck inside her lab coat over a brightly colored, calf-length dress, her pink tennis shoes matching its floral print. Gloria recognized the woman. Excitement quickened her unsteady pulse.

"Dr. Banerji." Gloria tried to sit up. Oracle nudged her back down.

"Gloria, my dear, what are you doing here?"

"Dying."

"Oh, please, let me see." Dr. Banerji knelt. Her delicate fingers probed the hole through Gloria's wetsuit. She wrapped her other arm around to the back.

"It's clean. Went right through your lung. I can patch you up. In the meantime, here, take these." She handed her two pills from her pocket.

"Happy Pills?"

"What do you think? I invented them, so I always have a supply on me." Dr. Banerji chuckled. She went over to the sink in a far corner and filled a glass with water.

"Are those the pills our agents use in the field?" Oracle had taken them once or twice. They were used by injured agents to dull the pain until they could receive medical help.

"Yes, they are. Oh, and here's some petroleum jelly. I'll seal the wound until I can get you downstairs."

Gloria popped the pills and sipped the water. Almost immediately, Oracle felt the numbness spreading across Gloria's chest.

"Who are you?" Oracle asked.

"I worked for TransGen many, many moons ago." Dr. Banerji began patching up the chest wound. "Is that Dama X's sister lying over there?"

"Sister?" Both women blurted out.

"You mean brother," Oracle clarified.

"Yes, that's right, even if Xalvadora won't accept it. I should check on him." The doctor crossed the room.

"What do you mean?" Oracle asked Dr. Banerji.

From Gloria's viewpoint, Oracle lost sight of the doctor when she bent behind a cabinet to where Reyes lay.

"Dama X's twin sister is not only a transhuman but transgender. Felicia completed the transition to Felix over twenty years ago before joining the military. Uncle Suarez used his influence to secure Felix a position and recast his past as a male. Dama X never forgave him for becoming a man. Thought her sister did it for male privilege or some nonsense reason like that. But I don't know any woman who would go through that procedure unless compelled by a deep need."

Eyes wide, Gloria peered at Oracle's face. Oracle lifted her shoulder in response. Nothing surprised her anymore.

"His kneecap was shot. And there are burn marks at his temple."

"Alessandra stunned him with her electric hands." Oracle shook her head at how ridiculous that sounded.

"Ah, well, that explains why he's unconscious. A good thing because that is a painful wound."

Dr. Banerji opened a small refrigerator.

"Oh, goodie me, I have backups in here. I like it when my past self was clever enough to help my future self. Luckily you got shot in a room designed to be self-sufficient in an emergency." She held up several vials, which looked familiar to Oracle.

Gloria's eyelids closed, putting her back in the dark.

"Gloria." Oracle touched her shoulder. Her eyes opened but her vision blurred.

"Will one of those help Gloria?" she asked.

"Let me see." The doctor squinted at the vials. "Hmph, this lighting is horrible, and I left my reading glasses upstairs. One is to knock them out and ready them for cryo. Another is for powering up a transhuman."

Gloria coughed. Her wheezing worsened. Oracle felt bone tired. She began taking deep breaths as if doing so would force Gloria to ingest more oxygen.

The doctor looked over at Oracle then back at the vial. "I guess it's no use asking your young eyes to read it."

"Put them in front of Gloria's eyes," she said.

"You're seeing through her eyes? How fascinating. I remember Vivas working on you but never saw your ability myself." Dr. Banerji sat on the other side of Gloria. She held up the needles and Oracle forced her boss's eyes to focus.

Oracle's breath hitched from the fire overtaking Gloria's chest. She reminded herself it wasn't her body, but it was impossible to separate herself from the pain.

"The left one is At-At . . . I think . . ." Oracle blinked away the tears from Gloria's eyes. ". . . and the right is Epi-Tra."

"Thank you. That is a huge help." Dr. Banerji grabbed cotton swabs and alcohol from a cabinet near them.

With a nudge of her power, Oracle tilted Gloria's head so she faced the doorway. She hadn't heard a peep from the hall since she made it back into this room.

"Don't worry. No one is coming. That grenade blew out the stairwell and the debris blocked the door." She felt a wet cotton ball being wiped across the inside of Gloria's arm.

"I didn't think a grenade was strong enough to take out a stairwell."

"Leftover prototype ammo from when Suarez and DERST used this facility as a testing ground. Xalvadora found them in the island's storage area after her uncle passed."

"How will we get out?" Especially with Gloria and Reyes, Oracle silently added.

"I had a lift built between my lab and this control room. It wasn't in the original plans, so I doubt Alessandra knows about it. And Lucy certainly wouldn't. Dama X cut ties with her before she moved here."

"Is that how you got to this room?" They hadn't passed anyone on the stairs.

"After Dama X disappeared with TimeTrap and Pax, I wanted to see about getting the lights back on and check on my backup medical supplies. Then the explosion occurred as I entered from the back corner. I didn't even notice these two in here. I really need to get my eyes checked. Don't grow old, my dear." Oracle flinched as Gloria flinched at the needle Dr. Banerji jabbed in her arm. The drug was a shot of liquid ice. Both women shuddered.

"You may want to exit Gloria's mind. She's about to go night-night. This drug will put her in stasis so I can move her to cryo. Fortunately for her, the chambers contain their own power source. We can repair her lung when the lights and equipment—and my eyes—are working again."

Oracle took her advice and withdrew.

"You saw Pax?" It took a moment for Oracle to catch up to the doctor mentioning him.

"How could you miss him? He fills a room . . . and jeans very well, I might add."

Oracle arched a brow. "Then he's fine."

"More than fine, even these old eyes noticed."

She found herself smiling in spite of their situation.

"Feel free to use my eyes if you want," the doctor offered.

"Then you know I'm not with Lucinda?"

Dr. Banerji's joints creaked as she stood. "Of course you're not. That woman is crazy. My goodness, I told Gloria long ago, Lucinda was a bad egg back when they roomed in medical school. But did she listen to me? No. Young people always know best, I tell you. Besides, I heard her yelling at you from the hallway. You're here for your agents."

The doctor's shoes shuffled away from where Oracle cradled Gloria, now snoring, on the floor. She relaxed against the cabinets, enjoying this down time to recharge her batteries before the next round of insanity ensued.

"How are we getting Gloria to the cryochambers?" Oracle carefully placed the sleeping woman on the floor.

"Felix." Dr. Banerji called his name, and then Oracle heard the sound of a gentle slap. Oracle felt her way toward the doctor's voice. Her fingers trailed along the glass surface of a desk and over the sharp edge of the glass monitor hanging over command central.

Oracle heard a sharp intake of breath from the floor not far from where she stopped to lean against a desk.

"I'm going to inject you with the cellular restructuring serum that Lucinda used to heal you in the past. Do you accept this?" The doctor paused and Oracle assumed Reyes agreed because she said, "Give me a moment."

Oracle considered sending out her power into the doctor, but the idea of seeing a blown out knee cap made her stomach churn.

"There, now give it five minutes to run its course, and you'll be right as rain."

"Thank you," Reyes gasped.

"Are you hurt?" A gentle hand lifted Oracle's elbow then released it. Fingers examined her neck and scalp. Oracle got an image flash of reddish-brown marks forming on her chin and right cheek. Above these bruises appeared a few scrapes, scabbing over.

"I could give you an injection as well." Dr. Banerji shined a penlight into Oracle's gray-white eyes devoid of a pupil or iris.

"No, thank you. I already had a power boost serum injection earlier. Then there are the pills I've been taking for anxiety, which Lucinda also laced with shavings from one of the skulls," Oracle explained. "I'm done with it all."

"Do you know which skull she used?"

"She said Tezcatlipoca."

"Anything else in those pills?"

"She didn't say."

"Probably Surefire's blood as a delivery method, just like with the serums." Dr. Banerji's hands dropped from her skin, and Oracle lost the vision of herself and the room.

"What do you mean?" Oracle's chest tightened.

"That's one of the reasons why Lucinda kept Surefire. Her blood is the key to enabling skull proteins to enhance transhumans. Has to do with the properties aligning with the cellular makeup of—"

"That's what Reyes was accusing Lucinda of when he came down here. Why he was so angry."

"Lucinda used the first cellular restructuring serum to heal Reyes. I helped her create it. But before you get angry with me, I assure you, I had no idea she was using Surefire's blood against her will. Lucinda lied to me, so I stole what I could from her lab and brought Surefire and Raven here with me. I flew in with Dama X yesterday."

"If you thought Lucinda was crazy, then why work for her?"

"Money, why else?" The doctor gave her a cynical laugh. "I also saw an opportunity to work with a woman leading the field in transhuman genetics. Science is still a boy's club. The old guard tolerates women as long as they don't challenge the status quo. I wanted the chance to work on my own projects without the drama men create, and she'd promised that to me. But I should've taken my own advice, and I aim to fix it."

"It's working," Reyes said. His voice was strong and full of excitement.

Oracle reached out with her power to see from the doctor's perspective. She got a slightly fuzzy image flash of Reyes sitting up on the floor. Legs stretched in front of him. A hole in the pant leg over his knee with charred stains around the edges. Blood caked his pants from the knee down to his ankle. Her nose crinkled at the iron smell. She wanted to step back, but what she saw was too fascinating for her to look away.

"I can feel the skin knitting together, but it doesn't hurt. It tickles." Reyes watched the wound healing. Amazement lit up his face. "This is working faster than before."

"I've added nanobots to speed repair. A piece of your kneecap was left. Those nanobots are multiplying its cellular structure to grow a new one. You need to be careful," the doctor said when Reyes bent his knee, "I've never done it before on someone your size. A mouse took a few days before it could leap and race around."

"A transmouse?" Oracle asked.

"Mighty Mouse." The doctor chuckled and then clapped her hands. "Oh, how I loved that cartoon as a child."

Oracle couldn't help but giggle in response. The doctor had an infectious positivity that spread to Oracle as she lingered inside her mind. She held back from prying deeper, as Oracle witnessed the miracle happening to Reyes.

"I thought humans were the only ones with the transgene."

"I created these mice, working the transhuman code into their genes after many generations. Made a pretty penny when I patented them for use by other transgenetic labs."

"I can stand." Reyes pulled himself up with the help of a desk behind him. He kicked his leg back and forth. He looked at Dr. Banerji with childlike wonderment. "It took months for Lucinda's version to heal me."

"You were far gone after that attack. Aged nearly twice what you are. Every cell in your body needed to be healed. Although I wouldn't put it past Lucy to have watered down the treatment to keep you needing her."

"Do you know what this could do for soldiers in the field? How many lives this could save?" he said.

"Don't get carried away just yet. There is still testing to be done, and it only works on individuals with the marker capable of cellular change," she explained.

"Like transhumans?" Oracle asked.

"We're still learning why your cells have this marker to make you more acceptable to mutation and bodily changes."

"Which is why one man died from the Diosa de la Venganza and others adapted to the change," Oracle said.

"Exactly."

"I'm feeling stronger already." Reyes rocked on his feet, testing his strength.

"Good. That means you can carry Gloria to the cryochamber in my lab downstairs," the doctor said.

Through Dr. Banerji's eyes, Oracle watched Reyes scoop a sleeping Gloria off the floor and into his arms. The doctor motioned them to follow her to the other side of a circular wall. She pushed a button, and a bookshelf on wheels rolled out of the way to reveal a metal door to an elevator.

As they stepped inside, Oracle remained in the doctor's head to see where she was going. She continued to count her steps and noted the button Dr. Banerji pressed inside the elevator.

"This is on the same backup generator as the control room, and it's a bit slow to get caught up. Once the lights come on and the rest of my equipment is working, I'll take care of Gloria's wound," the doctor reaffirmed.

The door closed with a *swoosh.* Gears churned to life and the elevator jerked. Oracle grabbed the bar behind her for balance.

"What would happen if you gave Gloria the nanobot injection?" Reyes asked.

"Did you ever see *The Blob?*" Dr. Banerji asked, and Oracle got a memory flash of a man with organs and skin liquefying on an operating table. She withdrew from the doctor's head and tightened her grip on the bar.

"Sorry, my dear, I forgot you were in there," the doctor said.

The elevator stopped abruptly. Oracle heard the *swoosh* of the door opening and then a man's voice.

"Out. Hands where I can see them," Smith growled. Oracle unwrapped her fingers from the bar to comply.

"My hands are preoccupied," Reyes replied. Oracle sensed he was motioning that he couldn't show his hands with Gloria in his arms.

"Put her on the ground," Smith said.

Oracle heard the doctor step out and the sound of Reyes placing Gloria on the floor.

"Stay where I can see you," Smith told Oracle before thick fingers grabbed her shoulder and shoved her into Dr. Banerji, who let out a surprised gasp.

"You get in my head, one of them dies."

Oracle nodded.

"Where are the others?" Smith bellowed even though Oracle stood close to him. Rubber soles squeaked against the floor. She smelled Reyes's cologne in front of her.

"You're hurt. Let me help you," Dr. Banerji offered in a sweet, motherly tone that didn't come out as contrived as it did when Lucinda tried it.

"Stay back." Feet scuffed against the floor. "Where are Lucinda and Alessandra?"

"I don't know. I lost them," Oracle replied.

"Shit." He paused before demanding, "Where's your satcom?"

"On the topside, in the comm room. They have several locked up for emergencies. But the stairwell is blocked and most power is still fried, so the elevator is . . . oh my, dear, what is wrong with your friend over here on the floor." Dr. Banerji's voice trailed away from Oracle.

"Stay away from him. We have our own medic to help him."

"He doesn't have much time. The shrapnel did a number on his organs."

"Don't be foolish. She's a doctor. She can save his life," Reyes said.

"Not the way she's planning. He's not with the Freak Squad, doc. He's an N-T."

Reyes backed into Oracle. She wasn't sure if he was shielding her—hard with her being taller than him—or if Smith forced him away. She touched Reyes's hand and saw an image flash of the room with two empty cryochambers. He turned to look behind them, his gaze lingering on a long counter with a sink, various vials, and glass containers she couldn't perceive in the dim light. A light shown on their right from the elevator. She could make out Gloria's body slumped against the wall.

Smith's attention was divided between her and Reyes and the doctor inspecting his soldier sprawled on the floor.

Get ready. I'm going in. Oracle whispered the words in Reyes's mind.

"What?" Reyes said out loud.

Smith swung the gun in their direction. But Oracle had already stretched out her power and buried its tentacle in the center of Smith's forehead until she exploded inside of him, filling every crevice.

He screamed and the gun went off. The doctor and Reyes ducked as the bullet hit the ceiling. Smith pushed and shoved at her energy, but her suckers had already latched on. She pried his fingers from the gun and dropped it to the floor. Reyes dove at him and held him to the ground. A loud crack, then a sharp pain issued from Smith's shoulder. Oracle and the soldier simultaneously cried out. She doubled over and snapped back into her own body. She heard flesh meeting flesh and realized she made it out before Reyes landed a knockout punch.

"That's what I call teamwork!" Dr. Banerji cheered.

"I'm sorry. You felt his pain, didn't you?" Reyes touched Oracle's hand and her power leapt into him. She saw through his eyes. He peered into her face, studying the patchwork of welts and scrapes on her cheeks.

"I got out in time. These are from the explosion in the stairwell."

Reyes squeezed her hand and let go.

"Is he dead?" Oracle nodded to where she last saw Smith struggling with Reyes.

"I pull my punches when fighting N-Ts. He'll have a headache when he wakes, but he'll live. What about the other soldier?"

"Not good," Dr. Banerji replied. "Shrapnel tore through his side and leg. I believe a piece cut the pancreas and for sure another nicked the femoral artery. He's lost too much blood for him to be prepped in time for the chamber."

"What about Gloria?" Oracle asked.

"Almost forgot about her. Felix, be a dear and place her in that chamber while I deal with this man."

Oracle took a tentative step toward the doctor's voice. "What are you going to do?"

"Thank you, Felix. Now I'm going to strip her down." The wetsuit was unzipped. Dr. Banerji huffed as she struggled. She felt Reyes holding back, unsure what to do. Oracle felt her way to the chamber and worked with the doctor to tug the suit from Gloria's body.

"Much obliged to you. Let me insert the IV and, Felix, you can hit that large blue button, please, to close it up."

Oracle heard what sounded like steam releasing, followed by a loud click and then a lock grinding to a close. The doctor didn't reply to Oracle's question so she asked again, "What are you going to do to that soldier?"

A whirring sound filled the room. Next came the buzz of fluorescent lights. A blast of cool air hit Oracle's face from a vent above.

"Now that's better. I can see what I'm doing and which drug to use on him." Dr. Banerji's quick steps echoed across the room and then back again.

"And I'm not ignoring you, Oracle. I just didn't want to alarm you." She paused, and Oracle reached out her power to see why she stopped talking.

The doctor leaned over Jones and injected a serum into his side. Organs that should never be exposed, she could make out in vivid detail. Oracle was going to vomit. She reeled back into her body.

"Will that work on him?" Reyes asked.

"I don't know. It's his only hope. If not, he'll go quickly and won't feel a thing. Be a bit messy in here though."

Oracle bumped into a wall as she retreated from the scene.

"Where are Surefire and Raven?" Reyes asked.

"They are doing better than expected. Bounced right out of cryo. Must be that goddess power she has. They left to speak to St. John, I believe," Dr. Banerji said.

Oracle recalled the commotion when Smith tried to contact his ship. Were Raven and Surefire attacking them or vice versa?

"He's looking good, Oracle. I believe this soldier has the transhuman marker," Dr. Banerji noted.

Oracle exhaled a long, relieved breath. "I'm going to find Pax, and we're going to get off this island."

Pax. She prayed his name, tapping into the high-octane adrenaline pumping through her veins from the struggle with Smith.

Pax.

Her power burned up her spine and exploded out toward the ceiling and higher, up through a layer of floors above them. Until she smelled Pax's cologne, felt the bulk of his strong body, and then saw what he saw.

Oh no, Pax.

Pax watched TimeTrap scuttle out of the room. She swept out her hand and pointed to an imaginary line outside the door.

"Not crossing this. I did it last time I encountered these things and almost got killed. One UltraAgent got sucked into a whirlwind and chopped into bits, and another is a goddess's bitch." TimeTrap hugged herself.

Pax blinked. The hair on the back of his neck stood on end.

Oracle?

Was she here again? Inside his mind? The warmth faded as fast as it came, bringing his focus back to the crystal skulls set on black pedestals inside glass cases. They formed a semicircle around the room. Track lights shone down on each one from above like a museum display.

"I don't have all thirteen skulls, so the ritual you experienced cannot occur," Dama X explained to TimeTrap.

Pax recognized three out of the eight skulls, including the one she had taken from TransGen.

The further he walked into the room, the more he felt small snaps of electricity against his skin. He wondered if it was a security feature. An electronic barrier that zapped anyone who tried to remove the glass cases.

"What are you planning to do with them?" Pax paused. Goosebumps prickled his exposed torso.

"Protect them. Study them. Respect them. In his later years, my uncle looked to the supernatural—the unexplained—to provide answers. He found a way to tap into their energy to design our special cloaking system. A system financed by several large governments, but he had a change of heart and decided not to give it to them." She walked around the room, weaving between the cases, running her hand along each one in a sign of respect.

"Near the end of his life, he became obsessed with the occult and legends of his and other cultures. Such as the Romans and Greeks. You noticed the statue of Diana in the island's center." She twirled her hand.

"It stood out to me," Pax replied.

She smiled to herself and looked down at her hands before lifting her head to address Pax. "She doesn't belong to my Aztec heritage, but I felt a connection to her and I named my Sisterhood after her. If you look hard enough, you'll see how humans across time and space are interconnected. Their legends hold similar lessons. Gods have similar histories. Diana was seen as a protector of women—the feminine divine. In one story associated with her Greek counterpart, Artemis, she'd turned a young boy into a girl for the violent thoughts he had toward her."

She stared out the window. Pax fidgeted. He glanced back at TimeTrap who shrugged. They were being attacked, and he was getting a history lesson. He wanted to interrupt Dama X but also wanted her to talk, gain her trust, and hope she would let slip information that could help them. But it was hard for him to be patient. He was built for action, not talking.

"My uncle saw the imbalance of the world and how he contributed to it," she continued. "This is why he left the island to me. He had a vision before he died. In it, Ometeotl, the Aztec creator god, named me as the protector and creator of a new Tamoanchan, where it all began for us." She ran her hand over a glass case containing a clear skull with flecks of turquoise that reflected a prism of colors from the light above.

"That's the one you took from TransGen," Pax noted.

"It was taken from me. It belongs to me. This is the first skull Lucinda had studied. When she learned about their ties to transhumans. I funded her, believing we had the same goals. But she used me, attempted to study me like Surefire even if I'm not a vessel yet."

Dama X pressed her finger against the back of the case. She lifted off the glass.

"See, that's what I'm talking about. I can feel its weird mojo from over here." TimeTrap pointed. "What are you doing with that thing?"

"Refueling my power." She held the skull to her face and kissed its sparkly forehead. The turquoise bits glowed, bathing her body in its unnatural light. She hummed with joy. A humming that rattled Pax's bones, vibrating his teeth, making his vision shake as if the earth were quaking around him. He backed up toward TimeTrap.

"I thought you were the one, Pax. Too bad." Dama X sighed, and he started to ask what she meant but she continued speaking, "In Aztec legend, Ometeotl served as both god and goddess. Lucinda used this skull's proteins to create a more potent version of Diosa de la Venganza. As I said before, the original serum didn't turn men into women. It merely made men's penises shrivel up."

"Hit them where it counts," TimeTrap chimed in.

Pax frowned at her, wondering whose side she was on. This male bashing was getting old. No matter how much Dama X said there were good men, Pax felt she was taking it too far.

TimeTrap lifted her hands in semi-apology. "Losing their penis is probably scarier than death to most men."

Pax shook his head.

Dama X placed the skull back on the mantel and the case over top of it. "The threat of Diosa de la Venganza is how I took over and disbanded the cartel after my husband died—and this threat kept my Sisterhood safe until I could secure this island for us."

Pax recognized an obsidian skull next to Ometeotl's as belonging to the god Tezcatlipoca.

He pointed at it. "How did you get that one? Surefire told me she'd hidden it."

"It resurfaced. I believe it's needed now, which is how we found it." Dama X inclined her head toward the skull.

"So that's the self-existing one. Closed loop theory and all. I'd take a closer look but that would require stepping over my line." The UltraAgent crossed her arms.

Pax had no clue what "self-existing" meant, and he didn't have time for her lengthy explanations. He pointed to the other side of Dama X. "And the light purple one. That's Xochi's."

"It is. I will give it to Surefire when she returns. As Xochi's vessel she should have it."

"And where is she? Any ideas?" TimeTrap chimed in.

A cacophony of voices rose from outside. Dama X ran to the wall opposite from the skulls. The white paneling flickered away to reveal a floor-to-ceiling window. Several women climbed down the hill at the sides of the window. Two paused to peer through binoculars.

"What's going on?" TimeTrap leaned into the room as far as she could go without crossing the line.

Pax squinted and saw a boat on the horizon. No, not a boat. A submarine. Sailors were evacuating it. Jumping in the water and climbing into rafts.

"Did your people attack the sub?" Pax turned on Dama X.

She shook her head. "Our weapons aren't operational yet after Alessandra disabled them. Magda and the others were to gather my security forces to meet me here to plan our strategy."

Dama X exited the room. A minute later, she returned with two sets of binoculars. She handed one to Pax. "My cameras are still offline as well."

Pax focused on the submarine. He recognized the markings. The uniforms. These sailors were from a special ops team—a unit run by Pax's friend and former commander who worked with Stephen St. John. They were brought in to fight supernatural and transhuman enemies of the state. Several men from Pax's ESP team worked for them. This Army unit had assisted Pax in extracting his agents in Mexico when Ari raised the god and attempted to use his UltraAgents as a sacrifice.

He refocused the binoculars on a raft filled with men, paddling closer. Their uniforms were different than the others on the sub. They wore black with berets containing an insignia he couldn't quite make out. It looked like a snake with a pitchfork but it was too small to tell from this distance. Were they from a new branch of this special ops team? Maybe from a black books operation?

"And you didn't call them here?" Dama X pinned him with an accusatory gaze. A cold gust pressed against his skin then retreated.

"Who's there?" TimeTrap called from the doorway.

"I didn't call them. Maybe U-Sec contacted them after we were kidnapped," he said.

Dama X peered through the binoculars again.

"Let me see." TimeTrap tapped Pax's shoulder. Her curiosity trumped her fear.

She scanned the horizon. "Why are they abandoning ship? Oh . . . I see."

Dama X uttered what sounded like a curse.

"Hey!" TimeTrap chirped when Pax snatched the binoculars back.

A purple light streamed from the hatch on top of the sub. In its wake, grass grew over the gray painted metal. White and lilac flowers sprouted from the outer hull. Vines slithered up and wrapped around the guns. Trees grew several feet into the air from the hatch, knocking two soldiers into the water as their branches stretched out.

"Gives new meaning to flower power." TimeTrap snorted.

"Surefire's on that sub," Pax said.

"More likely she called forth the goddess to do this type of damage." Dama X lowered the binoculars.

"Not a fan of that goddess but she does great work," TimeTrap said.

Dama X glared at her.

"If she tricked and then used your friend to get a foothold in our world, I think you'd have a problem with her too."

"Yes, I would." Dama X bobbed her head and scanned the water again.

Two women climbed down the slope next to the window, machine guns slung over their shoulders. Another three followed with bows and arrows. Pax watched as they took a position lower on the hill, hidden in the brush. The soldiers in the rafts paddled toward the island. A few others swam in their direction.

"Tell your people to stand down," Pax said.

Dama X continued to study the scene through the binoculars. She didn't acknowledge Pax's order.

"Are they going to kill those soldiers?" TimeTrap asked.

"If they threaten us. It is within our rights to protect our property and ourselves," Dama X replied.

"If you fire on them, you will bring down an entire military force on this island. Unless Surefire disabled it, as soon as that ship sustained damage, an SOS beacon would've resounded. Helping these soldiers will divert an attack you're not equipped to defend against," Pax said.

Dama X dropped the binoculars but continued to gaze out the window. Pax couldn't gauge her expression—part reflective, part determined. TimeTrap fidgeted next to him but kept quiet.

Finally, she placed her hand on a panel at the side of the window. It slid open about a foot.

"Jess," she called to a woman with a bow and arrow and curly hair.

"Dama, what's going on? Why did our systems go down? And who are those soldiers?" Jess knelt next to the window.

Dama X held up her hand. "They're here for Surefire and the skulls."

"We can't let that happen."

"We won't. I want you to take care not to harm those soldiers. Allow them on the island. Disarm them. But don't fire on them."

"What do we do with them?"

"Secure them until Pax and I can speak to them."

After I find Oracle and Gloria. Pax wasn't going anywhere else without them. If more troops stormed this island, he didn't want either one getting caught in the crossfire. He had half a mind to leave Gloria for dragging Oracle, still not one hundred percent, into this situation.

"What's he going to say to them?" Jess ducked her head inside.

"Yes, what are you going to tell them, Pax?" Both women turned to him.

"The truth," he replied.

An explosion rattled the cases and vibrated the floor. It appeared to come from inside the compound, outside of Dama X's room.

"What was that?" Jess's hand reached for her bow.

Dama X waved her back. "Tell the others what I told you. None of these soldiers are to die, yes?"

"Got it." She sprinted down the slope.

Dama X closed the window then hurried from the room. TimeTrap and Pax trailed on her heels. As they approached, the frosted glass doors to her room opened onto a metal walkway similar to the one Pax had used to flee from the guards. In the bowl-like valley below, the Sisters congregated around the harbor to form a barrier. Weapons drawn, they waited for the boats to come ashore.

Pax smelled the smoke at the same time Dama X said, "This way."

The walkway clanged with their steps.

"Down there." A group of women pointed as they pushed past them.

"Are we being attacked, Dama?" One woman asked, her voice frantic.

"We'll work it out. Check on the children. Keep them together while we get this fixed," Dama X replied.

The woman nodded and led the group down the stairs to the level below.

Pax and TimeTrap followed Dama X for a few more yards until they came to a set of metal doors. Dama X pried them open and a stream of smoke bellowed forth.

They coughed and waited for the smoke to dissipate. Then Magda and Kristina ran out, stopping themselves at the railing and leaning against it as they caught their breath.

"What happened?" Dama X asked them.

"It was Lucinda and several others on the stairs below us. They returned our fire. We sent a grenade down the shaft on the dumbwaiter. We got them, but Penny's leg was hit. We dropped her off with the medic."

"Who did you get?" Pax angled closer.

"Ah, God, no, no," TimeTrap muttered behind him.

Magda rubbed dust from her eyes and smeared her painted mask. "Lucinda and Alessandra. They were firing on us along with two soldiers."

Pax's stomach clenched along with his throat and his heart. "Who else?" He towered over the woman, not realizing how close he'd gotten until Dama X laid a hand on his chest to hold him back.

"A woman, I think," Kristina interjected. "She had black on like the others. Her skin was dark, and she stayed against the wall in the shadows, not shooting back but moving toward us. I couldn't see who—"

Pax took off into the stairwell. He ignored the smoke and dust burning his throat and eyes.

"Oracle!" he bellowed, and jumped to the landing then circled around. The railing rattled beneath his hand. Several steps crumbled under his heavy gait, as he bolted further down the stairwell.

"Oracle!" His voice faltered. His eyes teared up. He came to debris blocking his way and punched through a concrete slab. He hauled up large pieces of glass and concrete and tossed them aside, trying to clear the stairs. His hands bled but it didn't matter.

"Oracle!"

He swore he heard a voice below him. A cry for help.

Chapter 20
Short-Lived Mistake

I'm just like everyone else except I can travel through space and time. No biggie, really. It's not like I can affect anything in this universe. Because trust me, you all wouldn't have your jobs right . . . sorry, I've been told by my boss that I need to shut it down now.

—UltraAgent TimeTrap at the Senate hearing on transhumans

Oracle's eyes burned. Her hands felt swollen, as if she were the one hitting through the glass and concrete.

Pax.

Oracle's plea went unheard. His arms moved like a machine, hell-bent on finishing the task. Saving Oracle.

But she wasn't underneath the rubble.

Pax. Stop. I'm not there. I'm coming to help you.

"We have to find Pax now. He's tearing through the collapsed stairwell. He thinks I'm under there," Oracle told Reyes.

"The power's back up, so you can take the main elevator," Dr. Banerji said.

"I know where it is." Reyes grabbed Oracle's hand.

She received an image flash of the lab lit up with fluorescent lights. From the corner of Reyes's eye, she saw Gloria asleep in the cryochamber. Reyes pulled her into the hall. Outside, the undersea world was lit by a green glow from the circular glass hallway.

They reached the elevator and the doors opened. Once inside, Reyes dropped Oracle's hand, and she reached out to Pax again.

Her power bounced. A basketball hitting the backboard then ricocheting toward the shooter. Her head whipped to the side and hit the wall.

"Are you okay?" Reyes asked. The elevator traveled so quickly. The G-force pressed on her shoulders.

"Something kicked me out. I couldn't get in." Unless it was some*one.*

Oracle tried again. Concentrating on Pax. His body, his mind. The way his tone changed when he talked to her. How his arms enfolded her. Strong enough to crush her, yet gentle. Always gentle with her.

I still love you.

Inside his head, she saw memories float by. Of Oracle and him dating, laughing. Then there was another voice. Not someone she knew. Accented and husky, it said, *Pax, come back to me.*

Dama X. How dare she try to control him again.

An invisible force pressed against Oracle's power. She shoved past it and into Pax's mind. His muscles strained from the constant pounding. Cuts broke open across his knuckles. He huffed every breath as he tore apart the stairwell. But she wasn't fully inside him.

Get out of here. Dama X wasn't ordering Pax, but Oracle.

You have no right to be inside him. She countered with a metaphysical shove of her own. A test of her power. At first, Dama X said nothing, then she responded with a slap that caused a sharp pain in Oracle's head.

She gasped. Reyes grabbed her shoulders. She sensed he was into her face. "Oracle, what happened? You're bleeding."

Oracle sniffed then licked her top lip and tasted blood. She wiped the back of her hand across her nose then sent out her power again fueled by determination. Her energy traveled with a force she didn't think possible. She slammed into Pax's mind, and he let out a grunt and staggered. She'd knocked Dama X away. Oracle no longer felt her suffocating energy.

Far away, as if in another room, Oracle heard the ding of the elevator doors opening.

Pax, I'm not there. Oracle whispered in his mind, tempering her anxiety that wanted her to scream it.

"Oracle." Pax stood and blinked. Through the hole he had made, she could see several layers down.

You're hurt. You need help.

Pax raised his hands. Skin tattered. Forearms speckled with blood.

"Where—?" Pax pivoted and craned his neck to look up the stairs.

I'm on my way to you.

"How are you doing this?"

"Down here. Help us!" A woman cried from the opening at Pax's feet.

A hand reached up and Pax instinctively grabbed it.

No! This time Oracle did scream in his head.

He hesitated. The feminine hand wrapped around his.

Idiot. Dama X's cold energy returned and nudged Oracle's. *You're driving. Get him out of there or let me take over.*

Hell, no. Oracle forced her power into Pax. She tried to make his hand loosen its grip. But Pax was fighting for control. He was confused and angry.

Not that she could blame him for wanting to command his own body. Then Reyes took that moment to move Oracle from the elevator, and it split her attention. Her power slipped enough for Pax to regain control and haul up Lucinda.

"You." A vision crossed through his mind. Lucinda's neck under his hand, crushed and crumbling like an aluminum can. He wanted to kill her. His anger was overriding his logic. And there was Dama X, vying for control of Pax and fanning his anger.

Do it. Dama X prodded.

"No!" Oracle screamed out loud, and then forced that energy into Pax and stamped out Dama X.

"Oracle, sit down," Reyes pleaded. "You're bleeding even more."

Oracle tasted iron. Reyes had put a cloth over her nose and pinched, tilting her head forward. Her legs wobbled as her head spun. Reyes caught her and eased her onto the floor. She focused her remaining energy back into Pax to find Lucinda staring at him. Her eyes wide with fear. Mascara caked around them. Dust turned her hair and face gray.

He held her off the ground by her left wrist. She kicked against his thigh then winced, her water shoes providing no hard edge to dig into him. A gash on her right shoulder seeped blood.

"Pax, please. You're hurting me," Lucinda pleaded.

He tossed her into the wall. Hard enough to bruise her but not break anything.

"Where is Oracle? Gloria?" He loomed over her. She cowered on the ground, flattening against a slab of concrete and glass.

Lucinda shook her head.

Behind him debris shifted and crunched. Pax swung around to face the noise from the hole where he'd pulled Lucinda.

Pax, watch out.

A bullet grazed Pax's shoulder. He reeled back. Oracle pressed her body against the wall and groaned when she felt the bullet's sting.

"That's what happened to Gloria." Alessandra lifted herself up and out of the hole. She ducked as Pax swiped out his arm to grab her. She shot again and the bullet hit his chest.

Everything went black.

Oracle snapped back inside her trembling body. Head pounding. Nose gushing slick, warm blood past the cloth Reyes held there. Tears streaming down her face.

"Oracle, breathe through your mouth. You're in shock," Reyes said in a neutral tone, one she was certain he'd used on injured soldiers under his command.

"He's dead. She shot him." Oracle wanted to die. She wanted Reyes to leave her and let Dama X find her and do what she wanted. It didn't matter now. She should've let Pax kill Lucinda, let Dama X finish the job.

"Hush. You don't know for sure." Reyes stroked her hair.

"There's the one who killed him," Dama X's voice resounded along the corridor where Oracle slumped.

"Oh my God, Oracle. You're bleeding. A lot. What happened?" TimeTrap exclaimed, followed by rubber soles scraping against the floor in front of where she sat.

"I'll tell you what happened. She didn't have enough control. You strained yourself. Ay dios mío, you weren't ready for this or to go toe to toe with—Felicia, why are you here?" Dama X demanded when she came to a stop in front of them.

"Can you hold this on her face like so?" Reyes asked.

"Sure, yeah, I got it." TimeTrap's cool, long fingers felt nice against Oracle's clammy neck.

Reyes grunted as he stood. Oracle wanted to thank TimeTrap for her help and apologize for being a hot mess, but she didn't have the heart to speak the words.

"You left us to go to Lucinda. You knew she was here. You could've told me," Dama X spat.

"I wanted to hear the truth from her."

"The truth? You believe that woman over your sister?"

"I wanted to stop Lucinda myself before anyone else got hurt. Confront her about what she'd done to Surefire and Raven. Plead with the soldiers to call off St. John."

"That's true," Oracle interjected. She reached out, touched Dama X's ankle, and with the last drops of energy replayed the scene in her mind of Reyes confronting Lucinda, and Alessandra shooting him. Dama X moved out of her grasp.

"But you knew Lucinda was keeping them, didn't you?" Dama X insisted.

"Once the military forced me to retire, I no longer had clearance. I only knew what she and my previous commanders told me—that you'd stolen a weapon from them. I'm sorry, Xalvadora."

"It will take more than an apology to make this right."

"Dama X," two women called out in unison. Heavy boots thumped and vibrated the floor under Oracle.

"We checked the stairwell. None of them are there."

"They can't get far. We'll find them. But now I need to take care of this one. Pax went loco when he thought she was trapped. If she dies . . ." Dama X didn't finish the thought but instead said, "I owe it to him that she doesn't. Felicia, get Oracle and follow me."

Reyes picked up Oracle and cradled her to his chest. TimeTrap walked at their side, still sopping up the blood from Oracle's nose.

"Sorry," Oracle whispered.

"You have nothing to be sorry for," Reyes said.

Yes, she did.

Pax staggered from the bullet's impact. He clutched at his chest, pressing his hand against the wound. It didn't hurt as much as he expected. Probably because he was too angry and in shock for the pain to register yet.

The unsteady floor shifted underneath his feet.

"Alessandra," Lucy addressed the vicious woman with the gun. "We need to get out of here before it collapses."

"Lucy, why are you doing this?" Pax pressed harder as the blood ran down his chest.

"It's Lucinda, and my reasons are not your concern." She picked her way over the debris and shoved open the door.

Alessandra aimed at Pax's head and motioned for him to follow Lucinda. She was far enough away that she'd be able to get off one round before he could grab her. This woman was calm enough and knew how to handle a gun to make that round count. He opted to follow orders.

Pax raised his throbbing hands and walked out the door into a hallway.

"He's not necessary anymore," Lucinda said from his side.

"What?" Pax turned to her.

Alessandra shot him in the back. He collapsed.

"Fuck!" He punched the floor, which momentarily diverted the pain from his back and chest to his fist. The floor cracked from his punch. Blood splattered over it.

"Such language." Lucinda tsked.

Lying on his stomach, he stretched his arm around to his back to feel for the bullet hole. His legs numbed.

"Wow. Gloria told me about the yoga. It's really paying off for you. You couldn't even scratch your shoulder before," Lucinda said.

The bullet lodged in his chest was between the top of his pectoral muscle and shoulder. The bullet in his back appeared lodged next to his spine. The agonizing pain in his lumbar region and the pins and needles tingling his legs made him reconsider his choice to follow orders.

"What should I do with him?" Alessandra reloaded.

"It would kill Gloria if we killed him. Then again, she may be dead already, so it would be a wasted bullet."

"I'm low on ammo. This is my last magazine." Alessandra checked the gun's chamber. "I could zap him. Finish him off that way."

The crack and low hum of electricity sounded above him. He looked up to see blue light arcing between her fingers.

Lucinda squatted several feet in front of Pax. Far enough so he couldn't reach her.

"You know what"—Lucinda pursed her lips, appearing to give an idea serious thought—"I want him alive. Most of his platoon from ESP are experiencing rates of cancer that can't be cured by conventional treatments. Pax was an exception. Instead of developing cancer, he grew stronger. I'd like to dismantle him—chromosome by chromosome—to solve this mystery."

Pax set his jaw. He poured all his pain, all his anger, into the glare he leveled at her. "You better hope I die here."

She stood abruptly. "No, Pax, you better hope."

Alessandra and Lucinda took off down the circular hall. Pops and snaps followed in their wake, the sound of electronics being fried. Probably the security cameras. He heard the elevator doors open. There was a scuffle and a loud zap before the doors closed and the corridor fell silent.

Using only his arms, Pax crawled toward the glass wall overlooking the sea. Outside, brightly colored fish darted by, a small squid chasing them. The sun flickered against the blue-green water. This level was only ten feet or so below the surface, which churned with sailors swimming and rafts floating toward the island. He stretched out his arm and gripped the railing. He pulled himself up. His weak hand slipped, too slick from the blood covering it. He fell onto his shoulder, sore from where a bullet had grazed him.

"Dammit!" Stars exploded in his vision.

He rested his forehead on his arm and tried to even out his breath and push past the pain.

But Pax couldn't, because the pain went too deep. Had Oracle been in his head, controlling him like Dama X? He'd been in war zones with IEDs exploding along his path, and he never felt more afraid than having no control over his body. But did that mean Oracle was alive? Lucinda said Gloria was most likely dead. Pax fisted his raw hands and held himself back from punching the floor again. If Gloria was dead, then it wouldn't help anyone for Pax to be gone as well. Especially with the chance that Oracle was still alive.

Which she was. He knew it deep in his gut. He'd heard her voice call his name when he was punching a hole in the debris. Her warm, soothing energy encasing him, trying to to calm him.

And this certainty was enough to give him strength to reach up to the railing again and . . . why was that school of silver fish staring at him? Pax narrowed his gaze at the violet hue reflected in the glass. The glass had been green, reflecting the emergency lights lining the floor.

He peered over his shoulder.

"Hey, man, what happened?" Raven held out his hand to help. His eyes widened when he noticed Pax's knuckles were covered in blood.

Behind him, Surefire stood with a light purple glow emanating from her skin.

"Let's do it this way." Raven put his hands under Pax's arms and hauled him up. He had forgotten that Raven had goddess-given strength as well as many other talents.

Once on his feet, Pax tipped forward. His legs were paralyzed.

"Whoa, there, buddy." Raven caught Pax before he fell.

"Place him on his stomach," Surefire spoke, but it wasn't her voice. It was Xochi's sultry purr.

Raven lowered him onto the floor. Pax sucked in a breath at what felt like hundreds of needles sticking into his lower back at once.

"Shit. This doesn't look good. Can you feel your legs, Pax?" Raven asked.

Wincing, Pax shook his head.

"Go to Banerji. She'll have the resources to help," Xochi spoke through Surefire.

"What are you going to do?" Raven asked, skeptical.

"Get the bullet out." Her fingers danced along Pax's scalp and down his back. Wherever she touched, a soothing tingle followed.

"Why don't we switch? I'll get the bullet out and you go to the doctor."

"I can make him more comfortable and alleviate the pain, which you can't do." Her hand rested on Pax's lower back. The prickling sensation subsided.

"Xochi, remember this man is a like a father to Surefire."

"Not . . . that . . . old," Pax got out.

"Okay then, *older* brother. Don't do anything freaky, you got it?"

"Go." Xochi flattened Surefire's palm on the base of his spine. Her fingers spread across the top of his glutes and tailbone.

"Hang in there, Pax. I'll be back in a flash." Raven disappeared.

Soothing heat spread across his back and around to his abdomen. It traveled lower to his groin, causing a reaction that left him relieved he wore pants and was on his stomach.

"Everything important isn't damaged," Xochi spoke. Then she paused. Her hand lifted and she jerked back with an, "Ugh!"

"Fine. I will not . . ." She growled in exasperation, struggling against an unseen force.

"What?" Pax gasped. Was she talking to him?

"Will you . . . ?" Xochi trailed off.

Pax tried to turn his head, but she planted a hand to his cheek and he couldn't move.

". . . leave me be to save him? . . . Thank you." Xochi, still controlling Surefire, huffed. "It is a pain dealing with a vessel, having another voice in your head."

Was she talking to him now? Pax decided to wait it out and see.

"Surefire won't quit speaking until I tell you that she's in here. She's okay, and I promise not to ravish you. See . . . Surefire . . . I told him," she shouted then muttered, "Never lets me have any amusement. In the olden times, my vessels would never be so belligerent. Kids these days."

She circled the bullet hole with her finger.

"Not too deep. Bone fragments slowed it."

Pax didn't need to know that.

"Are you numb?"

He nodded.

Her fingers dug into his wound. "If it wasn't for Surefire, I could make you even more comfortable."

She laid her body across his back. Her small breasts pressed into his skin through the lab coat she still wore. "So strong. You could come at me with all your strength and it wouldn't hurt."

"Uh-huh," Pax replied, glad she couldn't see how uncomfortable this made him. He reminded himself over and over to not insult the Aztec goddess of love, especially when she was dislodging a bullet from his spine.

Raven cleared his throat.

"There you are. Back so quickly?" The goddess sulked.

"Dr. Banerji couldn't come so she gave me directions. She's prepping the operating room for Gloria."

"She's alive?" Pax tried to crane his neck and look at Raven but the goddess held him in place.

"Yeah, she's in cryo for now but will pull through. For you, I have a special dose of this cellular restructuring serum that should do the trick. Banerji said to inject it directly into his wounds."

Pax watched Surefire's reflection in the glass, as she took the syringe from Raven and held it up to her eyes. "My blood is in this."

"What?" Pax and Raven exclaimed in unison.

"No matter now." Her fingers slipped from the hole in his back.

"Yes, matter now. Why is your blood in there?" Raven demanded.

"I don't feel right about this," Pax told Xochi then added to himself, "and the potential side effects."

"I won't be possessing you. It merely contains a connector isolated from Surefire's blood mixed with the essence of Xochipilli's skull."

"And who would that be . . . ?" Raven spread out his arms.

"My brother, his essence heals."

Pax felt pressure on his lower back. He watched her stick the needle near the bullet wound.

"Didn't know you had a brother," Raven replied.

"You never asked."

Pax squirmed from a tickle that turned into a pinch as his skin stitched together. He lifted his upper body to get a better look.

"That's cool." Raven rocked onto his heels and stared at his back.

Surefire—well, Xochi—shrugged unimpressed. "If your society was ready, you would've had this technology sooner. But I don't like it being taken from me without permission."

Pax wriggled his toes. His heart leapt with relief.

"Turn over, let me get your chest." She knelt at his side.

He became acutely aware that the effects from the goddess's touch had yet to wear off.

"No need to do my chest now," Pax replied. "Give me a moment to test my strength."

She snickered then wedged her hands under him. "Don't be embarrassed. I have that effect on everyone."

"Umph!" Pax grunted as she flipped him over. She straddled his hips, and he averted his gaze. When she wriggled into place, he knew she could feel how much her love power had affected him.

Her nails trailed down the center of Pax's chest to his stomach. Raven cleared his throat when her fingers wandered lower.

"Never any fun for the goddess." Heaving a sad sigh, she dug out the bullet and injected the serum into his chest and side of his shoulder, then used the rest to heal his hands.

"Thank you for saving Pax, but I'd like to have the love of my life back again." Raven helped her up.

With small, careful movements, Pax rolled onto his side and bent his legs. Without Xochi's touch, his body was settling down.

"Synthia's going to interfere, and we've done enough damage to cause even more imbalance in your world," she argued.

"Of course she's going to interfere. Her friends are in danger," Raven shot back.

When UltraAgent Surefire had cornered Raven—her assignment for Operation Bird Catcher—in a warehouse, he'd been stealing artifacts from museums and private collections for Xochi to restore balance to the world. An imbalance the goddess claimed was the cause of wars and human strife. With Pax's help, they received permission from most of the artifacts' owners to return the pieces to the rightful cultures. Pax hadn't noticed any lessening of the world's problems or an end to Xochi's obscure threats of mankind's demise. Maybe he was expecting too much in a few months.

"I shouldn't be helping you," Xochi said.

"Then let Surefire do it," Raven countered.

The goddess glared at him.

"Please," he added.

"But I am here. I most likely cannot create more of an imbalance to this world than all of you have already done to cause the inevitable to happen."

"If it's inevitable then—" Raven began.

"Too soon," she interrupted. "We don't want to set it in motion too soon."

Using the rail, Pax pulled himself up onto his feet, relieved that he could stand and his jeans were no longer snug. "Lucinda is going for the skulls. Dama X has them, including yours and Tez's, in a special room."

"Lucinda has no right to them."

"That's impossible, we left Tez's skull in that time loop. The same one where Surefire and I retrieved your skull to stop Ari." Raven turned to the goddess, whose brow creased as she shook her head.

"It found a way back. Maybe the loop was destroyed when you disturbed it." Xochi stared into Pax's face. Surefire's eyes swirled an unnatural purple. "Where are the skulls? Take me to them."

She held out her hand. Pax was about to grab it when Raven threw a green shirt over his outstretched arm.

"Picked up this double x-large scrub from the doc. It was left by the previous staff. Thought you could use it." Raven nodded at Pax's exposed torso. "I got a set for myself. Felt like a flasher running around naked under that jacket."

He noticed Raven no longer had the white lab coat but green pants and a v-neck shirt that surgeons usually wore.

Pax slipped the scrub top over his head, marveling at how the bullet wound on his chest had scabbed over, partially healed. Underneath the blood caking his knuckles, his flesh was almost as good as new.

"I brought scrubs for you as well." Raven motioned to Surefire's body, the lab coat stopped just above her knee.

"No, thanks. I'm enjoying the breeze." She took Pax's hand and grabbed Raven's, and they were off.

Chapter 21
Once You've Tasted It

I once had a clear path, then I became blind and a clearer path opened to me.

—UltraAgent Oracle in an interview with government officials about being
a transhuman

"Put her here," Dama X said. Reyes knelt and laid Oracle onto a cold concrete surface.

Oracle didn't reach out with her power to find out where they had taken her. She didn't care. Although she became curious when the hairs on her arm stood on end. A small trickle of energy started to surge around her, increasing to a churning river with each passing second.

"Grab pillows and a blanket from Xalvadora's bed," Reyes ordered someone . . . TimeTrap . . . maybe?

"What are you doing with her?" the UltraAgent asked, her voice becoming more distant with each step Reyes took. "Why are you bringing her here?"

The agent's concern got Oracle's attention.

"Where am I?" She lifted her head.

"Don't sit up. You're still bleeding." Reyes coaxed her back onto his lap.

"You're dead center in Dama X's crystal skull room. Can't you feel the bad mojo? Which is why I'm staying outside this doorway," TimeTrap said.

"I feel something." Goosebumps broke out along Oracle's arms and chest.

"Get a blanket," Reyes requested once more.

"Fine. I'll get the blanket, but no funny business or else I will do something . . . not sure what . . . but I will do something bad to you . . . and you over there." TimeTrap padded away.

"Feisty, I'll give her that," Dama X murmured.

Mild electric shocks pricked Oracle's neck and face as if trying to find a way inside her.

"What did you just do?" Oracle stopped herself from touching Reyes's skin and seeing the room and Dama X. Her head ached with the force of a Beethoven crescendo. Blood crusted on her upper lip and continued to drip inside her nostrils.

"You felt that, did you? That was the fourth one I tried. Lucinda must've used proteins from—"

"Tezcatlipoca's skull. She told me," Oracle said.

Dama X's rubber soles squeaked along the floor closer to Oracle and Reyes, whose hand rested on her upper back, his thumb gently rubbing her tense muscles.

"I should've known since that god attacked you. His power left a mark that goes deep down to your genes. Lucinda assumed correctly that the proteins from his skull would work best."

Oracle moaned and arched her back. The electrical current that played along her skin dug harder into her body, feeling like a painful deep tissue massage after hours of intense dance practice.

"You need to take this. It'll recharge you." Dama X held an object over Oracle's chest. She could feel the weight of it even if she couldn't see it. The woman held a crystal skull. Oracle's cells buzzed in response. Her blood pumped harder as if wanting to burst from her veins and join with it.

"Oh, no, this is what I was talking about," TimeTrap spoke up from across the room. Quick, hard steps carried her voice closer. "And now you made me come into this circle of crystal creeps because I'm not letting what happened to Surefire happen to Oracle."

What Oracle assumed to be a pillow and comforter dropped next to her with a soft thump.

"She needs this power to help her heal. She has a brain aneurysm and is possibly beginning to hemorrhage," Dama X explained.

Oracle stiffened. Aneurysm? Reyes lifted Oracle's head from his lap and placed the pillow underneath.

"Oracle, is this true?" TimeTrap asked.

"I don't—" Her throat closed up, and at any moment, her head was going to split open from the pressure forming.

"There's too much interference in this room. I can't pop you out," TimeTrap said with alarm.

"You take her out of here, and she dies," Dama X stated.

"It's okay, Kali," she said, letting slip TimeTrap's given name. Reyes lifted Oracle with one arm and pushed the comforter below her.

While in the corridor, Oracle had wanted it all to end. The person she loved most had died because of her mistake. But now she wanted to live. Faced with the choice, she couldn't quit. Oracle needed to stay strong for her agent, who shouldn't see her boss, her leader, give up. She had more work to do. Her life should be defined on her terms. Pax wouldn't want her to die. In fact, he'd be pissed at her for doing so. She could almost hear his voice yelling her name, telling her to hold on.

She reached up and her fingers wrapped around the smooth crystal skull. Her arms jerked as a heated energy poured into them. It spread over her body, leaving a refreshing tingle in its wake. The energy hitched up her neck. Her thumbs rubbed along the sleek surface and inside the empty sockets. Oracle gasped when the migraine subsided, and she saw through her own eyes—for the first time in over fifteen years.

Dama X leaned over her, a knowing smile on her lips. Reyes studied her, a male copy of Dama X's face. Harder, lined with stubble. But the green eyes were the same.

A blue streak lit up the black skull that she cradled to her chest.

"Kali." The UltraAgent stood several feet from Oracle. Arms hugging her body. Behind her, a window let in the pink and orange rays of the setting sun.

"Can you see me?" TimeTrap inched forward and gaped at her. "Your eyes . . ."

"Oracle, stop!"

"Pax?" Oracle looked past Kali to find Pax barreling into the room.

He shoved Reyes aside. "What are you doing to her? This is how Surefire became . . ." He didn't finish his thought but grabbed the skull. Oracle's vision blacked out.

"It's not the same," Dama X said. "This isn't a full skull circle. There hasn't been a sacrifice."

"I don't care. Do you know what this thing did to Oracle the first time?"

"Pax, stop." She slowly sat up.

"What's on your face? Have you been bleeding?" He rubbed a finger over her upper lip.

She wrapped her fingers around his wrist to stop him. An image flashed of her face, upper lip bloody, color returning to her skin. "I thought you were dead. I saw you get shot."

"You were in my head then." He knelt next to her.

She nodded. She wanted to read his mind, learn if he was angry with her. Instead, she withdrew from him and moved her hand off his skin and onto the scrub top he wore.

She laid a hand on his chest over the material. "I saw you get shot. Felt your pain."

Her fingers sought out the wound and found the bumpiness of a scab. He recoiled when she pressed against it.

"Xochi injected me with a healing serum that Banerji gave Raven."

"I thought I killed you." Oracle choked on the lump in her throat.

"You controlled me, just like you controlled TimeTrap," Pax said.

Tears flooded her eyes. "I won't do it again."

"We'll discuss it later." He wiped the tears from her cheek. Through his eyes, Oracle received a flash of Pax gazing down at her. He started to lean forward to kiss her cheek but thought better of it and dropped back from her.

"Why are you standing out there?" TimeTrap asked someone.

"Tezcatlipoca's skull is tapping into my power. Put it away," Surefire ordered, but it wasn't Surefire. The intonation was Xochi's.

Dama X's curly hair sifted across Oracle's face as she reached over her to take the skull from Pax. She heard the other woman walking away and felt the energy moving away with her. A click signaled the glass case being secured over the skull.

"These cases include a special property that blocks most of the skulls' energy," Dama X said.

"I know. I can sense it." Surefire's voice now sounded from inside the room. Oracle never heard her enter.

"Lucinda used that skull to weaken us," Raven said.

"It's like your kryptonite," TimeTrap added. "Makes sense. Every powerful being needs one."

"Why do you have these skulls? Are you going to pull a Lucinda and trap us again? Because I'm sure I don't need to recite the whole 'fool me once' anecdote," Raven challenged.

"Surefire—" Reyes stopped, correcting himself. "Xochiquetzal, what are you doing?"

Reyes rose to his feet. Oracle heard his soft steps go from behind her and across the room.

She touched Pax's hand. The room flashed into sight. Surefire stood eye to eye with Dama X. Her hands cradled the woman's face.

Reyes stalked closer. His tenseness conveyed the concern he felt for his sister. Raven grabbed his shoulder to stop him. He shook his head at Reyes.

"You've been chosen, haven't you? I didn't notice it before when Surefire fought me for control. But you are the Keeper."

"My uncle passed it to me," Dama X said.

"Ometeotl. The Creator." Surefire nodded.

"What?" Reyes gasped.

"It's true. The Creator chose me." Dama X smiled at her brother.

"Both of you." Surefire's hands dropped from Dama X, and she pointed to Reyes. "Ometeotl is duality, like you and your brother."

"Sister," Dama X protested.

"No, the spirit is male. Has always been male. Ometeotl recognized this or wouldn't have chosen you both. Your brother is true to himself. Why can't you be true to him?"

A shot rang out in the room. TimeTrap screamed. Pax covered Oracle as she heard two bodies simultaneously hit the floor.

♥　☠　♥　☠　♥　☠

Pax balanced his upper body on his forearms as he stretched over Oracle to shield her. Across from him, two bodies lay prone on the ground.

"No, no, no!" Raven ran to Surefire sprawled on the floor. Dama X lay next to her. Both weren't moving. Blood pooled in the space between them.

"Xalvadora." Reyes dropped next to his sister and grabbed her limp hand.

"What happened?" Oracle whispered.

Before Pax could reply, a woman barked, "On the floor."

Pax spun toward the entrance. Two sailors—one man, one woman—entered, sweeping the perimeter. Alessandra marched in. She held a pistol steady in her hands. The three wore wetsuits like Oracle. The sailors dripped water onto the floor while they stormed across the space. From thin sliver chains around their necks hung vials containing sparking powder. As they entered the room, Pax noticed an insignia on their right arms, an eye of providence encircled by a snake with a trident. He wasn't familiar with this patch. Were those men in the black berets part of this group? The insignia on their caps could've matched this design. It was most likely a black books operation, separate from the military units he'd encountered on other transhuman cases. Yet another topic to discuss with St. John when this was over, if they both survived.

"That's her. That's who killed St. John." The sailor with red, spiky hair and the name Botts on her wetsuit motioned with her gun.

"She didn't kill him. Just turned him into a large daisy. He'll get better." Raven hugged an unresponsive Surefire to his chest. "But what you did to her—"

"She'll be fine. Only stunned. I would never kill her. We need her." Lucinda strolled in and then stopped, her expression slipping into one of awe as she took in the skulls displayed in the room. "Get the door."

Alessandra pressed her hand against the side of the entrance. A crack of electricity and the smell of burning wires followed. The heavy door slid shut, locking them into the room with a loud click.

"Lucinda, you're going to pay for this." Pax lifted his upper body off Oracle and raised his hands.

"I've already paid in years of service to those who never believed in me, who stole my ideas, like Vivas and my father." She leaned over the glass case containing Xochi's violet skull.

"You're the one who poisoned him and the others," Pax stated.

Her eyes flicked to Alessandra then back to him. She wasn't going to admit to this crime in front of the SEALs. They still believed Dama X was behind those attacks.

"Everyone has a purpose," she said evasively. "Dama X as well."

Pax wanted to keep her talking. The more she did, the more uncertain the sailors seemed. "James Donovan, too?"

She froze and turned but not before Pax caught the smirk on her face. "Everyone gets what they deserve."

"Like my sister?" Reyes clutched Dama X's hand.

"I needed a distraction. Besides, your sister will be fine. She has the power of the gods running through her veins. Both of them do. One to a lesser extent, but it'll all be good." Lucinda paused in front of the crystal skull, which belonged to Ometeotl. The light illuminating it created a prism effect in its cranium.

"If they'll be okay, then why aren't they moving?" Raven demanded.

"They were hit with darts laced with a transhuman beta blocker that neutralizes them. It won't last long, but long enough." Lucinda tugged on the case over the skull. She bent down to peer at the pedestal.

Pax's muscles twitched, longing to take her down, make her pay for what she'd done. The man with "Williams" sewn on his wetsuit must've read Pax's intentions on his face because he aimed the barrel of his gun squarely at Pax's forehead and yelled, "Down! On the floor!"

He laced his hands behind his head and laid flat next to Oracle. He could scan the room if he lifted his head a bit.

"Anyone know how to open this?" Lucinda looked around the room, pausing on TimeTrap who was on her stomach, eyes screwed shut.

"You shot the one who did," Reyes bit out.

Lucinda felt around for a switch.

Pax stayed close to Oracle's side. He watched the movements of both sailors and Alessandra, who always had her finger hovering over the trigger. Williams was just under six feet. Swimmers build. Lean muscle. He favored his left leg. Botts squinted and kept rubbing her right eye. Pax guessed her to be about hundred and forty pounds. Strong legs, build of a soccer player. She kept a tight grip on her weapon, focused on Reyes and Dama X.

Get those necklaces off them. They protect them from my power.

Oracle's voice sounded loud and sure, as if she were speaking into his ear. He didn't feel her touching his skin.

The anxiety pills were laced with dust from Tez's skull. It enhanced my ability. When I'm strong, I don't need to touch to see. I don't have to concentrate as before.

You're seeing through my eyes now?

She nodded.

"Shit. It's DNA encoded with a fingerprint reader. I just got pricked. We need Dama X's blood to open it." Lucinda sucked on her finger.

Are you strong enough to take them? Oracle's hand touched the wound on his lower back. He sucked in a breath as the pain resurfaced. It wasn't quite healed.

This is nothing.

You can't lie to me when I'm in your head.

"Do you want me to try?" Alessandra offered. A blue current playing along her fingers.

Lucinda shook out her hand. "That really smarts. No, I'm afraid it may make it worse if we try to fry the circuits."

The sailors watched as they discussed ways to open the case. Their attention divided, Pax nodded to Reyes, who was staring at him, waiting for direction. Reyes tapped Raven in the thigh. He glanced up from where he cradled Surefire's head in his lap.

Alessandra pressed her gun against Reyes's head. "Carry your sister to the case."

With small, careful movements, Pax turned to TimeTrap. She opened one eye, saw Pax nodding to her, and then closed it.

Are you kidding me? Pax shook his head.

She's not a fighter, Pax. Let me talk to her.

TimeTrap's lips moved as though she were talking to herself.

Reyes drew Dama X into his arms. Limping, he carried her body over to the case where Lucinda stood.

The skulls are messing with her mojo, Oracle explained.

What does that mean? Pax cringed when he jerked up to look at Oracle, which reminded him that his pectoral muscle was still healing.

Blocking her ability to teleport, bend space/time. The glass cases help diffuse energy from the skulls, but she doesn't know if she has the strength to teleport herself or anyone else.

Tell her to stay out of the way.

"It's not working. Why isn't it working?" Lucinda asked the room.

"If she were awake, she could tell you," Reyes replied.

Alessandra zapped Reyes with a jolt of her power. He fell into the case and dropped his sister.

Raven can take the woman closest to him. But his power was drained by the skulls. The crystal powder in the vials may be affecting him too.

Then we rip them off.

What's the plan? Oracle remained on her back. Her eyes closed. Hands on top of her stomach. The SEAL standing over her probably assumed she was unconscious.

Shit. He'd been counting on Raven's supernatural strength and ability to phase out. He could also heal quickly, but a severe injury—say a gunshot—would slow him down. One to the head would stop him. Would it kill him? According to Surefire, he had died once and was resurrected by the goddess whose power kept him alive—but could he rise again?

Three with weapons. Lucinda appeared unarmed. Alessandra may be the only transhuman. He couldn't tell if the others had abilities. He'd need to go easy on them and not use his full strength, which was good since he didn't have full strength.

We need a distraction, Pax sent thought to Oracle.

"No, no, God, no." Lucinda held out her hand. It was bubbling. The skin expanding, growing.

"What's happening to you?" Alessandra backed away in disgust. Reyes slid toward the wall.

"A needle pricked me, injected me—" She screamed, clutching her arm to her chest.

"Possibly the serum Dr. Banerji used to heal my knee. Only works on transhumans. On N-Ts, the cells over multiply," Reyes said.

"Get that doctor now!" Lucinda screamed.

Pax grabbed the ankle of William's bum leg. He lifted and flipped him over onto his back. Leaping up, Pax felt a sting as a bullet skimmed his bicep. He ripped the gun from Williams's hand as the sailor landed a foot in Pax's solar plexus.

He reeled back to catch his breath. Another shot whizzed by Pax's ear. In his peripheral, he found Alessandra aiming at him. Reyes tackled her, the gun sliding from her hands. Behind them, Raven broke off the necklace from Botts's neck. He slammed a palm into the side of her knee.

Williams flicked his wrist and a knife flipped out of a compartment hidden in his sleeve. He sliced at Pax's forearm. When he followed through with another swipe, Pax twisted and landed an upward jab and heard the crunch of the sailor's jaw breaking.

Williams grabbed at his jaw. A zap of electricity stole Pax's attention. Reyes's limbs quivered, his teeth ground shut, eyes rolled back into his head. Alessandra pushed Reyes off her and lunged for the gun.

"No." Pax dove at the same time but he was too late. Alessandra grabbed it and rolled toward TimeTrap.

"Stop, or this one dies!" Alessandra pressed her weapon against TimeTrap's temple.

Out of the corner of his eye, he saw Raven crush Botts's necklace in his hand. The sailor limped to her feet and nabbed her gun from the floor. With a wide sweep, she slammed the handle into the side of Raven's head. He fell to the floor. His hand rested on Surefire's cheek. His eyes fluttered close.

Alessandra hauled TimeTrap to her feet. "Take Lucinda to Banerji."

"I can't. These skulls block my ability."

"Bullshit." Alessandra's finger twitched over the trigger.

An arc of electricity leapt from Alessandra to TimeTrap's temple. She squealed and doubled over.

A harrowing scream echoed in the room. Lucinda fell to her knees, holding out her arm. The skin melted to reveal her forearm muscles and the tendons in her hand.

The gun ground down into his agent's temple. Pax considered his options. He glanced at Raven, whose skin had paled. He appeared sick, drained. The tattoos on his neck slithered and shifted on his skin. Pax blinked, believing it was a trick of the light.

Reyes moaned and tried to lift himself from the floor. When this didn't work, he began crawling toward his sister.

Botts kept her gun focused on an unconscious Raven and Surefire.

"Take her now!" Alessandra's hand tightened around TimeTrap's upper arm.

Another zap of power shook the agent's body.

"Ow." TimeTrap tried to pull away but was too weak from every shock. Her knees wobbled. "No need for the shock therapy. I'll do it. Just get me out of this room."

"No."

"Over there. Near the windows. Away from these cases. It may be far enough." TimeTrap pointed across the room.

"Just get her." Lucinda held her deteriorating arm aloft.

Alessandra dragged TimeTrap toward the window, and Lucinda shuffled after them.

"What's this?" Botts lifted her feet. Vines snaked up her legs.

"Shoot Surefire, again," Alessandra ordered, but Botts threw her gun down.

"Oracle." Alessandra's wild eyes landed on her. "I will kill—"

A shot fired. Alessandra dropped her gun. Blood poured from her wrist. TimeTrap ducked away and disappeared. Surefire stood in the center of the room with Botts's discarded gun in her hand.

Pax pushed himself up as Williams snatched the gun he'd drop during their scuffle. He fired at Pax, who ducked. The bullet nearly hit Alessandra as she knelt down to retrieve her gun with her good hand. Reyes leapt from behind Williams and wrapped his arm around the man's throat.

Another shot and Pax swung his head toward Alessandra, who swore as the bullet punctured a hole through her palm. A blue current snapped then faded, along with the color in her face.

"Don't threaten my friends. Do you want to try again? I can keep hitting important bits until there is nothing important left of you," Surefire, no longer Xochi, said.

Oracle sat up. Her head turned to Botts, who stared at the wall. Vines stretched up her calves to her knees.

"They're afraid of us," Oracle said.

Surefire lowered her gun. "They should be."

"Lucinda tricked them. They believed Dama X was going to use Surefire to threaten world leaders. They feared her having the skulls and the power to do so," Oracle explained.

Pax realized Oracle was inside Botts's head, relaying the sailor's thoughts.

Once Reyes ensured Williams was unconscious, he moved to Alessandra, who cradled her hands against her stomach. Her cheeks twitched and her jaw was set tight, but she didn't cry or shake or display any distress.

"You are wrong. Lucinda was protecting us. Dama X doesn't deserve this power. She will use it for her own gain, doling out punishments as she sees fit." Alessandra pressed her lips into a firm line.

"Lucinda has a funny way of protecting people." Pax's shoulder and chest ached in agreement.

"You'll see," Alessandra sneered.

"You know nothing about my sister." Reyes removed a knife from the holster around Alessandra's waist.

"I know she killed my husband, Miguel. She invited him to a dinner where she unleashed Diosa de la Venganza on the guests. He suffered greatly before he died, and I will see to it that she does too."

"Those guests worked for the Mictlantecuhtli cartel and terrorized Mexico for decades. Your husband was a killer for Estabon. The Mexican military called him Puño del Diablo, the devil's fist."

"Lies. Made up to disparage him and me. We did what we could to survive just like your family did." Blood surged between her fingers.

"Did Miguel use you to steal secrets from Suarez Tech? Was that why you left, or did my uncle fire you?"

"I didn't take anything from Suarez that didn't already belong to me. I trusted Dama X with what I'd done and she squealed to her uncle, using my secret to reconcile with him. She betrayed me twice."

"It doesn't negate your betrayal. Lying about my sister."

Alessandra snorted. "You were quick to believe those lies. You knew what your sister was capable of doing." She glared at Reyes standing above her with the bowie knife, almost daring—no, beseeching—him to kill her with it.

He twisted the knife in his fingers. Pax wondered if he was going to use it on her.

"Reyes," Pax said cautiously.

"She's right, Pax. When my sister married Estabon, I thought what Xalvadora had experienced had corrupted her, making her become that which she despised in order to survive. But she was stronger than I gave her credit for. I won't make that mistake again." He turned his back on Alessandra and put the blade away.

"I found her." TimeTrap popped into the far corner by the window. Next to her, Dr. Banerji stood a head shorter than TimeTrap with her gray hair pulled back in a loose bun.

"I'll have my work cut out for me. Glad Gloria is somewhat healed and able to help." Dr. Banerji wagged her head at the scene before her.

Everyone turned to the case next to Ometeotl's skull, where Lucinda lay unmoving in a pool of liquefied skin and muscle and bone. Her right hand and forearm gone, skin beginning to bubble at her elbow.

"Ah, and that's what it does to N-Ts." Dr. Banerji walked over to Lucinda.

"I'm going to be sick." TimeTrap cupped her hand over her mouth.

The doctor removed a needle from her pocket and stuck it in Lucinda's bicep above the severed forearm. Her body jerked than stilled again.

"What will happen to her?" Pax asked.

"She'll be our human test subject. See if we can reverse the effects, maybe neutralize it so N-Ts can benefit from this."

"Don't touch her," Alessandra said.

"You aren't in a position to make demands," Dr. Banerji said. "And here I was going to use my serum to save your hands."

"I want nothing from you."

The doctor shrugged and then motioned to Botts, still staring into space. "What's wrong with her?"

"I was inside her head, keeping her still," Oracle said.

Surefire raised her hand and the vines grew higher around Botts's legs and stomach. Botts exhaled as Oracle released her. She pulled frantically at the vines.

"We're not going to hurt you. I just want to ensure you won't hurt us," Surefire said to Botts, who was too busy throwing a fit to acknowledge her explanation.

Surefire fell to her knees by Raven as Pax helped Oracle to her feet.

"What's wrong with Raven?" Pax motioned to him. Was he even breathing?

Surefire caressed his cheek. "He transferred his life-force to me so I could heal."

"He's not . . . ?" TimeTrap trailed off. She laid a comforting hand on her friend's back.

"He'll live. But I need Xochi's skull to power him back up."

"I will get it." Dama X wobbled onto her feet. Reyes gripped her elbow to help her balance.

Dama X pressed her hand on the back of the pedestal and the case opened up.

"You're bleeding." The doctor hurried to Dama X, who waved her away.

"It's nothing. The bullet grazed my thigh. It was laced with a drug that stunned me, but the effects are fading. Help the others."

Dr. Banerji complied. She threw a roll of gauze at Alessandra, who made no move to use it. The she handed Oracle a wad of wet wipes for her nose and gave one to Pax for his hands.

"I need help getting Lucinda down to cryo," Dr. Banerji said.

"I can take her." Surefire grabbed the skull from Dama X. As soon as it touched her hand, it glowed a light purple.

"What about the others?" Dr. Banerji asked.

Pax took in the room. "Williams has a broken jaw. Alessandra—"

"Don't touch me."

"—doesn't want to be touched," Pax finished.

"They can stay here, out of the way. I'll have my people stand guard," Dama X said.

"Don't hurt them, they aren't bad. Just scared and misinformed," Oracle said.

Pax squeezed her hand.

"Oh, no," TimeTrap interjected. "That one is bad." She pointed to Alessandra, who glared at her.

"And that one"—she pointed at Lucy's unconscious body—"is super bad. If assholes had a queen, she'd be the one."

"What about Dr. Vivas and Cook? Lucinda knew the cure for Diosa de la Venganza. She needed Ometeotl's skull to create the remedy," Pax said.

"I was the one who created it for Circe," Dr. Banerji said. "I can create another batch and have it ready in a few hours. Can someone get it to Dr. Vivas and Cook?"

"I will." TimeTrap raised her hand. "I need some of my protein bar stash, but I should have enough juice to make it once I'm out of this room."

"I can give you a power booster shot," Dr. Banerji suggested.

"Yeah, I'm good." TimeTrap's eyes flicked to Lucinda.

"We'll come back for the rest soon," Dr. Banerji said.

Raven lifted his hand to Surefire's hair. She kissed his forehead. "We're ready."

Surefire, Raven, Lucinda, and Dr. Banerji disappeared from the room.

"Alessandra destroyed the door's keypad when she broke in here. We'll need to go through the window." Dama X laid a hand against the wall and the glass slid partway open.

"It's quiet," she noted.

Pax walked over to the window and scanned the ocean. The terraformed submarine floated somewhat farther away from where he last saw it. No sailors or boats remained in the water.

Far in the distance, what looked like a flock of large birds appeared.

"Can you get your cloaking ability back online?" Pax asked.

"Depends on how badly it's been damaged." She cut a look at Alessandra then flagged down a woman jogging along the slope toward them.

"Dama, we tried to get into the room to help you but the door was locked. I came out here to try the window." She stopped near them. "Are you okay?"

"I am now, Patricia. Where are the others?"

"U.S. troops have come ashore. Some of our Sisters are holding a group of unarmed sailors peacefully, and others are engaged in a battle with those who won't give up without a fight."

Dama X nodded.

A distant explosion got everyone's attention.

The woman started to move toward the sound when Dama X stopped her. "Help these men"—she motioned to Reyes and Pax—"secure the prisoners here. Oracle and I are going to stop this attack together."

"You're not taking Oracle with you." Pax moved out of Patricia's way as she climbed through the window.

Dama X ignored him and walked over to the crystal skulls, opening two of the cases.

"Pax, it's okay." Oracle touched his back.

"No, it's not." Another explosion like a distant firework. A grenade. Pax recognized the sound all too well.

"Once you secure them, then you can help us," Dama X said to Pax, and then turned to her guard. "Patricia, contact tech for an ETA on getting our cloaking back online."

She nodded and removed an old school walkie-talkie clipped onto her belt.

"Hold out your hands." Dama X handed Oracle Tez's skull. The fading sunlight revealed blue sparkling highlights along the cranium.

Dama X grabbed Ometeotl's skull for herself.

"Oracle." Pax wanted to tell her not to go, to be careful. But he couldn't say the words. Then he noticed her eyes were no longer a grayish white. She had pupils and irises, brown with yellow flecks, as he'd seen in her childhood photos. "Your eyes are . . . beautiful."

A tear trickled down her face. Pax wiped it away. He couldn't stop staring into her eyes as she continued to stare into his, as if they were looking at each other for the first time. "This is allowing me to see."

Pax shook his head, needing to wake from this daydream before he forgot about the real world and the real fight going on outside. "What's the plan?"

"You don't want anyone to get hurt so we're using an alternate weapon. Our power. Combined, we can end this fight. And this skull will boost her ability. Don't worry, she won't be in the line of fire." Dama X motioned for Oracle to follow her through the window.

"Can you do this?" Pax asked, remembering what Gloria had taught him about asking first and not making assumptions, not making decisions for her.

"I won't know until I try, and she is experienced with this power that I possess. I'm scared, but I want to help and stop anyone else from getting hurt." She kissed his cheek.

Then she turned on her heel and waltzed over to the open window, her steps more certain than he'd ever seen her take before.

Chapter 22
To Seek, To Find, and Not to Yield

I regret only one thing.

—Pax to Jaybird during an ESP troop reunion

Crystal skulls held against their chests, Dama X and Oracle stood along the railing and looked into the bowl-shaped valley below. Her guards had corralled a group of sailors from the sub onto the archery field. On the other side, twenty or so Sisters surrounded sailors who had taken refuge in the gardens on a plateau above the practice fields.

"They have a radio." Oracle pointed to a man in a black uniform and beret, speaking into a comm device.

"If the Sisters get our systems back online, then we can scramble the signal." Dama X studied Oracle's face. "You can see through your own eyes?"

"When I touch the skull, I can."

Dama X nodded, but Oracle didn't like way her brow furrowed.

"Although, my vision's not as clear as before," Oracle said.

"It's the skulls. They feed on each other's energy. In the room, the glass cases blocked most of their power. We'll need to keep our distance when we do it."

"Do what?" she asked, but before Dama X could reply, Oracle noticed two guards setting up a rifle on the hill above the sailors. "Are your people going to kill them?"

"Pax was right. We can't kill them. They are misinformed. That's not a reason to die." As Dama X stared at the snipers, a chilled air gathered around them and then blew past Oracle.

The women waved at Dama X in response. Once they crawled away from the rifle, Oracle reiterated, "What do you want me to do?"

Dama X watched as several men and a woman fell back into a large shed in the center of the garden. "What Alessandra accused me of, what she wanted to kill me for, I did only two times with the aid of this skull before it was stolen from Lucinda, who had been studying it for me. Then I tapped into its power once more when I retrieved it from TransGen. The first time, I made a room full of my husband's associates turn on one another. Those who didn't die by the others' hands, I used the original version of Diosa de la Venganza to make them suffer first. They were fifteen of the most sadistic devils ever birthed. I did it to save myself and my country. Was it wrong?" She half-shrugged. "Depending on the side you're on. But I was in the middle of a war where you take lives to save lives."

Oracle tightened her grip on the skull. Its energy throbbed, aroused by Dama X's story.

"The second time was with men who had been assaulting women at my club. Then I retrieved the skull from TransGen and used it to make that guard and officer attack Pax. But I need your help for this. I counted twenty trained fighters using the garden's shed as a shield as they fire upon my Sisters. We need to make them drop their weapons and surrender."

"To reiterate, your guards won't kill them," Oracle said.

"I told them not to. Unlike men, they listen." Dama X limped down two flights. Oracle followed, growing concerned at the blood soaking the right side of Dama X's pants.

When they stopped on the lower walkway, Oracle said, "You're bleeding."

She glanced at her thigh. "A flesh wound. But I should wrap it up."

She set down the skull and removed her V-neck sweater. Underneath she wore a gray tank top over her leggings.

Dama X tied the shirt tight around her leg. "My bruja outfits are for show. I find it easier to fight and maneuver in this. Much more comfortable and easier to underestimate me when I look like a fitness instructor."

Oracle surprised herself by laughing. Dama X appeared so normal—so human. She grinned in response. She noticed a necklace—like Surefire's—resting on her chest where a tattoo of black butterfly wings spread across her breasts and disappeared under her tank top.

Dama X picked up her skull and then dipped her head toward the garden. "Look over there."

They stood at mid-level on a metal walkway that lined the sides of the valley. From this vantage, they had a clearer image of the sailors within the garden area: two women and eighteen men. As they watched, all but two of the sailors fled inside the large shed. They had enough ammunition to defend their position and do damage to the Sisters fighting against them.

Below the garden plateau, a woman with a long ebony hair, wearing a flowing white pantsuit, bandaged several guards lying outside a grenade's blast radius. Oracle spied another area of seared grass where a second grenade had hit, although it must have been a dud because the area wasn't as large. No casualties surrounded it.

"Focus on the sailors closest to you," Dama X said. "I'll take care of the others. Use one person's mind at first, and when you feel comfortable, go for the others. Do what is necessary to unarm them. I'll move closer onto the field. You stay on the walkway two levels below where we are now. That should keep you out of their line of fire if they spot me, and you need to finish it."

She tried not to let the worry show on her face but the other woman saw it and laughed.

"Don't worry. I won't let it come to that."

Once more, Oracle trailed Dama X down the stairs until she motioned her to remain on the designated floor. Then the leader hobbled down the last two flights and entered the wide grassy field.

She didn't have time to be anxious or consider whether she could or couldn't do this. The closer she came, the more the sailors' desperation wrapped around her in a chokehold. Their fear tasted of bitter chocolate. In response, the skull buzzed, growing hot. Without much effort, their voices bounced inside her mind. They waited for the extraction team about thirty minutes out. Her gut churned.

What would the military do if they found this island? The memory of St. John's blank mind boosted her into action.

Oracle inhaled, filling her lungs with the scent of gunpowder and tropical flowers and sea air. When she exhaled, the power spilled forth with an urgency that caught her off guard. Not a floating spirit that flittered out to the world, but a poltergeist able to shake the foundation of a house.

She focused on a sailor along the fringes, leaning against the entrance to the shed. A mix of gun oil, body odor, and rich soil filled her nose. The man was afraid and angry and wanted to go home to his child. He propped his back against the doorjamb of the garden shed as he reloaded his weapon.

Oracle pushed her power into his limbs. She opened his hand and let the gun slip to the ground.

His mouth gaped in mid-yell. The power spiked, becoming stronger the more afraid he became. She forced him to lie on the ground.

"Have you been hit?" A female sailor leaned over and shouted over the gunfire. "Flint, answer me."

She touched his neck to feel for a pulse. Oracle's power leapt into her while still maintaining a connection with Flint. She forced this woman to lie down next to her battle buddy. Her fear also energized Oracle's power, and she savored the succulent taste.

If she didn't concentrate, she could see from both sets of eyes. It was disorienting, reminding her of a spider's vision.

"Don't touch them!" An officer ordered another sailor, who had stopped firing and moved to check on his fallen buddies.

Oracle's power leapt from the female, named Polaski, to the soldier inching away. She made his arms go limp. His weapon slipped to the ground next to a discarded rake.

She closed the eyes of the first two sailors then stretched out her power across the wide shed to the commanding officer in the black beret. He pointed his gun.

"I'll shoot him," he said.

Oracle paused at this unexpected threat.

Three sailors from the far end of the shed dropped to their knees. Dama X's ice cold power brushed past Oracle's. Her vision wavered then cleared. The commander's finger rested on the trigger.

Oracle slammed into him, pushing him back against the wall. The gun dropped from his hands onto the dirt floor. The energetic thread she'd woven across the three wrapped around this man's body, pinning his arms to his sides and his legs together.

He struggled against her, and Oracle's grip began to slip on the others. The first sailor yelled for help and the second gasped.

Concentrate. She visualized the power thread becoming thicker until it grew into a corded rope.

A sailor called out from the other side, "Aim for the woman up there with the skull. She's—"

He choked on his words as Oracle's power looped around his throat and tightened and tightened more until black spots floated across his vision and . . .

Stop. No. This isn't you. Oracle released her grip and the man gasped for air from his burning throat.

She shook her head and the four sailors' heads swayed in unison. In her hands, the skull pulsed with a preternatural heartbeat. Thump. Thump. Thump. It pumped a searing power into her blood, and with it, a dark force she'd felt once before. Last time it had tried to crush her, and it weakened her spirit. This time it was a symbiotic force, weaving inside her and embedding a darkness that grew the more fearful her victims became.

Oracle wanted to drop the skull but couldn't. She'd lose her grip on the troops. She could only hope she wouldn't lose a grip on herself.

An object whizzed by her cheek and struck the glass door behind her. She sidestepped and another bullet missed her. She spied the barrel of a rifle sticking out from the shed's doorway.

The dark energy longed to crush those under her power. It expanded and nudged and shoved at Oracle's conscience, persuading her to kill them, unleash the power on the shooter and then everyone around her.

The thump, thump, thump became kill, kill, kill.

Oracle stepped to the left and avoided another bullet. The power balled up in her throat. It rose like the gentle ebb of an ocean tide that turns into a riptide without warning, sweeping unsuspecting swimmers away.

Through her own eyes, she spied Pax and Reyes along with two guards crouching low behind the shed before moving inside. The shooter's barrel disappeared. She refocused inside the shed to find the shooter along with the remaining sailors surrendering.

Pax and Reyes disarmed the sailors. The Sisters handcuffed them.

"We got it." Pax looked into the eyes of Polaski and Oracle withdrew. Her attention no longer fractured, she realized how exhausting it had been to be spread so thin. She leaned against the railing, taking stock of what had happened and what she'd done—and almost done.

Oracle stared at the skull in her hands. Flecks of red and blue sparkled against the shiny black crystal. Sweat dripped from her face as she poured the power back into the skull, like shoving slime into a jar. It slid against her skin, trying to seep around her fingers to return inside her.

She wanted to drop the skull, but she wanted to see the scene even more— through her own eyes. It was a freedom Oracle had missed so much. She wondered if it would be worth it to sell her soul to this god to have her sight back.

Pax, Reyes, and two Sisters marched their captives to where the others were penned up in the archery range and forced them onto the ground, hands secured behind their backs.

Dama X handed her skull to the woman in the flowing outfit. They didn't speak—not out loud—and the woman took the skull away and into the level below, disappearing from Oracle's sight.

She turned her attention back to Dama X, who glanced up and gave her a triumphant smile. Then she walked over to the prisoners. Even in workout attire, Dama X had a regal flair, emanating authority with every certain—but limping—step toward her loyal guards.

Oracle sought out Pax, who stood with his hands on his hips. He stared at her with an expression even her god-given eyesight couldn't make out. An overwhelming urge to touch him, talk to him, forced her into a sprint down the stairs, where she nearly barreled into Raven and the woman with the flowing outfit.

"Give the skull to Gracie." Raven blocked the flight of stairs down to the grassy valley—and to Pax.

"Why?" Oracle flicked a glance at Gracie with her shiny, blue-black hair parted in the middle and the serene oval face of an angelic hippie. Her skin a shade lighter than Oracle's, eyes were brown—or maybe green—it was hard to tell with a light glowing behind them that slightly changed their color.

"Because I can feel its power tugging at my own. When I first saw you, I could sense Tezcatlipoca's power inside you. But when you're holding his skull, the energy's concentrated. You're powering it up." Raven pointed to the skull and continued to keep his distance.

"I can't see without it." At least, not through her own eyes. Oracle hugged it to her chest.

"Yes, you can. Maybe not how you'd like to view the world, but there's a price for this power, trust me."

Oracle caressed the smooth crystal. Her fingers dipped into its sockets. In the distance, but drawing closer, she heard the sound of helicopter blades.

"They're almost here, and Surefire needs to do her thing and that douche god doesn't play nice with others." Raven pointed his middle finger at the skull.

Gracie stepped around Raven and laid her slender hands over the smooth dark crystal.

Oracle snatched it away. One more step and she would smash the skull into Gracie's face.

"No," she yelled, but not at Gracie—at herself. Her arms held the skull aloft, ready to make the desire a reality.

"No." Oracle shook her head. She wouldn't sell her soul for this power. Even if a piece of it had already been given for this ability without her consent.

She lowered her arms. Hands shaking, she held the skull out to Gracie, who hugged it to her chest. Then Oracle's vision turned black, like the final scene of a movie. The skull's energy tugged at her. She turned in its direction, the prickling power fading as Gracie exited the walkway.

"I'll take you to Pax . . . or maybe not . . . because here he is." Raven's warm power pressed along Oracle's skin then dissipated. With that, he was gone.

Heavy steps bounded toward her, rattling the metal walkway. Muscular arms enfolded her. Her feet lifted off the ground. She nuzzled her cheek against Pax's stubbled jaw. She breathed in the lingering scent of his cologne, the one she'd bought for him years ago.

As if remembering they were no longer lovers, Pax set her down as quickly as he had lifted her.

Her heart fell. Oracle sensed him moving several feet away. Too far. Stepping forward, she closed the gap between them.

"I'm sorry. I was just happy to . . ." Pax stumbled to find the right words before giving up and asking, "What did Raven and that woman want?"

Oracle fought the urge to kiss him. Take his face in her hands and plant a long, deep kiss on his lips. Instead she said, "They wanted to take Tez's skull away, so Surefire can do her thing. Whatever that is."

"Your face. I didn't notice the scrapes and bruises before, but it looks like they're fading." She sensed his hand hovering near her face as if debating whether it was safe to touch her.

She pressed her cheek against his palm. Holding her power inside, she focused on the warm comfort of his hand caressing her skin. "It doesn't hurt anymore. They felt raw earlier. The skull's energy helped heal me, maybe it's still healing me."

"I'm so glad that you're okay." His hand dropped from her face. "I want you to see what's happening."

Lacing his fingers with hers, Pax gave Oracle his view of the archery green, where the sailors continued to sit in groups circled by the sugar-skull-painted Sisters. Dama X and Reyes conferred with Surefire, who gripped Raven with one hand and Xochi's skull with the other. A helicopter appeared over the edge of the hillside.

Oracle drew back.

"It's okay. The shields went up in time. They're seeing the ocean, not an island." Pax tilted his head and watched the helicopter fly over. In the fading sunlight, Oracle spied a spider web of laser lights, crisscrossing above the island.

"What is Surefire going to do?" she asked.

"She's calling forth Xochi to transport those sailors back to their sub. She needed them in one place to do it, and we wanted them unarmed."

"But can't they find the island again?"

"Surefire and Raven disabled the sub's navigation and fried the controls, erasing any saved coordinates. The sub has already floated further back, thanks to the currents. Another helicopter is circling the sub in the distance. As soon as she transports them, they'll be rescued."

"And the helicopter that just flew by?"

"The island has a magnetic force that is scrambling the controls for the helicopter. They can't pinpoint their location let alone ours. As for St. John, I don't think he'll be back for Dama X. She's no longer a threat to him. It's Surefire he wanted, according to his men. Owning her island would've been a bonus."

"I don't understand why he didn't ask for our help in the first place."

"According to one of their officers, he wanted Surefire and Raven to remain in cryo. He knew we wouldn't let him do that. That's why he used Lucinda and didn't tell us. Afraid we'd sabotage the mission."

"I don't trust him anymore. Not that I trusted him to begin with, but I thought he was on our side." Oracle recalled the blank void in St. John's mind.

"In his opinion, he is," Pax said with a snort.

Oracle shook her head then realized with a start that one of their agents was missing. "Where's Kali?"

"Putting away several protein bars to renew her energy so she can transport the serum back to TransGen. She's spent."

"I know how she feels." Oracle let out a relieved sigh. Out of habit—an old habit—Oracle laid her head on Pax's shoulder.

He arm twitched, and he grunted.

"The bullet, is it still in there?"

"No, just sore, back in the skull room a bullet nicked my arm." He shrugged it off.

Static electricity tingled along Oracle's scalp. Across the green grass, a purple mist surrounded the sailors and thickened into a sparkling smoke, obscuring the field and everyone on it. The fog swirled before evaporating and revealing empty ground where the troops had been.

They're on the sub. A chopper is circling them. Dama X sent the words into her mind.

"The sailors are safe," she related the information to Pax.

"How–?"

"Dama X told me in here." She pointed to her head. "It's a bit odd when someone else does it."

Pax chuckled. "I have no idea what you're talking about."

Oracle gave him a light punch on the forearm and laughed.

The crowd on the field roared in victory. On the walkways, across the valley and below, people streamed out of doors and balconies to gather together. A cheer erupted. Multiple languages combined to become one voice proclaiming victory.

A purple explosion lit up the archery range like a firework. Oracle looked for Surefire and Raven but couldn't find them.

"Where did they go?" Oracle asked.

"Somewhere safe," Pax said.

Oracle received a memory flash of Surefire telling Pax they were going to The Old Ones, where Xochi lived, a place Surefire referred to as the Garden.

"I have to admit that this island is an awesome setup. Wouldn't mind getting a place like this for U-Sec."

"Do you think we need to hide ourselves? Have this type of security?"

Pax's thumb stroked her hand. "I hope not. But as soon as we return, I'm having a talk with St. John about honesty."

"I don't know if he'd get it." Oracle told Pax about what she encountered when she entered St. John's mind.

"I have no idea what that means," she said.

"Me neither, but if he's wants to continue working with U-Sec, we have a right to know what he's about."

Footsteps rattled the metal walkways above them. A flock of women and a few men galloped down the stairs to join the celebration on the fields.

"Let's find someplace quiet to talk," Oracle suggested as the first group made it to their landing. They voiced their appreciation in multiple languages and excited gestures. Oracle and Pax smiled, nodded, and backed into a corridor, which—to their relief and delight—led to a glass door and a solarium. Overstuffed chairs and a couch surrounded a rustic table painted with sugar skulls along the edge. The room was so tranquil and removed from the raucous celebration in the valley that if Pax told Oracle the battle had been a fantasy, she might've believed him. Far in the distance over the choppy water, they spied the sub—appearing like a child's toy bobbing in a tub. Two helicopters hovered above them against the purple and pink sky. Pax touched the lock button on the keypad.

With a loose grip on her fingers, he led her to the couch and then noticed a mini-fridge in the corner.

"Maybe they'll have something to drink." Pax dropped her hand, but Oracle remained inside him, seeing through his eyes. He opened the door to find well-stocked shelves.

"Water?" he asked.

"Beer," she replied, mouth watering at the prospect.

"You're still in my head?" Pax grabbed two beers and popped the tops off.

"Sorry." Oracle took the beer and retreated into herself and the grayish black void.

"It's okay." He settled onto the couch, and his fingers settled on top of her hand, giving her a view of the setting sun.

"It's not okay. I almost got you killed." She took a drink then licked the bitter taste from her lips.

Oracle slid her hand onto her lap. She didn't want to touch Pax and hear his thoughts. Instead, she wanted him to reveal what he chose to.

"Back in the stairwell, you were controlling me like you did Kali." His words were measured. She couldn't tell if he was disappointed or angry or both.

"Yes." Oracle dug her nails into the wetsuit material covering her thigh.

"How did you do it?"

"My anxiety meds were laced with proteins from that god's skull. It strengthened my ability, which is how I could go in so deep with Camille, the first person I'd ever controlled. Then Lucinda gave me a booster shot before we arrived at the island. It was like a steroid for my power. I have no idea what chemicals comprised it and if I need another booster to be a tele-marionettist."

"A *tele*-what-a?"

"It's a term Gloria made up about my power."

Pax's beer sloshed inside the bottle. "We'll have Gloria check into the pills. I'm sure Dr. Banerji can shed some light too. She mentioned Lucinda was using Surefire's blood to make her treatments effective."

"The pills I've been taking were made using Surefire's blood. Banerji told me all about it and how her blood was also used in the serum that healed Reyes and TimeTrap."

Oracle took in a long, chest-expanding breath and exhaled slowly. When that didn't calm her, she took another drink and wished she had something stronger than beer.

"Don't worry until our people run tests," Pax offered in reassurance.

"I wanted to stop taking the pills when I found out that Tez's proteins were inside them—and now inside of me. But this . . . this is worse. Gloria told me I need to be weaned off, but I can't continue taking those pills knowing what was done to Surefire and Raven to create it. I don't care what happens to me." Oracle understood Surefire's fear of being used for her power. Now she had benefited from it.

"If Gloria says you need to stay on them, then you do. Surefire will understand."

Oracle smoothed a hand across her hair, bits of which had fallen out of her bun.

"I'm also concerned about how this drug is affecting me, affecting my decisions. When you were in the stairwell searching for me, I was afraid Dama X was going to hurt you when she entered your mind. But it was me, instead. I distracted you and got you shot—and almost killed. I won't do it again."

He blew out a breath then cleared his throat. "I don't have to tell you how much I didn't like it."

Oracle cringed. She pressed back into the cushions, wishing to disappear. "I need to talk to Kali and apologize. What I did to both of you was a violation of trust, no matter the reason."

Pax didn't correct her or agree with her. Instead, he took a long swallow of his beer, as if buying time or finding the courage to say what he truly thought.

Oracle fidgeted, drawing her legs up under her.

Finally, Pax said, "I hate to think what would happen if an enemy had your power. When Dama X was controlling me, I was afraid . . ." He paused, his weight shifted on the cushion. "I could've killed Kali, if she was Dama X's target instead of Reyes, who luckily could take a punch from me—and give one too." She heard his fingernails scratch his stubbly jaw. "I couldn't do anything to stop her, no matter how hard I fought for control. I'd take a room full of armed enemy combatants over that experience again. We'll need to create mental armor for the field to defend against this new kind of threat. I'm hoping Oliver will have some ideas."

"I can be the test subject." Oracle picked at the label on the bottle sweating in her hands. "Besides, it may buy me brownie points with St. John since I used my amped up ability to control some of his N-T soldiers."

When Pax didn't say anything, she continued, "St. John kept tabs on me before this power surge. I've sensed his men trailing me on occasion, making sure I didn't cross the line when using my ability on N-Ts to get image flashes. I'm afraid of what he's going to do now." She didn't have to remind Pax that doing so was against a law passed this month.

"Nothing. That's what he's going to do."

"I wouldn't be so certain. Someone will take the fall for Surefire disappearing again, and Dama X fighting off his people and then literally dropping off the radar with the skulls. He'll put the pressure on us to turn them in."

"Trust me about this. St. John's sailors attacked civilians on a mission that wasn't on any official books." Pax resettled on the couch. His knee rubbed against hers. "Plus, St. John needs us. He needs U-Sec. He can't risk jeopardizing our relationship or putting any of our agents out of commission."

"What do you think he just did today? I'd call that harming our relationship." Oracle set her empty bottle on the coffee table.

"He just witnessed how much he needs our help. Maybe the outcome wasn't what he expected, but a travesty was averted. He bet his chips on the wrong person. And we gained an ally."

"Dama X?"

"Yeah."

"She's powerful."

"And we need that power on our side."

"She helped us. She came through for us. But I don't fully trust her." Oracle stretched her stiff back.

"At this moment, I trust her more than St. John."

A spike of jealousy cut into Oracle's chest, which she knew was ridiculous. "I saw how she looked at you when you were on her bed. I believe she has a crush on you."

Pax snorted. "Yeah, right. I think her mind is on other things."

And Oracle's should be too, but with Pax sitting so close, she was all too aware of his body. How he could easily wrap his arm around her shoulder and draw her into an embrace. If he wanted to.

"On the plane to Mexico, Gloria admitted she broke us up, and she did it because she still wants you," Oracle said.

"Why doesn't it surprise me that Gloria told you this?"

To Pax's credit, he didn't question why Oracle broached this topic. She didn't know herself. Perhaps it was comforting to talk about something normal like their relationship after this abnormal event.

"Gloria said you were afraid of hurting me or of someone hurting me to get to you. However, you never asked me if I was afraid—what I wanted."

"I wanted to protect you," he said, as if it were the most obvious reason in the world.

"From you?"

"Yes."

"That's a decision I can make, as a grown woman with experience in relationships. I know now when one is good and when one will hurt me."

"My strength. I still break things by accident. The other day, I flushed the toilet too hard in the stall at work. Sean had a hissy—which was actually worth it. Then there's Matthews and the security guard. I nearly killed them."

"But you didn't. You held back even under attack, you had control." Oracle placed a hand on his shoulder and squeezed.

"Not enough. I put them in the hospital."

"Matthews understands. He knows you didn't mean it. He's forgiven you."

"That's because he's a good guy."

"He is and so are you."

"We're not the same. Matthews won't—"

"Hurt me?" Oracle dropped her hand. "Pax, you didn't need to touch me to hurt me."

That got his attention. "I didn't want to hurt you. That was the last thing I ever wanted to do."

"Is that why men keep breaking up with me? So I don't get hurt?"

"What do you mean?"

"Matthews broke up with me because he knows I'm still in love with you." There she said it, tired of skirting the elephant in the solarium.

"Oracle, I—"

"Gloria said you still felt the same."

Oracle pushed her next words into his mind. *I dare you to say you don't. You've always known how I felt. It hasn't changed.*

"Then say it out loud," Oracle challenged.

♥ ☠ ♥ ☠ ♥ ☠

"I love you." Pax rubbed away a tear at the corner of Oracle's eye.

"Then why aren't we together?"

All the reasons he used in the past seemed inadequate, unreasonable, stupid. "I don't know."

"Didn't I prove that I can handle myself in the field?" She unfolded her legs and stood.

"Yes." Pax sucked in a breath as she planted her knees on either side of his lap to straddle him.

"We make a good team, professionally." Oracle kissed his right cheek. "And personally." She kissed his left.

He swallowed a groan. The last time a woman nuzzled him was in a very vivid dream. Reality with the same woman was much sweeter.

"I should find Dr. Banerji and check on Gloria. Maybe get some Happy Pills. I'm still pretty sore." His hands betrayed what he really wanted as they caressed her thighs before resting on her sides, holding her in place.

Oracle placed her hand on his chest. "Does it hurt here?"

"A little." He sucked in a breath as she laid a kiss there.

"What about your shoulder?"

"Yes." Her soft lips skimmed the area above the wound.

"Your jaw." She rubbed her thumb over his jawline.

"Yes."

Oracle flicked her tongue over his pulse and up the side of his neck to his jaw before brushing her lips across it.

"What about here?" She placed a finger on his mouth.

He leaned into her, pressing his lips against hers. Her mouth opened and his tongue tangled with hers. His fingers dug into her wetsuit and tore holes in it.

Pax broke their kiss. "I'm sorry, I—"

"Rip it off," Oracle commanded.

He obeyed, tearing the suit from her chest to her belly button. She stood and he shredded the lower half, revealing her lean dancer's legs. He reached for her bra.

"Not yet." She slapped his hand away. "This off now." She tugged at his shirt.

He obliged.

She smoothed her hands along his chest, carefully avoiding the still healing wound. Her hands dropped lower over his abs, which quivered in response.

Oracle hooked her fingers into his belt loops and yanked. "I want to feel all of you."

Working quickly, he unzipped and lifted his hips to shimmy out of his jeans and underwear. She helped him slide his pants from his legs. He kicked off his shoes.

"Now you." Pax eyed her breasts, which strained against the bra they filled too well.

She knelt between his knees where her hands rested. The sides of her breasts rubbed his inner thighs, teasing him.

You remember the rules. No touching until I say so. Her voice ebbed and flowed through his mind.

"Screw the rules." His fingers itched to unlatch her bra and to bend her over the sofa, tearing the thin cotton panties . . .

I get to do what I want first. Her hands ran over his thighs, down his calves, and back up to his knees as if cataloging his body.

I don't know how long I can last like this.

Try. She kissed his inner thigh. Skimmed fingertips over his hairs. Her tongue darted out, tracing a line up his leg.

His breath hitched.

Not yet. A whisper, a threat, echoed inside his thoughts.

Her hands wedged between his legs, pushing them further apart, stopping short of his most sensitive area.

"You're killing me," he moaned.

"Why?" Oracle smiled, trailing her lips along his skin but avoiding where he wanted her to touch the most.

"Because I want you."

She leaned closer. Her breasts suspended over him. If he raised his hips, he could grind against the lacy fabric. Maybe brush his hard tip against the soft skin overflowing from the bra. But she held him in place. The throbbing pain in his groin growing more painful than the bullet he'd taken.

He closed his eyes. "Cassandra, please."

That's what I wanted to hear, Levi.

She kissed him where he'd been begging her to touch.

"Please." Pax lifted his hips and shook with pleasure at the feel of her soft, luscious lips.

♥ ☠ ♥ ☠ ♥ ☠

The sun toasted Oracle's skin. Too much longer lying on the ship's deck and she'd need to reapply lotion. She caught herself nodding off. The sound of the waves lapping against the boat was nature's lullaby.

A fishing reel whirled. Water splashed at the bow. Pax's feet hit the deck from the chair he'd been lounging in.

"You catch something?" Oracle called over to him.

"Almost. Broke the line."

A tackle box rattled from Pax's direction. Oracle laid her head back down on the towel. She relished doing absolutely nothing and thinking about absolutely nothing. She could never repay Dama X for letting them use her boat to take a few days' vacation.

Gloria decided to stay as well but with Dr. Banerji, learning about her research and performing tests on Lucinda. They were only able to slow the transhuman drug, not stop it from from boiling her skin off.

"Not having much luck. Maybe I'll join you." Pax sank down on the large blanket Oracle was lying on.

He kissed her lightly then shifted to cover her.

"Be careful. You didn't apply sunscreen to your butt last time." She chuckled.

Pax kissed her throat. "It does still burn. We should go inside."

"And now you two." TimeTrap huffed, surprising them both.

Pax rolled off Oracle. "What are you doing here?"

"I stopped at the island of Dama X. She did her little mind thingy and showed me where you were."

"I thought you went back to the office." Oracle checked her bathing suit, making sure everything was in place.

"I did and Dr. Vivas has recovered, meaning his bits are still in place. Dama X was right. The fake version was used on Dr. Vivas, so he didn't need the antidote. Although there is a debate about Cook. He's tested positive as a transhuman, so he could survive the change, which was his choice to begin with. Dr. Banerji has offered to transport him to her lab to oversee his transition."

"But why are you back here?" Pax shifted on the other side of Oracle.

"I finally figured out what Sean does with those ugly ties of his. I surprised him in his office—close to midnight, mind you—with a woman straight out of an Amazonian epic. It's too traumatic to recount, but let's just say I was issued an office of my own that I can use to QT." She applauded and let out a whoop.

When Pax and Oracle didn't join in the fun, TimeTrap said, "So, you two are a thing again? Because that's cool. I won the bet on that one."

"Bet?" Oracle exclaimed.

"Talk to Gloria," Pax replied, then to TimeTrap he said, "Yeah, we worked it out."

"So . . . I guess three's a crowd here. I'll make a pit stop at the all-female club over there then head back home." TimeTrap didn't move or pop away. "Did you know that island is actually a ship? Kind of weird how it can just detach and float away . . . feel like I can relate to it . . ."

"You're welcome to stay," Oracle offered.

Pax pinched her side. She smacked his hand.

"Maybe I will for a bit. Not in a rush to get back to good ole Baltimore. Just dropped that chick Naomi off with Matthews to debrief and book."

"Naomi?" Oracle asked.

"Camille's dealer who pulled a vanishing act."

"I forgot about her."

"Used to work for Estabon until Dama X took over and put the kibosh on her Maryland drug business. She played the victim card and got on the island to spy for Lucy. Camille's defense lawyer is hoping Naomi's testimony about all this craziness will get her off." TimeTrap plopped down next to Oracle on the large towel. "Do you have anything to drink?"

Oracle turned in Pax's direction and lifted a brow. She didn't have to reach into his mind to know what he was thinking.

He stood. "What do you want?"

"I'll take a Manhattan. Heavy on the bourbon."

"I can get you a beer." Pax jumped from the sunbathing deck on the bow of the ship where they'd been sitting.

"That'll work, I guess."

"I'll take another beer." Oracle called after him with a smirk.

Pax grunted in response, not hiding his irritation. Oracle was going to pay for this later. She smiled, thinking how she'd make it up to him.

"Geez, what got into him?" TimeTrap leaned into Oracle.

"Don't worry about it," she said with a smile then changed the subject. "Have you heard anything about Surefire?"

"Haven't seen her. I'm going to check with Dama X before I head home. With her being the 'keeper of the skulls' I'm wondering if she can set up a phone line to the other world."

"I'm glad you're here." Oracle stretched out next to her agent. "I wanted to personally apologize for what happened on the island, when I used you to stop Pax."

"It did freak me out to not be in control of my body. Very trippy for sure."

"I won't do it again."

"No big thing."

"It was a violation."

"It was, but desperate times and all that." Without seeing, Oracle knew TimeTrap flapped her hands for emphasis. "You have my permission to use me again. I trust you. Besides, we're part of a team. Now that I know about your power evolution, I can expect this possibility if we're in a jam."

"Thanks for understanding." Oracle gave the other agent a quick squeeze to show her appreciation.

"Just promise to keep it within business hours and when on assignment . . . Holy smokes, is that Gloria?"

An engine's low murmur coasted closer. Oracle stretched out her power to TimeTrap, finding it easier, second nature, like moving a limb without a conscious thought of doing it.

Oracle's mouth dropped open, mirroring TimeTrap's. Reyes's heli-boat pulled next to theirs with the tall drink of cerveza standing port side.

"Is that Roberto, my side-of-the-road savior?" TimeTrap murmured.

"What is this?" Pax stormed the deck with beers in his hands.

"Gloria," Oracle said.

"Hola!" Gloria exited the control room with a wave of her hand.

The wind blew her brown hair across her face. A red and yellow sundress that belonged on a cruise ship whipped around her legs. Underneath the cotton material was an outline of a bandage over her chest still healing from the gunshot wound.

"I'm taking a break from working on Lucinda. Reyes said I could take the heli-boat for a spin. I convinced Roberto to join me."

He saluted them with a pineapple concoction replete with paper umbrellas.

"You know how I am when under stress, Oracle," Gloria said with a knowing smile.

"No need to say anything else." Oracle got her hint loud and clear.

"Pax, I'm sorry I never told you about the Circe contract. But my hands were tied."

"I'm sure they were," Pax replied under his breath. "We'll discuss it when we get back."

"I look forward to it." Gloria's tone implied she meant the opposite.

"Hey, Roberto, I'm doing much better, thanks to you," TimeTrap chimed in.

Oracle rolled her eyes.

"Want to join us? We're picking up his younger brother, who Roberto claims is way better looking than he is. Figured I'd be the judge of that. His brother offered to give us a tour—"

TimeTrap leapt over Oracle and nabbed the beer from Pax. The next moment, Oracle was looking through TimeTrap's eyes watching her and Pax while standing on the other ship.

"I'm ready!" TimeTrap chirped.

"And don't forget to do your timesheet. I'll make sure the DoD, care of St. John, gets the bill," Pax called out as the boat turned away.

"Do I get overtime for almost getting killed?" TimeTrap asked.

"Pad your hours as much as you want," he said.

"Cool beans," she exclaimed as the boat chugged away.

"Remind me to thank Gloria for that one." He touched the chilled beer to Oracle's hand.

"Did you hear from St. John after his crew was rescued?" Oracle took the bottle.

"Sean did. Some sort of apology veiled as a threat, topped off with an excuse about protecting the country and transhumans being dangerous. Whatever. Should've kept him as a flower."

"But we are dangerous." Oracle thought about her power and the implications of this ability falling into the hands of someone with bad intentions.

"That's not for him to decide." Pax leaned over her. "I don't want to talk about work. This is my first real break in months. I want to not think, just be with you."

Oracle's cell phone rang from her bag with the "Like a Virgin" tune. She turned her phone to silent. "I'd asked Matthews to call when he was released from the hospital. We spoke yesterday, and I told him I'd give him a full report when we return."

"Huh," Pax replied, sounding agitated.

"What?"

"Why did you use that song for him?"

Oracle shook her head. "You and Gloria both think alike."

"Don't ever say that again." He trailed a finger down her back to her sweet spot then pulled away. "Answer the question."

"Ask Matthews." She smiled coyly. "He's the one who picked it out for me. Although he did laugh at the idea of you finding out about it."

"I should give him more credit. What ringtone do you have for me?"

"I plan to update it. Any suggestions?" She rolled onto her back.

Pax rubbed his thumb over her lips. She licked the tip. He leaned over and kissed her, placing small delicious kisses down her jawline to her neck.

"Oh, Pax," she groaned.

"That's what I want for my ringtone," he said next to her ear. The deep bass of his voice sent shivers to her lower deck.

"Now where were we?" Pax scooped Oracle up as if she were a bag of sweet potatoes, as Gloria would've said.

"Nothing will be the same when we go back," she whispered, the call from Matthews reminding her of what was waiting when they returned.

"I know. But right now, I don't care." He carried her into the cabin and shut the door.

About J.T. Bock

When J.T. Bock was a child, she wanted to be James Bond or Indiana Jones or a vampire hunter or Wonder Woman. Whatever brought her the most action, adventure and romance while play acting on her stage—otherwise known as her grandmother's basement. Now J.T. has assembled her own team of action heroes, supernatural creatures and maniacal villains and set them on adventures far from her basement to exotic lands and alternate dimensions.

From a secret location outside of Washington, DC, J.T. conjures these pulse-pounding tales to share with those kindred readers looking for an exciting escape. Her alternate identity enjoys spending time with her workaholic husband and their sidekick rescue dog, traveling to interesting locales (San Diego Comic-Con), and enjoying life to the fullest with an amazing group of family and friends and a good glass of wine.

Twitter: @jtbockcom
Facebook: J.T.Bock.Author
Group Blog: Romance on the Rocks

J.T. is an active member of WRW and RWA. She regularly speaks at conferences and contributes to panels about writing, self-publishing, and pop culture. You can view J.T.'s past and current schedule on her News/Events page.

A Surefire Way—UltraSecurity Book 1

UltraAgent Surefire's plan is simple: Capture the transhuman thief Raven. Win back the respect of her father. Get a raise.

Easy, right?

Except Surefire just broke the number one rule of her employer, UltraSecurity, a niche security firm that solves crimes committed by genetically enhanced humans like Raven. She trailed Raven into a warehouse without backup. And something more powerful than any transhuman is waiting inside.

Raven's plan is simple: Atone for his past crimes. Return stolen spiritual artifacts to restore the world's balance. Don't get caught by UltraSecurity.

Easy, right?

Until a spunky UltraSecurity agent is suddenly on his tail, although Raven wishes she was on ... well, never mind ... he can't get distracted from his mission. Because she's followed him into a warehouse filled with his reclaimed relics, and Raven's ex-partner in crime is about to unleash a supernatural-sized complication into his plan.

His old partner has accidentally summoned an Aztec god who will destroy the world unless Raven stops this spirit with a superiority complex. To do this, Raven must team up with Surefire and reveal the truth about his powers, exposing her to a force that can either save the world or destroy them both.

Following Raven into that warehouse throws Surefire into a surreal world filled with moody gods, day-glo skulls, dizzying dimensional portals, maniacal half-roach magicians, and a sexy thief who is more than he appears under his snug t-shirt. Is Raven a criminal, or is he working for a higher power? Surefire needs to be certain, because if she joins him on this mission, she'll have to surrender everything she believed in for a surefire way to save the world, discover her destiny and find true love.